Karen paid my couple of days wo..... .. .. .uiiing room, which would close soon and move to Los Angeles. Allen had me pull sound effects from his cassette library and showed me how he laid them in, improving scenes with sound and subtle picture changes.

He'd snap a short rough-cut sequence into the Moviola gate, press the pedal, and send the film clacking through. Stop the Moviola with the hand brake. Trim or add frames, splice the pieces together, and repeat the process until the sequence pleased him. He worked so fast—whir, screech, cut, splice, whir, screech, cut, splice—that I pictured him as an editing Rumpelstiltskin, spinning film straw into gold.

Reel by reel, Allen transformed our corny story into a scary, fast-moving adventure. He amazed me when, by moving one shot, or by shortening or lengthening it a few frames, he could alter the sense of a moment or a scene—or the whole story. I loved that notion. Wished I could do something similar—alter, remove, or replace an event, or a thing I had said or done, or failed to do—and give my life a different meaning.

Praise

Arthur won the Novel Prize at the Southern California Writer's Conference in June 2005 for Rough Cut.
He won a local Emmy for a documentary he wrote about land use and environmental planning in Washington State.

Murder in Concrete

by

Arthur Coburn

Murder in Concrete

Cover Art by *Lea Schizas*

The Wild Rose Press, Inc.
PO Box 708
Adams Basin, NY 14410-0708
Visit us at www.thewildrosepress.com

Publishing History
First Edition, 2024
Trade Paperback ISBN 978-1-5092-5338-8
Digital ISBN 978-1-5092-5339-5

Published in the United States of America

Dedication

To my mother, who mesmerized me with stories of her childhood. From my earliest years, I'd sit beside her ironing board as she ironed pants and sheets, all the while recounting experiences of raising orphaned piglets, living in Minnesota with a father who lost job after job, and a mother who raised three girls in a family that spoke German until the First World War. She loved stories, and passed that passion on to me.

Acknowledgments

Clair Lamb gave me useful early feedback; James Thayer read an early version and, in addition to notes, gave me valuable rules for writing; Lisa Fugard offered invaluable notes about character and pacing and keeping it real; my ex-wife Julie read it and encouraged me; as did Christine Wilson; Trudy Catterfield offered truly helpful insights. I learned a lot from Tod Golberg's class at UCLA; Bob Dugoni's classes at PNWA gave me a great foundation.

Chapter 1

I was strapping my stuffed cougar onto my bike when Dad rushed from the house and said, "Charlie, you can't take that animal to school."

I grinned. "He's harmless. Just a way to give the uptight teachers a reason to remember us."

"Not happening."

"He attacked a hiker last year. Would have killed someone sooner or later. It was a public service to take him down."

"You'd upset the school administration, get arrested, and give your mother conniptions."

Crusty eyes, day old beard, hints of bourbon and coffee on his breath—he'd had a tense morning. My parents split the days. Mom up until midnight, doing the books. Dad out of bed at dawn and off to measure, saw, and wrestle thousand-pound logs into place.

I said, "Why are you such a grump?"

He pulled the cougar from my bike. "Mind's on business. Put yours on finding a summer job before they're all taken."

At the sound of a distant explosion, Dad stared down the road a long moment. I looked but didn't see or hear anything special.

He wrapped an arm around my shoulder. "You're still my favorite daughter."

"*Only* daughter. That joke hasn't gotten funnier

since second grade."

"I hope you enjoy the assembly, even without your ferocious trophy." His grin told me he knew I had something on my mind besides the teachers.

Bringing the cougar into the school might have reduced my chances for admission to Bellingham University in the fall. But when I woke at four, the idea of adding a little fun to our final assembly looked like a winner. A way to get Tony Crane's attention before we all split.

Dad said, "Do you know how smart and pretty you are?"

"Maybe not." My grades said I was smart, but nothing in my life told me I was pretty. Not my yearbook picture with my hair clumpy all the way to my shoulders, not the girl with thin lips I viewed in the mirror every morning, not the boys in class who seemed to forget my phone number around prom time. I grabbed a ball and threw it. Scout, our golden lab, bounded off the porch and across two lawns after it.

Dad said, "Don't be late for supper. I'll pull some elk from the freezer. Make a stew the way you like it, tender and spicy." He gave me a serious look—brow lowered, eyes hard on mine. "Even if you don't get what you want today, you can be a winner."

"Not sure what cereal box you read that on, but I know winners go after what they want until they get it."

He carried the cougar inside and shut the door.

I put on my helmet, slung my purse across my chest, and pedaled my bike north along Challenger Road as it paralleled the gray-green Skagit River, winding its way down from Concrete. I turned on Superior Avenue, left my bike in a rack outside the high school, and trooped into the auditorium with the other sixty seniors.

I had just taken my seat when Tony Crane came down the stairs. As he walked by Mary Sue, my rival for everything, especially boys, she held out a small packet tied with a ribbon. Flashed her sexiest smile, lots of teeth, extra lip gloss. "Tony," she whispered, "I brought chocolate chip cookies in case you get hungry. I'll make us a basket lunch for the senior picnic."

"Thanks," he said. "But I'm heading east of the mountains to go coyote hunting in Coleville."

My palms went sweaty. I wanted to ask if he had room for one more. But except for class discussions in History and English and a couple of times when I bumped into him in the hall and mumbled something dumb, Tony and I hadn't talked. So, I kept quiet and waited for him to walk on.

He turned to me. "Your father's Jefferson Purdue, right?"

I thought of saying, "I haven't hunted coyotes, but I bagged my pheasant limit last fall and shot an elk and a cougar the year before." A warning of Mom's played in my head: "Bragging to boys in Concrete about your hunting skills makes them remember there's somewhere else they need to be."

I nodded at Tony. "Yeah, Jefferson's my dad."

"I'm going to start a contracting business. Do you think he'd hire me to work on his log cabins this summer?"

"You think a forty-five-year-old man would like a high school boy doing all the dirty work?"

Tony grinned. "Got it."

"You and Dad would get along great. He can down

a buck from 150 yards and field dress it in fifteen minutes. Eats his venison steaks rare."

Tony gave me a thumbs up and sauntered down to his seat.

Principal Dalton stepped under the podium spotlight. "Greetings, Concrete High Class of 1986. Are you ready to graduate next week?"

Whistles and foot stomps filled the room. We quieted and listened to an hour of announcements. Mary Sue kept giving me the death glare, but I didn't care. I pictured a perfect summer. Fishing, hunting, and a chance to spend time around the coolest boy in class—handsome and nice, even to the dorkiest kids.

At the end, Dalton said, "When you go out into the world, if anyone makes fun of your hometown, you can tell them concrete from the limestone processed here built the Grand Coulee Dam and skyscrapers in Seattle. Two thousand years ago, the Romans used concrete like ours to make the Pantheon dome, which stands today, still amazing and beautiful. You students are like our concrete, strong enough to weather troubles that would undo most people." After our final cheer, he said, "Be on time for rehearsal tomorrow."

Tony hurried out with a few buddies. I left with the rest of the class—most kids in cars, a few on foot.

I slung my purse under my arm, put on my helmet, and coasted my bike under the school archway and down Superior Avenue toward the center of town. I had to wait at the Loggers Landing grocery on Route 20 while a truck and trailer of Douglas fir logs roared past, raising eddies of gray powder. Until it closed in 1969, the Worldstar Cement plant spewed gray-white dust that covered everything. Most of it had blown or washed away, but the town still had a faded look, like an old painting that needed restoring.

I cycled across the highway, pedaled hard up to Burpee Hill Road, and followed it west, then headed north about three miles and cut off on a dirt two-track. Spears of sunlight flashing through the trees half-blinded me as I navigated the ruts and practiced. "Dad, I know you think teen guys are lazy. But a boy in my class wants to start a contracting business. He's dying to learn from you. I'm sure he'd work hard."

Dad's half-finished demo log home loomed at the end of the cul-de-sac.

"His name's Tony and he's in terrific shape. So, do you..."

From the nearby woods, a dirt bike engine screamed, screamed again, and faded to silence.

Dad erupted from his Airstream trailer-office and dashed toward his Ford F-150, doing his duck step, hip sticking out each time his left foot hit the ground. He often moved quick time, as he put it, but today he limped faster than I'd ever seen him.

He scrambled into the front seat, his Vietnam dog tags flying from his open shirt and bouncing on his chest. The V8 coughed to life, and the red 150 came roaring down the road so fast I knew he hadn't seen me. At the last moment, the truck skidded to a stop. Dad jumped down and hugged me. "Charlie, I screwed up."

I pointed to a bruise on his chin. "You get in a fight?"

"You're a brave girl, tough as a fox caught in a trap, chews its foot off to get away."

"There's a scratch on your neck. Blood on your sleeve." I grabbed his arm. "What happened?"

He fished dollar bills and coins from his pocket and slapped them into my hands. I stared at his wounds, and the money fell to the ground.

"Pay attention." He scooped it up, shoved it into my purse, and gripped my shoulders. "Every second counts."

"Counts for what?"

"Your future. Focus on what I tell you."

"Damn it."

He kissed my forehead. "Call your Grandma Lottie from a phone booth and have her come get you. I'll explain when I can. Leaving now is the only way I know to keep you safe. If anyone asks, this conversation didn't happen." He hugged me again and squeezed my hands, his callused fingers rough as sandpaper. "I know you'll want to go home. Please don't."

"Why?" I searched his eyes for an answer. They were red and swollen, his pupils glassy. "Dad, talk to me."

"No use. Too many complications." He made me repeat his instructions, said, "I love you," and drove away, spinning gravel against my bike like buckshot.

"Wait!" I shouted, racing after him. I sped around a corner and hit a patch of gravel. The bike skidded and turned on its side. I slid five feet on my hands and arms, screaming and swearing as I picked myself up. I couldn't catch Dad, so I pedaled to our house.

Gasping and light-headed, I dropped my Raleigh in the driveway. Mom's Toyota Corolla sat on the street. No sign of Dad's 150. Nor of Scout, who rarely left his spot on the front porch.

I tried to look through the living room window, but

the curtains were closed.

I tried the front door. Locked. When my key didn't work, I bent two bobby pins the way Dad had shown me and wriggled them in the lock until it clicked.

I threw myself against the door, tumbled into the dark living room, and tripped on a tangle of wires. I smelled a stink like when a hunter guts a deer and nicks its bowel. Tried the light, but it didn't work. In the gloom, I made out the smashed stereo speakers, moved past them, and climbed over the couch and chairs.

"Mom?" I called.

Silence. Except for the drip, drip, drip of the kitchen faucet Dad never got around to fixing. I checked the stove. Cold as stone. No elk meat in the fridge or in the Dutch oven. I climbed the stairs, where a dim shaft of light from a side window played over fresh stains on the carpet. Tensing, I stepped over them.

At the top, unsteady on my feet and still breathing hard, I inched along the dark upstairs hallway, my tennies tripping and sliding on cosmetic jars and curlers.

"Mom," I called, "what happened in the living room? Are you all right?"

Another sniff of deer gut. I kept going, slipped on a wet spot, and lurched into the dark bathroom. My foot ran into something solid. In the glow of the night light, I made out a man's body on the floor. Nudged his leg. "Dad?" No response. I bent forward for a better look. Not a man.

A female stared past me, mouth open, hair a bloody tangle. My heart raced, and the room swam. I held onto the sink.

"What do you want?" the woman asks.

7

I whisper, "Why are you wearing Mom's bathrobe?"

"She loaned it to me."

"You're not taking good care of it. There's blood on the collar."

"It's not my fault."

The room, still swimming, slowed enough for me to recall Dad's instruction for emergencies. I took a deep breath and reached under the robe to check the woman's carotid. No pulse. When I drew my hand back, my fingers snagged a delicate chain. I pulled it and drew up a silver locket, sticky and engraved with "J.L.P." on the front.

Mom's name was Janine Louise Purdue. J.L.P…

The room swam faster. I couldn't think, couldn't figure out what to do. So, I stood and tried to leave, but my feet wouldn't move. I forced them: left…right…left…right…left…right…along the hallway, my eyes zeroing on each bloody carpet stain and squashed hair roller, seeing them clear as close-up photos.

Confused about where I was, I followed the sound of faucet drips to the stairs and down to the kitchen. Found the counter phone, dialed the operator, and mumbled, "Help."

"What's your emergency?" a woman asked.

"My…mom."

"Your mother's injured?"

"No pulse…blood."

"Is she breathing?"

"No."

"Are you hurt?"

"No."

"How old are you?"

"Nineteen."

"What's your name? Where do you live?"

"Charlotte Purdue, 43 Cedar Lane, Concrete."

"Are there relatives close to you?"

"My grandma lives in Bellingham." I gave her Lottie's number.

"Help's coming, Charlotte. Find a safe place to wait."

"A safe place?"

"In case the attacker comes back."

I hung up, rushed to Dad's gun safe for my Remington 870 shotgun, and punched the code. The safe wouldn't open. I tried again. No luck. Had Dad changed the combination, or was my mind too addled to do it right?

I hurried to the open side window and wriggled out, blinking in the light as I fell onto Mom's marigolds and petunias. I skittered on all fours to the carport and flattened myself on the ground beside Dad's snowmobile.

The world swam again. I shook my head to make it slow down and peeked around the snowmobile. No one in sight.

A northern hawk owl swept across the yard, wings rising and falling, rising and falling. *Whoosh, whoosh, whoosh.* Strange. When I hunted with Dad, owls flew by without making a sound. "They're silent fliers," he told me. The owl rose to the carport rafters and landed on our furled Sunfish sail.

I grasp the tiller and lean back to balance the boat's heeling. Waves slap the hull, and cold spray splashes my ribs.

Mom points at the flapping sail. "You're luffing. Head off the wind or trim the sheet."

A crimson stream trickles from a gash on her throat and down across the bra of her two-piece.

I try to hug her but can't. Try to get back to the carport. Can't do that either. Feels like I'm plodding through a gelatin swamp which slurps and clicks as I walk.

Clattering engine valves replaced the gelatin sounds, and I raised my head to check the road. A mile away, a car raced toward me, swerving and screeching. The killer coming back.

Chapter 2

Our neighbor, Mrs. Donner, fishtailed her old Volvo into their driveway. Red-headed, tall, and usually nervous about something, she leapt from the front seat, juggling three grocery bags. She glanced my way, screamed, "It's true. God help us," and dropped her bags. As bottles, apples, and eggs tumbled across the grass, she ran to me, pulled an alcohol wipe from her purse, and scrubbed dirt and gravel from my arms and palms.

Wailing sirens approached. An ambulance pulled into the driveway, painting our house with red and blue flashes. Paramedics got out and hurried inside.

I longed to see Scout's honey-colored body race from behind the house, but he didn't appear. A police car skidded to a stop beside the ambulance. I hurried to the officer getting out, a big man with a round belly and sad, basset hound eyes. I said, "You have to find my dad right away. His name's Jefferson Purdue."

"You live here?"

"I'm Charlie. My mom is…"

He nodded and touched his name tag. "Officer Shanahan, Concrete PD. I'm here to find out what happened and to help you feel safe." He studied my arms and hands. "Where did you get those scrapes?"

"Fell off my bike."

"When did you see your dad last?"

"I…uh…before school."

"What did he say?"

"Nothing."

"I know you're upset, but you're safe now. Can you wait here until I check things out?" I nodded. While he hurried inside, I stayed close to his patrol car, hoping for a radio call about Dad. But there was only static and police talk I couldn't understand.

After a few minutes, the officer came out, strung yellow crime scene tape around our house, and walked back to me. "We haven't located your father, but city and county units are searching everywhere."

"He must be in backcountry," I said.

"I hate to bother you at a time like this, but do you know of anyone having conflicts with your family?"

I shook my head.

"Any new people? Threatening phone calls? Disturbing events?"

"No."

He patted my hand. "I'll have to go for a while, but someone will be here."

Mrs. Donner beckoned to me from their front door. I didn't know what to do, so I followed her into their den and sat on the couch, hugging my knees.

She sat beside me. "Let's pray for your dad's safe return." Mrs. D went to church a couple of times a week and spoke with God a lot.

Usually, I ignored her religious talk but I nodded, bowed my head, and prayed. "God, please bring Dad back safe."

"Amen," Mrs. Donner said.

I went outside and stared down the road. Mrs. D joined me. "I know your dad has a CB in his truck and I bet the police tried to reach him. Strange he hasn't come home."

"Sometimes the logs Dad orders don't show up. He has to drive all over the county looking for replacements. Reception stinks out there. He misses plenty of calls."

The officer drew Mrs. Donner aside and whispered. "I've seen a lot of trauma. This girl's hanging by a thread."

Mrs. D said, "We'll take care of Charlie while you find her dad and her grandma. But first, we have to get her a change of clothes."

"The house is a crime scene, but if she wants to go pick out—"

"No," I said.

Mrs. D squeezed my hand. "I'll find a few things for you."

The officer ushered her under the yellow tape and into our house.

In a few moments they came back, Mrs. D carrying a small bundle of tops, pants, socks, underwear, and pajamas. The officer made a list of the items in a notepad. She signed it and gave me the clothes.

"I'll need to take her bloody shirt in for testing," he said.

After I'd changed to a clean top and jeans in the bathroom I sank into the big couch pillows, pressing the fresh clothes to my chest and inhaling the scent of Mom's laundry soap. I knew I should have been crying but I felt numb, not weepy.

Ginny, the Donners' daughter, came in. A senior like me, but a foot taller, with frizzy blonde hair like a troll doll. She had always been pleasant and kind, but so serious and by the book I'd never felt close to her.

Ginny wiped her eyes. "I want to say the right thing, but all I can do is be here." She sat down. "You can borrow anything you want while we wait for your dad. Since you're into hunting, you'll think it's dumb, but I saved money and bought a used microscope and a big magnifying glass. I've got slides and specimens."

"Thanks," I said.

"Plus, a cassette player and lots of albums: Beatles, Carpenters, and a bunch of others."

"We can listen later," I said, but I couldn't imagine liking any music.

At dinnertime, I didn't eat. Stayed in the den until the evening news, when Mrs. Donner urged me and Ginny to go to her room for the night, adding, "I've set up a roll-out bed and fresh towels."

After we got ready for bed, Ginny turned to me. "We can talk if you want."

When I didn't answer, she rolled over, and her breathing slowed.

I leaned back on the bed, and the next thing I knew, the ten p.m. news was playing on the TV downstairs, the newscaster saying, "Police found Janine Purdue murdered today in the bathroom of the family's Concrete, Washington home. Detectives are looking for her husband, Jefferson Purdue."

I rushed down to the Donners' living room. On TV, two men were rolling a gurney away from our house, with a body bag on it. I shouted, "You can't throw a person away," and went to the stairs and sat down.

The big officer came in, talking on his radio. When he finished, he said in the kindest voice, "We still haven't located your dad. But I know he can take care of himself. He'll come find you for sure. I have to leave again and take the clothes with the blood on them, but my partner will be outside all night."

I went upstairs, lay down, and listened as the exhaust sound of his car faded, leaving the scuttling, chewing, and snorting noises of animals in the nearby woods. I'd never heard them so clearly.

Dad's truck roars away, spinning gravel at me.

I gripped the sides of the bed, trying to hold onto the present.

Dad's truck roars away again. I race after it, pedal to our yard, and stumble through the front door. Weave between stereo speakers, climb the stairs, and start down the hall. "Charlie's mom is in the bathroom," a play-by-play voice announces.

"Please don't make me go in," I say.

I bolted upright at the sound of ringing from my house next door. I climbed down the tree outside Ginny's window, ducked under the yellow crime tape, and crawled in through our side window.

I groped my way to the kitchen counter and grabbed the phone. "Dad, it's me. Where are you?"

A breath ghosted from the earpiece.

"Dad, if that's you, say something."

Another breath.

"If you're hurt, I'll come take care of you. I know where Mom keeps the Corolla keys."

A sigh.

"I'll help you find out who attacked her."

The phone clicked and went dead. I dialed Grandma Lottie's number, but after it rang and rang, I hung up.

Crouching below the windows in case the killer

was outside, I hurried to Dad's gun safe and tried the combination. The safe opened—I'd pushed the wrong buttons earlier. I removed my Remington 870, picturing 20-gauge pellets ripping into the killer. Grabbed my Smith & Wesson Shield. The semi-automatic pistol could pump eight rounds into the guy before he took a step.

I went upstairs. Looked out my bedroom window at an officer behind the wheel of his car on the dark street. I gathered all two hundred dollars of my odd job earnings from my bureau and stuffed them into my purse. Went down, wriggled out the side window, and sneaked to the Donners' yard. Settled onto their lawn chair and set the weapons on my lap. I waited all night. The phone didn't ring again.

Chapter 3

A red-orange glow was inching up the hills as I climbed the tree and into Ginny's bedroom. She didn't wake when I slid both weapons under my mattress.

I went downstairs and tried calling Grandma Lottie from the Donners' phone. No answer.

Mr. Donner went to work, and Mrs. Donner drove Ginny to Concrete High for graduation practice. I spent the day pacing the yard, waiting for Dad to come back, and scanning the neighborhood for strangers. I called and called for Scout, but he never came.

That night, Mrs. Donner tried to convince me not to watch the news, but I planted myself on a chair in the living room and stared at the TV.

On the screen, a tow truck winched a red pickup from the flowing waters of the Skagit River. The pickup twisted in the air, giving me a view of Dad's license plate. I held my breath as water gushed from the open driver's door, followed by a mass of mud and weeds. Nothing else.

I stared ahead, sapped, as if all the blood had drained from my body.

Mrs. D said, "Looks like your dad got out in time."

When a car pulled up outside, I went to the front yard but kept my distance from two patrol cars parked driver-to-driver, the heavy police officer telling the other one, "We have the results on the girl's clothes.

Some of the blood is hers: AB positive from her slide on the gravel. Some is her mother's: B negative because the girl touched her mom. If the mom had been alive, it would have been tough to get her a transfusion—B negative's super rare. There are also smudges of A positive blood."

The heavy officer stayed at our house while the other one left. I went inside and tried to watch an episode of *Knots Landing*, but I kept picturing the empty front seat of Dad's pickup after the mud and weeds drained out.

****

The day after graduation, when Ginny left with her dad to catch a bus for a summer school course, a *Skagit Valley Herald* thumped onto the Donners' porch. I picked it up. The front-page story began, "The Kelly twins, Donny and Brian, fishing the Skagit downriver from Concrete, pulled in the body of a 45-year-old white man."

In a photo, the boys puffed out their chests and grinned, as if they'd accomplished a heroic feat.

The article went on, "The man's hands, jaw, and most of his skull had been gnawed away by a coyote or a bear. Police identified him from his military dog tag." The article didn't include a photo of the tag and said the police were withholding the man's name pending notification of the next of kin.

About to throw away the newspaper, I noticed, in the photo, a sun reflection off the spoon lure hanging from one boy's rod. Smaller and of a different shape than the ones Dad and I used in the river.

I tore out the photo, went to Ginny's room, and placed it under her microscope. The enlarged image showed a maze of unreadable dots. I switched to her magnifying glass and read the words stamped on the metal tag: "PURDUE, JEFFERSON, A. 425-23-8604, O POS, NO PREFERENCE."

Chapter 4

I hated those cocky boys. Showing off Dad's dog tag like he was a steelhead they'd reeled in.

My brain swirled with images of women's throats, sliced and dripping blood. Men with their jaws and hands gnawed off. For several days I hardly slept, unable to think of my friends or Tony or my plans to go to the U. Life was cruel. Ready, without warning or reason, to strip you of everything.

One morning after a night of flashbacks and terrifying dreams, and with no memory of having left the house, I found myself biking across the old Henry Thompson Bridge outside of town. My brow feverish, my mind and body wrung out, I pumped hard up the hill past the Baker River Dam and into the parking lot in front of the crusher building of the abandoned cement plant.

The structure looked like a simple box, but I knew from childhood war games and high school beer parties that it contained a warren of passageways, chambers, and a conveyor tunnel. The company had boarded over the entry. Plywood spray-painted with neon graffiti and cartoon figures covered every surface. I slid down a bank at the side and crawled through a break in the wall into the dark, musty basement. Piles of charred firewood smelling of urine and old beer made me gag, but the silence promised there'd be no one to stop me.

I started up a concrete stairway, water drops landing on my head and shoulders. *Drip, drip, drip*—a steady beat, like drumming. As I climbed, the beats grew louder.

When I reached the first floor I clamped my hands over my ears, but the drumming continued. Was it in my head? I lowered my hands.

Guitar chords, earsplitting as Dad's power saw ripping through nails, joined the drumming. A boy sang, "She's a gym class hottie and loves to flaunt her body." I kept climbing and reached a catwalk forty feet above the floor—perfect for what I had to do.

From somewhere below, after a blast of drumbeats, boys chanted, "Check out her calf. Feel her thigh. The girl's so hot she'll make you high."

My face burned. Less from embarrassment than anger. A gang of town jerks was messing with me.

They sang, "To hell with manners. Check out her jamas."

The last thing I needed was teen-boy sex drivel. "Whoever you are, shut up!" I shouted.

But on they went. "Her flirtin's high skirtin' when she leads the school cheers. Shakes her pom-poms fast 'cause she's fishing for leers."

I bounded down the stairs. Thumped onto the first floor and surveyed the chamber—half the size of our high school gym. Graffiti decorated concrete columns, supporting a high ceiling above a wall of six-foot chutes and hoppers. Giant words: "BUZZ, WEED, FEAR, AND NOTHING" covered the flat spaces.

Four boys—barely fifteen by the look of their hairless chins—marched from the far side of the chamber and halted. One kid carried a three-foot boom box, blasting, "Take a tour; you'll be hooked for sure. She's sweet as a peach with sexy lessons to teach."

I sliced a finger across my throat, movie style. For a moment the boys froze, like they hadn't expected to see me, and they lowered the volume.

I said, "Are you guys so mindless you can't sing real lyrics? Have to make up smutty crap?"

The short lead kid—he couldn't have been five feet—swiped a flap of green hair from his eyes. "We don't make up squat. Borrowed these lyrics from garage bands in Mount Vernon."

"Why copy trash?"

"Why not? Teachers are jerks. Parents are jerks. Concrete students are jerks. We love to piss on their ears."

He boosted the volume again. Guitar scrapes blasted from the boom box as the boys sang, "She's no granny by the look of her fanny."

I swiped a finger across my throat again, and the short kid cut the sound fast, as if he thought I'd attack him. "Why play in here?" I asked.

"We record in my dad's barn. Need to check the tracks with better acoustics." He gestured at the cavernous interior. Pulled cassettes from his hoodie pocket and plopped them in my hands. "On the house. We're 'Acid Reflux.' Do lots of covers." He handed me a poster of the boys, clutching smashed guitars. "Tell your friends."

The boom box blasted again. "Check out her calf. Feel her thigh. The girl's so hot she'll make you high."

"Lame," I said.

"Try this." He plopped in a new cassette. "Don't go wussy. Be proud of y—"

I punched the stop button.

The kid grinned. "Must be sad to be a prude."

"Are you guys artists and musicians, or losers with nothing better to sing than demeaning lyrics?"

"They're just words. You afraid of words?"

"I'm not afraid of dog shit but I don't wallow in it."

"Dog shit can give you an infection. Words make you smile."

"You see me smiling?"

"Maybe you should. Like the two girls I heard laughing at school about hoohas and tatas."

I dropped the kid's poster and cassettes to the floor and headed to the stairs. "We aren't angels and sometimes we swear, but girls get grabbed in their privates all the time by boys, and men, too. That language makes the guys think it's all right. And it's *not*." I scrambled up the stairs to the highest level, climbed on a rail, and leaned out.

"Hey, wait!" the short kid shouted. "We'll stop!" He pushed a button, and the chamber went silent. "Jumping's not the answer to whatever's bothering you."

"You have no clue what's bothering me."

He scrambled up to a spot below me. "Sorry I upset you."

"We all are," the others behind him said.

"Please don't jump and make us feel guilty for the rest of our lives."

"Don't flatter yourselves. Your music's the last and least important of all the shit the universe has dumped on me."

He extended his hand. "I'm so sorry. Would you

like us to walk out with you? We can go to town, get burgers, my treat, and joke about the Concrete High teachers."

I wanted to stay mad at him, to rekindle the will to jump and tell the universe to go fuck itself. But the little guy's attempt at repentance (slumped shoulders, an extended lower lip, and a grin he seemed unable to hide) flipped a switch in my brain. I looked down at the concrete floor where machinery, and kilns in other buildings, had turned limestone into concrete. Closed my eyes, clenched my teeth, and imagined myself made of cement, sand, and gravel. Strong and enduring, a true Concrete girl.

"Come on," he said.

I stepped down from the rail. "I appreciate the offer, guys. And don't worry. I'm going to hang around this planet a while longer."

They cocked their heads the way Scout used to when he didn't understand me, descended the stairs, and looked back.

I said, "Go. Write wild songs. And feel free to piss on my ears."

They laughed and marched toward the conveyor tunnel, the boom box blasting, "Check out her calf. Massage her thigh. The girl's sexy as hell. Well worth a try."

Their lyrics were childish and gross, but their attitude struck a chord. Lots of people were jerks—life was worse. Mean, and ready to kick you in the place I hated boys joking about. Made me want to shout their nastiest words—the vulgarity matched my disgust with a world where one monster could slice my mother's throat and another drown my dad in a river.

I went down to the floor where the boys had been. Gathered the cassettes and stuffed them into my purse with their poster, folded four times. I went outside and biked to the Donners'. Looked for Scout along the way but couldn't find him.

Chapter 5

When I got back, Mrs. D was folding a pile of shirts, pants, shorts, skirts, and socks for the family. Fresh and squeaky clean, as if that mattered.

I brought the poster, cassettes, and my clothes to Ginny's room and settled onto the floor between our beds. I put on Ginny's earphones and inserted a cassette in her player.

The songs were all gross and juvenile. But, to my surprise, when I played them several times, their coarseness began to work like the sulfuric acid in my last chemistry experiment. Dulling the jaggedness of my anger, the way the acid etched away the sharp edges of the copper strips in the dish on my bench.

****

That afternoon the heavy police officer came to tell me Dad was dead.

"I know," I said.

"How?"

"Those stupid fishing boys showed his dog tag."

"Oh...Would you like to ID the body?"

"I don't need to. They can bury Dad next to my mom, or wherever my Grandma Lottie wants."

"We haven't reached her yet," he said.

"When you do, tell her she's free to arrange a service for both my parents, but I don't want to go."

The officer nodded and left.

Before dinner, a TV newsman announced, "We're still hoping for an explanation of the Purdue tragedy."

"Bullshit," I said.

Mr. Donner glared. "*What did you say?*"

"There's no explanation for what happened to my parents."

Mrs. Donner reached toward me. "Charlie—"

"No meaning to anything in life."

"What happened to your parents was a tragedy, but instead of concentrating on what you lost, count your blessings and pray for guidance."

I said, "I'd better go to bed." I hurried upstairs, checked the weapons under my mattress, and realized I hadn't brought ammunition from my house. When Ginny fell asleep, I slid the Smith & Wesson into my purse and climbed down the tree outside the bedroom. I kept low, ducked under the crime scene tape, and crawled through the unlocked side window.

To mask the kitchen faucet's *drip, drip, drip,* I tore bits of paper towel from the roll, stuffed them in my ears, and started up the stairs. I cringed as I stepped over the carpet stains but continued to the second floor.

At the sound of a breath, I pulled the Smith & Wesson from my purse. A board creaked. I whirled. "Who's there?"

Out of the darkness, a whisper: "Charlie, it's me. Don't worry."

"Is that you, Mom?" I hurried to the bathroom doorway. No body on the floor. Just Mom's tile drawings, glowing an eerie purple under the night light. Another breath. I pulled the paper from my ears.

A soft voice: "Are you okay?"

"Prove you know me. What's my birthday?"

Clothing rustled. I aimed the Smith & Wesson at a tall figure in darkness near the top of the stairs. "Drop to the floor, or you're dead."

"It's just me." The figure stumbled, and dim light fell on frizzy blonde hair.

"Ginny?"

"What's going on?" she asked in a quavering voice.

"Why did you follow me?"

"A noise from your house woke me. I came looking for you. Why do you have a gun?"

"The killer's bound to come back." I lowered it.

"Do my parents know?"

"Don't tell them. I have to protect myself."

"Charlie—"

"Please."

"I won't say anything as long as you keep it out of the house."

"Okay, but go home. I'll be there in a few." She left. I went to Dad's safe and opened it and got a box of cartridges for the Smith & Wesson and a dozen 20-gauge shotgun shells. Put them in my purse. I trusted Ginny as a friend, but worried she'd feel honor bound to talk about my gun.

I went outside, hurried to our car port, hid the Smith & Wesson and the ammunition in a compartment in Dad's snowmobile, and slid the 20-gauge underneath.

****

After breakfast the next day a car stopped outside. I headed for the door. Ginny beat me and peered out a window. "It's Tony Crane in his father's convertible. He canceled his hunting trip, so I called him. Thought it might help to have a friend stop by."

"Tony and I aren't close. He barely knows me."

"At the assembly he said he wanted a job with your dad, but I know he already had two lined up. I'm sure he asked so he could hang around you for the summer."

Ginny meant well, and two days ago I would have sprinted out to see Tony, but Ginny didn't realize after I found Mom's dead body, nothing in my life would ever be the same. Not my dream to get a college education. Not my feelings about Tony who had both made me want to hunt coyotes with him and kiss him. I had landed on the other side of a line no one else could see or understand.

I said, "I'm not going out."

"Charlie," Mrs. Donner said, appearing in the kitchen doorway. "You don't have to, but it might do you good to connect with someone from your class besides Ginny."

The car honked.

I said, "Tony's a nice guy, but I don't want to see him."

Ginny went to the door. "I'll tell him it's a bad time." She went outside. After they exchanged a few words, the engine revved, and the car roared away.

Mrs. Donner said, "Charlie, I understand."

"No, you don't."

"I guess you're right. With that negative attitude and your language, I don't recognize the girl I've known all these years." She sighed, and her expression softened. "I do have news you might like. The police located your grandma in a Bellingham hospital. They admitted her a few days ago with a case of bronchitis, but she's well now and driving down this afternoon."

I loved my grandmother—from my earliest years she had spoiled and fussed over me. When I slept at her house she'd baked hot buttery rolls with orange frosting which I loved so much I ate too many and added extra pounds.

Years ago, I made peace with Lottie's toughness. She had been a high school English teacher and always corrected my grammar. "You can't say, 'Me and Mom went to the movies.' *Me* cannot be the subject of a verb. *Me* cannot do anything, neither can *him, her,* or *them*."

I felt as distanced from Lottie as I had from Tony, and I had no idea if I could warm up to her. But my family had been shipwrecked, my parents lost. She was a lifeboat in a treacherous sea.

Chapter 6

When Lottie's Chevy rattled to a stop in front of
the Donners' house, I stood in the yard, doing my best
to feel enthusiastic. Lottie opened the door, and a hint
of her favorite perfume drifted my way, bringing
images of her antique dressing table with its army of
perfume bottles decorated with silver floral designs.

After a muffled cough, she slipped a lozenge into
her mouth and walked toward me, wearing a black
dress and black shoes with short, wide heels. When she
dabbed her eyes, I longed to cry to let her know I
shared her grief. But I couldn't coax out a single tear.

I felt twice bad, first for not easing Lottie's pain,
and second for failing to weep for my mother. Any
normal girl would cry about her mother's murder. How
had I become a freak? Lottie wiped her eyes and pulled
something from her purse. A fresh hanky, I thought.
But it was a small, rudely made figure with burlap arms
and legs, corn silk hair, tiny agates for eyes, and a dress
sewn from scraps.

Lottie smiled. "Your mom lent this doll to me
when I was sick in bed a week ago. 'It always cheers
me,' she said."

Lottie held the figure out, and I clutched it,
recalling my fifth Christmas.

****

Snow fell outside my window when I jumped out

of bed at five in the morning. I rushed downstairs, placed my small package under the tree, huddled on the couch, and waited. Mom came in and joked about me being awake so early. She pulled my gift from beneath the branches.

"Open it," I said.

Mom folded the wrapping back and held the doll. "Oh, darling," she cried. "You're amazing." Her eyes sparkled, and tears moistened her cheek. She pressed my little creation to her breast. "I'll call her Twinkle and keep her always."

Mom and I ran into the yard and let falling snowflakes melt on our faces.

****

I blinked away a tear, and several more rolled down and fell to my chest. I threw my arms around Lottie, and we sobbed together.

When we were quiet, I stepped back. I tried to hold onto our closeness. But the emotional curtains closed, and I felt cut off from my grandma. I gripped her hands.

She dried her eyes, grabbed something from her car, and went into the house.

After I scanned the neighborhood for danger, I retrieved the Smith & Wesson and the ammunition from Dad's snowmobile along with the shotgun, wrapped them all in an old bath towel, and stowed the bundle in Lottie's trunk.

I found her inside the house, assuring the Donners her bronchitis had passed. She thanked them for their kindness to me and handed Mrs. D a jar of plum preserves.

Ginny approached me with her cassette player and her old daypack. "These are for you."

"The player's too much."

"Don't worry," she whispered. "I'm lobbying my dad to buy me one of those new Walkmans. And I know you'll use this because you were listening with earphones. A Beatles song?"

"Octopus's Garden," I said, though I'd been flooding my gray cells with the teen boys' lyrics. Their cynicism and vulgarity made my bleak outlook seem normal.

Ginny hugged me. "I hope you find someone as nice as Tony Crane where your grandma lives."

"Thanks," I said, though I couldn't imagine being entranced by any boy.

I stuffed the player, the rock group poster, and the clothes Ginny's mom had brought me into the daypack along with the cassettes. I slung my purse over my shoulder.

"You've eaten like a bird the last few days," Mrs. Donner said. "Take these for the road." She slid a half dozen small bags of almonds into my purse.

After we all said good-bye, Grandma Lottie and I loaded my Raleigh into the trunk of her Chevy and drove off. I looked back, scanning the neighborhood a last time, wondering if the killer was watching from behind a bush and waiting to follow us in his car.

As we drove west on Route 20, paralleling the Skagit, Lottie said, "I'm so sad you're going through all this, sweetie. It's not fair."

"Anyone who thinks life's fair is an idiot."

"You're being dogmatic."

"My mistake. It's fair for one maniac to slash Mom's throat and another to make mincemeat of Dad's hands and face."

"I don't have an explanation for what happened."

"There isn't one, but if I find the killer, he'll have five seconds to come up with something amazing before I finish him off. If you're arranging for Mom and Dad's funerals, thanks. But I can't go. I refuse to be a target for a butcher."

Lottie said, "Charlotte, I know you're grieving and angry, but the police are investigating this. The best thing for you now is to show some character."

"Too bad I don't meet your standards."

I expected a harrumph or a cutting remark. When Grandma Lottie said nothing, I turned to her.

She wiped her eyes. "I miss her as much as you do."

"I know."

We drove west in silence, turned right onto Interstate 5 at Mount Vernon, and headed north.

****

Twenty silent minutes later, we left the interstate in Bellingham, made a couple of turns, and pulled into an overgrown yard. Lottie steered between two vegetable beds and parked under a plum tree a few yards from her gray clapboard house. Most of the paint had peeled from its walls. The gutters sagged, and the structure leaned like an old drunk.

Before getting out, I studied the yard, noting places where someone could hide: among the berry bushes, behind a copse of fruit trees, or in my grandfather's long-abandoned station wagon parked in a patch of weeds. He had died before my third birthday. Lottie resisted getting rid of a reminder of the man she loved.

I slung my purse and the day pack over my shoulder, leaned my bike against a peach tree, and walked ahead of Lottie.

"Come look," she said, catching my arm and turning me around. She spread the branches of a rangy azalea. Behind it, a metal fin stuck up from a round bronze dial mounted on a pedestal.

I said, "We have to check out the yard. See if the guy is here."

She pulled me closer to the pedestal. "This sundial fascinated you as a toddler. You loved knowing it tells time by the sun."

"Why hang onto a hunk of scrap metal when you have real clocks all over the house? I'm sure it's wrong, anyway."

"What time do you imagine it is?"

"Noon."

"And what time does my sundial say?"

"The shadow is between eleven and—"

"Twelve, so it's almost right. That hunk of metal will be telling time when the rest of civilization has crumbled to dust."

"Or, when the killer comes to get us, which will be any minute."

"Ah, the heady cynicism of youth," Lottie murmured, as she led the way past a rhubarb patch.

The wood creaked as she mounted the porch steps. We went inside, past the grandfather clock in the hall. I headed up to the second-floor bedroom, where I'd slept when I stayed with Lottie.

She followed, saying, "I put out fresh towels, a toothbrush, and toothpaste. Do you need anything else?"

I shook my head and retreated to my bedroom. Sat for a long time, watching the three-legged squirrel on the branch outside the window. It had been a resident of Lottie's maple tree for years.

I said, "Life screwed you, too. I bet hobbling around on three legs makes it hard to get enough to eat." From my purse, I took one of Mrs. D's bags of almonds and scattered the nuts on the sill. The squirrel leapt down, stuffed its cheeks, and bounded away.

For supper, Lottie served homemade vegetable soup and fresh bread, hot from the oven. I thanked her but didn't touch mine. I went upstairs and listened while Lottie washed her face and brushed her teeth. When her bedroom door closed, I tiptoed out to the Chevy. Pulled my 20-gauge, the Smith & Wesson, and the ammunition from the trunk. I loaded both weapons, put the handgun in my pants pocket, and cradled the shotgun. Started a circuit of the house.

The moonless night left the yard dark and featureless except where a streetlight's glow painted the bushes yellow. Partway around the house, at the sound of rustling in the bushes, I drew the Smith and Wesson. A cat darted out and raced away.

When I finished my circuit, I opened the door of my grandfather's Plymouth and sat behind the steering wheel. Some creature had died in the old car, and the odor made me want to throw up. Why did smells that hadn't fazed me during years of cleaning fish and gutting game disturb me so much?

I went up to the bedroom, lay with the shotgun at my side, and tried to relax. But a hint of the odor from the car drifted through the bedroom window.

I slip and stumble down our hall in Concrete. Pause at the bathroom doorway. I smell the deer gut odor and want to leave but can't remember the way out.

I backtrack along the hallway, listening for the dripping faucet. Can't hear it.

I lay back and closed my eyes. Without an awareness of time passing, or of rising from the bed, I stood before the front window, staring at Lottie's yard, the loaded 20-gauge in my hands.

A shadowy figure leaned into the Plymouth's front seat, turned away, and headed toward the house. I threw the window open and shouted. "Stop, or I'll shoot."

Lottie looked up. "What in God's name are you doing with a gun?"

"Protecting us." I hurried to the bedroom, shoved the 20-gauge under the mattress, and ran down to Lottie. "You saw him in the yard, right?"

"The Plymouth door squeaked."

"That was me."

"*I*," Lottie corrected. " 'That was *I*.' Predicate nominative."

"Perfect grammar's not going to save us."

"Neither are guns."

"If Mom had one, she'd be alive."

"Even your father didn't carry a gun around the house. We'll be fine."

The teen rockers were right. Everyone (including my grandma) was a jerk. I retreated to my bedroom, lay down, and stared at a spider running a web from the ceiling light to the wall.

A knock rattled my door. "Tomorrow is Sunday," Lottie said. "We're going to church."

"Mom and Dad didn't. Me either."

"Then, you're overdue."

****

At seven, Lottie opened my door, dressed in a tan

summer suit. "Time to go."

I put on a top and pants. Recalling her services lasted forever, I slid the cassette player and earphones into my purse and followed her out.

She drove to a department store, bought me a pale green skirt-and-sweater set and black flats. I doubted I looked church-worthy, and didn't care, but Lottie beamed and let me choose underwear, tops, shorts, jeans, cotton skirts, two sweaters, socks, and tennies.

It started to rain as we arrived at the church, a New England-style white clapboard building with a copper-sheathed steeple and yellow stained glass sanctuary windows.

We went in, and Lottie led me to a pew near the front. Raindrops plopping on the windowsill outside sounded like the dripping kitchen faucet the day I found Mom. A wave of body odor drifted from a large man in the pew in front of us.

I stand on the bank of the Skagit, inhaling a musky breeze off the river. A boy hauls in a sockeye salmon shaped like a man, a dog tag hanging from his mouth. I shove the boy aside and reach for the dog tag.

Lottie nudged me. "Pay attention."

In the pulpit, her pastor, with a boyish round face and a plump body, adjusted his glasses and opened a bible the size and color of a wedge of split oak. "Second Corinthians 11:25," he began in a resonant voice. "Thrice was I beaten with rods, once was I stoned, thrice I suffered shipwreck, a night and a day I have been in the deep."

The fish-man's dog tag twists, shimmering in the sunlight as I struggle to read it.

Lottie nudged me again.

"In journeyings often, in perils of waters, in perils of robbers, in perils by mine own countrymen, in perils by the heathen, in perils in—"

"Blah, blah, blah," I grumbled. I put on the earphones and hit play on the cassette deck. In my ear, a teen rocker sang, "Check out her calf. Caress her—"

Lottie pulled off the earphones and pointed at the pastor.

"Everywhere," he continued, "mankind suffers disasters, tragedies, misery, torment, and loss. How does the Lord want us to respond? What is he trying to teach us through these difficulties? In Second Corinthians 11:23-28 Paul tells of the misfortune that befell him in his service to Christ. In weariness and painfulness, in hunger and thirst, in cold and nakedness. Why would the Lord allow Paul to suffer like this?"

"Because He doesn't give a shit," I said, surprised to hear my thoughts aloud.

The pastor's head snapped toward me.

Lottie grabbed my arm. "Charlotte Purdue, you hush."

The pastor raised his voice. "Paul's suffering may seem unfair, but God used his hardships and pain to bring about His will. During his imprisonment in Rome, Paul wrote Ephesians, Philippians, and Colossians."

The teen boys' lyrics swarmed in my brain like hornets, buzzing for release. I pressed my lips shut as the pastor droned on. "And his letter to the Philippians was filled with joy because he understood through adversity God accomplishes His divine purposes and works for our ultimate good. Great problems bring great opportunities."

I suppressed the boys' lyrics as long as I could.

Finally, a verse rushed from my lips. "Check out her thigh. Give it a squeeze. Do it right, and she's sure to please."

I glanced at Lottie, hoping she hadn't heard. But she rose from the bench, grabbed my arm with more strength than I knew she possessed, and towed me down the aisle toward the door and out to her car. "It's one thing to embarrass me, or my pastor."

"Sorry," I said, without conviction. The pastor, to borrow the boys' jargon, was another jerk, making alibis for God's heartlessness.

Lottie got into the car. "It's another thing to attack God."

I slid in on the passenger side. "Didn't He make this world and everything in it?"

Lottie exhaled a long breath. "You dismay me."

"I dismay me too, but strange things keep happening in my head. I see Mom and Dad's mutilated bodies over and over. I have to find out who killed them."

"Sounds like you're inventing excuses." She started the motor and sat back. "No, I'm wrong, that was uncalled-for. But please, Charlotte, for the hundredth time, there is an ongoing police investigation. We'll be safe."

"Speaking of making things up," I said, "I doubt your pastor picked his bible passage by accident. I bet you called, told him about Mom and Dad, and asked for a special reading and sermon to convince me to accept what happened."

"We can't change the past. All we can do is create the best future." She stomped the accelerator, and we zoomed down the street.

I said, "If God knows everything, He knows how awful life is. Pretending His meanness is for our benefit is as perverse as my words."

Lottie stared ahead as she drove to her house and parked.

I expected an angry lecture, but her eyes turned moist, and a tear slid down a crease in her cheek.

"I want to help," she said, her voice quaking, "but I don't know what to do with you."

"Me either."

Her hand trembled as she reached to turn off the car.

Before my eyes, my grandmother aged twenty years—she had been so vital I'd forgotten she was seventy-five. "I don't like to be mean," I said. "I relax by listening to music on my cassettes."

"What music?"

"Ugly songs some boys recorded. Bits sneaked out. I'm sad I embarrassed you."

"I'm sad as well, but too upset to talk." She marched toward the house, picked up a *Bellingham Herald* from the front steps, and passed me the movie section. "You can't stand the real world. Maybe you can handle a made-up one. Pick something you'll enjoy so we don't scrap like alley cats all day."

I surveyed the offerings, looking for *Back to the Future*—the idea of leaping back in time sounded perfect. But I couldn't find it. *Witness,* about a young woman in mortal danger in a rural Amish community, had an unsettling resemblance to my own situation.

"Friends have told me this one is wild." I pointed to an ad for *The Terminator.* "It might take our minds off our quarrels. Arnold Schwarzenegger plays a cyborg assassin, disguised as a human, who travels from 2029 to 1984 to kill Sarah Connor. Her son will lead the fight against Skynet, an artificial intelligence system with plans to start a nuclear holocaust."

Lottie made a sour face.

I said, "*The Terminator* is so over the top, it'll be more like a comedy than a serious movie."

"I'll believe that when I see it, but okay."

I changed into jeans and a sweatshirt, and Lottie put on a casual dress. We drove to the theater, bought popcorn, and settled into seats near the back. As soon as the movie started and Arnold Schwarzenegger appeared nude, I stood. "My mistake, Gram. We should leave."

She sat me down. "This is an awful time for me, dear. Something absurd as this film might distract me for a while."

I was going to argue, but Lottie took a handful of popcorn.

"Sure," I said. "Let's have an adventure."

The movie rolled, and Sarah Connor met Kyle Reese, the man from the future. In car chase after car chase, cyborg Arnold Schwarzenegger careened around corners, chasing the pair. Kyle blasted Arnold away, but he came back to life and bore down on them with a huge tanker truck.

Toward the end of the film, Kyle attacked Arnold with a giant explosive. Arnold turned into a metallic monster, swiping with titanium arms and metal fingers, grasping for Sarah.

I leap into the scene with Kyle and Sarah and realize Arnold murdered Mom. I charge him, kicking and punching.

Kyle grips my hand. "Stop."

"He killed my mother," I scream. "We have to destroy him,"

Kyle grasps my shoulders. "Everything will be all right. You can relax." He pulls me away from Arnold, but I keep flailing at him.

An usher grabbed my arms. When two of them pulled me away, I realized I'd been punching the screen. "Calm down," one said. "You're safe. It's a movie."

While they led me off the stage, through the lobby, and out to the street, a police siren approached. A patrol car screeched to a stop.

When two officers got out, the ushers described what I'd done. The officers escorted me to the rear door and opened it.

Lottie pushed between them. "My granddaughter's upset because her parents were murdered a few days ago."

"You can explain that to the judge," one said. He tried to ease me into the cruiser.

Arnold's titanium fingers grope for my throat.

I punch him.

I punched the officers, too. They cuffed me, shoved me into the car, and closed the door.

Chapter 7

I plucked a miniature driver from a foot-tall golf bag on a table by my chair. I gave the club a wicked swing and raised my hand to shade my eyes as an imaginary ball sailed down an imaginary fairway—not a hallucination, my expression of contempt for the session.

The man in the leather executive chair facing me said, "Charlie, the club's a decoration."

I continued to follow the ball until it splashed into an imaginary lake. "Damn," I said. "A girl can't get a break."

The man wrote in a notepad and said, "You need to take this seriously if you want to get better."

"The way for me to get better is to be in the real world, finding out who killed my parents."

"Let's not get off track."

"We've been off track since we started chitchatting."

"In case you've forgotten, your grandmother chitchatted you out of going to jail." A fellow alumna from Bellingham University had given Lottie Dr. Kraig's name, and he talked the law enforcement people and the university into substituting psychotherapy for a judicial procedure.

"I need to watch out for my grandmother."

He motioned to the chair.

I sat.

He said, "I realize events kicked you in the gut. The most important thing in life isn't what happens to us, but how we react."

"Shrink-babble."

"Therapy isn't babble to one patient of mine. She suffered a paralyzing spinal fracture from an auto accident. Learned to leave the bitterness behind and put her energy into playing basketball in a tricked-out wheelchair. Earned a chance to compete in the Paralympics. She has friends galore."

I stared out the window.

He said, "Make me look stupid. Ask a tough question."

"Can you stop the scenes repeating in my head and the things I see that aren't there?"

"I can give you a chance to get better, but you'll have to work at it."

"What if we quit now and pretend you've given me your whole speech?"

"If you have another episode like the one where you punched a movie screen—"

"I didn't kick a movie screen. I kicked an Arnold Schwarzenegger cyborg."

"That's how your mind works now. If you attack a screen again or a person, you could be arrested, convicted, and locked up. You might be tough enough to survive that, but—" His eyes locked on mine. "How would your jail sentence affect your grandmother?"

"So, teach me a psycho-gimmick to stay out of jail."

"First, we'll have to agree on what's going on with you."

"I'm upset because my parents were murdered, and my grandma doesn't believe we're in danger."

"I wish it were that simple. You've told me you have troubled sleep, weird visions, and time lapses. You're always searching for the place where your mom's killer is hiding. Your vision is hyperacute. You're sensitive to noises, sounds, and smells, especially the ones from your horrible day. Those cues keep yanking you out of the present to another reality. You relive scenes without being sure if you've experienced them before."

"Anybody who's had a big shock would go through that."

"When veterans show those symptoms, we call it post-traumatic stress disorder."

"Never been in the military."

"PTSD afflicts all kinds of people, including victims of natural disasters and rape."

"I've never been through an earthquake. No one has assaulted or raped me."

"Your symptoms tell me you have PTSD. The good news is you're determined and smart. The bad news is your reactions to the triggers are baked into the cake of your psyche. That makes your brain like an ape's—your body makes decisions before your mind knows what's going on."

"You're saying you can't help me."

"I can prescribe medications, but they have downsides. Instead, if you're up for it, we can try a reenactment exercise."

"Why would I want to repeat the horrors I went through?"

"Think inoculation. Small doses of discomfort over

time desensitize you to upsetting stimuli."

"Sounds like shrink nonsense, but I'll try it once."

Dr. Kraig led me into the hallway. "You'll experience one or more triggers. Try to avoid violent responses. If we repeat the exercise enough, your reactions will diminish."

"This hallway isn't anything like the one in our house in Concrete. I'm not going to get upset here."

"Start at the far end by the elevator and head toward this bathroom." He pointed to a nearby door. "No matter what you hear or smell, no one else is on this floor today."

When I walked to the far end, Dr. Kraig turned out the hall light and stepped into his office, closing the door behind him.

Piece of cake, I thought. I started forward, detected a foul odor, and tensed. "Charlie," I mumbled, "You're in an office building, not your house."

As I pushed on, the smell grew stronger. I went ten more steps. Water dripped in a sink.

No one else is here today. Unless…is the doc tricking me?

I edged forward. The drips grew louder. Was there a rainstorm? Shaking, I stepped to a window and spread the blinds. The sun blazed in a cloudless sky. A seagull landed on the sill and pecked the glass.

Maybe the doc hypnotized me. Maybe he knew Mom's killer. Maybe he murdered her himself. Maybe the killer hired him to confuse me.

I step over stains on our hall carpet. Mom's bloody robe beckons from the bathroom. I hurry to the doorway and look in. Mom lies on the tiles, her blank eyes staring past me.

47

Did I have this vision before? My eyes blurred. I lost my balance and fell, struggled to my feet, ran from the building, and got into Lottie's car.

She closed a *Romeo and Juliet* paperback. "Your session lasts another fifteen minutes."

"I want to go home, Gram. The guy's playing tricks on me."

****

At the house, I pulled out another of Mrs. D's bags and scattered almonds on my windowsill.

The squirrel hopped into view and eyed me.

"Are you real?" I asked. "Or a PTSD delusion?"

The squirrel brushed its face with its remaining front paw.

"Do you keep remembering the animal chewing off your leg? Was it a dog? Do you see your leg even though it's gone?"

The squirrel scolded me with squeaks and clicks. It jumped to my sill and stuffed its cheeks with almonds, leapt to a higher branch, gripped it with three paws, and scrambled out of sight. Two gray hairs floated to the sill. I picked one up and rolled it between my fingers. It felt real. I hoped it was.

****

Two days later, Dr. Kraig asked, "What brings you back so soon?"

"A squirrel with three legs mocked me. But I guess the poor creature couldn't help it. I bet a dog attacked it." I winked at Dr. K. "He could have squirrel PTSD."

"Often people in your situation lose the ability to empathize. So, good work."

"Don't try to butter me up. Let's do the hallway again."

"Close your eyes and picture the squirrel."

I gave a frustrated sigh and imagined him standing on a branch.

"Ask this squirrel what he thinks about your fears."

I asked...waited...nothing. I ad-libbed, "He told me you're as clueless as everyone else."

"Smart squirrel. He doesn't need therapy. Try again."

I did. The squirrel's lips didn't move but a tiny voice in my head whispered, "Don't be a brat."

I tried another ad lib: "He told me to stop asking stupid questions and do the hallway exercise." I started for the door and turned back. "If we're taking the squirrel's advice, how come Lottie's paying *you*?"

"If the little guy sends me a bill, I'll split my fee with him."

I did the hallway exercise again and experienced the same sights and fears.

I went back to Dr. K. "When will I be normal?"

"Give yourself time."

"I don't have time. There's a killer out there." I left and went to the street.

When I opened Lottie's car door, she put down her book. "You're leaving early again."

I got in. "Let's go home."

"Do you still think the doctor's playing tricks?"

"He wants to know what the squirrel outside my bedroom window thinks. So, you tell me."

Lottie nodded. "Another appointment?"

"No."

But I kept going and always panicked partway down the hall. Though I went a few steps farther each time.

****

One day, after I'd made it all the way to the office bathroom, Mom reached out from the floor, calling, "Help me."

I went to the doc. "This isn't working."

"Have you fired any weapons?"

I shook my head.

"Punched any movie screens?"

"I'm always on edge."

"Don't worry. You're making progress. Each effort to make decisions and move forward in the face of pain will bring rewards even though you feel like you're falling short."

"You're sounding too much like the sermon my grandma's minister gave."

"Think about why that is."

I left the session early again. But I continued to meet with him because of the squirrel's taunts ("Stop wasting time." "Be the brave girl your father believed you are." "Honor your mother's life with risks, not anger."). And because I had to beat my demons.

On a humid night midway through July during mental reruns of my horrors—Mom's gashed neck, Dad's body hauled out of the Skagit—a yowling cat woke me. I rushed to Lottie's upstairs window and spotted a human form in the dark yard—female with a girl's hips, boyish breasts, and locks of shoulder-length red-orange hair.

She crouched behind a bush and looked at me, grinning as she turned away.

I got the shotgun from my bedroom and hurried outside.

There was no sign of the girl, just a lingering floral

scent. I kept watch the rest of the night, but she didn't return.

The next day, I prepared to hear Dr. Kraig tell me to suck it up. He said, "I wouldn't discourage you from being vigilant. But we're trying to give you new ways to react to possible threats."

"You're saying I screwed up."

He handed me an eight-by-ten piece of cardboard with columns and rows. "This is a self-report card patients have found useful. Whenever some trigger sets you off, give yourself a score for how well you handled it. I've marked a C plus for your reaction to the female in the garden. You didn't fire a weapon, but rather than pausing to think, you rushed down to confront her." He handed me the card.

"I need a faster way to heal."

"The trauma did a number on your brain. Got rid of the old 'present.' Left you with 'over-remembering.' Your rational mind wants that to go away but it's a deep-seated survival mechanism, stored in your amygdala, part of your brain that's not amenable to reason."

****

I pestered Lottie to let me bike downtown to look for the girl I'd seen, but she insisted I work in the garden the whole week. Each night we watched several of her favorite movies, including lots of old ones.

After my "garden week," biking to my next therapy session, I noticed a slender redhead disappear into an office building.

I dismounted and raced inside but couldn't find her.

****

The girl seemed to materialize every time I rode those streets, but I never got close to her. I gave myself C pluses because, though I didn't carry or use a weapon, if I'd been able to, I'd have tackled her and forced her to admit what she was up to.

One afternoon, I watched her enter a movie theater. I chained my bike to a lamppost, bought a ticket, and ran inside. After my eyes adjusted to the dark, I spotted her in front, sitting with a guy. I crept toward them. The redhead began coughing and hurried out. I couldn't find her in the lobby or the ladies' room. When I returned to the theater, the guy had gone.

I went to the seat where they'd been and sniffed but detected no floral scent. I pulled a paper scrap from between the bottom cushion and the back—a torn receipt showing "$100" and the letters "elta."

****

"I'm giving you a D minus," Dr. Kraig said the next day.

"Gave myself a B. No gun. Didn't tackle her. Didn't—"

"The girl's not following you. You're following *her*. Correction, you're stalking her. That's a crime."

"But—"

"You do it repeatedly, with the intent to assault her."

"Maybe she killed Mom and Dad. Maybe she knows who did."

"Too many maybes. Drop it. For your sake as well as hers."

I didn't argue but kept wondering if the girl might be a student at the University. I studied an old campus map of Lottie's. One batch of dorms had Greek alphabet endings to their names: Ridgeview Alpha, Ridgeview Beta, and Ridgeview Delta. They formed a double line along a ridge overlooking the university grounds from the west.

I biked to campus, pedaled north past the baseball and soccer fields, climbed the long hill to the ridgetop. I turned right and rode north past the backs of Ridgeview Gamma and Beta to the parking area behind Ridgeview Delta. I left my bike and went inside.

A girl monitoring the entrance told a guy, "No key without your student ID."

"It's at home," he said.

"You have to show your ID."

Afraid someone would demand to see mine, I rushed ahead and collided with a guy emerging from the men's room. He fell, his books scattering. I bent to pick them up.

"Hey," he said. "You trying to steal my physics book?"

Someone shouted, "Call the campus police."

I hurried away, spotted a redhead in a crowd of students, and raced toward her. She broke from the group, headed down a side corridor and up a stairway.

I followed, reached the top, and pushed through a door into a hallway beneath a banner announcing WELCOME TO NEW VISTAS OF LEARNING. Beyond it, the doors were decorated with paper footprints: "Patty and Darlene," "Donna and Lucy," "Ann and Sally."

Without the redhead's name, I couldn't find her room.

I sensed figures approaching. Expecting campus police, I whirled around, ready to fight, but faced an empty hallway—a PTSD false alarm.

****

Gathering the last of our Hubbard and acorn squash with Lottie, I said, "I have a plan to keep me from going rogue and get me a college education at the same time."

"The 'I have a plan' part makes me nervous."

"I'll finish the application for the U. and enroll as a freshman, if you back me."

"How do I know you won't go wild?"

"I need to look for a killer, not get barred from campus. My one hesitation about enrolling involves money. I can't let you spend all yours or risk losing your house to pay my tuition and expenses."

"While your dad built cabins, your mother made sure they both had wills. The law firm she chose is handling everything. Your parents' assets were limited, but some of their savings are available for you now."

I didn't know if Lottie believed I'd stay out of trouble, but she made phone calls on my behalf and helped me write a letter and a long essay.

****

At my next therapy session, Dr. Kraig said, "If you go off to college, your amygdala could be a problem."

"I'll have tons of reading to keep me out of trouble."

"Won't you worry being on campus and not at home protecting your grandmother?"

"I'll sleep at home most of the week."

"You're bound to have stressful moments and be at the mercy of your triggers. You'll get upset and do something that might harm yourself, your grandma, or someone else."

"So, if the university wants a statement from you that I'm fit to enroll, you'll—"

"Say they'd be lucky to have you, on the condition you continue your therapy with me or another professional familiar with PTSD."

Did he want to help? Or keep his fees coming?

"Great," I said, though I bet he wouldn't keep his promise, and I'd lose my chance to go to the U. to search for the redhead.

Chapter 8

Doctor K. must have come through. Three months later, after Lottie's phone call and letters, submission of my Bellingham U. application, my high school records, and my Scholastic Aptitude Test scores, I received an acceptance letter.

The last week in August, I packed toiletries, basic clothes, plus a dozen novels, two sports bras, biking shoes, biking shirts, and pants. I hid my Remington 870 and the Smith & Wesson Shield under my mattress. I didn't want to risk being caught with them on campus.

As I carried my suitcase and portable typewriter downstairs, the hall phone rang. I set both by the front door, picked up, and said, "Hello?" A feathery breath came through the earpiece and sent a chill up my spine. "Hello," I said again, shivering as I remembered the strange call at our house in Concrete after Mom's murder.

Silence. "Dad?" Another breath in my ear. I lost my grip. The phone fell and bounced off the floor. The oven banged shut in the kitchen, and Lottie joined me.

"Another weird call," I said—I'd told her about the first one.

She picked up the phone and said in her disciplinary teacher-voice. "You don't scare us."

The line went dead.

Lottie hung up and put her arm around me. "You

sure you want to live alone on campus with thousands of strangers, looking for some mystery girl you've never met but are sure is stalking us?"

"Maybe that was Dad. The newspaper report about him could have been wrong."

Lottie said, "I didn't tell you, but I identified his body for the authorities."

"Seeing a jaw and hands gnawed by some animal must have shocked you. I bet you were mistaken." I carried my suitcase and typewriter out to the Chevy, loaded my road bike into the trunk, and slid into the passenger seat. Lottie got behind the wheel, and we left.

****

As we approached the Bellingham U. campus, I avoided thinking about the phone calls by focusing on the red, orange, and yellow foliage mantling the hills of Sehome Arboretum. We followed the route I had biked, climbing the hill, turning north at the top, and driving toward Ridgeview Delta.

We passed three girls walking—a blonde, a brunette, and a redhead, their chests, arms, and legs tanned beneath spaghetti strap tops and cut-offs. The redhead had the muscular build of a gymnast, so I eliminated her as the stalker. The three chatted and laughed as if they were coming from a party. Before Mom's murder I would have joined their conversation, offered my opinions about bands, movies, and boys. But today I felt as distant from them as I did from Tony and Lottie.

When we parked, I unloaded my suitcase, typewriter, and bike.

Bells rang on a tower across campus as Lottie came around the car to me. Sunlight slanting through the maples by the dorm played over the cornflowers she had pinned to the silvery braid circling her head. She leaned close, her blue-gray eyes as vibrant and clear as they had been when she invaded my kindergarten class to see if they were teaching to her standards.

"You're stronger than you know," she said. "Make this a fabulous experience."

"Thanks for the ride...and everything. This isn't much, but..." From my suitcase I pulled a box of her favorite Aplets and Cotlets, like Turkish delight.

"They're perfect. I'll ration myself to one a day." She hugged me and drove away. I gazed up at Ridgeview Delta, imagining the redhead behind one of the windows, grinning as she decided what trick to play on me next.

I carried my suitcase and typewriter through the dorm entrance, showed my new Bellingham U. ID card, and got my key. I climbed the stairs to my single room on the second floor, with a set of paper footprints labeled "Charlie" on the door. I left my first load and went down for the bike.

On the way back, wearing my helmet and wheeling the bike, I passed the threesome in the parking lot, waving at someone on the third floor. I spotted a flutter of red hair behind an upper window, lost my balance, and bumped my bike against the blonde's leg.

"Hey, what are you doing?" she said.

"It's...I...uh..." I hurried into the dorm, wondering if I was up to going to college.

Alone in my room, the door locked, I tried to tamp down my worries by cleaning and oiling my bike chain, opening my Olympia portable, and installing a new ribbon. I put my clothes in the beechwood dresser and armoire, arranging the novels I'd bought—works by Camus, Kafka, and Sartre—in ascending order of bleakness, *The Plague* topping the list. I considered them my equivalents of the teen band's ugly songs. I added my high school philosophy notebook.

Over my bed, I hung the poster of the Acid Reflux guys, holding their smashed guitars and glaring, the short boy winking at the camera. "Wish me luck," I said.

In the bottom of my suitcase, I found a tuition check Lottie had promised to mail. Did she forget, or had she hidden it amongst my things, hoping by the time I turned it in I'd be too late to be admitted this quarter, and give up on college for the year?

I hurried outside, down the hill, and across a plaza called Red Square, dodging spray from the fountain. I passed the University Library and arrived, damp and disheveled, in the registrar's office.

When I started toward the woman behind the counter, a hand grabbed my arm. I spun around and faced a girl about my age. I squinted, trying to place her.

"You don't recognize me?" she asked.

She had a slender face, the almond eyes of a model, and a pert nose. All familiar, but my PTSD brain failed to connect her features to a person.

She grinned. "Guess I can't blame you for forgetting, after what happened during our last month at Concrete High." The lip-glossed smile nailed it—Mary Sue Brasher. She added, "And of course, Tony taking a pass on dating you must have been tough. Guys, huh?"

"Cut the crap. That's not what happened."

"I apologize if I upset you, Charlie. Such a tragedy

about your parents. But my mom says the way to move past a problem is to face it. Despite what your dad did."

"What my dad *did* was get murdered."

"Mom swears he attacked yours when he found her with a lover. Like a Hollywood thriller," she said.

"Your mom's the biggest liar in town." I turned away.

Mary Sue clutched my arm. "It wasn't only my mom."

I stand in our bathroom, staring at the bloody gash on Mom's throat. Mary Sue hovers behind her.

I say, "Do you have a napkin of cookies for my dead mother?

Mary Sue furrowed her brows. "You knew what people said, right?"

The teen boys' lyrics buzzed in my brain. Desperate to avoid a PTSD blowup and expulsion from the U., I clamped a hand to my mouth and started for the registration counter.

Mary Sue pulled me back. "Didn't your grandma tell you? Everyone in town knew your dad murdered—"

"Check out her calf and squeeze her thighs. Keep on going and you'll get a prize," came out before I could stop myself.

She gaped. "*What was that?*"

Despite an effort to keep silent, I heard myself say, "Flaunt your tatas and treasure your hoo-ha."

Mary Sue's face reddened. Spittle formed at the edges of her mouth. She inhaled a long breath, and her outraged expression relaxed into a beatific smile. "I know those slutty words are your pain talking. I'll tell the University Wellness Center about your problem.

I'm sure they'll help." She walked toward the door.

I pleaded, "Don't talk to the U. I need—"

"What you need is counseling."

"No, please, I—"

"You'll thank me in the end." She strode out.

Chapter 9

After handing in my tuition check, I left the registrar's office and called Dr. Kraig's number from a phone booth.

While I waited for his machine to answer, I spotted a slender girl with persimmon hair jogging across campus in sweats. I hung up and followed, keeping my distance.

She ran to Sehome Arboretum and went in. When I reached the trailhead, I couldn't see her. I jogged on, surveying the woods and checking side paths. After several minutes, I arrived at a three-story observation tower at the summit, hurried up the stairs to the top deck, and scanned the woods in all directions. I saw no sign of the girl.

I gazed at the campus, spread out below like a Lilliputian landscape, tiny human figures and cars moving past Bellingham U. buildings and along the city's streets.

The three-legged squirrel popped into my head. "Stop wasting time. You have a redhead to find."

I descended the stairs and started back along the trail.

A female screamed, "Help!" Hurried steps crunched on salal ground cover and faded in the distance.

"Amygdala, keep quiet," I said. "Your fantasies get

me in trouble." I walked on.

"I'm talking to *you*," the female said.

I looked everywhere but saw no one. "Prove to me you're a real person."

"I don't have to prove anything."

I pushed through a thicket toward her voice.

I trip over a pair of legs. Mom stares up at me, hands clutching her throat, a bloody locket in her wound. I gather her in my arms.

"Put me down," she shouts.

"We have to get you to a doctor."

"No," she says, thrashing.

I grip her tighter. "Don't worry. I'll save you this time."

"Are you deaf?" she screams. "Put me down."

I said, "Why are—"

Mom slapped me, pulled free, and dropped to her feet, leaving me face to face with a girl about my age in a blood-stained Rum Runner T and white capris. Her face looked beautiful, except for a bloody scrape on her forehead. Eyes flashing green, brown, and blue, she snapped, "I don't need a damn doctor. The guy just scraped my forehead."

"Apologies. I'm confused these days. I thought you were...never mind."

Her expression softened. "Sorry for being rude. If you hadn't come along, that pervert would have raped me."

I pulled a tissue from my purse and wiped blood from her hands and forehead. "We have to get you to the infirmary and call the campus police."

"They'd tell my mother, and she'd pull me out of school."

"How can I help?"

"Walk me to Ridgeview Delta." She teetered and clutched my arm.

"Delta's my dorm, too. I'm Charlie."

"Nina."

"Cool name." If I had a sister, she'd be like you— smart, pretty, and bristly.

As we walked, I said, "I hate to bother you, but did you see a redhead in the woods this morning? Slender figure, quick on her feet."

"I was concentrating on sunlight streaming through the leaves. Didn't notice anything else until that asshole jumped me."

"Have you come across any redheads in the dorm? I'm looking for a girl I know."

Nina stumbled.

I steadied her. "Guess I should explain about before. I spaced out for a second, thought you were my mom. Sometimes I act weird."

"Who doesn't?"

"My friend Ginny from Concrete. Normal as peanut butter."

"You're funny."

****

Nina's Ridgeview Delta room was on the second floor, down the hall from mine. I paused outside my door and said, "I need to locate the redhead from the arboretum."

"I'll jog my memory. Let's meet for a bite at the Commons, unless you run across someone else who needs to be carried to safety."

I loved to trade sarcastic jabs with Dad, and it comforted me to hear one from Nina. "I can be ready in

64

an hour."

When Nina headed to her room, I found a phone booth and called Dr. Kraig.

"How are you doing?" he asked.

"C plus. I got angry when a girl from Concrete hit me with ugly gossip about my parents."

"Don't get discouraged. Cs are better than Ds or Es. I take it we're not talking about punching or kicking."

"No, though I almost abducted a girl in the woods. Mistook her for my mom and tried to carry her to the campus infirmary. She didn't like it and slapped me, but she cooled off. In fact, I think she might be my first friend since Mom and Dad died."

"Your work is paying off."

After I hung up, I went to the University Bookstore, bought my textbooks, and brought them to my room.

To keep from obsessing about the redhead, I filed and painted my toenails and checked the mole between my right pinky toe and the next one. The tiny brown mark usually made me think of a hawk diving to kill a rabbit—today, I pictured a ladybug.

After washing my face and hands and shelving my books, I went to Ridgeview Commons, behind the dorm. It was a bright, airy place with big windows, birch paneling, and paintings by local artists. In addition to salad bars, there were platters of cooked vegetables and meats.

Nina sat at a table with a pair of dark-haired girls with broad faces, prominent cheekbones, and high nasal voices. They talked so fast in a foreign language laced with Zs and CZs and SKIs that the threesome sounded like five people.

When they finished, Nina left them and joined me.

I asked, "What language were you speaking?"

"Polish. My major. Those two are exchange students from Warsaw. I started learning it a couple of years ago after seeing Andrzej Wajda's films." She pronounced it "Vaida" and told me her favorites were *Ashes and Diamonds, Man of Iron,* and *The Promised Land.* "All his movies are wonderful, or as my Polish friends might say, 'vonderful.' "

"I love movies—watched tons with my grandmother. By the way, did you recall seeing the girl in the arboretum?"

"No. Wish I could help." She lowered her head the way I did when I'd screwed up.

"Don't worry." I liked this girl who spoke Polish and had traits like mine.

A skinny young man with an electronic calculator half out of his back pocket limped across the dining room on orthopedic shoes. A book bag hanging on his shoulder bore a stenciled "SLIDE RULES RULE" caption beneath a silkscreened image of one of the old devices. Slide Rule Guy dropped a notebook. Nina picked it up for him.

"Thanks," he said. "Your movie suggestions were fantastic."

She bowed, and he walked on.

I ate a salad with Nina, roamed the halls of Ridgeview Delta, and checked out several girls with reddish hair. Not finding a match for the girl I saw in Lottie's yard, I began to fear the "elta" ticket stub belonged to someone else. I also feared Lottie had been right, my amygdala creating all my bogeymen. If I lived in a mirrored reality of reflections and illusions, how would I figure out who killed my parents?

Chapter 10

The next morning, I went to the University Library and found the newspaper room. I located the 1986 issues of the *Concrete Herald*. My hands shook as I flipped through the months to the May headline, "Tragedy Visits Our Quiet Streets." Tensing, I turned to the obituaries section and pored over details about Mom's early years in Washington State, Dad's in Minnesota, their graduations, and marriage. After mentioning me as their daughter, and Lottie as Mom's mom, the copy described Dad's luxury log cabins, constructed in Concrete, disassembled, and moved to the buyer's site. The writer finished with, "The Purdues were respected community members whose brutal deaths shocked the town and the region."

Without any awareness of going there, I found myself in a library phone booth, listening to a woman's voice on the line, saying, "*Concrete Herald.* How may I help you?"

"I'm Charlotte Purdue, the daughter of Janine and Jefferson Purdue. I need to speak to the person who wrote their obituary."

The clerk said, "He moved out of state to take care of an ailing relative." She gave me the writer's phone number.

I called it and reached a man with a tired voice. I introduced myself and asked, "Did you come across any unusual questions about my parents' deaths?"

"Yes. But no satisfactory answers. Concrete's a small town and that means rumors. I ignored them when I wrote the obituaries, but a writer in the area likes rumors. Her last name starts with a P."

In the main library, I searched for northwest nonfiction writers dealing with crime. I came up with a *Seattle Times* interview with a woman named Elaine Prescott, a writer researching unsolved murders in the area.

When the reporter asked what she knew about the Purdue deaths, Prescott replied, "Though I'm saving most of the details for my book, I can give you a taste. Some people in Concrete speculated an outsider killed Mrs. Purdue. But police identified Jefferson Purdue's fingerprints and his wife's blood on a knife found in the neighborhood."

Dad's fingerprints on a bloody knife? I shuddered.

"Local rumor has it," Prescott told the reporter, "sometime before the murders, Purdue tried to sell one of his log cabins to Hollywood movie people. Had a flirtation with the sexy star, which inspired Purdue's wife to have an affair with the movie's producer. Rumors further suggest Purdue, who had grown fond of his whisky, caught the pair in the act and killed her in a drunken rage. The producer, fearing backwoodsman Purdue would track him down, managed to escape and later followed Purdue along Route 20 toward Mount Vernon. He ran Purdue off the road, murdered him, and pushed him and his truck into the Skagit River."

Prescott's version sounded as suspect as Mary Sue's gossip. I didn't buy it. Dad had been in Special Forces in Vietnam. Killed men with his bare hands. He would not have been a pushover for some Hollywood producer. And, I'd never had a hint he'd fooled around.

"In an interesting side note," Prescott added, "Purdue had borrowed a hundred thousand dollars in the sixties when he bought fifty acres of timber, a small sawmill, and the land for his residence. By the seventies he had missed too many payments, and the bank was in the third year of foreclosure proceedings. They stopped when Mr. Purdue satisfied his loan in full by repaying the total amount in cash."

Where had Dad found a hundred thousand dollars? We'd eaten game he hunted and food Mom bought in bulk from a discount supermarket in Mount Vernon. She recycled jelly jars as drinking glasses.

****

In one of the library's phone directories, I located a number for E. Prescott in the town of Welcome, twenty miles northeast of Bellingham, in the shadow of Mount Baker. When I called, an answering machine picked up. An edgy female voice said, "If you're selling something, go away. If you're my agent, relax. I'll finish this manuscript before you know it."

I waited, hoping she'd pick up, but after several clicks the phone went silent.

I phoned Lottie from a booth. "Did Mom have affairs?"

"Why would you ask a question like that?"

"People say she and Dad argued a lot."

"I won't dignify foolish gossip with an answer. Concentrate on your therapy and your classes."

"I love you, Gram," I said, and hung up.

I phoned the Concrete Police Department and asked for the officer who had handled my parents' murders.

The clerk who answered said, "Jim Shanahan took the calls. He retired on disability."

"Where can I find him?"

"He doesn't see people."

"Who else knows details about my parents' deaths?"

"Skagit County Sheriff's detectives handle our big investigations. We're a three-man force in Concrete."

From a phone booth, I called the sheriff's office in Mount Vernon, said I was a murder victim's daughter, and asked to speak to a detective. The operator transferred me, and a deep voice said, "Bremmer."

I introduced myself, gave my parents' names, and told him I wanted to know about their murders.

"It's an open case. I'll connect you to the Victim's Liaison Office."

After a buzz, a woman answered. She confirmed it as an open case, didn't have any news, and said she couldn't give out Shanahan's location.

When we finished, I dialed the Concrete PD, made my voice chirpy and pretended to be a niece from Chicago, desperate to find her Uncle Jim Shanahan. The clerk gave me an address for an assisted care facility named Lake View, located outside Ferndale, about twenty miles north of campus.

****

I used a yellow highlighter to mark a route on a map and brought it on my ride the next day after English class. With a fresh bag of almonds in my pocket, nibbling as I went, I biked northwest from the U, passed west of Bellingham Airport, then north and west between farm fields. After twenty-two miles and several wrong turns, I found a sign for the Lake View facility. I rode up a winding drive past vegetable beds gone to seed and a wooden bench beneath a tall evergreen to a two-story building with cracked stucco walls.

Hoping the place didn't have loud dripping faucets, or hallways with stained carpets, I pulled the front door open and wheeled my bike into a reception area painted pea soup green and decorated with posters of Dutch canals and fancy stilted huts at a Fiji vacation resort.

Across the lobby, five white-haired women, wearing velour leisure suits and sneakers, peered at me over their *Life* magazines and *Reader's Digests*. One studied a *Time* she held upside down.

At the reception desk, a woman in a pale green uniform turned to me and smiled.

"Hello, Ruth," I said, reading her nametag. "I'm here to visit Jim Shanahan."

"Are you a relative?"

"We have a close connection."

"That should please Mr. S. He doesn't have visitors except for a cousin who's come twice during the last couple of months."

I signed in, and she led me along an antiseptic-smelling hallway. I pictured Shanahan sitting in geezer attire—coffee-stained shirt, baggy sweatpants, and a discarded Concrete PD jacket—his face creased in a frown.

Ruth and I passed through a sun porch filled with white wicker furniture and watercolor paintings—a mallard in flight and a trout rising for a fly. We continued onto a deck toward a plump man in loose khakis, a plaid shirt, and an expression as placid as the lake stretching out before us. Shanahan sat in a wheelchair and gazed toward a figure on the far shore, casting a lure into a bed of lilies.

Ruth said, "The Department of Fish and Wildlife stocks Lake Terrell. People come all year to fish. The residents love to watch."

She removed a smoldering cigarette from Shanahan's fingers and crushed it out on the deck railing. "Jim, you know Doctor doesn't want you to smoke. Nor to be out here alone."

My PTSD brain struggled a second before I recognized him as the large officer who came to the house in May. His eyes looked sadder and older and his facial features asymmetrical. He raised a hand to a recent palm-sized scar above his left temple but gave no indication he noticed my presence.

Ruth tapped my shoulder, mouthed "Good luck," and left.

I edged closer. "Last spring, when I lived in Concrete, you arrived at our house after a killer murdered my mom. My father had disappeared, and nobody knew what to tell me. You said in the kindest voice, 'We still haven't located your dad. But I know he can take care of himself. He'll come find you for sure.' Your words comforted me more than you can imagine."

When Shanahan didn't respond, I said, "Looks like your luck has been as bad as mine. I'm sorry for whatever happened."

He continued to stare past me as a mallard and its mate winged low over the water.

I said, "I imagine you know my dad disappeared last May. Right afterward, two boys fishing the Skagit hauled in a mutilated body wearing his dog tags."

Shanahan shaded his eyes and followed a bald eagle doing aerial maneuvers to avoid two attacking crows.

"You were the first officer to arrive. You must have found my mom in our bathroom. And I'm betting you were present when the two boys pulled Dad's body out of the river. If you know something about his death or Mom's, but are nervous about telling me, don't worry. We Concrete girls are tough."

Shanahan continued watching the eagle.

"If you can't speak when I ask a question, blink once for yes, twice for no. Okay?"

His eyes met mine for a second, then he bent forward to stare at a raft of coots a few yards offshore.

"Do you remember coming to our house?"

He sighed.

"Taking my bloody shirt to be tested?"

He neither moved nor made a sound.

I said, "I hate to keep asking for answers, but I have to know why my parents were killed."

After he remained motionless and mute, I said, "Sorry to bother you." I went to the doorway and turned back.

He kept studying the coots.

On the way out, I asked Ruth if Shanahan had dementia or had suffered a stroke.

"No," she said. "But he hasn't spoken in several months. The doctors say he never will."

Chapter 11

The next morning, two guys in my philosophy class started a fistfight over the existence of free will. I made use of my sessions with Dr K and didn't get sucked back to our hallway in Concrete or into seeing Mom's body—B plus on my progress chart.

After class, I checked E. Prescott's address in a phone book, grabbed a fresh bag of almonds, pumped my tires to sixty pounds, and biked toward Welcome (population 1,050). I planned to apologize for disturbing her writing with my phone call, plead for mercy, and ask her about Mom and Dad's murders.

A few miles out of Bellingham, Mount Baker looming in the distance, I passed barns and farmhouses with frosted roofs steaming in the morning sun. The skies shone blue and clear until I neared Welcome, where gray smoke rose and flattened into a hazy blanket over the town.

By the time I found Ms. Prescott's road and stopped behind the fire truck parked in her driveway, the only large items left on the acre-sized lot were a charred trellis hung with singed grape vines, a scorched Toyota Land Cruiser, and a crumbling brick chimney. A portable typewriter, keys and roller melted into a Salvador Dali-esque mass, lay half-buried in wet ash.

"What happened?" I asked a tall fireman in calf-high boots and a heavy jacket, rolling up a hose by the truck.

He pulled off a glove and wiped his face with a sooty kerchief. "The owner had a wood stove. Lit her first fall fire last night without cleaning creosote from the flue. Chimney went inferno and the old house burnt up in a flash."

"Where is she?"

"The flaming roof fell in. Smoke finished her off. The paramedics carried her body away an hour ago."

I didn't try to look for Prescott's notes in the slushy ashes where her first floor had been. Heading for my bike, I ducked under burned wires dangling from the nearest utility pole and thought about the clicks on her line the day before, and the mysterious calls at my house in Concrete and at Lottie's.

"Ms. Prescott," I said as I rode away, eating an almond, "I'm sad you had to die in a fire. Even sadder I'm out of leads."

When I got to school, I called the obituary writer to see if he had any other ideas. A phone system message said the number had been disconnected.

****

A few days later, a light drizzle falling on the campus, I went to the Ridgeview Commons dining room and ordered a dish of double-chocolate-coffee ice cream for a caffeine and sugar jump-start.

A girl ran in, calling, "Person-to-person for Purdue at the dorm."

I ran to Ridgeview Delta, stepped into the phone booth, and picked up.

"Charlotte Purdue?" the operator asked.

When I said yes, she left the line.

"Gram," I said. "I miss you."

The line went silent.

My heart beat faster. "Lottie?"

Faint breaths drifted through the earpiece.

"Dad?"

No answer.

"Talk to me, please."

The squirrel popped into my mind, shaking its paw. "Charlie, grow up. They found his body. You saw the dog tag photo."

"Mary Sue, if that's you, I apologize for grossing you out. I've been—"

A click and a dial tone.

I dropped the receiver into the cradle.

At the sound of tapping, I turned to see Nina outside the booth. She said, "I've found a few redheads. They'll say I'm nosy, but I don't care. I like to meet new people."

I followed her around the dorm. Each candidate came to the door when we knocked, but from their size and stature, I knew none was the mystery girl.

Nina bit her lip. "I wanted to help, after you saved me from that bastard in the arboretum."

"Don't feel bad," I said, though I felt disappointed Nina didn't ask why I wanted to find the redhead, why I'd mistaken her for my mom, or anything else. That's the way girls in Concrete bonded with their girlfriends. But then, I hadn't asked her many questions and hadn't volunteered much personal information. I ranked my frustration a PTSD side effect and decided I was lucky to have a new friend.

Nina said, "Since I didn't come through, the least I can do is invite you to see a few cool films."

"That's a risky idea. A few months ago, I attacked

a movie screen in the middle of *The Terminator*."

She grinned. "Wish I'd seen that, but don't worry. I had brothers who were always attacking someone or something. Besides, the movies in the series I'm talking about are super low budget. You'll laugh at the screen rather than attack it."

****

I gazed at a marquee announcing "NOIR GALORE" as Nina and I wedged our way through a throng of students in T's, shorts, and jeans, jamming the entrance of Bellingham's Pickford Limelight Theater. While Nina went to the concession stand, I studied the vintage movie posters on a wall—I'd rented half the films with Lottie.

As Nina came back with a package of red licorice, the student with ortho shoes who'd passed us in the dining room walked by, cradling an armload of round cans the size of jumbo pizzas. Nina tapped his shoulder. "You have a film to make us laugh?"

"Six low budget oldies from a Hollywood vault, and one that may not make it into a theater—taken away before it was finished."

Nina opened a door marked "Projection." The guy entered and climbed a stairway while the crowd, munching popcorn and slurping drinks, swept us into the theater.

"Hi, Charlie," a girl called. Mary Sue waved from the balcony and shouted, "We have to talk."

I nodded and turned away, hoping after the movies I could escape before she dragged me in for counseling.

Nina and I found open seats and settled in. The lights dimmed. On the screen, a man murdered rodeo cowboys, encased them in resin, and sold them to carnival sideshows.

I groaned. "These films are going to cheer us up?"

Nina offered me the red licorice. I chewed one until the smells of melted butter and sweaty T-shirts made me queasy.

I try not to inhale the deer gut smell as I edge along the upstairs hallway. The hem of Mom's robe beckons from the bathroom doorway.

Time spools back to the road. Dad roars to a stop. He hugs me. "Call your Grandma Lottie from a phone booth."

I pedal home...climb the stairs...creep down the hall toward the bathroom... "Mom?"

The events unspool and start again: Dad, the house, Mom's body, Lottie's arrival, and our drive north.

An elbow jabbed my ribs. "Earth to Charlie." Nina waved her hand in front of my eyes. "You spaced out through the whole movie. Try to stay awake for the next one."

On the screen, opening credits rolled. Over the logo of a dead dog, all four legs in the air, blood-red letters announced, "Famous International Films presents *Dead Girls Don't Lie.* Producer, Zolton Baron."

Moody shots from odd angles filled the screen. The grainy color print made it hard to make out faces. Light stands and stray arms and legs invaded the edges of the frame. Actors in overdone makeup and ill-fitting wardrobe missed lines and cues.

The characters went from arguments in corridors to dark alley chases, all to a synthesized score with eerie sax solos and loud drumming.

Students around us clapped and cheered.

As a man opened a door, a girl behind me shrieked, "Don't go inside."

A guy said, "If you see a girl, give her mouth to mouth."

"Mouth to anything," yelled a chorus of male voices.

The students hushed as a man in a trench coat, features obscured by a low-brimmed hat, dragged two platinum blondes in black waitress uniforms to a rooftop parapet. One elbowed him. "Screw you, asshole."

He tossed her over the edge. She fell four stories, slammed onto the pavement, and lay still.

The second blonde, a star-shaped mole on her cheek, struggled as the man yanked her off her feet. "Put me down, before I make you a soprano," she yelled in a New York accent.

"Sure thing, doll." He wrestled her to the edge. After she kneed him in the groin and doubled him over, she broke free and sprinted across the rooftop.

I jumped up. "I can't take any more."

Nina grasped my hand. "Don't wuss out. Hang a few minutes."

I pulled free. And hesitated, remembering Dr. K's words: "Each time you resist the urge to act out, you get stronger." I forced my attention to the screen.

The blonde with the star-shaped mole sprinted out of the building's first floor doorway and past the camera, the man right after her.

She leapt into a taxi. It veered in front of an oncoming truck.

A crash. A ball of fire. In a close-up, she scrambled

from the burning taxi and ran off through traffic. The man followed, firing a pistol at her.

I said, "Nina, this movie's absur..." My voice trailed off as I stared at the man running away from the camera. His hip stuck out each time his left foot hit the ground.

Chapter 12

Nina stuck with me as I stumbled into the aisle, down to the lobby, and out to the street. "I feel terrible," she said. "Had no idea a corny low budget movie would upset you so much."

"Where can I find a print?"

"I'll check with my projectionist friend."

I kept going, turned right at Railroad Avenue, and headed toward campus.

Nina said, "Please tell me what's going on."

"I thought my parents were murdered last spring. But my dad didn't die, at least not then. He was the man running and shooting the pistol."

"How awful about your parents, but how wonderful your dad is alive."

"Some people said he killed my mom. Which seemed unlikely when I thought he'd been murdered, too. Now I know he survived, I can't help wondering if he did it."

"That must be driving you crazy."

"I have to see my therapist."

"In the meantime, you can unload on me, if it helps."

I told her the few things I knew about my parents' deaths. I said I lived with my grandmother and described Prescott's *Seattle Times* article and her speculations about my parents' affairs. Nina listened, rapt, and I was thrilled to let someone in.

****

At our next session, when I told Dr. Kraig about seeing Dad in the movie, he said, "Charlie, you often have warped, unreliable perception."

"I know what I saw."

"You've seen lots of things that weren't real. When faced with horrible events, the mind seeks out facts to form a story to explain them."

"My friend Nina was there."

"You don't know she saw what you did. Consider the time frame. Your father left a few months ago. Movies take longer than that to finish."

"The projectionist said it was low budget. A movie with rough edges, taken away before it was finished. I have to go to Hollywood, check it out, and find my father."

"I doubt a cabin builder would get hired as an actor."

"Harrison Ford worked as a carpenter before he got his big break."

Dr. K asked my permission to contact Nina. I agreed. Surprised I didn't know her last name, I gave him her first name and room number. He ended our session and made an appointment for the next day.

When we started again, he said, "Your friend Nina described the film much like you did, but she has no way to know whether the actor was your father. She didn't say you were hallucinating, used the word euphoric. The *Dead Girls* film is no longer here so we can't check it against photos of your dad."

"It was him. I know it."

"Even if that's true, it doesn't make sense to go

83

find him. By walking out after your mom's death he proved he's irresponsible. He might be dangerous."

"Dad said he had to leave to keep me safe."

"And you believe him?"

"I want to."

"What will you do if you meet and decide he killed your mom?"

"Turn him in. Shoot him. Something."

"Awesome decision for a young woman beginning to deal with PTSD."

"Are you saying forget about my father?"

"I'm saying you'll have a better chance to navigate the wilds of Hollywood and face your father after another six months of therapy."

****

I found Nina in Ridgeview Commons, sitting alone, sucking a blackberry shake through a straw. "I like your shrink's advice," she said when I described our session.

"Why?"

She finished her shake with a slurp. "I hesitate to tell people—my parents don't believe me—but I plan to become an FBI agent. I read true crime and how-to cop books by the stack. It would be good practice for me to go to Hollywood and do reconnaissance. Your dad doesn't know me. I could find him and suss things out. Tell you where he is without you seeing each other— until or unless you're ready."

"I'd worry about you."

She licked the straw. "I get it. Dumb idea."

"Not dumb, generous, but I won't put you in jeopardy while I take care of myself."

She cupped her hand to her ear. "Listen to that

shouting. The soccer field's a good place for you to chill and get your head straight. On the way, you can tell me about this dad of yours, and we can figure out a plan."

While we hiked across campus, I told Nina about Dad's hunting, fishing, and hiking. She said, "Does he have lots of guns?"

"A Glock 17, a Beretta, and a Czech CZ-75 an army buddy brought him from Eastern Europe."

"Sounds like a movie hero."

"He can be tricky. Taught me to pick a lock with two paper clips or bobby pins."

"How?"

"You bend and twist and jiggle."

She grinned. "You're an outlaw family. I love that."

"We liked to play a game. I'd yell 'Heads up' and toss a knife at him. He'd flip it in mid-air and snag the handle. Never cut himself. Learned the trick from a Special Forces buddy."

"Did your mom mind you two being so close?"

"Sometimes she'd tease him about the way he talked—pronouncing 'root' like 'foot.' 'Root beer' as 'foot beer,' the way people did where he grew up in Minnesota. I didn't kid him because when I added a few extra pounds as a girl, he never joked about it."

As we approached a women's soccer game, two young men headed our way along the sidelines.

I said, "If by chilling you meant dating, you can forget it."

"I'm not trying to set you up. But it won't hurt to meet a couple of nice guys." She hugged the taller one. "Tim, this is my friend Charlie."

Arthur Coburn

Handsome and tanned, wearing a numbered jersey and shorts over muscular arms and legs, he looked like he'd stepped off a Wheaties box.

"Nice to meet you," he said, and flashed me a Wheaties box grin.

I checked my gut for a twinge of attraction. Zero.

"I'd also like to introduce Stephen," Nina said, turning to the second guy. His sandy hair peeked from under a long-billed baseball cap hiding most of his face. His skinny frame didn't fill his T-shirt and khakis, and he stood hunched over.

"Tim plays varsity soccer," Nina said. "And Stephen's a math whiz who can multiply huge numbers in his head, or cube them, or whatever mathematicians do."

I didn't have a good view of his face, but as he turned to watch a girl score, I made out black-marble eyes behind steel-rimmed glasses and a pointed nose.

When he gave my hand a clammy shake, I said I had studying to do and left.

Heading toward the dorm, I regretted abandoning Nina at the soccer field. I went to the library and found a few things to help her prep for her FBI career. I found a Fortune Magazine article naming the "50 Biggest Mafia Bosses," from Anthony "Fat Tony" Salerno of New York to Frank "The Horse" Buccieri of Chicago. It also listed Russian mobsters. I photocopied the article and a dozen other crime stories and took them to my room.

After four, I was sitting on my bed, asking the three-legged squirrel if I'd been silly to turn down Nina's offer to check Dad out. Before the squirrel answered, someone knocked. I opened the door.

Mary Sue stood there, kneading her hands. "You rushed from the theater, upset. Sorry. My fault for making comments about your dad."

Tony stepped from behind her. "Please forgive the intrusion. Mary Sue told me you'd been having trouble, so I came up from Concrete for the day."

Nina hurried down the hall to us and ushered Mary Sue and Tony aside. "Nice of you both to come, but Charlie's had a shock. A visit later would be better."

Tony stepped past Mary Sue. "I'm so sad about your mom's death. That must have been horrible for you. I would have come earlier to express my condolences but I figured you needed time to collect yourself."

Warmth flooded my chest as he talked.

Mary Sue said, "Charlie has other problems so—"

"I haven't started my contracting business yet," Tony said, "but I appreciated your encouragement." He seemed as genuine and handsome as ever. I loved his cutting Mary Sue off, and I cursed my PTSD for distancing me from him and Lottie.

I said, "Thanks for thinking of me, but Nina's right. Later would be better."

Mary Sue lingered a moment, her mouth open as if she wanted to say something, but Tony led her away.

When they'd gone, I said, "Nina you're a life saver. Mary Sue makes me nervous. Sorry for running away from the soccer field. I know you wanted to take my mind off my dad, but guys make me uneasy."

"Except Tony. Your face went red when he talked to you."

"Even Tony. He's special, but I can't connect with any boy now."

"My friend Stephen's not handsome but people say he's a sweet guy, and I could tell he liked you. He'd be a good friend."

"I have to focus on whether to stay in Bellingham or go search for a father who might be a killer."

Chapter 13

Goosebumps stood out on my arms as I rummaged through Lottie's storage closet.

I opened a box marked "Jefferson-Hunting" and pulled out an old decoy—a mallard with one glass eye missing and a tail chewed by mice. I shuffled through a bunch of hunting photos without seeing a familiar face, except Dad's.

I packed his duck call, the decoy, a camouflage vest, and dozens of photos into the panniers on my bike.

****

At the Lake View facility the next morning, I got Ruth's blessing to exhibit what I'd brought. While I laid everything on the sunroom table, Shanahan sat in his wheelchair outside the door on the deck, smoking and staring at an island in the lake where a pair of trumpeter swans were flapping their wings.

I blew the duck call, and Shanahan wheeled inside to the table. He laid his smoking cigarette on the edge, raised the call, and blew it several times. After he ran his fingers over the decoy, he surveyed the snapshots and pointed to a close-up of Dad hanging a deer carcass between two trees. In a crackly voice, his words starting and stopping like an old engine coming to life, he said, "Skinned…cleaned…fast. Great…with deer…geese… any game."

"Oh, my God. You remember my dad? Did you

know him well? What can you tell me?"

"Lots...blood...bruises."

From the gash on Mom's throat? Was Shanahan offering his cop's opinion that Dad killed her? He pointed to a photo of Dad slicing out a buck's innards. His finger moved to a blurry form in the background. "Me," he rasped and touched images of himself in other photos. "Your dad...terrific shot." Shanahan grinned.

No wonder he had comforted me and said Dad would come back.

I said, "I hope you didn't think I questioned what you told me about my dad."

"Haven't...talked...long time...staff...don't think I can." He sucked his cigarette. "A man...came...few times...asked about your dad."

"What did he want to know?"

"I'm not sure. Strange. Made me...nervous...my cop instincts kicking in...so I've kept mum." Shanahan's droopy basset eyes blinked. "Your parents' murders...my fault."

"What do you mean?"

He stared at the lake, and I suspected he either didn't remember what he'd been thinking or felt too ashamed to tell me.

I said, "Some people claim Dad killed my mom. I've wondered myself. A writer from around here says Dad drank too much and went nuts when Mom had a fling with some Hollywood producer."

Shanahan coughed smoke over the photos and spoke with growing confidence. "When you were a child a fidgety movie producer...came here...bragged about his action films." Shanahan cleared his throat and went on. "The guy had read about your dad's log cabins...wanted to buy one. He'd put gun battles in all his films...but hadn't fired a serious weapon or gone hunting. Your dad and I...took him. Had a ball."

"Did a female star go on your trips? Did my dad flirt with her?"

"The blonde?" He chuckled. "That honey could make a pair of jeans...look like they'd shimmied straight out of *Playboy*. Can't say your dad didn't find her sexy, but he never chased her. The cabin sale fell through...she and the producer went back to Hollywood."

"Why did you say my parents' deaths were your fault?"

He wheeled his chair out the door to the end of the deck.

I followed, hugging my arms across my chest against a cold breeze blowing in as lightning flashed in the distance. Rain dimpled the lake, and big drops splatted on our arms and heads.

Shanahan massaged the scar on his temple. "Your dad drank more and more in the days before your mom died." He lit a fresh cigarette. "Don't recall details since my accident. I do know one afternoon your dad drove through town, face bruised...blood on his shirt, on his knuckles. Mumbled about fighting with some guy. If I'd locked him...in the tank a night or two...neither of your folks would have died."

"Dad drove through town the day some guy murdered my mom?"

He nodded.

"Coming from our house?"

"From the other side of town, going fast."

"Did you tell anyone?"

"Told Bremmer, the county detective. He said he'd check into it. Complained to my boss. Accused me of sticking my nose into his case, tried to have the city fire me. I started drinking heavy. Crashed one night during a call on Highway 20 near Sedro Wooley. Crawled out right before the cruiser caught fire. I swore someone sabotaged the brakes."

From a bag on his wheelchair, he pulled a handful of cracked corn and dropped the kernels to several ducks on the water by the deck.

"Did you have other ideas nobody listened to? What about the bloody sketches beside my mom's body?"

"Reminded me of Lower Skagit Indian bird designs. But I couldn't find Indian connections to your folks."

"Anything else?"

Ruth came to the doorway and motioned us in out of the rain.

I stayed put after she left, preferring to keep our conversation private.

Shanahan puffed his cigarette until the rain put it out. "I didn't find skid marks…on the pavement or the shoulder where your dad's truck went into the river. Just shallow indentations on the grass."

"You saying my dad didn't go out of control? Somebody got him to stop, killed him, and pushed his truck into the water?"

He shrugged. "Nobody wanted to hear from me."

"Any other details bother you?"

"Bremmer and the Medical Examiner claimed an animal had chewed away your dad's hands and jaw. I didn't see tooth marks on the bones. But I'm no doctor."

"You were on target about plenty. I hope you can help me understand something. Dad acted in a movie made after everyone thought he'd died."

Shanahan's eyes widened. "Your dad's alive?"

"I hope so, but I'm upset he didn't contact me. Do you know why?"

He shook his head.

The sun broke through the overcast and glinted on something shiny at the far side of the lake. A male figure in a tan jacket, binoculars hanging around his neck, pointed a parabolic mic at several areas along the near shore.

"Birder," Shanahan said. "They come to photograph and record bird calls. The guy showed up the other day. Same jacket."

Several men and women with binoculars stood farther away on the lake edge.

When the man in the tan jacket panned his microphone along the near shore, I thought about Prescott, and bells tinkled in my brain. Was the guy recording birds, or us?

I asked, "Do you have a theory about who killed my mom and who tried to make it look like my dad died?"

"Nope. Big Shot Bremmer didn't either." Eyes twinkling, Shanahan added, "But I got to kiss the movie star. Bremmer didn't."

"Tell me about the kiss."

"After I taught her how to shoot, she bagged a deer. Jumped around like she'd won an Oscar and gave me a big smacker." He pointed to his cheek, tugged a wallet from his pocket, and pulled out a faded photo of a woman with wavy hair, large expressive eyes, and a teasing smile.

"You know her name?"

"Lynn Hannah—she wrote it on my arm in ball point. Told me if I ever came to Hollywood, to say hello. Sunset Villa Studios. Famous place, she said. Gave me photos of herself and the producer."

"Can I see them?"

"Lost 'em somewhere."

"You remember the producer's name?"

"Sorry."

"Would anyone in Concrete know?"

"The pair didn't mix with town people."

****

At the dorm, I called Los Angeles directory assistance from a phone booth. They didn't have anything for Lynn Hannah. Did she die, or have an unlisted number? I found no entry for Sunset Villa Studios either but noticed one for Sunset *Vista* Productions.

I had decided to major in philosophy and opened my textbook to study. I was reading the forward when Nina knocked and came in. "My projectionist friend says a guy he knows found the *Dead Girls* reels and sent them to him. Most of the opening credit section was missing, the end credits, too. My friend hasn't a clue where to look for personnel lists. He says it may not matter because actors and crew use phony names on sleazy movies, the way authors hide behind pen names."

"Don't worry. I have an actress's name and a studio to check."

Chapter 14

"I met a man who knew Dad well," I said on the phone to Dr. Kraig. "The cop who came to our house the day of Mom's murder. What he told me changes everything."

Dr. Kraig said, "I'd hate to see you get ahead of yourself."

"He gave me leads to find Dad. So, I won't be lost in LA. I'd like to come see you again to prepare for the trip."

"I'd be glad to give you a session. But I'm canceling office appointments for the next couple of days while a forensics team goes through the place."

"You've been attacked. Now you see why—"

"No one attacked me. Someone broke into my office and stole patient files."

"The redhead."

"We haven't proved she exists except as a character in your mind."

"She does exist and she's closing in."

"I don't know if the intruder stole your records or viewed them. I have lots of patients, including scientists from the U. The breach could relate to any of them. But let's have a phone session now."

I said, "Your break-in makes it more urgent I find Dad before the redhead or whoever she's working with. I bet she knows I'm after her. That's why she followed me, why she snooped around Lottie's house, why I kept seeing her in Bellingham, why—"

"If this redhead presents a danger to your grandmother, won't going away be risky for her?"

When I didn't respond for several seconds, he said, "Charlie?"

"I'll stay and watch out for my Gram."

****

I went to the bookstore to buy a copy of *Wuthering Heights* for English class and came across Nina in the comparative literature section.

"You look stressed," she said.

"Someone rifled my shrink's office and might have taken my files. Had to be the redhead."

"That's a leap, Charlie."

"After what happened to my parents, I have to assume the worst."

"It must be awful to feel so exposed."

"Like I'm naked. Ever felt that way?"

"Once when I wore a super-skimpy bikini to my brother's pool party." She bit her lip. "I shouldn't be joking when you're upset."

"Don't worry. My dad and I joked all the time about embarrassing subjects."

"If there's the slightest chance of a connection between the redhead and your dad—"

"I can't bail on my grandma right now. I'll live at her house and ride my bike to class."

"I like that. Means I'll see you all the time."

When Nina left to prepare for her history class, I dropped the *Wuthering Heights* book in my room and went for a swim in the Rec Center pool. After twenty laps I shuffled to the dressing room, stripped out of my swimsuit, and stepped into the shower.

Through the water cascading onto my face, I noticed a girl with reddish hair pass my stall, wearing shorts and a halter top. I peeked out and glimpsed her leaving the locker room.

Wrapping a towel around me, I hurried into the hallway and hid behind a partition while she joined a guy thirty feet away. My PTSD hearing made out whispered fragments of their conversation.

The guy: "...have a lead...should be able...find him...so we can finish..."

The redhead asked, "Where?"

"Hollywood. I've got...address here somewhere."

While he searched his backpack, I moved behind a crowd of students heading their way. The guy pulled out a slip of paper. "Here it is." As he opened his mouth to read, someone yanked my towel off. Howls erupted behind me. A crowd formed, boys whistling, girls giggling. The commotion covered up whatever the guy said, and the pair climbed on a motor scooter and rode away.

I snatched the towel from the sidewalk, rewrapped it, and hurried to the locker room. After a long, steamy shower, I dressed and went to the dorm.

I rapped on Nina's door for twenty seconds without getting a response.

She hurried toward me from the bathroom, wearing a robe and flip flops, her hair turbaned in a towel. "What's the emergency?" she asked, opening her door and stepping inside.

"I'm going to Los Angeles to find my dad as soon as I get to Lottie's and pack."

"I'll be ready in half an hour." She pulled a

suitcase from her closet.

"I'd love you to come but—"

"I have to help."

"I won't be here to watch out for Lottie. I know it's horrible to ask, but after your talk about becoming an FBI agent, I'd love it if you stopped by her house from time to time to see if anyone's lurking in the neighborhood."

"I could move in."

I pictured Lottie's conniption at the thought we were babysitting her. "Peek in once a day."

"I'd rather be helping you in Los Angeles, but if Grandma-minding will make you feel better, I'm in." She smiled, but her shoulders sagged.

Nina was so poised and able. I shuddered at the prospect of braving Hollywood without her. I'd find out if I had the Concrete toughness Principal Dalton had promised.

Chapter 15

Lit by a waning moon, the distant Mount Baker glaciers glowed like pale blue neon under a black sky. Bugs attracted by my hissing camping lantern swarmed before my eyes. I waved a hand through them and continued tightening the cables on a new battery in my grandpa's 1954 station wagon.

The Plymouth hadn't moved in years, its turquoise body dented and rusty, the engine caked with grime. I'd ridden home from the U. and made two bike runs—to buy a battery, a can of starting fluid, new spark plugs, and a plastic jerrican of gasoline. In four hours of tinkering the car hadn't started.

My wrench slipped off the battery cable, scraping my knuckles on the air filter. I whacked it. "Goddamn."

"Taking the Lord's name in vain is a sure road to trouble." Lottie strode toward me, her long skirt swishing across the last of our mustard greens and rhubarb plants. She kicked a tire with her sandal. "I should have had this heap towed away the day your grandpa died."

"I'll get it running. Dad taught me engine mechanics," I said, proud to be praising his skills, despite my uncertainty about what he might have done to Mom.

"Teaching you he respected his family would have been more like it. Finding a decent job instead of leaving your mother to pinch every dollar until it screamed." She broke off a wilted rose and tossed it under the Plymouth.

I said, "Dad hated office work, but he built fabulous cabins." I'd spent countless afternoons from age four on, watching from a sawhorse while he cut and wrangled heavy logs—if one fell, it could have crushed his spine.

Lottie said, "Too bad he didn't use his guns and hammers to protect your mother."

I met her angry look. "Did he mention any Hollywood movie people?"

"No."

"Do you have order slips in his papers for a cabin a producer was going to buy?"

"Your dad complained about losing some special deal, but I didn't keep track of his business."

"Did you ever hear Mom or Dad talk about a woman named Lynn Hannah? If I can find her—"

"A few weeks ago, you were out of your mind, worrying about some local girl attacking you. Now you're planning a trip to Los Angeles where you'll be up to your neck in wild and dangerous people." She exhaled a long breath and lowered her voice. "I know you're doing your best with Doctor Kraig. Someday you'll be ready for a trip like this but not yet."

I sprayed another burst of starting fluid into the air filter, slid behind the steering wheel, and cranked the engine. It turned over, whining and coughing, but didn't start. I sprayed another blast of fluid. Turned the key. More coughs. Loud bangs.

Lottie slammed the hood closed. "Enough."

I kept cranking. The car shook as the engine

caught, and oily exhaust swirled around Lottie.

I got out, grinning.

She waved the smoke from her face. "This wreck won't even make it to Seattle. Besides, you have no way to find your father in Los Angeles."

"I have the address and the personnel roster of the company that made his film," I said, hoping the fib would calm her fears.

"Don't leave school. Your fall quarter will be over before Christmas."

"I'll be gone ten days at most and finish my assignments when I get back."

"You don't have any money."

"Enough from odd jobs to buy gas for the trip."

"What are you going to say if you find your father? 'How's life?' For all you know, he killed your mother. The police found his bloody footprints all over the house and his fingerprints on a knife they pulled from a storm drain."

"I have to find out what happened."

"If he's guilty, he won't let you get close." She took my hand. "You may think you're all grown up, but you don't know about the men a girl can run into in a place like Hollywood." She dabbed her eyes with a hanky.

I blinked away a tear of my own. "I promise I'll be careful and hurry home."

Lottie opened the car door, turned off the motor, and grasped my arm. She towed me into the house, settled me on the sofa, and fished through piles of papers in her roll-top desk. She brought out a wooden box and removed a picture of Mom in a white wedding dress, Dad in a tuxedo. She passed me the photo.

"You can get married to a worthy man if you're sensible now."

I nodded to make her feel better but I couldn't imagine marrying.

She held up a box of VHS tapes. "I rented *The Third Man* and some wonderful Katherine Hepburn films: *Stage Door, Bringing up Baby,* and *Woman of the Year.* Work on your class assignments here between movies."

"We'll do that for sure when I get back, Gram."

She sighed.

In her desk, beneath pictures of Mom, I found one of Dad in his fatigues, posing with a dozen army buddies in a Vietnam jungle clearing. I found advertising pamphlets with color photos of log houses he'd built. Beneath all the papers I unearthed Dad's .45 caliber Colt, an empty, seven-round magazine, and an old driver's license with a faded photo.

Lottie put the gun back. "Forgot I kept that awful thing. You should, too." She returned the box to her desk. "Stay here and finish school. Your future will depend on your education, not on some hare-brained trip."

When Lottie went to bed, I searched her desk without success for Dad's old address book. In the back of a drawer, I found a pile of family doctor bills and medical records, which I packed in my suitcase along with the .45, its magazine, and Dad's driver's license.

I went upstairs, filled the claw-foot tub with hot water, and tried to soak away Lottie's doubts. But when I grabbed a hand mirror beside the tub what met my eyes, between the dark patches where the silver backing had broken down, were glimpses of Mom's eyes, searching mine for an explanation for what happened to her life.

Chapter 16

The next morning, I awoke to rain pelting the roof and water dripping from a ceiling leak into a pan by the window.

The squirrel chattered from the tree. I tossed a few almonds onto the sill. "If you can survive on three paws, I can make this LA trip with three quarters of a psyche."

He said, "Don't screw up, Charlie."

I searched my bedroom for my Remington 870 and the Smith & Wesson Shield. They were nowhere to be seen. Lottie must have confiscated them. No point asking—she wouldn't say where she hid them. I hurried down to the kitchen with my suitcase. Lottie set a plate of fried eggs and sausages in front of me at the table.

"I'm too excited to eat. Be home soon, Gram." I grabbed the suitcase, headed outside...and halted. The mangy Plymouth had gone, leaving a muddy patch and a set of wide tire tracks across the garden.

I stomped up the porch stairs to Lottie. "What the hell happened?"

She hugged her terry cloth robe to her chest. "Your grandfather, God bless him, wouldn't forgive me if I let you run off to a place like Los Angeles. I had the car towed away to the crusher first thing this morning."

Swearing under my breath, I carried my suitcase to my room. Lottie's ploy made me more determined to make the trip to LA. I transferred my clothes and toiletries into my two panniers.

Retrieved the .45 from my suitcase and shoved it to the bottom of a pannier along with Dad's license and the papers.

I changed into Spandex biking shorts, a biking shirt, and biking shoes. I put on my helmet and rain jacket, carried my bike across the mud to the road, and headed into the downpour.

Seconds later, the Chevy rumbled alongside me. Lottie shouted over the thrumming rain, "Biking to California will take you weeks."

I kept going.

She cut me off. I planted my feet astride the bike. "I'm nineteen. You can't stop me."

"This trip is a fool's errand. Your dad was too ornery and tough to pal around with movie people. You imagined he was on that screen."

"Go home, Gram."

She got out, the rain plastering white curls to her forehead. "I can see you're determined. With all the college expenses, I can't afford to fly you, but this should be enough for a bus ticket." She passed me a roll of bills. "At least give me a hug."

We embraced, her tears warm against my neck.

She said, "I hear Hollywood is full of ruthless people. Call and let me know you're all right."

I thanked her, stuffed the roll of bills with my other savings into my purse, and stowed it in a pannier along with a half-dozen peanut-butter-and-cheese-cracker packs Lottie handed me.

The rain eased. I mounted my bike and pedaled away. Lottie followed me the two miles to the bus terminal, which shared space in Bellingham's red brick Amtrak station. A heavy freight roared by so loud it had me swerving all the way to the station entrance.

After Lottie waved good-bye and left, I walked my bike into the waiting room. Travel posters offered views of snow-capped Cascade Mountains and sailboats crossing Puget Sound. A half dozen people sat on a wooden bench. A couple with a child ordered cocoa and cookies at the snack counter. Keeping Lottie's money in reserve, I used some of my savings to purchase a bus ticket, moved to a window, and gazed at Mount Baker, fifty miles to the east.

The summit lay half-hidden in gray clouds. The glaciers, cliffs, and forests around the ancient volcano stretched out like wilderness petticoats. My throat tightened at the thought of leaving Lottie and the northwest I loved.

I called Nina from the waiting room phone booth and told her I'd be taking a bus to Los Angeles in a couple of hours.

She wished me luck, and we said a tearful good-bye.

I fished a few more coins from my purse, telephoned Lake View, and asked to speak to Officer Shanahan.

"That's not possible," Ruth said in a hushed tone.

"I promise I won't bother him. I want to say thanks for his help."

"Since you were so kind and got him talking after his long silence, it pains me to tell you last night he missed bed check. He sneaked out for a late-night smoke, wheeled himself to the end of the deck, went through a weak section of railing, and drowned."

My heart stuttered. Had the poor man grown tired of life trapped in his wheelchair? Had my questions depressed him? Or had someone rolled him off the deck into the lake?

I asked, "Did he leave any papers or letters?"

"His cousin picked up everything this morning."

"His cousin?"

"The man who's been coming to visit from time to time."

"You know his name?"

"Robert Smythe. He brought a letter from a lawyer listing him as Shanahan's executor."

"Don't you have protocols for releasing a patient's things?"

"Of course, but Mr. Shanahan hadn't listed relatives when he arrived."

"You didn't make Smythe show a court order or a driver's license?" I asked in a steely tone.

"Our protocols don't require…Oh dear, I hope we didn't make a mistake."

I closed my eyes, realizing I deserved the anger I'd aimed at her. When Shanahan first mentioned the man who had showed up and unnerved him, I should have quizzed him and Ruth for more information. I'd have to be more attentive in the future.

I gave a long sigh. "I'm sure it's been a traumatic time for everyone. Apologies for my harsh tone."

When we hung up, I recalled the birder across the lake and how his parabolic mic had panned past Shanahan and me while we talked. I pictured Elaine Prescott's incinerated house. Her death and Shanahan's could have been unrelated. Perhaps viewing Hollywood noir films with Lottie had made me ready to imagine foul play. But two lethal events coming so soon after my inquiries made the hairs on the back of my neck stiffen.

****

Two hours later, I stowed my bike in the bus's baggage compartment, changed into jeans and a cotton top in the ladies' room, and boarded. I walked past an assortment of passengers, ages seven to seventy, and went to a seat toward the rear.

A thin young man with close-cropped strawberry blond hair advanced along the aisle, wearing a gray Bellingham T-shirt, his head inclined forward, face covered by the bill of a baseball cap, steel-rimmed glasses obscuring his eyes. Those details, his slumping posture, and hesitant step pegged him for me as Nina's math whiz friend Stephen, from the soccer field.

I sat and draped my arm over the place beside me to discourage him from sitting there. As the front door whooshed closed, he glanced my way before taking a spot three rows ahead. Nina had said Stephen liked me. Had he talked her into telling him my itinerary?

"Get over yourself," the squirrel chided from a branch in my mind.

Indeed. If Nina wanted to nudge me into dating, she'd have been too respectful to reveal my plans, knowing how uncomfortable I felt around boys. Stephen was probably heading for a math conference in Seattle or somewhere farther south.

I tried to relax by tilting my seat back, closing my eyes, and imagining the chairman of Sunset Vista Productions greeting me from behind his mahogany desk. We'd talk about his actress, Lynn Hannah, and her trip to Concrete with a producer to buy a log cabin.

The chairman would invite me to watch the crew shoot a scene on his studio lot and tell me, between takes, how to find Dad.

Chapter 17

When I opened my eyes, Stephen sat three rows ahead, reading a newspaper.

Though his lack of attention to me calmed my nerves, my fingers gripped the armrests. Heading to Los Angeles felt like sliding toward the bottom of the continent. I envisioned my ties to Bellingham like rubber bands, stretching farther with each mile. When I got to California the bands might be so weak, I'd never get home.

I huddled under my jacket and tried to stay calm, but my amygdala danger warnings, as Dr. Kraig called them, were like burglar alarms that kept going off.

As country vistas whizzed by outside, I rubbed a patch of the foggy window clear. Across a field, a farmhouse leaned in the wind. A dog tore about the yard, inspiring a scenario in my mind: Scout barks as the killer enters our house; the man threatens him; Scout runs away—I refused to imagine the gruesome alternative.

I tilted my seat back and took a deep breath but couldn't relax. The bus was carrying me away from Mary Sue, but also away from Lottie, Nina, and the northwest I loved—to look for a father who might kill me if he had murdered Mom and I confronted him. Lottie's voice echoed in my brain: "Someday you'll be ready for a trip like this, but not yet."

After more miles of countryside, suburban neighborhoods flashed by, then Seattle skyscrapers. Had Dad taken the same bus to Los Angeles last spring?

The bathroom door snapped open behind me, releasing a foul odor, like the deer gut smell.

As we rumbled along, it had me drifting in and out of consciousness.

Dad throws a waitress off the roof. She runs from the building toward a waiting taxi. It bursts into flame. She runs away, Dad shooting at her.

I follow bloody footprints up the stairs...and see Dad in camouflage gear, flirting with a beautiful blonde.

A phone rings. I race to it and answer. A soft breath plays on my ear. "Mom," I say, "is that you?"

"Don't be silly, dear. My hands are too bloody to hold a phone."

****

The bus schedule had us arriving thirty-six hours later at nine p.m. the next day. But mechanical problems kept delaying things. We spent most of a night getting roadside repairs and arrived at the bus terminal in Los Angeles at seven the second morning.

I changed into biking clothes in the ladies' room, collected my bike, wheeled it outside, and gazed at palm trees towering three stories into an azure sky.

I walked my bike to a shoebox of a snack shop smelling of burnt coffee and greasy hot dogs and bought a Los Angeles street map.

Outside, his face turned away, Stephen waited at a city bus stop, studying a schedule.

On my map, I found the location of Sunset Vista

Productions, twenty miles away in Van Nuys. I marked the route in yellow, lathered sunscreen on my face and arms, and went north a mile on Alameda Street into an area of rice-paper-screened windows and Japanese pedestrians. I rode another mile to a neighborhood with orange hip-and-gable roofs, Chinese lanterns, and shop windows displaying strings of roasted ducks. A sweet soy aroma in the air made me ravenous.

Worried about money, I held my hunger at bay, rode another half an hour, and stopped at a restaurant called Mort's Deli. Inside at a window table, a tanned, silver-haired gentleman in a linen sport jacket chatted with a young woman about twenty. She had amber eyes and a flawless complexion, and she tossed waves of her coffee-brown hair for effect every few moments as she spoke.

I locked my bike to a lamppost, carried my purse inside, and walked past a wall of movie star photos with greetings written in Sharpie: "Mort, you're the best," "Tastiest breakfasts in LA," "Keep the brisket coming."

At the hostess's station I checked the menu and decided I couldn't afford the corned beef sandwich, cabbage roll, or omelet.

The couple I'd seen from outside occupied a nearby booth. The man patted the brunette's hand and said in a soothing tone, "You'll be an amazing surgeon."

She blushed. "I won't disappoint you; I promise."

That's what a dad should do, I thought. Stay around and encourage his daughter's dreams.

The young woman pulled a movie script from a shoulder bag. "I love the scene where she goes to the housing project to find the blind boy."

The three-legged squirrel appeared in my head and snickered. "Get with it, Charlie. She's an actress, buttering up a producer."

Before I could step forward to ask the man if he knew about Sunset Vista Productions or Zolton Baron, he slid his hand under the young woman's skirt and up her thigh. I expected her to startle and push him away. But she opened the script to a folded page, and gushed, "The scene where she operates and restores the boy's sight makes me cry every time."

The man's hand inched farther up her leg.

Lottie one, Charlie zero.

The chance of being vulnerable like this actress inspired me to pull out Lottie's roll of cash. Inside it I found a photo of my grandma in her twenties, wearing a one-piece bathing suit and reclining on a beach towel. Three boys stood near, eyeing her. On the back of the photo she had written, "Charlotte, my sweet girl. I remember the pleasures of being young. Stay clear of unscrupulous people but try to find some joy along the way."

Reading Lottie's note reminded me that during the bus ride, awash in memories and concerns about what I'd find in Los Angeles, I had not reviewed the documents and medical records I'd brought. I pulled them from my pannier, went inside, and settled in the restaurant's phone booth. I found a page from an OBGYN visit of Mom's with an invoice for an "SAB," listed as a spontaneous abortion.

I called Lottie from the pay phone. "I'm safe in Los Angeles. Thanks so much for the photo and the money. But I'm stunned. Why did Mom have an abortion?"

"Don't worry about that."

"I want to know."

Lottie went silent.

"Gram?"

"A spontaneous abortion is another name for a miscarriage. Your mom had several."

"When?"

"Before you came along. They distressed her so much she gave up trying to conceive for a while. Your parents wanted to adopt but found it expensive and difficult."

"Who did they try to adopt from?"

"You mean, 'From whom did they try to adopt?' From some man with a foreign name. The main thing is, your mom was delighted when you came along."

I doubted Lottie had told me everything, but pushing her didn't work. I said thanks and hung up, wondering what else—besides the miscarriages, Shanahan's revelations, and Prescott's—I didn't know about my parents.

I put more coins in the pay phone, rang Ridgeview Delta, and asked for Nina. When she came on, I said, "I think your math whiz friend Stephen rode on my bus. Did he ask you about my plans?"

"No way."

A man banged on the phone booth door, twirling his finger for me to wrap up the call.

I nodded and asked Nina, "Have you run into Stephen on campus?"

"I've been busy studying—didn't realize college would be so hard. You positive the guy was Stephen?"

"My mind whipsaws so often with PTSD fantasies I can't tell what's real and what isn't. I'd bet money it was Stephen, though he never approached me. When I left, he was waiting at a city bus stop." I told Nina about Sunset Vista Productions. "If they don't know where I can find Zolton Baron or my dad, I'll be out of luck."

"Where is this Sunset Vista place, in case I need to reach you?"

I gave her the address.

"Speaking of strangers," Nina said, "Your friend, Mary Sue, found out my room number. She's been by, asking me to talk you into coming to get help."

"If you see her again, say I'm fine."

The man knocked louder. "Not your private office."

I told Nina I missed her, and we hung up. I pushed the door, but it wouldn't open. Pushed harder. No luck.

I stand in our bathroom, Mom's body at my feet. I grab the princess phone from the floor and listen to the dead earpiece. I want to run but don't know the way out.

The man knocked again. "Come on."

Sweat beading on my forehead, I pushed the door. It didn't budge. Struggling to breathe in the clammy booth, I pushed harder. Nothing. I braced my back against the phone and slammed both feet against the door. It flew open. I burst out and escaped to the sidewalk, determined to avoid tight spaces the rest of my life.

Chapter 18

Commercial jets from the nearby airport roared into the smoggy sky above Van Nuys Boulevard as I biked by stores and restaurants.

My route to Sunset Vista Productions went down a side street, past stucco bungalows with modest lawns landscaped with palm, lemon, and avocado trees, to a ranch house surrounded by a bamboo fence. Not the grand movie studio I had imagined from Shanahan's description. Perhaps a boutique operation making quality, low-budget films.

To break the ice with the company president, I planned to mention a few off-beat titles Lottie and I had rented, like *Husbands* and *One-Eyed Jacks,* or *Rebecca*, Lottie's favorite Hitchcock movie.

I pushed the intercom button. The gate buzzed open, and I walked my bike into a yard of plants with wide, striped leaves, buds with curled tips, and red and orange bird-beaked flowers. Through a tall hedge I glimpsed a pool. The air smelled of cocoa butter—my first taste of enchanting Hollywood.

A young woman in tight black jeans and a striped top opened the ranch house door and nudged a garden slug off the step with her tennis shoe. Heavy liner circled her large brown eyes. Her scarlet lipstick stood out against bone-white skin—shades of Elvira, the actress I'd seen introducing horror films on Halloween.

I thought, please don't let this be a slasher studio.

"If you're in the water scene," Miss Scarlet Lipstick said, "Change in there." She pointed to a hut on the far side of the pool.

I tried to still my trembling hands and said, "I need to see your producer."

"Name's Ray India. He doesn't interview talent on shoot days." She ran her eyes up and down my body, pausing at my chest. "Hmmm. One of our kittens is missing in action, and Ray likes a variety of body types, so he'll talk to you. Follow me." She led the way through a living room with a faux zebra skin sofa and chairs and deposited me in an office with a desk made of a sheet of thick glass on aluminum sawhorses.

Behind it, a skinny, balding man wearing a green silk shirt puffed on a cigarillo as he shuffled through eight-by-ten face shots.

A poster board on a side wall displayed pictures of men and women in various stages of undress— buttocks, crotches, and breasts in lush color.

I'd come to a porn studio.

Maybe Shanahan's mind had been so fogged or dazzled by memories of the blonde he had given me the wrong studio name. Perhaps Lynn Hannah had been a tavern waitress in Concrete and not an actress at all. Or maybe she hadn't existed.

The seamy quality of Sunset Vista hung in the air like the smell of a week-old trout. About to rush out the door, I spotted, leaning against a filing cabinet, a faded poster featuring a blonde with electric blue eyes and the pleased expression of a woman sure of her beauty. A boa constrictor twined around her naked torso.

Large neon letters announced, "Hannah Lynn, in

Serpent's Lair. Opening June 1975."

Not Lynn Hannah. Shanahan had reversed the blonde's first and last names.

He and Dad were pals with a porn star.

India studied me. "Right age. A demure librarian might work in the junior high scene. But your hair's a mess. Who sent you?"

"I'm not here for an audition."

India jetted a stream of cigarillo smoke and flicked an ash off his desk. "Then you're wasting my time."

Thinking of Mom's courage dealing with her miscarriages, I summoned a bit of my own. "Do...you know anything about a movie called *Dead Girls Don't Lie?*"

"I'm trying to shoot a picture, and everybody's screwing with me." He leaned to the side, peered around me, and shouted, "Vikki, you got a replacement for Terry yet?"

Miss Scarlet Lipstick answered, "I thought this girl..."

India turned to me.

I said, "I'm looking for my father, Jefferson Purdue. He had a small part in a movie called *Dead Girls Don't Lie,* produced by Zolton Baron. If you can tell me anything about him or the movie, I'd appreciate it."

India opened a drawer and pulled out a handful of business cards. "Baron, sure. Card's in here somewhere. I'll find his phone number. Now I think of it, I'm sure I met your dad."

"Really?"

"No time to look. I'll check later—if you help me. We shoot in twenty minutes. Terrific part. We'll fit you with a sexy wig."

Stomach tightening, I turned away. My eyes landed on a second poster. The film's title, *His Favorite Girl,* glowed in orange neon. A nude woman bent over a muscular man wearing a thong and a wolf's head.

"No thanks," I mumbled.

India dropped the cards into his desk drawer and shouted past me, "Wake Tootie Conners. If she's half sober, get her butt here ten minutes ago." He returned to his head shots. "Find your way out."

I asked, "Does Hannah Lynn work here?"

"No."

"Did she die?"

"Not as far as I know." India waved me away with his cigarillo.

"How can I locate her?"

"You can't."

My lead was evaporating. No chance for help finding Dad unless I acted in a sex film. I started toward the door. The squirrel popped into my head and growled, "You won't endure a little humiliation to locate your father and find out who murdered your mother?"

I cleared my throat. "In your movie..." Am I saying this? "...what would I have to do?"

"A couple of shots. Cash in your pocket. One of our sexy actors will fondle your ass."

No one had ever fondled my ass. And in my PTSD mind, no one ever would. I averted my eyes from *His Favorite Girl.* "What if you find my dad's card, then I do the part?"

India tapped his cigarillo on an ashtray shaped like a girl's open mouth. "I didn't just pop out of the cabbage patch, Miss—?"

"Becker," I said, inventing a name. "If I do your shot, do you promise to tell me where to find my father? First name's Jefferson, handsome, walks with a limp."

India's smile widened to reveal a set of glistening teeth. "Cross my heart."

He frowned at something behind me.

A fortyish woman in a long-sleeved silk blouse and gray slacks stood in the doorway at the back of the office, her green eyes studying us, fingers toying with an ash-blonde braid hanging down her chest. She pressed her lips together in a thoughtful pout as if trying to remember if she'd left food out for her cat.

"You're late," India told her.

For what? She didn't have voluptuous breasts or a seductive expression.

"Pileup on the 101."

"Candy Star's waiting for you."

She backed out of the doorway.

"Where do I go?" I asked. Before I had to see any naked bodies or take off my jersey and sports bra, I could ask crew members if they knew about my dad or *Dead Girls*.

India told Vikki to get me a wig, horn-rimmed glasses, and "the usual."

She crooked a finger.

I followed.

On my way out I glanced at Hannah Lynn's poster. Her heavy eye makeup and coquettish smile couldn't hide a sweetness that must have entranced Shanahan and my dad.

Vikki led me into a studio throbbing with a disco

beat. In a corner, two honey blondes in skimpy bras and G-strings primped. One, with a round face, double Ds, and buttocks the size of Christmas hams, applied turquoise eyeliner.

The other—slender and toned as a marathoner, with a modest chest and lemur eyes, rouged her nipples.

I studied the floor tiles while Miss DD said, "Baby, I need you so bad," with all the emotion of a woman reading a hardware catalogue.

Braid Woman said, "Try again. Take your time."

"Baby, *I*...need you. *I* need you so bad."

"Don't emphasize the 'I.' Add emotion. Picture your favorite lover."

Miss DD stuck out her chest and purred, "Baby, I need you so bad" with more feeling than I would have imagined.

At the sound of male voices, I pictured myself half-naked in front of the camera, all the men leering. My face burned. I wanted to run but, imagining Mom's horror in the seconds before the killer slashed her throat, I kept my head down and my feet planted until Braid Woman finished coaching. I stepped forward to ask if she knew Zolton Baron, but she turned away.

Vikki ushered me into a curtained-off space, handed me a string bikini, and left.

I pinched the tiny garments between my thumb and forefinger.

A paunchy man with a day's growth of beard and heavy circles under his eyes stepped in, cradling a camera in his left arm. "You lie on the bed. Commander pulls off your G-string with his teeth and gets down to business while Zeus does Candy Star. Give me lots of hip action and moans."

A wave of nausea launched my last peanut-butter-and-cheese snack onto the dressing table. I imagined Lottie watching and threw up again.

"You don't look ready," the cameraman said. "You've got to look like you enjoy getting turned on or it won't work."

I asked, "You know about a film called—"

"You're a hundred miles from turned on which begs the question, do you want to get paid? Or walk your ass out of here and never work for us again?"

"You mean *raises* the question."

"What?"

"You mean it raises the question," I said, reciting one of Lottie's favorite lessons. "To beg a question is to answer it with information contained in the question itself. For example, if I ask, 'Why do you make so much money' and you say, because my paychecks are big, that would be begging the—"

"Drop the English lesson, sweetie, and get ready to work."

When he left, Braid Woman passed me a folded note, retreated, and after a few tries got Miss DD to make "Baby, you make me so hot" sound enticing.

Braid Woman's note read, "LEAVE. India wouldn't know your father from Eddie Murphy. Black Cat Café. Twenty minutes."

I peeked through the curtain, past a variety of fleshy body parts to a half-open door. I dropped the bikini and hurried through the forest of oiled bodies, knocking over a tray of cookies and a pot of coffee. I collided with the camera tripod, tipped over a light stand, and dashed outside.

"Hey, come back," Vikki called after me, but I

jumped on my Raleigh and pedaled off, veering to avoid a cat scrambling out of my way.

A horrendous experience avoided, just.

Lottie two, Charlie zero.

Chapter 19

I locked my bike to a light pole and entered a café filled with blue-haired women and balding men seated at Formica tables. They nursed cups of coffee and nibbled donuts covered with rainbow sprinkles. Crepe paper ghosts and pumpkins decorated the back wall where a sign invited everyone to "Join us for the Black Cat's Halloween party."

I picked up two coffees and sat at a corner table.

Braid Woman hurried in and joined me. Crow's feet made her look older than she had in the studio—but refined, like my English professor.

"Wise choice, leaving," she said.

"Do you know my father, Jefferson Purdue? After my mom was murdered a few months ago he disappeared and came down here. Might have used a different name."

"Lots of name-changing in LA. I'm Laurel, but people know me as Sally at the studio. I don't want carryover from India's world into my regular dialogue-coaching career." She stirred cream into her coffee and sipped. "Haven't met your dad. Why is he in LA?"

I told her about Mom's murder and about seeing Dad in *Dead Girls Don't Lie*. "Do you know anything about that film?"

"Rumors."

"Have friends who worked on it?"

"Dale Henson, the DP, director of photography. He's about to start a new film. If you want to pick his brain, get a job on it as a gofer."

"Why can't I ask if he worked on *Dead Girls?*"

"People say weird things about Famous International and about that movie. Dale might be reluctant to admit he'd worked on anything sleazy or shady. You'd have to get him to trust you." She scribbled an address on a paper napkin.

"Would he remember a bit part actor from last spring?"

"Crews and actors make connections with lots of people on productions. This town's like an extended dysfunctional family."

"Do you know an actress named Hannah Lynn?"

"Again, rumors."

"Where is she?"

"Living with the man she fell in love with a few years ago. Changed her name and persona. Didn't want anyone in her new life knowing about her past."

"What about her producer friend, Zolton Baron?"

"I hear he died earlier this year. Entombed in a cemetery vault in Hollywood."

A black box clipped to her purse buzzed. "They need me on the set," she said and finished her coffee.

"I'm curious. Why does a porn producer hire a dialogue coach?"

"You'd be surprised how many people in Hollywood think they're making art."

She rose. "Better not tell anyone on Dale's movie crew who you want to find. If your dad went AWOL, he had a reason. Nosing around might put him in a bad position or unearth things dangerous for both of you."

She went to the door, opened it, and turned back. "Things aren't always what they seem in Lalaland. Keep your wits about you."

****

As I walked my bike into the Burbank warehouse where Sally had sent me, four beefy guys pushed an eight-wheeled apparatus onto a lift gate at the back of a twenty-foot truck. Two others loaded coils of cable and lights into compartments beneath a semitrailer.

Three women wearing layered tops and rows of silver bracelets tugged racks of clothing up a ramp into a long van.

At the driver's door of a truck labeled "Camera Dept" a young guy with scraggly sideburns was brushing food wrappers and paper napkins into a trash bag.

I asked, "Where can I find Dale?"

He pointed toward the rear of the truck. I walked around it and found four twenty-ish guys in T's and cargo shorts clustered near a six-foot man with rugged features, gray hair, and a trim beard—Dale, I gathered. A female assistant half-hidden inside the truck was labeling film cans.

Dale opened an aluminum case and checked several lenses. "Any of you hear the tragic news from Australia?"

A sarcastic chorus of, "Gosh no." "Please tell us." "Can't wait to hear."

"The inventor of the boomerang grenade died."

I laughed. The guys didn't.

Dale said to me, "If you're one of Ivan Shervek's minions, wanting me to give up more of our pitiful camera package, tell him to find his savings someplace else."

"Your friend Sally said you might have a job for me. I'll work free."

"We're full. Try Windstorm Entertainment. They're starting a comedy next week in Culver City."

"I want to work for *you*."

He winked at his crew. "Doesn't everyone?"

A few chuckles.

Dale opened a box of glass filters.

I left and walked to the far side of the warehouse, where a rail-thin woman with spindly arms issued orders to six young people so fresh-faced and wide-eyed they looked like they'd been bussed in from a 4-H meeting.

While they stacked file boxes, typewriters, and supplies on handcarts and loaded them into a van, the woman paced. "We're late, people. Hustle, hustle, hustle."

"No problem, Karen."

"Sure thing."

"You got it."

When I asked about a job, Karen said, "Can't even afford you as a freebie. Try Ivy Films." She put two fingers to her mouth, whistled, and pointed at me.

A muscular security guard in a tank top, mermaid tattoos on his biceps and a Bic lighter in his ear lobe, approached and walked me outside with my bike.

After shouts and door slams, engines came to life in the warehouse, and the semi rumbled onto the street, followed by a string of smaller trucks.

"Where are you going?" I called to a passing driver.

"Barstow."

"Where's that?"

"Halfway to Vegas."

So far, I had nothing to go on but Sally's recollection that Dale had worked on *Dead Girls.* That was not enough reason to follow the caravan across the desert on my bike—until the camera truck passed a few feet away and I spotted a black baseball cap swaying beneath the rearview mirror. The cap had an embroidered figure like a dog on its back, legs up in the air. And lettering that looked like "Famous International Films."

"Wait," I shouted, but the truck roared off.

I hopped on my bike and rode after the caravan until the trucks pulled away too fast for me to follow.

Tires screeched behind me. A gray sedan swerved onto the street.

I turned to see if any more trucks were coming. The gray sedan darted into a parking space three cars back. The driver, a priest with glasses and a reddish beard above his clerical collar, stepped out and talked with a female letter carrier. He got into the sedan, a rosary swinging from his hand.

A PTSD alarm rang in my head. I biked a few blocks and stopped at a hardware store. Wheeled my bike inside, leaned it against a power tool display, and peered out the front window.

The sedan pulled up and parked at a bakery across the street, and the priest went in.

Heart accelerating, I walked out and approached the sedan. I peered through the front passenger window, expecting to see a bible and feel foolish for being suspicious.

A dark green file folder lay on the seat. A

photograph extending part way out showed an arm and a hand with long slender fingers. Was it mine? Or a PTSD mirage?

Sending a cleric friend of her minister to look out for me was the kind of protective thing Lottie might have done. Though I doubted any clergyman would have the time or patience to follow someone's granddaughter around Los Angeles.

I memorized the car's license number, 1BJZ782, and hurried through the store and out the back. I pedaled down an alley, turned onto a series of narrow streets, and stopped after several blocks. I couldn't spot the sedan, but an engine whined and brakes squealed in the distance.

Chapter 20

Five minutes of fast riding brought me to a gas station mini mart. I bought a California road map and located Barstow—a hundred and fifteen miles out in the desert. I'd biked a hundred miles, but not in burning California sunshine. I bought two sports drinks, downed one, and filled my bike's bottles from a tap. I bought and ate a protein bar and a handful of nuts.

Seeing and hearing no sign of the gray sedan, I pedaled away.

Another short ride and I stopped at a phone booth, used a bunch of change, and called Ridgeview Delta. When Nina came on, I told her about the priest. "I haven't had a good view of his face, but his walk and posture say Stephen. I can't shake the feeling he followed me onto the bus and has changed outfits. Have you seen him recently?"

"No, but how terrified you must feel to have a strange man shadowing you. I doubt it's Stephen and I can't imagine how a priest is connected to your search. Is this guy real, or are you having one of your hallucinations?"

"I'm not sure. My PTSD visions always seem real."

"Where are you?"

"In Burbank, about to follow a crew off to film a movie in Barstow. My dad might be working on it.

What's the latest from my grandma's house?"

"She plays Texas Hold'em with a few old guys. Cleans them out, from what I could see through a window. I'm more concerned about *you*. I read Barstow is the most dangerous city in California. I'm afraid hanging out there will give you jitters. Make you do something weird."

"I'm fine. Delighted you'll be getting stellar grades."

Nina said, "I hate not helping."

"Watching out for Lottie means more than I can say."

"I have to pass on sad news. When I went to tell your friend Mary Sue you were okay, her roommate said Mary Sue got stressed, took drugs, and freaked out. Left school a few days ago."

Relieved to be free of her, I recalled my own moments of panic and delusion and wished her well.

After we hung up, I rubbed on more sunscreen. Highlighted a route from Burbank to Barstow, avoiding Interstates 805 and 215 as long as possible. Biking might not be legal on them, and I didn't want to get pulled over with a .45 in my pannier.

****

I rode east through Glendale's tree-lined neighborhoods and the commercial part of Pasadena and cruised residential streets in Arcadia, the sun blazing overhead, as though Los Angeles was a broiler and I was a flank steak. I downed a bottle of sports drink and continued along back roads into Ontario, where my route veered northeast toward Barstow.

Double checking the map, I decided Interstate 15 offered the shortest way over Cajon Summit, so I switched to 15, and started off. Steep, scrub-covered hills on both sides trapped the heat. Two thirds of the way up, I was puffing like a steam engine, sweat soaking my body, every muscle screaming at me to quit. I slowed as I approached a man walking on the shoulder. He wore a daypack, hiking boots, and a fisherman's hat with trout flies around the brim.

As I passed, a voice like Dad's said, "Don't give up, Charlie." I swung around, lost my balance, and toppled to the pavement.

The man extended his hand.

I waved him off and rose. "Why did you say, 'Don't give up, Charlie'?"

"Heat must be getting to you, miss. Drink some water. I said, 'Don't get a charley horse.' "

After he walked on, I finished my sports drink and rode by him, my brain foggy.

The summit still out of sight, I strained in granny gear as the interstate climbed between mountain ridges hundreds of feet above me.

I pulled onto the shoulder, drank the last of my water, and looked around. A mile behind me, a gray sedan rounded a curve.

I rose from the saddle and pedaled on, sweat running from my nose and chin.

A black Dodge pickup with double drive wheels rumbled past, towing a horse trailer, leaving a wake of diesel exhaust and manure fumes. The rig pulled onto the shoulder, and the passenger window rolled down.

"Sun won't set for hours," a dusky female voice said. "Lot of hot climbing to go. You want a lift?"

I approached the cab. Inside, a woman with a tanned oval face, coral-blushed cheeks, and Jackie-O glasses studied me. Lines creased her face, but waves of copper hair and an enigmatic expression gave her a timeless beauty.

She raised her Jackie-Os and seemed to appraise me with eyes like blue ice on fire. A familiar quality about the woman rang a bell in my head, though I had no memory where I'd seen her.

Blue Eyes nudged the driver. "To finish our conversation, you know he killed her."

My gut tightened, and a peanut-butter-and-cheese snack rose in my throat.

"Did *not* kill her," the driver said. He tugged at his white Buffalo Bill van Dyke and adjusted a hollowed vertebrae that centered a string tie on his buckskin shirt. Hot air flowed through the cab, twirling an eagle feather hanging from the mirror. The driver faced me and raised his brows, as if inviting my opinion about their "he killed her" argument.

I tried to swallow, but couldn't.

The woman said, "He wanted her out of the way, the bastard. He'll get his comeuppance. Wait and see."

The man turned to me. "What do you say?"

I licked my dry lips. "Killed...who?"

"His wife, of course," the woman said. "Men can be so sneaky."

I stepped back. "Not sure I should trouble you."

"The girl doesn't trust us," Blue Eyes said. "Guess they don't make 'em brave as they used to."

I said, "They've made some cowardly men."

"Can't argue with that. But not my Clint." She kissed him and patted the space beside her. "Get in, if you're gettin'."

The gray car, a half mile away, was closing fast.

I stowed my bike in the truck bed and climbed into the cab, my arms and legs glistening with sweat.

Clint studied me with steel-gray eyes, half hidden in a sea of leathery wrinkles. "What do you say? Killed her or not?"

I pictured Mom's slit throat and struggled to keep from sliding into a PTSD sink hole. "Killed who?"

"Sunny van Bülow," the woman said. "You didn't follow the trial?"

Clint said, "Women on the jury were suspicious of his good looks." He poked Blue Eyes. "You were too."

"Not for a second."

The papers had followed the story for decades. After Sunny van Bülow spent twenty-eight years in a coma, a jury convicted her husband, Claus, of attempted murder. He had been acquitted on appeal a year ago.

Feeling relaxed now I knew what they were talking about, I closed the door.

As Clint shifted into drive and we pulled out, the woman edged toward him. She looked my way and pinched her nose.

I'm so smelly she doesn't want to touch me. She regrets they stopped. "How close can you drop me to Barstow?"

"Can't get closer than we're going." She smiled. "Pleased to meet you. Name's Della Canyon."

"*The* Della Canyon? I loved *Lost Corral* and *Longhorn Lady*. Thought your face looked familiar."

"Those were my first movies, when I had blonde hair. What takes you to Barstow?"

"Trying for a job on a movie, but they don't want to hire me."

"What's your specialty?"

"Philosophy, I guess."

"Same here," Clint said.

"Where'd you study?"

"University of Cow Manure, Quarter Horses, and Stunts. Fallen off more ponies than I can count."

A gray sedan whizzed past—no priest inside—a young couple with two kids.

Relieved, I took a deep breath and looked to Clint. "I bet you've been in tons of movies."

"Not so's you'd notice. I'm the geezer gets hit with the fake whisky bottle. Or falls into a watering trough outside the saloon. Comic relief."

Della ruffled his white hair. "Don't you believe it. Clint was the glue that kept fifty westerns together." She glanced at me. "Not much call for Socrates and Plato on this movie, except to make sense of the insanity. I've spent most of my life in the film business, but the plot of this one beats them all. A gold mine, a cowboy, romance, betrayal, explosions and, believe it or not, zombies."

"Any Martians?"

"Bite your tongue." She patted my arm. "On what they're paying, I can't afford to hire you. But help Clint and me, and we'll say you're part of our team. Might get you free meals for a few days and a peek at the glamorous world of the silver screen." She raised her eyebrows, mocking her words. "What's your name?"

Recalling Sally's warning not to reveal things right away, I made one up. "Tanya."

"Pleasure, darlin'." She shook my hand, starting the silver bracelets on her forearm clinking.

I liked this woman, kept sneaking looks at her on

135

the way down from the summit. The golden desert light haloing her face recalled for me idyllic close-ups in her westerns.

While we roared along in the truck, Clint glanced at Della with a softness in his eyes that said, after all the years, he was as entranced as ever. Dad had often gazed at Mom like that on a Saturday night. He'd put on one of her favorite albums, and they'd slow dance.

We cruised into Barstow on Interstate 15, paralleling a fast, mile-long train of box and tank cars squealing and rumbling into the freight yard bordering the small desert city. Miles of low, sandy hills covered with scrub brush flanked the highway. We drove by two-acre plots with ranch houses, pickups with jumbo tires, and horses grazing in half-acre fenced pastures.

Feeling more at ease, I said, "Della, do you know any gossip about an actor who—"

"On gossip, I go with W.C. Fields: 'If you can't dazzle them with brilliance, baffle them with bullshit.' Or, as Clint puts it, leave it be."

Chapter 21

We turned off the freeway, passed a park and blocks of homes. As the sun sank toward the horizon, we cruised city streets in front of stores and restaurants, some boarded up.

Della said the production office had been set up in a defunct Ford dealership, the film shoot to take place farther north in the desert. As we approached a building with the oval outline of an old Ford sign over the showroom window, a young man aimed a camera at us, then panned to follow other passing cars.

"Are they filming already?" I asked.

"A test," Della said.

We parked and went inside. Tire marks and oil stains on the showroom floor showed the places where the last models had been displayed. The production assistants I'd seen in Burbank bustled between sales cubicles along the back wall, setting up typewriters and file boxes, and organizing the office.

A teenage boy wearing a black Metallica T escorted Della toward a small office with a faded SALES MANAGER sign on the door.

I detected the aroma of roasted chicken. Dying for a taste of real food, I followed the scent to the adjoining building, the gym-sized former service area. Crew members were unpacking and checking gear from the trucks.

Beside a food van, a slender Latino teenager wearing wrap-around sunglasses cleared silverware, salt and pepper shakers, and napkins from a long table covered with a red-checked cloth. His shoulders and hips moved to Latin music from a portable radio.

Another man about twenty, muscular arms shining with sweat, cleaned the catering van counter. When I stepped to the service window, he said, "*Finito. Closed.*"

"*Por favor. Tengo hambre.* That's about it for my Spanish."

He pointed to my biking shorts and said, "I ride, too." He got together a plate of chicken and vegetables, which I carried to the table.

A brunette wearing a bloodstained nurse's uniform alighted on a seat across from me, a knife protruding from her chest. Her eyes were circled with heavy purple makeup, like a psychedelic raccoon.

"Wh-who are y-you?" she asked in a perky voice. "I'm Annie P-P-Porter."

The girl, about my age, stood as tall as me, but with the stick-like limbs of a preteen and the upright bearing of a cadet. She looked at me so directly with unblinking eyes I wondered if she'd ever told a lie.

"I'm Tanya." I held out my hand.

Annie shook it. "I p-play a z-z-zombie. Because of the w-w-way I talk, I can't get big roles. But I'm a p-p-perfect ghoul. The nurse's uniform and m-makeup are my ideas."

Relieved Annie's outfit and the pretend blood stains weren't sending me into a PTSD delusion, I said, "Let's have lunch soon."

"F-for sure." She beamed and waltzed out of the

service bay.

As I reached for the drumstick, Karen grabbed my plate. "I told you in LA. We're full. Not running a soup kitchen."

"But I met—"

"Don't care." She whistled, and the security guard with the Bic lighter in his ear lobe stepped toward me.

I snatched the drumstick and ate two bites before he ushered me toward the front door, his tattooed mermaids wiggling as he walked.

I was getting on my bike when Della emerged from the sales manager's office and said, "Karen, where are you taking my new assistant?"

Karen turned to a thin man about sixty. "Ivan, this girl bugged me in Burbank to give her a job. I already told her no."

He frowned, and his sallow face swiveled back and forth, reminding me of a sci-fi movie raptor, looking for someone to eat.

"I need Tanya's help," Della said to Karen. "Can't we work something out?"

Karen's bony chest heaved beneath the V of her top. She lit a cigarette and exhaled a plume of smoke.

Ivan gave a movie raptor growl, as if my employment was the worst of a string of annoyances. "Okay, Della. Off the books. No fringes or taxes and not a word to the state."

Karen said, "Economy room. Per diem, no salary, and she works wherever I tell her."

"Fine," Della said. "Now, I'd like to see my motor home."

Karen handed me a welcome packet. While I checked out the crew list, Ivan led Della into the repair bay. She grumbled, "What the hell. You gave me the clown-car version. I need something bigger."

Ivan chuckled. "Join the club."

I followed them into the service area, the clicking of my bike cleats lost under AC/DC's "Who Made Who" blasting from a truck speaker.

At a counter against the far wall a half dozen crewmen in jeans and Ts were filling cups from a coffee urn and munching donuts while they studied a dog-eared *Penthouse* centerfold taped to the sheet rock.

A brunette in jeans and a black leather jacket strode past me to a big metal box inside a van and opened a nylon bag. "Damn," she said, as she pulled out knee pads, hip pads, a mouth guard, a plastic knife, harnesses, and nylon cords. "I'd swear I packed three sets."

An arm patch on her jacket read, "Stunt Women's Association of Motion Pictures."

"Wow, stunts," I murmured. "This could be an exciting movie."

I found the camera truck—no baseball cap, just a collection of paper cups and candy wrappers.

Dale's assistants crowded around a tripod-mounted camera while he aimed it at a piece of white foam core printed with geometric designs. He adjusted the focus, shot a few seconds, and looked my way. "Didn't we leave you in Burbank?"

"I followed on my bike. Got hired to help out. If there's anything I can get you…"

"A Dino Ferrari." He focused and shot a few more seconds. "Or a condo on Maui."

Hoping to gain his trust, I asked about lenses, cameras, and how he'd started in the business.

After a string of quick, gruff answers, I asked, "Are my questions stupid?"

He filmed another burst. "You can't barge into my crew and expect a tutorial. These people have gone to film school or taken any job available. If you want to learn, pay your dues."

Lottie three, Charlie zero.

I turned away and tripped over a cable.

Dale's female assistant grasped my arm and ushered me away, whispering, "Don't take the grousing to heart. A girl your age, a production assistant on a shoot last year, played up to him and claimed she wanted to be a DP. She flirted him into tutoring her. He pulled in favors to land her a second unit camera position on his next film. A month ago, some hot shot producer offered her a gig on a bigger project. She ditched Dale."

"Romance can be tough," I said, wondering if I'd ever want one.

Two females unloaded a light the size of a bass drum from a semi. I said, "I didn't know women worked on tough physical jobs in film."

"As assistants. Not many DPs, gaffers, or grips."

"In the Los Angeles warehouse there was an upside-down dog embroidered on a baseball cap in the camera truck. You know who it belongs to?"

"Producers give souvenirs to crews after every show. Leather valises or jackets on major films, baseball caps or T-shirts on low budget ones like this. I don't know about your dead-dog cap." She smiled. "I'm Lori."

"Tanya."

"Good luck. I'm off to work."

As she headed toward Dale, Karen approached, a walkie-talkie pressed to her ear. "When? Shit, okay. I'll ask the kid." She squinted at me through a veil of smoke. "You have a driver's license?"

I hadn't driven since my PTSD episodes. "In my wallet," I said.

"Our regular drivers are on runs, and the leading man has shopping to do yesterday. Pick up keys from the transportation captain." She pointed toward a heavyset guy in jeans and an "I love Las Vegas" T-shirt. "Get out of your sweaty biking outfit and go to room 1203 in the hotel. You'll recognize the actor—he's handsome. Don't ask for an autograph."

"Is he a star?"

"He thinks so."

Convinced Karen viewed everyone with jaundiced eyes, I imagined I'd be telling Lottie and Nina I'd met Michael J. Fox from *Teen Wolf*, quizzed Tom Cruise about his wild dance in *Risky Business*, or asked Anthony Michael Hall if he fantasized about designing a woman on a computer like he did in *Weird Science*.

Chapter 22

The key for a Taurus station wagon in my purse, I walked my bike outside and watched a gray sedan pass. I couldn't read the license number in the evening darkness but glimpsed a clerical collar and beard on the driver—the priest. I didn't care if it was a PTSD fantasy. I ran after the sedan, but it skidded around a corner and sped away.

I went to the Desert Hacienda Hotel, a block away, and walked through the lobby past a mannequin dressed like a cowboy—boots, chaps, plastic six-shooters, and Stetson hat.

After signing in at the reception desk, I brought my bike up in the elevator and found my room. It came with a hard double bed, a view of the rail yard, and a cheap desert print of a bird perched on a saguaro cactus. I showered, changed into black slacks and a white short-sleeved top, ran a brush through my hair, and added a touch of eyeliner, blusher, and lipstick. Not my usual style, but when a girl gets a chance to meet a star, she has to glam up a little.

So Lottie would know where I was, I chose a picture postcard from the front desk, printed a greeting and left a dime for a stamp to mail it.

I drove the Taurus to the hotel portico, found room 1203, held my breath, and knocked.

The door opened, and my star fantasies evaporated.

Instead of Cusack, Cruise, or Hall, a six-foot, twenty-something guy faced me wearing white pants and a sea-green shirt decorated with palm trees and parrots. His bright eyes, tanned face, and boyish grin were the stuff of movie billboards, but I hadn't seen him on one, or anywhere else.

"I've got a car outside for you," I said, smiling to hide my disappointment.

He waited what seemed like forever before saying, "Brett Winner."

I smiled again.

"From *Cop Crusade,* top-rated TV show," he said. "Detectives rooting out corruption in the Beverly Hills City Hall. Great review in the *Hollywood Reporter.* You haven't seen *one* episode?"

"*Cop Crusade*...oh, sure."

He stood taller. "Going to be in a thriller with an A-list actor next spring." He positioned his wristwatch under a ceiling light by the door, where the stainless body glistened, and numbers glowed on four mini-dials.

"Impressive," I said. "How deep have you dived?"

He reddened. "Gift from my agent. Ten grand." He grabbed the room phone, dialed, and said, "Karen, someone else has to take me. The girl you sent is an idiot."

I clasped my arms across my chest, expecting to be fired. Crap, I hadn't even had a PTSD blowout.

Brett growled, "There's got to be someone."

Apparently, there wasn't. He hung up, grabbed a Nike sports bag, and walked past me. "Close the door. We're already late."

****

We headed off in the Taurus through darkened

downtown Barstow, passing an old man with a white beard and a black cowboy hat. I tried to figure a way to get on Brett's good side on the remote chance he might know something about Dad. No ideas came.

"What's your name?" he asked as we pulled into a parking area in front of a shopping mall.

"Tanya."

"Exotic. Ever work as a dancer?"

"This is my first job."

He directed me to a spot near a department store, and we went inside past a banner announcing a Halloween sale. He walked between racks of suits and sweaters. "This place is a dump. They have better things at Penney's in Burbank."

I followed him through the men's department while he selected expensive shirts, a silk sport jacket, a cashmere sweater, and two bottles of French cologne. He slipped them into the sports bag and handed it to me. I dropped the bag when I spotted the red-bearded priest near a coffee maker display halfway across the floor. I blinked several times, suspecting he might be one of my visions and would disappear. He didn't.

I took off toward the priest. When I was fifteen feet away, he exited through a side door.

"Hey," Brett yelled. "What are you doing?"

I pushed through the door, hurried down a hallway, and exited onto a parking area filled with cars, but no evidence of the priest.

"Get back here," Brett shouted from the sales floor.

I sprinted inside to Brett and grabbed the bag. "Thought I saw a priest I know."

Brett grumbled and led me through the electronics department, where he added an expensive shortwave radio to the bag. I expected we would stop at a register and pay for everything, but Brett headed toward the exit. I wanted to walk away but I needed to stay on the film.

We were halfway out the door when an alarm rang. A tall, stocky man in a dark gray uniform with a SECURITY OFFICER patch on his arm and "G. Trumbull" on his name tag blocked our way. Trumbull ushered us inside and stopped at a sales counter. "Let's see what's in your bag."

"Nothing important," Brett said and flashed his movie billboard grin.

Trumbull emptied the bag.

Brett turned to me. "Oh my God. What have you done?" In response to my frown, he said, "Officer, it's not her fault. She put those things in by mistake. I just said I liked them. I'm Brett Winner from *Cop Crusade*." He held out his hand.

Trumbull shook it. "I'm sure you do a wonderful job on TV, Mr. Winner, but you need to explain the items you were carrying out."

"As I said, Tanya here must have—"

"Did you put them in there?" Trumbull asked me.

Brett held his hand out of Trumbull's range of vision and rubbed his thumb and forefinger together—I'd get a reward if I played along. I stared, amazed at his arrogance.

Trumbull raised his brows. "Well?"

Brett winked.

My mind raced. I pictured a huge fight with him and Karen banning me from the movie.

I struggled to keep control but couldn't stop one of the teen boys' lines from leaking out. "When you're *naked* and spread on the *bed*, you look more *dead* than ready for *head*."

While Brett shot me a fierce look, a smile creased Trumbull's lips. "Your friend's a pip, Mr. Winner. Brightened my day and earned you a break." He guided us to the manager's office, where Brett wrote a check for the stolen items plus a generous donation to the store's Christmas fund.

On the drive to the hotel, Brett fumed. "You were gloating in there. You're working for Della. She tell you to sabotage me?"

"I'd never do that. You were the one cheating, trying to rip off the store."

Della's kindness to me and her diplomacy with Karen had made me wonder if an acting class might be a way to control my PTSD episodes. But Brett's behavior proved you could be a card-carrying actor and have no more self-control than a five-year-old.

When he got out and started for the hotel, I asked, "Why shoplift? You can afford a thousand times what you stole."

He stalked away with his bag. "It's no fun if you have to pay."

When I brought the car to the production office I approached Karen, standing by the transportation captain's podium, writing on a clipboard. She said, "Congratulations, Sunshine. Our star's agent called five minutes ago. If you aren't off the show in the morning, his boy is walking. Guess how that's going to turn out."

Chapter 23

I went to the hotel bar, hoping for an epiphany about how to find Dad before the producers packed me off to Washington. A ten-foot historical photo hung on a wall. Grim-faced men sporting thick moustaches and women in long black dresses stood on an unpaved town street, scowling as if they knew my prospects were dismal.

I detoured around a rusted mine car display and waved to Della, who sat in a booth, wearing a brown silk top. With fresh makeup, her hair swept up in a twist, and two spiral curls framing her face, she looked captivating.

"You live on the edge," she said, motioning me to sit.

I slid in across from her. "Guess you know what happened with Brett."

"Rumors on a set move like brush fires in a windstorm."

Nearby crew people were paying no attention to me. I suspected the scuttlebutt said the new girl had pissed Brett off and was on her way out. I ordered a root beer from a waitress in a cleavage-revealing dirndl.

"I wasn't trying to be offensive," I said. "If they kick me out, I'm screwed."

Dale entered the bar with his assistants, sat in the next booth, and leaned over, smiling as if he'd forgotten

I was a shiftless freeloader. "Give us the real Brett story," he said.

"Nothing to tell."

He pressed a cocktail napkin to his forehead and closed his eyes—Johnny Carson doing his mind-reading bit as Carnac the Magnificent. "Hmmmm. I see it all. The guy came on too strong, and you had to cut him down to size."

Chuckles from his male assistants.

Came on too strong. Cut him down to size. Sounded like he was talking about the PA ditching him.

He whispered, "Tanya, your public wants details."

Dale would bug me until I said something. And, no matter what I answered, Brett would win. I switched to offense. "When your camera truck pulled out of LA, there was a baseball cap with an upside-down dead dog image on the rearview mirror. Who does it belong to?"

"I don't keep track of those things. They float around like Frisbees at a beach party." He leaned closer. "So, what about Brett?"

"I can be strange sometimes. Misinterpreted what he said and got mouthy. I understand why he's angry with me."

"Your bullshit meter is peaking." He turned to his assistants.

Della pressed my hand. "Love your spirit, hon. I'd love to keep you, but I gather the boss wants you gone." She pulled out her wallet and offered me sixty dollars.

"Thanks, but I can't accept the money."

When she went to find Clint, I hung around, hoping Dale might loosen up after a few drinks and give me an opening to ask about Dad. But as soon as he and his crew finished the next round, they left.

Annie Porter, wearing faded jeans and an oversized T, shuffled toward my table, her perky grin replaced by a defeated expression—eyes half-closed, button mouth turned down. "You w-want to have dinner?"

"Be happy to, but why aren't you eating with your fellow zombies?" I motioned toward a booth across the room where several men and women sat drinking, telltale smudges of stage blood on their sleeves and collars.

"They complain I r-ruin our scariness."

"Sorry to hear that."

"It's r-r-ridiculous. The way I talk makes me extra frightening," She contorted her features and gave a ghostly moan.

I shrieked in mock terror.

"Very f-funny. Y-you don't know w-what it's like to be d-different."

"I've been different for months. Rebuffed an approach from a guy I'd been wild for. Attacked a movie screen. And punched a cop. Quite a pair, aren't we?"

"T-total maniacs. But we'll mow 'em down."

After we each had a burger and a soda, she skipped out with a wave of her fingers.

Annie's pluckiness inspired me. Ivan might send me packing tomorrow, but for a few hours I'd follow the one lead I had, the priest. I left the hotel and did a circuit of downtown Barstow. Searched two hours without success.

Until the gray sedan with license number 1BJZ782 stopped at a traffic light. I rushed to it. A middle-aged woman behind the wheel frowned when I knocked on the window. I asked, "Where's the priest and where did you get this car?"

"I don't know about any priest," she said. "I rented this down the street."

I went to where she pointed and found a car rental office. The agent refused to give out customer information, so I headed toward the hotel—downgrading my priest sightings to PTSD fantasies.

I passed a curbside trash can and spotted inside it a reddish-brown beard and a clerical collar mixed with an assortment of paper cups and food wrappers. I hadn't been hallucinating. The priest following me was a real person.

I called Nina from my room and told her about the fake priest. "I'm more convinced than ever Stephen is here. Were you worried and sent him down to look out for me? Or did he charm you into telling him where I am?"

"Neither. Be careful. The guy could be dangerous."

"From what I could tell about Stephen at the soccer field he wouldn't win a tussle with Grandma Lottie."

"You better buy a knife. Sometimes the people who seem harmless are the most dangerous."

Chapter 24

The next morning, my second on location, I swung out of bed at five a.m. and called Karen's office. "I know I screwed up with Brett. I'll apologize or do whatever I need to. I've got to stay on this film."

A lighter flint buzzed in my earpiece, followed by Karen's hoarse voice. "He's in the makeup trailer. Give it a try, but don't do anything stupid."

Rehearsing my apology, I walked through the Ford service bay, past the two Latinos loading crates of vegetables and meats into the catering van.

In the makeup trailer three beauty shop chairs faced a wall of mirrors decorated with snapshots of two pre-teen girls in comic poses. A stack of *Cosmopolitan, Vogue,* and *Elle* magazines lay on the counter beside jars of foundation, eye makeup, and tubes of blusher. A lingering cloud of lacquer-tinged hairspray made my eyes water.

Brett sat in the middle chair while a curvy woman about thirty, with dimples and pale blue eyes, applied foundation to his face while he berated her.

"Don't cake it on so thick." "You missed a spot." "That's the wrong shade."

I raised my eyebrows.

She gave a careless shrug, as if to say, "He's an asshole, but I roll with it."

When I approached Brett's chair, he said, "Doreen,

leave us alone."

"They've told me to finish you in five minutes."

"Get out before I have you fired."

She rolled her eyes and strode from the trailer.

The apology I'd imagined offering Brett evaporated, and I said, "You must be a huge star if you can treat people like that." I stepped back, expecting him to shout or swing at me.

"Easy does it. I want you to be my driver."

"Yeah, sure."

"You're a royal pain, but I appreciated you keeping mum about what happened at the store and telling people *you* mouthed off to *me*. A shit storm of stories would have hit the trades." He put down a copy of *Variety* and grinned. "You have a wild side beneath your school-girl exterior?"

"I don't gossip."

"I'll get us a fancy BMW. You can use it when I don't need you."

I had a smidgen of interest in what it would be like to hang around even a minor star, though I doubted I could tolerate Brett for more than a few hours. And being an arrogant actor's flunky would not make crew people open up to me about Dad. "I owe my job to Della," I said. "Have to be ready whenever she needs me."

"Della was old news ten years ago. Her last job was a commercial for a bank in Reseda. I asked Ivan to get Ellen Burstyn, but he paid himself a bundle for the script and had zip in his budget, so we ended up with Della."

Spotting a small can of hair spray to aim at Stephen's face if he came too close, I put it in my purse.

"I'd be glad to drive you when I can, but—"

"Get out." He chucked a hairbrush at me. "This time you're really fired."

As I exited, a curler box hit the doorframe and spiky cylinders bounced down the steps.

Dale approached me, grinning. "You have to cut our leading man down to size again?"

"He wanted me to be his driver. I said no. I'll stick to what they hired me for. But I'm curious. Are all actors like kindergarteners?"

"More than you'd imagine, emotions right under the surface. They claim it gives them authenticity."

Karen pulled me aside and asked what had happened with Brett. When I told her, she offered her glowing cigarette. "If you're determined to self-destruct, feel free to put this out on your palm."

My best way to keep from self-destructing was to connect with my patron. "Does Della need any help?"

"If you're comfortable with horses. She's riding today."

The only one I'd ridden—on a field trip in junior high—threw me into a gorge and fractured my arm. "I love horses."

****

I jogged to the hotel, my mouth dry as I scanned the street, wondering what new persona Stephen would assume and how I could find out if he was a threat to Dad. I pictured Dr. Kraig warning me I was in PTSD mode, but I couldn't stop.

I told the driver of a waiting van I needed to go see Della.

Backfires shattered the silence in the parking lot. My heart raced as a skinny guy with slumping posture like Stephen's sat astride a Harley, gray exhaust popping from the tailpipe.

The Harley followed us out of the lot, staying several car lengths behind, but when I looked back after a few blocks, it was gone.

****

The van drove me across a stretch of the Mojave Desert carpeted with cheat grass.

When the van stopped, I opened the door and stepped into sage-infused air, vibrating with the wingbeats of hummingbirds, feeding on a sea of lush, red Catalina snapdragons.

From fifty yards away, Della cantered toward me, erect in the saddle. Her silk blouse clung to her figure and made her look like the leading lady she'd played in her westerns. She reined her bay mare to a halt, raised a pistol, and fired at a line of rusted cans on a log. She hit all but one.

She faced me, eyes unreadable behind dark sunglasses.

I said, "I thought you might want some help."

She holstered her gun and pointed to a chestnut horse tied to a runt of a tree. "Saddle my gelding."

"Not sure I know—"

"His bridle's already on."

I glanced toward the horizon. There was no sign of the Harley or Stephen, but Dad's shimmering figure rode toward me on a black horse, waving a greeting.

A PTSD illusion, but I waved back—love-hate; hate-love. Dad and the horse disappeared in a dust devil.

"If you're here to help, get to it," Della said.

The mount she indicated had a dark mane and tail,

a white diamond patch on his forehead, and white up to his knees. He towered over me. His shoulders quivered with muscle and his rear legs looked so massive I pictured him leaping a two-lane road in a single bound.

"Well?" Della said.

I hadn't saddled a horse but had seen it done in dozens of cowboy movies. I hefted the saddle from a stump and swung it onto the gelding's back. I reached under, grabbed the strap, ran it through the metal ring on the near side, and tightened it. His middle swelled.

"He's fighting you," Della said. "Put your knee on his side and cinch it tighter."

I did.

"Now let out the stirrups."

I lengthened the near one and ducked under his head, smelling grassy breath.

After I slacked off the other stirrup and came back, I put a foot in the near one. He shied sideways and dragged me, hopping behind him. I clambered up and hauled my butt into the saddle. The gelding skittered backward.

Della moved her mare closer, grabbed the reins, and stilled him.

The van drove away.

I asked, "Ever hear of a movie called—"

"Here's our epic." She handed me a script.

"*Zombies from Gold Mountain,*" I said, reading aloud. "Doesn't sound like a western."

"Think restaurant menu. Science fiction and horror from column A, cowboy scenes, romance, and adventure from column B." She flicked the reins, and her bay began to walk. My gelding fell in step.

"It's the best script my agent's sent in a while," she

said. "Don't have the choices I used to."

"What's the story?"

"A young couple try to cheat an old miner woman—me—out of my gold claim, but zombies in the mine kill the woman and turn on my partner and me. Hot stuff, huh?"

"Maybe it will earn you a bundle."

"Pay my hay and vet bills until I get a better part. You don't know what it's like out there. It's hard enough for actresses when they're young and pretty like you. Helluva lot tougher when you add a few years. At least I'm not cooking oatmeal and washing some geezer's sweaty long johns."

I didn't feel pretty, but Della, with her luxuriant hair, high-boned cheeks, and creamy complexion, looked like a vision right off the screen.

I asked, "Why did Ivan put so much western lore in this story?"

"He grew up in Brooklyn, always wanted to be a cowboy."

Della settled her dark glasses on her hair. "My agent found out what happened at the department store yesterday. You were a straight shooter, didn't spill a word to the crew. Give that attitude an encore." She slapped a bug off her neck. "I've been in twenty-five movies. But Brett doesn't give a damn."

"I love old films. Did you ever hear of one called—"

"Read my cues." Della pointed to the script.

I read the yellow-highlighted lines.

After Della made mistake after mistake, she pulled a silver flask from her saddlebag and drank.

I said, "How about if we take a break from the

157

lines, and you talk about your favorite films? Strange ones, like—"

"If I mess up, I'm history. Brett didn't want me in the first place. Keep reading."

I did. She got more cues wrong and drank again.

"Won't alcohol make learning your lines harder?"

"You my babysitter?"

"Just a PA."

"Tell Brett I'm going to have these lines down cold."

"I don't report to him."

"How much I drink is none of Brett's business, or yours."

She spurred her horse to a trot, then a gallop.

Mine reared and bolted past her, tossing me about in the saddle. When I grasped the reins, the script flew from my hands and spooked the gelding, sent him leaping over branches and stumps. The harder I pulled the reins, the faster he flew. I grabbed the pommel horn. The gelding's mane whipped my eyes, and hot air whooshed past. Flying insects stung my face like sleet.

Della caught up and galloped alongside. "You're feeding me bad cues, not a straight shooter."

"Then pull out your six-gun," I shouted over the galloping hooves, "and plug me like one of those tin cans."

She grabbed the gelding's reins and slowed our horses to a walk. "I don't shoot people."

I took the reins from her. "You know I can't control him."

"Seems I don't know anything today."

If they replaced Della because of memory problems or drinking, or if she complained about me to

Karen, I'd lose my connection to the film.

I scanned the desert and tried to use my PTSD eyesight and hearing to locate Stephen in the cheatgrass. I didn't see him, but after two distant pistol shots, a circling vulture tumbled from the sky. If Stephen had downed it with a handgun, he could take Dad out before he saw the man coming.

Lottie four, Charlie zero.

Chapter 25

Clint scowled. "You want me to buy *what*?"

He'd arrived with the Dodge and, while Della loaded the horses into the trailer, he stood by the driver's door, an imposing figure in a black shirt with a jeweled guitar design on the front. His broad chest and long white hair were pure Buffalo Bill.

"A box of .45 ammunition," I said. "You have to be twenty-one to buy it here. I brought my dad's old .45 and want to do target practice."

"How do I know you won't wing somebody?"

"I hunted with my dad for years. Never had an accident."

"From what age?"

"Six."

He massaged his Van Dyke. "I'll see." He climbed into the cab, and Della slid in beside him. I followed and nodded to her, but she stared ahead while we drove to the highway.

****

The Dodge bounced and rumbled up a mountain road through a steep-sided canyon, a dry creek bed below, brush and acacia trees clinging to the rocky walls.

"How far to a bathroom?" I asked.

"Another half mile," Clint said, "By the way, Ivan owns this parcel. As a young man, he worked on a thriller up here, *The Gold Mine Murders.* Suggested a bunch of ideas to the director, Leo Dvorak, but the man brushed them off. When Ivan won the land in a poker game, he decided to direct the story his own way. Came up with our epic, *Zombies from Gold Mountain.*

When we arrived in a clearing between two granite peaks, Clint said, "Used to be a busy mining town." Dilapidated buildings faced the dirt street, some leaning at steep angles, others missing windows, roofs, and front doors. They'd lost their paint, as had a rusted thirties sedan with deflated whitewalls, half-hidden in a mass of milkweed.

Five hundred feet higher, halfway up the taller peak, a shed-roofed structure bearing the faded title Ajax Mine clung to a granite outcrop.

The crew must have arrived hours earlier. Trucks, trailers, three motor homes, and cars sat parked in neat rows, people setting up cameras and rolling out lights. With all the skills—welding, sewing, carpentry, car repair, and a dozen more—we made up our own little world. It felt like I'd run away and joined a circus.

I asked Della, "Where are the bathrooms?"

"In the honey wagon." She pointed to a long white van with six doors.

Clint stomped the brake and stopped us inches short of a grotesque man. The red, lumpy skin on his forehead had the look of a half-cooked cheese pizza. His eyes lay hidden in scarred crevices. A hole penetrated his head where his ear would have been. His face had a rosy translucent cast as though he'd had recent surgery after a catastrophic accident.

"Jeez," I said. "That makeup's way ugly even for a zombie."

Clint raised a warning finger. "It's not makeup. He's Jake Kinsler, the special effects coordinator. Handles explosions and fires."

Clint pointed to an actor with a giant hypodermic sticking into his skull, and to another with an arm severed at the elbow. "Those are zombies."

I jumped out of the Dodge and rushed to the honey wagon where I found actors' names taped on four of its six doors. I entered one labeled W.

"Emergency," I said, squeezing past Lori, Dale's assistant, and ducking into a stall.

I finished in a hurry and stepped out, anxious to question her about crew people who might have been on *Dead Girls.*

After Lori took her turn, she hurried out to the camera truck and started loading magazines.

I walked to the set and surveyed the male crew, looking for Stephen. I couldn't see him. I spotted a grip with a limp like Dad's, but he was Asian American.

Twenty yards away, Della entered a thirty-foot RV. I walked to it and opened the door. The interior had a couch, a TV, and wood-paneled cupboards above a stove and sink. Oranges and apples filled a basket on the counter.

Della pulled an ice tray from her refrigerator and dropped cubes into a glass.

I said, "Can we start fresh? I'm sure life is harder for actresses. I'll do anything I can to help."

She poured brandy from a pint bottle over the ice. "I don't need a lecture."

I opened her script. "What if we go over your lines again?"

She glanced out the window to where Clint chatted

with a security guard while he took a cookie from the craft service table stocked with cold cuts, veggies, and fruit.

I said, "It's inspiring how much you two care for each other."

Her face relaxed. "Love of my life. I wish we'd met twenty years ago, but I'm grateful for the last ten. Sorry I lit into you. Clint made me promise to go easy on the brandy. When you two were talking by the truck I figured he was pushing you to monitor my drinking."

"Didn't mention it." I opened the script and ran a scene with her.

She missed a half-dozen lines and drank more brandy. "You must be giving me the wrong cues."

I showed her the pages.

Della went through the scenes again, making more mistakes. She grabbed the script. "You weren't looking at the words."

"I can recall text once I read it a couple of times."

"Trying to make me feel stupid?"

I said, "You want me to pretend to be less competent than I am?"

She shook her head. "Women have done too much of that."

After we practiced an hour and Della had her lines cold, I went outside to look for the phony PI. Checked out the carpenters adding planks to the mining town sidewalk and grips hoisting four-foot-square boards covered with aluminum foil. There was no sign of Stephen. A few times I spotted slender guys with light brown hair, but they didn't wear glasses.

I scanned older men for a limp like Dad's but didn't spot one. I headed for the camera truck to talk to

Dale, but he was on the move, sighting through a viewfinder and giving orders about lights and reflectors.

While I scribbled notes about what he did, I drifted toward a man sitting behind an aluminum cart with a tape recorder, coils of wire, and microphones. The guy wore a baseball cap with an emblem like an upside-down dog.

I went closer. Instead of dog legs, four middle fingers stuck up—a quadruple obscene gesture.

A sign on the cart read, "SOUND RULES—DOMINICK." The short man behind the sign perched munchkin-like on a high folding chair. He leaned forward and peered at me through smoke rising from his soldering gun. "Tell camera to stop bugging me. I'll be ready before they are."

"I have nothing to do with camera. I'm interested in baseball caps. Ever see one with an upside-down dog?"

He shook his head, put on earphones, and waved to the boom man, who was holding a long pole with a fuzz-covered mic over two teenage assistants.

After Dominick flashed the boom man a thumbs-up and pulled his earphones off, I said, "You've got a perfect eavesdropping setup."

"This is nothing compared to what I could do with radio mics." He showed me two bumblebee-sized devices.

A muscular assistant director with a buzz cut and aviator sunglasses barked orders into a walkie-talkie as if he was directing an amphibious assault. He nodded at Dominick, who said, "Sound's ready."

The AD walked to Brett's motor home and knocked. "We're up in five." He repeated the message at Della's RV.

I worried she'd be tipsy, but she stepped out wearing a paisley western shirt, cowboy boots, and tight jeans. She walked toward the set as sure-footed as a ballet dancer. Brett emerged from his motor home, checkered shirt unbuttoned, cowboy boots scattering dust as he caught up with Della in front of the set's tavern.

Dominick's boom man attached radio mics inside Brett's and Della's shirts.

Ivan, on a high folding chair like Dominick's, said, "Let's get something in the can."

An assistant held a slate labeled "Zombies fr G M" in front of the lens and called out, "Scene 27, apple, take one." He closed the clapper with a bang.

Ivan said, "Action."

Della took Brett's arm, and they strolled along the street set while Dale rode beside them on the dolly.

Della said, "You left here last week to take our gold samples to Sacramento for testing. Should have been back days ago."

"I had a problem."

"Word is your 'problem' had a busty figure and the IQ of a spaniel."

"A fire closed the gold assay office for a couple of days, so I went to see my cousin in San Francisco." Brett caressed her cheek and kissed her.

She pulled away. "If you want to chase some young thing, have the guts to say so."

"Wouldn't ever cheat. You're the sweetest, prettiest woman I ever knowed."

Della shoved him away and stared into the camera. "Shit, Ivan."

"The line's wrong," said a young woman seated on a folding stool, a stopwatch and script on her lap.

Ivan pulled off his earphones. "Cut. You two want to run the scene again with script?"

"I have my lines," Della said. "His are off. He's got the cities mixed up, he doesn't kiss me at the right time, and what is this 'ever knowed' nonsense?"

Brett shrugged. "A little western feeling." He and Della faced each other, inches apart.

Ivan stepped between them. "It's a first take. Let's reset."

The dolly followed Della and Brett to the starting position. This time Brett said the correct city names but kissed Della at a different time and added lines about a train wreck and a robbery.

Della said, "Jesus, Mary, and Joseph. How about doing what's on the page?"

Brett said, "Got distracted."

In succeeding takes, he switched words, named the wrong city, and kissed Della after different lines. He always apologized, but by the end, the subtlest change threw Della.

Doreen, the makeup artist, her dimples deepening with exertion, dabbed perspiration from Della's face and patted on fresh powder.

After Della flubbed more lines, Ivan said, "Let's take ten" and drew her aside.

I followed Brett to his motor home and slipped inside as the door closed. More deluxe than Della's, it had a bigger TV, leather seats, a larger kitchen, an alcove stocked with drinks, and a guest basket with cheese, apples, peaches, and grapes.

Brett turned to me. "What do *you* want?"

"I'm worried about Della."

"You should be. She's drunk and blowing her lines."

"She had them half an hour ago."

"She doesn't now." He poured a club·soda, squeezed in lime juice, and downed it.

"You're changing things on every take."

"Mind your own business. You're on this show because I didn't have you fired."

"Because I didn't tell the crew you're a thief."

"You blackmailing me?"

"Asking you to stop sabotaging Della's performance. Give her a chance. She's a good actress."

"Been second rate for years."

I glared. "You signed on to work with her."

"Under protest. I'm supposed to be in love with a crone like that?"

"Seen any Julie Christie or Jacqueline Bisset movies? Those women are more than a couple of years past twenty, but sexy as hell."

"Della's no Julie Christie."

"But she has something you never will. Class."

"Let her have 'class' somewhere else. She's ruining the movie. I'm going to make her screw up when we start again and in the next scene and the one after that. She can ride her horse into the sunset, and they can replace her."

Two men roll a gurney from our house with Mom's body in a black bag. I shout, "You can't throw a person away."

I grabbed an apple from Brett's guest basket and threw it. The apple thumped against his chest.

He knocked it away. "Are you nuts?"

I hurled an overripe peach. It hit his stomach and oozed down to his crotch.

"That's it!" He stepped toward me.

I barraged him with apples, oranges, and bunches of grapes.

"That the way you fight, little girl?"

I expected to shout an *Acid Reflux* obscenity, but what came out was, "Women have served all these centuries as looking glasses, possessing the magic and delicious power of reflecting the figure of man at twice its natural size."

"Spare me the feminist bullshit."

"Shakespeare had a sister. But do not look for her in Sir Sidney's life of the poet. She died young—alas, she never wrote a word…"

"Unbelievable."

I threw a water bottle.

Brett knocked it away with a table lamp, yanked the window open, and shouted, "Security, get this crazy bitch out of here."

"You scared of a little girl?" I punched his shoulder. He whirled. The lamp, still in his hand, struck my head, shattering the bulb. Pain seared my scalp. My vision clouded.

As I sank to the floor, Karen shoved the door open. "What have you done, you silly child?"

Ivan hurried in and went to Brett.

"She's insane," he said.

Della arrived and knelt beside me.

"And on drugs," Brett added. "Did you hear that crap?"

Della said, "It's Virginia Woolf, *A Room of One's Own.*"

"Right," I said. "I memorized it for an English class."

Brett growled, "I don't care if it's William friggin' Shakespeare. Get this maniac away from me."

Della wiped the blood from my face and helped me up and outside. Clint ushered me to his truck and into the cab.

A female zombie nurse with purple eye makeup, shredded clothes, and a jumble of spiky, green hair stumbled to Clint's truck. She climbed in and sat beside me, groaning and clutching her stomach. "Oh, T-Tanya."

"Annie? Are you sick?"

"On my first day, too."

"What happened?"

"The zombies who say my stuttering ruins our performance gave me a hard time at breakfast. I asked if they had spiked my food because I felt queasy. A nice kitchen man brought me a special plate from the cooks."

"What man? Describe him."

"My tummy hurt. I didn't notice."

Clint drove us to the Barstow Community Hospital and told a nurse we were covered by the production company's insurance. Two orderlies placed Annie on a gurney. I gave her shoulder a squeeze as they wheeled her away.

A nurse showed me into a curtained cubicle. A doc in green scrubs entered, cleaned my wound, and applied butterfly strips.

At the pharmacy, I picked up pain and antibiotic prescriptions the doc ordered. I downed two of each, and Clint drove me to the hotel. I went to my room, curled up on the bed, and buried my head in the pillows. My thoughts scrambled into a woozy pastiche.

Chapter 26

I awoke to loud pounding and feared it was Stephen breaking in. I grabbed my unloaded .45 and aimed at the door.

It opened, and a chambermaid removed her key from the lock and walked away.

I slid the .45 under my covers as Karen came in, blew cigarette ashes from her sleeve, and sat on my bed. "Tell me about your tantrum in Brett's motor home."

"When I'm upset, I say and do weird things. It's a medical condition."

"Stop the bullshit. You're not from Seattle. There's no one with your name at the address you gave us or anywhere in the area. The police after you?"

"I'm trying to get away from a father who treated me like shit."

"Not buying it." She sucked her cigarette to a sputtering glow. "But I can use your talent for keeping Brett off balance. I refuse to let a wet-behind-the-ears TV actor sabotage Della. I'll keep you around on one condition."

"If the condition is I sleep with him—"

"Don't worry." She smiled. "We'll hold your siren charms in reserve. Just keep the boy on edge so he leaves Della alone."

"How's Annie doing?"

"Still in the hospital." She exhaled a swirl of smoke and walked out.

Ivan entered. "There's no excuse for your nonsense this afternoon. Karen and Della want to keep you around, and I've given the okay, but you've got to grow up if you want to make it in this business."

When he left, I phoned Nina and described my fight with Brett.

"Go, girl," she said. "I'm glad you stood up to that jerk."

I called Lottie and repeated my story, expecting an I-told-you-so lecture. She surprised me by chuckling. "That's the type of hullabaloo your mother created in her teens."

Lottie's support boosted my spirits. After we hung up, I held a cold compress on my forehead until my mind cleared. I got ready to look for Stephen, and imagined Doctor Kraig shaking his head and telling me I was suffering from a PTSD delusion based on someone I'd seen for a few moments on a soccer field and on a stranger I'd glimpsed on a bus.

But PTSD delusion or not, the guy was all I had to go on. And I still suspected his appearance in town had something to do with my dad.

Since Clint hadn't brought my ammunition, I slid Dad's unloaded .45 and the can of hairspray into my purse and walked the streets of downtown Barstow, glancing over my shoulder.

I checked stores, restaurants, and bars for two hours without seeing him.

Legs wobbly and head aching, I walked toward the hotel. After a few blocks, I passed an alley where Loretta Lynn's "Honky Tonkin' " wailed from a bar's open doorway. I approached and looked in.

Seated at a booth, his back to me, a young man with sandy hair studied a newspaper as he drank clear liquor from a shot glass. When he turned to watch a bald guy playing a pinball machine, I made out steel-rimmed eyeglasses. The hair, glasses, slender frame, and slumped posture convinced me he was Stephen.

The bald guy ran out of quarters, thumped the machine, and stomped off to the men's room.

Stephen slid his newspaper into a briefcase, locked it, left it on the table, and moved to the pinball machine. He snapped a ball into play and hit the flipper buttons.

I closed my fingers around the .45 in my purse. Heart speeding, I stepped forward, dividing my attention between Stephen and his briefcase.

He jostled the machine, which dinged and clattered as his score climbed. When several men crowded around and cheered him on, I stepped to his table and picked the briefcase lock with two bobby pins. I pulled out a green folder like the one I'd seen on the seat of the sedan in LA.

My jaw dropped at the sight of two dozen black-and-white, artistic shots of me, my hair soft and flowing, my eyes evocative, my lips full, and my cheekbones shadow-sculpted to appear as classic as Della's.

Wide shots showed me running across Red Square on the Bellingham campus. Other angles captured me biking. Telephoto shots through my dorm window caught me undressed and made me wince. Though, to my surprise, the photos had none of the cheap qualities of the porn studio posters.

He had created the me I wished I'd been in high

school, instead of the plump ordinary girl I'd viewed in the mirror every morning. I shuddered and closed the folder.

In another folder, I found legal documents and papers about Dad's bank loans, plus newspaper articles.

One page contained, after a paragraph in English, a word in Cyrillic letters—a 3, an O, an M, something like a 6, and a backwards N. From a history class, I knew Cyrillic type was used in Russia and had been the language of the Russian Orthodox Church centuries ago.

Why would a math-whiz from Bellingham have papers using that text? I needed to translate the Cyrillic writing.

By the time the guys at the pinball machine quieted down, I had checked the rest of the folders. I slid them into the briefcase, locked it, and moved away as Stephen turned from the pinball machine.

As he approached the booth, I tried to see his face, but he slipped onto the seat, looking away from me.

I went outside and hid behind a dumpster across the street, hoping to follow him.

He came out as a plane passed low overhead. When he glanced up and I got a clear view of his face, I froze—the guy was not Stephen. He hurried off between two apartment buildings, and I followed but when I arrived at the first corner, I couldn't see him.

To check the Cyrillic writing, I looked for a bookstore. I found one open near the Barstow Community College and bought a Russian-English dictionary which included entries in Cyrillic script. The backwards E, O, M and something like a 6, and an N translated as "zombies." The man had come to Barstow to check out the shoot.

****

Though I had no proof, and Dr. K would have scoffed, I decided Dad was nearby, and my Stephen-look-alike had followed me, hoping to find him. His use of Cyrillic text meant he was Russian, or involved with Russians.

Hanging around campus taking photos, he must have followed me to my room, tracked Nina and me to the screening, to the soccer field, and later followed me to the bus terminal. But why did he want to find Dad?

While a freight rumbled through the rail yard across the highway, shaking my room, I pictured what I'd seen in the briefcase, including a blurry photo of a man emerging from a storefront on a sunny street lined with palm trees. On the back of the photo someone had written, "Bought explosives several times in September."

If he was my father and if he had bought explosives in the last month, he was alive. The note continued, "Seen at the FBI's LA field office."

I recalled newspaper articles about recent West Coast FBI and DEA crime syndicate busts, including a photo of a bloody corpse face-up on the street, two men in FBI jackets standing over it, with the caption, "Tip leads agents to confrontation with Russian mobsters near Canadian border."

Why and how had my cabin-building father gotten involved with Russians?

Chapter 27

At seven the next morning, day three on location, I called Nina from my room and told her the guy-on-the-bus/phony-priest was not Stephen. I recited what I recalled from clippings about criminal gang busts and Russian organizations. "Stephen has to be one of their people," I said, and described the Cyrillic letters for "zombies."

Nina said, "I'll ask the Russian Studies profs if any know what those groups are up to. In the meantime, stay away from that psycho." Someone knocked on my door. "What's that noise?" Nina asked, alarm in her voice.

I stretched the phone cord and peered through the security port. Clint stood in the hall. I told Nina a friend had arrived, and we hung up.

Clint handed me a box when I opened the door. "An instinct told me to trust you. Don't screw up. Something tragic happens, I'm in big trouble."

When he left, I opened the box and found a carton of .45 ammunition, a notched rod, patches, and oil.

Later, as I finished cleaning the gun, the phone rang. I answered with a nervous "Hello?"

Karen's voice rasped, "Transportation had to bring the makeup trailer to the production building for a repair. Go down there. Find Brett and tell him he's late. Put him on edge for his ride to the set."

"Any news about Annie?"

"Gastritis. No one else got sick, so I guess it wasn't a food issue."

"Will she come back to work?"

"We'll see."

I wanted to warn Karen a stranger had been hanging around and had poisoned Annie. But I had no evidence.

I hung up, washed my face, and pulled my hair into a loose ponytail—my scalp still hurt. I rummaged in my cosmetic bag and dabbed concealer on my bruises, put on a burgundy knit top and jeans, and went to the makeup trailer.

Doreen's apple cheeks glistened with perspiration as she applied foundation to Brett's face.

"*You*," he growled when I entered.

"They said to tell you you're late."

"You need to stay in whatever burrow peons hide and leave me alone."

Doreen checked the butterfly strips on my head. "Your wound is seeping, hon. You should have it re-dressed."

"Right," Brett said. "Go to a hospital far away, in Cleveland, for example. And stay there."

"Brett…" Doreen said.

"The girl's crazy."

"Yeah, I'm the crazy one."

I ducked out of the trailer and passed Jake, the scarred special effects man, talking with Karen. She pulled me aside. "With the bleeding around those strips you look like a crash victim. It's time for an easy day."

"I don't want an easy day. I want to go to the set." Where I can quiz Dale and other crew people about my dad.

"What *I* want is for you to avoid another freak-out. The editing room's in the old Ford parts department. Dark, quiet, and isolated." She pointed. "Go work with Allen, our editor."

****

The parts department exterior was painted battleship gray, and the door was closed. Something behind it clattered like Lottie's old treadle sewing machine.

I knocked.

"Go away," growled a voice like the bridge troll in my favorite childhood record, *Three Billy Goats Gruff.*

I said, "Karen sent me."

"Tell her she'll get my 1099 later."

"I'm not here about paperwork."

"Bye." More clattering.

I knocked again.

The door opened a crack, releasing a puff of marijuana smoke. An eye stared from the dark room, reminding me of Mom's dead gaze.

I stepped back.

"Get in here," the troll said. "I'm up to my ass in crap."

"You're Allen?"

"Usually."

The door opened halfway. A stooped figure, backlit and hard to see, retreated into the gloom.

I stepped inside and made out a bench against the far wall.

Allen settled onto a high, wheeled stool, propped his sandals on the foot rail, and leaned over a silvery green machine the size of a standing mailbox. Two metal arms holding reels, the bottom one full, the top empty, extended back from the machine.

He pressed the foot pedal, and the machine clattered again. Film snaked in a jiggly loop around sprocketed rollers, behind a viewing box, and onto the upper reel. The index-card-sized screen flickered with an image of Brett's face, moving forward and back, turning right and left.

"Makeup test," Allen said.

A few bright flashes…darkness…moments of Brett's face in different makeup, his forehead black-and-blue, blood trickling from a wound on his scalp.

Light reflects off the bloody gash on Mom's throat.

I held onto the editing table for support. "Is…this for the scene when he's attacked by the zombies?"

"Who knows? Someone gets attacked everywhere in Ivan's scripts." Allen ran more film through the machine and gestured around the windowless space, which had dozens of cubbyholes and a jumble of empty Ford parts boxes. "If you're my assistant, move those things outside."

"Okay, but I'm just here for the day."

"Figures. Cheap bastards."

I moved the boxes he indicated. When I got back, the editing machine's screen was casting a dim light on Allen's face, illuminating dark eyes half-hidden under bushy brows. A few bits of scrambled egg nestled in his thicket of a beard.

Allen toked again.

I waved my hand through the smoke. "Don't they mind?"

"On my salary, they can take what they get." He put the joint down. "What's your name?"

179

"Tanya Becker." I pointed at the machine. "What's that?"

"A Moviola. The production won't spring for a flatbed, so I'm stuck with this antique. But it works. They cut *Casablanca* on one like it." Allen moved the full top reel from the Moviola to the bench. He slid it onto a spindle on the right and ran the loose end to an empty reel on the left. Cranked them to a whirring, clattering blur.

The darkness and the noise of the spinning reel made me dizzy.

"My assistant should be doing this," Allen said, retrieving his smoldering joint and sucking it to life.

He would be a pain to work for but a good source for information. "You must have seen lots of strange movies over the years."

"What are you looking for, Mary? Kinky sex stories?"

"The name's Tanya. And not kinky, *dark*. Come across any grisly films?"

"Once you learn how special effects are done, see the fake scars and pretend bullet hits, it's routine. An editor's like a surgeon. The director has half-killed the poor movie. It's on the operating table, and you're trying to save its life and his ass before the backers take over and kick him out."

Allen, in a blue surgical smock, stitches Mom's gashed throat.

I knotted my hands into fists. "Did you see a scene showing a woman dragged across a rooftop?"

"Your mother raise you to go for rough stuff?"

"My mother…"

I stumble out of the bathroom, tripping over

scattered bottles and makeup jars, and stepping around bloody footprints.

I shook my head and brought my mind to the present. "For a school project I need to research scary movies."

A strip of film dangled from a small roll on the bench. I picked up a plastic tube with a magnifying lens at one end. "Okay if I look at it with this?"

He nodded. "Called a loupe."

I held it to the film. "An animated Thanksgiving story."

"We've got cartoons, westerns, everything." He pointed to piles of boxes on the floor.

"Can I look through them?" I asked, thinking there might be *Dead Girls* reels inside.

"They're for leaders. Leave 'em be."

A UPS driver wheeled a foot-high stack of round, twenty-inch tins into the room on a handcart and left.

"The dailies from what they shot yesterday," Allen said. He mounted a roll of track on a split reel and ran it over a sound head on a rig with four sprocketed wheels. He listened for pops and, using a Sharpie, marked pop frames with Xs.

"I'm serious about gory movies," I said. "Ever see one where a woman is thrown off a roof? Or chased into a taxi that crashes and burns?"

He kept working.

When he finished the sound rolls, he opened a can of work print, cranked through it, and studied a section of film with the loupe. "I mark the slates. Use them to establish sync points." He handed me the loupe. "Crank down a few feet and tell me when the clapper falls."

I tried, but my gaze wandered to the stack of old

movie boxes and film spooled onto the floor. Bending to retrieve it, I kneeled on a spiral of picture.

"Pay attention," Allen grumbled. He edged me out of the way and took over.

Either too drug-addled or too ornery to help me, he completed the rest without mentioning a single gruesome film.

"I'd better see if Della needs me." I walked out and went to the Ford showroom entrance, where drivers were delivering coffee, bottled water, and office supplies. While PA's scurried about, collecting the supplies, a hand grasped my arm.

I whipped around. "Don't you dare—"

Doreen stumbled back, blushing. "Sorry. I wanted to say how inspiring you were, standing up to Brett yesterday."

"I hate bullies."

She studied me. "Let me fix your hair, give it some style."

"Style's not my thing these days." Don't insult the woman, I thought. She takes enough abuse from Brett. "Thanks for the offer, but I'm broke."

"I do it free for the crew. A snip here, a curl there, and you'll be a new woman."

Her offer gave me an idea. "Let's see what you can do."

"The makeup trailer is still being repaired—they're working from a tent on the set." She led me inside, bent me over the sink, and rinsed and washed my hair.

I said, "You must hear lots of gossip, like which people have worked together before and what movies they've done."

"Bits and pieces." When she finished shampooing,

she sat me on a chair. She handed me an *Elle* with a cover photo of a doe-eyed girl wearing a wide straw hat. I put the *Elle* aside—I avoided comparing myself to models.

Doreen cut, thinned, and curled my hair, added concealer under my eyes, eyeliner, a touch of foundation, blusher, and lipstick. She turned me to face the mirror.

I stared, astonished. She had evened out several locks I'd cut short in moments of PTSD frustration. She teased long curls to frame my face and shaped the back—the tousled me replaced by a girl looking a bit like the one on the *Elle* cover. "You're a magician," I said, taking a last look. "If you don't know about crew backgrounds, who does?"

"Karen's got all the resumes."

****

When Karen exited a van arriving from the set, I hurried to her.

She said, "Looks like you went AWOL from the editing room and ran off to a spa."

"I went to Doreen's trailer after a quick stint with Allen. We didn't get along."

"That old hippie's as laid back as they come. You must be a pain in the ass."

She headed into the Ford showroom. I followed her to an office paneled in fake mahogany plywood, decorated with old Ford posters, and furnished with a desk, chair, and a file cabinet, one drawer labeled "CREW."

While Karen went through her in-box, I studied a black-and-white photo on her desk—a girl about seven pulling a wagon full of stuffed animals. Karen turned the photo away.

I asked, "Anything I can do to help?"

She got a walkie-talkie call and rushed out. I opened the CREW file drawer and found a folder of resumes. I leafed through them, looking for *Dead Girls* crew members and anyone who had worked with Zolton Baron.

Neither *Dead Girls* nor Zolton's name appeared anywhere, but I discovered something puzzling. Though Della and Ivan must have been in the business for two decades, I didn't recognize any of the early titles listed in their CVs, except for *Longhorn Lady* and *Lost Corral* which Della did years ago.

I returned the resumes to the file drawer seconds before Karen came back, followed by a chocolate Lab that tried to sniff my crotch.

Karen pulled him away. "Damn mutt keeps sneaking into the building. Take him to animal control and have them put him down."

Ribs sticking out, legs scrawny, he looked pitiful. I scratched behind his ears. He licked my hand and rested his chin on my lap.

"Do it quick," Karen said. "He'll get run over or catch rabies from a coyote and bite somebody. Break your heart either way."

I nodded but had no intention of taking him to be killed. He made me think of Scout.

Karen lit a cigarette. "By the way, your friend Annie is out of danger, but the doc won't okay her for work. We've already hired a new zombie. An unsolicited resume came in. The movie gods must be looking out for us."

I suspected those gods might include my stalker,

but telling Karen my suspicions about him would make her think I had gone off the rails again.

I led the lab to a far corner of the repair bay, laid out a piece of carpet, and set down a dish of water and a leftover stack of cold cuts. While he wolfed down the food, I tethered him to a water pipe with a rope. "I'm calling you Royal," I said, "because your coat is the same color as the colas I loved when I was six. Now, stay here. I don't want anyone taking you to animal control."

I headed toward the Ford showroom between two rows of parked trucks.

Something poked my back. I jumped and whirled. The phony PI stood behind me, wearing a black sport coat over khakis, his hands raised in mock surrender. "Sorry, Charlie. Don't worry. I'm here to help."

My breaths coming fast, I glanced around for a weapon but couldn't see anything to grab.

He smiled. "Hope I didn't frighten you by tagging along from time to time. You might have seen me at the U., taking snapshots for our company files. All confidential." He handed me a card reading, "Peter Zamos Investigations. Discreet and Reliable. Seattle, Washington."

I squinted.

"Your grandmother hired me to look out for you."

"And President Reagan asked me to be his ambassador to Sweden."

He pulled out a Western Union money order made out for $500 to Peter Zamos Investigations, Lottie's name in the purchaser box. "If you won't agree to return home, which is what she'd prefer, I've been asked to help you find your dad."

What he said made vague sense—Lottie had towed away the old Plymouth and tried to talk me into staying in Bellingham. But why would she have hired such a strange, inept man. "Prove it," I said. "Let's call her together."

"Your grandmother will deny everything. She knows you'd hate her looking over your shoulder."

True. Besides, Lottie didn't have enough money to hire a high-priced investigator. "Let's talk to my friend, Nina."

"Your dad's enemies are keeping an eye on her. If we scare Nina and she rushes down here to help you, I can't be responsible for what happens."

"Who are my dad's enemies?"

"That's what we need to find out."

I stepped toward the office.

"Wait." He pulled out a .38 Smith & Wesson and offered me the handgrip. "If you suspect I'm lying, turn me in to the local police."

Royal charged from the shadows, growling, and stood beside me, a gnawed piece of rope hanging from his neck. He sniffed Zamos and growled again. I leaned down and whispered, "I'm okay, boy. He isn't going to do anything while you're here. I'm impressed you knew to protect me. Were you a guard dog? A police dog?" He licked my chin.

Keeping a nervous eye on Royal, Zamos offered his weapon again.

I shook my head—contacting the cops would put my name on record in town. Any hint of police involvement might convince Ivan and Karen to send me away and scare Dad's enemies into attacking.

"We need to think about this." I patted Royal's

head.

"Don't think too long. Other people are looking for your father."

"How do you know that?"

"PI instinct." He walked away.

Chapter 28

In my room, I relaxed, figuring I'd be safe as long as this guy believed I would work with him. Though he unnerved me, he hadn't triggered a PTSD outburst or a vision of Dad's mutilated jaw or Mom's slit throat. Progress, perhaps.

After changing into clean clothes, I went to the Ford service bay. Royal leapt toward me, wagging his tail. I was pleased he didn't leap up and put his paws on my chest. After I fed him, I walked across the repair bay to a makeshift screening area and helped arrange three dozen folding chairs to face a fabric screen mounted on the wall. A 35mm projector stood in a plywood enclosure facing a window in the front.

I printed *"Dead Girls Don't Lie"* on scraps of paper and left them on various chairs. I studied the crew as they came in, grabbed pizza slices and beers from a table, and sat. Neither Dale nor any of the others touched my paper scraps.

Brett and Della didn't show up. The lights dimmed, the projector whirred, and images flashed on the screen. Brett was more handsome on film than in person, the camera capturing sureness in his movements and intensity in his eyes. His voice on the soundtrack resonated with strength.

In her shots, Della had leapt back ten years. Soft lighting, diffusion filters, and subtle makeup muted the lines on her face, and accented in her eyes the icy blue fire I'd seen when we met. Hollywood could create magic after all. The camera and the pair's acting—no traces of their mutual animosity appeared on the screen—made it look as if romance burned between them.

With illusion so ingrained in this movie world, I doubted I would recognize my dad if he walked up to me and said hello.

Dale left as soon as dailies were finished. I followed him to the hotel bar, where two waitresses in bustiers and red skirts puffed out with crinolines wound their way between the tables, carrying trays loaded with plates of fries, burgers, and beers. Strings of colored lights and a huge black-and-white rodeo poster hung on a side wall.

While Dale's crew clustered at the bar, he sat alone in an empty booth, eyes downcast, shirt collar turned up as if to ward off a raw wind. He was shredding a cocktail napkin into strips and drinking from a mug of beer.

I grabbed a dish of pretzels from a wait station and set it on his table. "I don't blame you for being irritated by my questions the other day."

"It's fine, kid." He motioned toward a space opposite him.

I sat, ordered a beer from a passing waitress, and slid the pretzels toward him. "I have no ambition to be a cinematographer. I'm not trying to sneak onto your crew, so, please don't get nervous when I say your dailies amazed me."

He shredded another napkin. The waitress brought my beer, and I drank. "Your images made me realize you're a painter—with a camera instead of brushes. You made Brett and Della look like stars and transformed a low-budget, desert movie set into something atmospheric and beautiful. It reminds me one of my favorite movies, *McCabe and Mrs.Miller*."

"*McCabe,* it's not." He lobbed a wad of napkin strips at his beer and missed.

"Looks exciting to be a cinematographer. But I suppose it bores you."

"Not if the director gives me room to follow my instincts. And, for all of Ivan's faults, he does that." Dale grabbed a fresh napkin. "Your hair and makeup's different. Very becoming."

I crumbled a pretzel and stared at my beer.

Dale drained his glass. "You might as well come clean. I know you've been spying on me."

"No way."

"You took notes on the set. Ivan's got you writing down everything I do so he can whittle away at my lens-and-lighting package to save a few bucks."

"I'm not a spy for Ivan."

"Show me your notebook."

As I pulled it out, I realized it would confirm his suspicion. I had written, "Why is Dale using so many lights? What's the purpose of all those glass filters? How will he use ten lenses?"

I handed it over. "This isn't what it looks like."

He snorted, turning pages. "I suppose Ivan told you to butter me up. Flirt and sweet-talk me into caving on whatever he wants."

I laughed so loud the tables around us went silent.

"That would be a joke, huh? Running a seductive con on me?"

"The joke would be on Ivan. I haven't flirted much. Never had sex. Kissed a few boys in high school but fooled around less than most girls. I wasn't Miss Popularity."

He frowned. "Ivan must be paying you."

"You movie people gin up more fantasies than the girls in my college dorm. I wrote notes on the set so I wouldn't sound stupid when I asked you questions about your work." In a moment of PTSD impatience, I ignored Sally's advice not to reveal my situation. "If I tell you the truth, will you keep what I say private?"

"Are you capable of telling the truth? I know you didn't give out the real story on Brett."

Noticing no one was listening, I said, "I met a woman who told me you worked on a film called *Dead Girls Don't Lie*."

"Applied for the job. They hired someone else."

"When you were at their production office did you run across a man named Jefferson Purdue?"

"No."

"Ever see *Dead Girls*?"

"Nope. Why do you care?"

"I recognized someone in it I thought had died. I'm here to find out what happened to him."

"Like I said, I didn't work *Dead Girls*."

"Know anyone on the crew who did?"

He shook his head, finished his beer, and leaned closer. "A piece of advice. Be smart. Lots of guys on crews look for quickie romances. A bad one would screw up a nice girl like you."

"Not interested in guys these days. But I am interested in what you use for visual inspiration."

His eyes brightened. "Edward Hopper and

191

Caravaggio. Hopper likes muted images with thoughtful or sad people looking away from the viewer. Caravaggio loves mysterious frames with tortured facial expressions. Bodies in uncomfortable positions. If you're not bullshitting about your interest, I'll show you my art books."

Dale's assistants slid into the booth. Lori had brushed her hair and changed into a white top over black pants. Dale asked, "Any of you know about a film called *Dead Girls Don't Lie?*"

The guys said no, and their talk turned to the large breasts on a girl in the wardrobe department. Lori groaned.

I slumped in my seat. Dale had been my main link to *Dead Girls*. His denial he'd worked on it and my failure to see a crew member with Dad's lopsided gait made me suspect the PI and I were both wrong about Dad being here. Perhaps, as Lottie had suggested, at the college screening I saw my dad because I wanted to.

I put three dollars beside my drink and walked toward the lobby, daunted by the prospect of questioning more crew people, who would deny knowledge of my dad. I worried about the PI. If he had told me the truth and I didn't keep him informed, I'd have missed a chance to get his help. If he'd lied, he could do his worst to Dad before I knew it.

As if reading my mind, the PI joined a small crowd ahead of me, leaving the bar. I continued to the lobby, rode the elevator up one floor, and came down.

The PI had crossed the main drag and was heading down a side street. I followed a few blocks and hid in a doorway as he entered a small motel. A light went on in a second-floor room. Moments later, he emerged, and I followed him. When he approached the pinball bar, I returned to his motel.

It had no reception desk, so I went to the second floor and used bobby pins to pick his lock. His plain room had a single bed, a colorful spread, and an amateur oil painting of a man on a horse.

Folders, papers, and photos lay spread on the desk. I gathered a stack and hid them under my top, jogged to the production building, ran everything through the copy machine, and left the papers where I'd found them.

****

In my hotel room, reviewing what I'd copied or memorized, I abandoned any notion the PI had my back, or that he was a PI at all. One photo showed a rustic cottage exterior, Elaine Prescott's home before the fire. Close-ups, taken at night through a window, showed a sturdy gray-haired woman typing at a desk. Other photos had angles of the same woman on the floor in a pool of blood. In several, taken outside, flames curled over the roof.

A singed page of Prescott's book manuscript read, "Chapter 7 - Jefferson Purdue, Mountain Man/Shit Magnet." One partial paragraph said, "Purdue attacked a man shouting in Russian."

Paragraphs of Russian names and sentences in Cyrillic text were scorched beyond readability but several pages in English contained financial data, including dates and Russian names. In a blurry photo, Dad had his arm around Shanahan's blonde actress friend, the pair posing in front of one of Dad's log cabins. Even on these black-and-white copies, her eyes glinted, and her full lips shimmered.

Another series of telephoto color shots, taken from the far shore of Lake Terrell, showed me with Shanahan on the Lake View deck. A half dozen pictured Shanahan's body floating face down, his wheelchair beneath him on the bottom.

I returned the photos to their folder and tried to forget I slept a few blocks from a man who probably murdered Shanahan, Prescott, and Mom.

A clipping from a Vancouver newspaper included a picture of a young man covered in blood and lying on the pavement. Cyrillic letters on the margin included a backward 6, an O, a P, a backward N, and a C. My Russian dictionary said those letters spelled "Boris."

Who was he? A Mafia pal of the phony PI? A threat to Dad?"

I found a blurry wallet-sized glossy of a fortyish Hannah Lynn. On the back she'd written, "XO, Jim. Call me if you come to town. 213-555-6252."

The phony PI must have stolen the photo from Shanahan's body when he killed him, showed up the next day, posing as his cousin and executor, and collected Shanahan's papers after presenting a phony attorney's letter.

I called the 213 number and reached a woman who didn't know Hannah. It figured—Sally said she had changed her name and contact information. The woman said, "The phone company split the 213 area code to accommodate more customers. If the person you want lives in the San Fernando Valley, the number might have an 818 area code now."

I dialed 818-555-6252, which got me a woman who ran a dog-grooming business.

I said, "Any chance you have information about the

person who had that number? I'm desperate to find an old friend of my dad's and learn why someone murdered my mom."

The woman said, "I don't usually do this, but I think the person assigned this listing might not mind." She gave me a new 818 number.

When I called it, an answering machine picked up and a silky female voice said, "I'm out of town. Leave a message."

"My name is Tanya," I said. "Please call me." I left my hotel and room number.

It was midnight when I phoned the dorm. Nina was still awake, cramming for an exam. I told her I was sure the phony priest, calling himself a private detective, had killed Elaine Prescott and Officer Shanahan. "He pretended Lottie hired him to make sure I was okay."

Nina said, "I'm concerned. I know you want to find your dad, but you should call the police in Mount Vernon and see if you can push them to work harder on the case."

I was surprised at her suggestion. She knew how useless they'd been in finding out who killed Mom. I told her so, adding, "They'll insist I come for an interview even though I've told them all I know. I've hit dead ends, but I'm getting close, Nina. I can feel it. I'm going to find my dad."

"I'm sure you're right but I worry about you. I'll do whatever I can to help."

We hung up, and I decided to be more appreciative of Nina's concerns. I checked the hallway outside my room before I got back to reviewing the papers I'd taken from Lottie's desk and the ones from the phony PI. Phone records for Dad's trailer-office showed he had made no calls to Mom on the day she was murdered. Mom's records listed one call to his trailer, five seconds long. Neither of them had called the police. But both their bills included an incoming call shortly before her death from a number I didn't recognize, 604-555-3719. My phone book put 604 in Vancouver, British Columbia.

Who had called from there? If Mom sensed danger, why hadn't she phoned the police? If some outsider's call or Mom's had drawn Dad home, he seemed less a murderer than a victim. I closed my eyes and tried to picture what Mom had sketched in blood on the tiles. A faint image came through—kite-shaped marks, ragged and hard to make sense of.

I phoned Lottie, woke her, mentioned the area code 604 calls to Mom and to Dad's trailer on the day of her murder, and asked if she knew who made them.

"I didn't keep track of your parents' acquaintances."

"Have you seen any strangers in your neighborhood during the last week or two?"

"Not even your mystery girl."

"But if there was one—"

"*Were* one. If there *were* one. Uncertainty calls for the subjunctive."

"If I find out the subjunctive can stop a killer, I'll use it in every sentence. I'm worried about your safety. How about living with friends for a while?"

"I won't be a lodger in someone else's house."

"At least lock your doors and be on the alert." I described my conversation with the PI.

"Piffle," she said. "I didn't hire anyone. I've been taking care of myself for half a century. I'll be fine. But since you're distressed, I'll ask the police in California to check on you."

"If they start poking around in Barstow or on the set, and if Dad is here, he may leave."

She gave a frustrated sigh but agreed to hold off. "A friend of yours named Mary Sue stopped by, asking how to contact you. I said I'd pass on the message."

I went to bed and left the TV on to keep from feeling alone. I dreamed Mary Sue was dragging me back to Bellingham to fix my psyche.

Toward dawn, I awoke to hear a newscaster say, "FBI agents raided a house in central Los Angeles where they found a Russian Mafia prostitution and counterfeiting operation run by the California branch of the Odessa Mafia out of Brighton Beach in New York."

Was there a Barstow branch of the Russian Mafia?

Chapter 29

The next morning, day four on location, after the crew left for the set, a delivery truck pulled up. The driver unloaded a stack of film boxes marked "Editorial." My mind went to the *Dead Girls* boxes, and I showed the driver the way.

When I unloaded the new ones beside the Moviola, Allen said, "What do *you* want?"

"To help."

"Thought syncing dailies didn't interest you." He spliced two shots together, slapped the clip in the Moviola picture gate, and ran the cut. He made a mark, trimmed a frame, and ran it again.

"Do you want to remind me how immature I am, or teach me?"

He slipped off his editing chair. "See if you can mark picture slates and check the shots against the camera reports."

I picked the top roll from the pile, mounted it, and fumbled my way through the first slates. After I made several mistakes, he took over and whipped through to the end of the roll. We traded off for an hour, doing all the work print.

When we'd synced the rolls, we added leaders Allen had made from the old movie stock. He asked me to print labels on strips of white tape, checked my first one, and said, "I've seen fourth graders do better."

Forming neat letters, he printed the film's name and the screening roll number on the tape.

I tried to copy his example, but my mind went to possible *Dead Girls* reels in the boxes on the floor, and I messed up again.

He nudged me aside. "Can't you pay attention for ten seconds?"

"I'll stay late, redo this one, and make a bunch more."

"All right, but take pride in your work." He pulled a rumpled joint from his shirt pocket, lit it, and left.

After lettering new leaders for the rolls to be projected for the daily screening, I cranked through the fill stock, bypassing anything in black-and-white. I rolled through a color print with dark, grainy images and stopped on a shot of two platinum blondes in waitress outfits. In my high school audio-visual club, I'd learned movie sound appeared as a wavy line on the edge of the film.

I located the Moviola's optical reader, threaded the film around its metal drum, and pressed the foot pedal. Above the machine's clacking, the soundtrack played, staticky and muffled. But I recognized one blonde's raspy New York accent and her star-shaped beauty mark I'd seen in the *Dead Girls* screening at the U.

The second blonde's voice had a sultry, appealing quality, but neither that nor her beauty were enough to raise the movie above the low-rent level I recalled. Lights hovered at the edge of the frame and the microphone often bobbed into view. I cranked on, looking for my father, but didn't see him.

I found five more *Dead Girls* rolls, each a thousand feet, or ten minutes long, and spooled through them, but didn't find the rooftop scene. I had no proof from the footage that my father was alive, or that *Dead Girls* had a connection to people on our zombie movie.

I went through all six reels a second time. Finally, I spotted Dad, not as a character in a scene but popping into frame in the background for a couple of seconds, as if he hadn't known the camera was running.

He ducked out of frame and said, "Sorry" off camera.

I played the moment again, touched the image of Dad's out-of-focus body, and grinned. But when I played the clip a second and third time, I clenched my fists and said, "If you were alive, why the hell didn't you contact me?"

During my syncing sessions with Allen, sometimes a camera magazine ran out, leaving more sound than picture. If the sound was usable, he left it. In place of the missing picture, he inserted a piece of fill stock. One of those picture runouts occurred in the coming night's dailies. Allen had slugged in a piece of an animated film about dogs. I substituted two minutes of *Dead Girls,* ending with the clip showing my dad slipping in and out of frame and saying "Sorry" off camera.

The dailies played as usual. My altered roll screened last. When the *Dead Girls* clip appeared, the key grip glanced at Dale and nudged him. As the lights came on, I headed their way.·

Allen stopped me. "Who promoted you to editor?"

"You recognized the added clip. And you worked on *Dead Girls*."

"Why is that your business?"

"People on this shoot claim they know nothing

about *Dead Girls*, but when we project a few seconds of it, the key grip nudges Dale, and you get angry." Either because I sensed an opportunity, or again from PTSD impatience, I disregarded Sally's advice. "The man who stuck his head into the shot was my father. He was the actor who threw the blonde off the roof. Since last spring I've thought he was dead."

Allen led me to the editing room, pulled a bottle of scotch from a filing cabinet, and poured himself a drink. When he offered me one, I declined. He downed a long swallow.

I said, "You knew my dad, didn't you?"

"I worked· on the movie but spent all my time in the editing room. I did hear about a man named Alec Hudson, hired off the street for a minor part as a heavy."

Allen drank again. "I got sick and had to leave before shooting ended. Didn't meet any actors and didn't cut the roof scene. Show it to me."

"It's not in the rolls we have."

Allen scratched his beard. "An actor on the film got killed. Might have been your father."

I showed him Dad's driver's license.

"I don't recognize the face," Allen said. "Hudson had a rep as a decent guy, but when someone dies on a film, everyone wants to pretend it didn't happen. So, people avoid answering when you ask about your dad."

He finished his scotch. "Sorry about the pain you've had. If it's weird for you to work here, you should go home."

"I have to find my father. I'll go through the fill stock again."

He put away the bottle. "I hope you find

something."

When he left, I locked the door and, using the guillotine splicer—its hinged blade swung down to chop the film—I removed the clip of Dad and spliced it into a loop. I played it five times and started to feel a new connection to him, hearing his "Sorry" as an apology. I rethreaded the first reel (missing the title and opening credits) and inched through the footage.

I had checked the second reel and was halfway through the third when someone knocked on the door. Picturing the phony PI, I grabbed the heavy film splicer and yelled, "I'm busy. Can't stop to talk."

"Tanya?" Brett said, "It's me. Open up."

"The last time we were alone, you broke a light bulb on my head."

"By accident. After you barraged me with everything you could grab. Come on. I want to check something in the dailies."

"You need to talk to Ivan or Allen about that."

He knocked again.

"I'm working."

"I'm not leaving until you let me in. Won't do anything mean. I promise."

I unthreaded the roll and opened the door.

Brett stepped in, wearing boot-leg jeans and a denim shirt. His casual outfit, mussed hair, and day's growth of beard gave him the look of a whisky ad model. It was more appealing than the usual neat-and-tidy Brett. But I didn't trust him.

He pointed at the Moviola. "Let me see my last takes."

"Not allowed to show dailies."

"I'm allowing you."

"You're not my boss."

He said, "You want to get in trouble?"

"You want me to send a note to *Variety* about your shoplifting?"

He studied me. "I thought you were a nice person. You look nice. Classy haircut." He walked out.

I was impressed Brett wanted to see his dailies. I'd underestimated his dedication to his craft. With him gone, I relaxed and rethreaded the third roll in the Moviola. I went through it and was starting the fourth when the door opened—I'd neglected to lock it.

Brett stepped in.

I said, "I told you, I—"

"What are you looking at?" He tried to push past me.

I blocked his way. "Nothing important. You need to leave."

I figured he'd argue, but his bluster faded, and he sagged against the editing bench. "I was a jerk the other day. To Della, to you, to the crew. Wouldn't complain if you sued me for battery. You still can, for lots of money."

"I don't want money."

"What do you want? Fame? Life in the fast lane?"

"I want you to go to your room."

He peered at the Moviola screen. "I had a part in that movie."

"Prove it. Tell me the title."

"It's like a dream I've had. What's it called?"

"Déjà vu. Please go to bed before I get in trouble."

"I mean what's the film called? I had a few drinks, feel a little foggy." He stepped closer and stared at the Moviola image of a man wearing suspenders and a white shirt and pointing a gun at one of the waitresses.

"Do you know the title or not?"

"Sorry. I've blocked it."

Like you blocked the need to pay at the department store. "Please leave."

"I didn't get to see the film after…" He closed his mouth, dropped his hands to his sides, and walked out.

Leery about his motives and reliability, I was glad to be rid of him.

****

I finished going through the reels without finding another shot of Dad. I trudged to my room, flopped on my bed, and turned the TV to a news channel. After car accidents, convenience store robberies, and sports clips, a story came on about a Russian sex-trafficking ring in Vancouver, British Columbia.

Los Angeles, Vancouver, Barstow—Russian crime was all around me. Was Dad in more danger than I'd imagined?

My thoughts went to the Russian Mafia articles I'd found at the University library to support Nina's FBI plans. I hadn't given her the information, but one term stuck with me, *Torpedos,* or contract killers.

Was the phony PI a torpedo? He seemed too unprofessional and strange to belong to a real crime family. He could have been an oddball with a grudge because he suspected Dad had informed on some guy he knew named Boris. It was a lot of speculation, but if I was ever going to make progress with my PTSD therapy, I'd have to push through events when I was uncertain about their reality.

Pounding shook my door. I rushed to the security port.

Brett stood in the hall, wearing a bathrobe and stepping from foot to foot, like a kid who had to pee.

I opened the door a crack. "Go to bed."

"*Dead Girls* was a weird deal, but I had a minor role in it. My mother's acting career was underwater. She asked me to help her get one of the waitress parts, and I did."

"What was weird about the movie?

"The day of her big scene with the burning taxi, I had to go to LA to audition for a role in another movie. When I got back, her scene had been shot, but no one wanted to talk about it. While I was in the office, a call came in from my mom. She said there had been a problem. She'd been injured and was heading home. I told her I'd come see her. 'No way,' she said. 'Stay and finish the movie. I'll see you when it's over.' That was the last time I talked to her. A week later she was dead."

"Did you ask Jake about it?"

"He said the stunt people on the safety crew did their jobs, but everyone was warned not to talk about what happened because the production company was worried about a lawsuit for damages or a criminal investigation."

"Where is your mom buried?"

"Her ashes are in my apartment. I haven't been able to learn how her injury happened."

"Was Jake responsible?"

"I don't know. My distress about her situation put me in a basket. I had to gobble tranquilizers for a while, but the crew supported me and helped me keep working."

"How do I know your story's true?"

"How do I know yours is? You say the dad you were super close to was killed six months ago. Then he appeared in a movie but hasn't gotten in touch with you."

"Fair point." I decided part of what Brett said might be correct. Either way, I felt sad for him. My mind kept replaying images of Dad throwing one blonde off the roof and chasing the other toward a car that crashed in a ball of flame, the actress emerging unhurt a moment later and running away.

Brett said, "Can we see the scene?"

"I don't have the footage, but you can see my dad." I went with Brett to the editing room and played the shot of Dad's face peeking into frame. "Do you recognize him?"

"We didn't meet. But the shot of him must freak you out. Is he here?"

"I'm not sure. For a while I suspected he murdered my mom. Now I don't know. I need to find out why he pretended to be dead. Why he ran away and didn't call or write."

"I bet he's here somewhere."

I stiffened. Of all people, why had I blabbed to Brett? Out of despair? Fear? For companionship, I decided. Carrying secrets made me lonely. Having someone to share the load, even a self-absorbed actor, comforted me.

He said, "Let's look at the reels again."

"It's dangerous for us to discuss these things." I told him about Prescott's house fire and Shanahan's dead body in the lake. When I mentioned Annie's situation, he said, "The poor kid? Why would anyone hurt her?"

"You may want to go to your room and forget we talked."

"I have to find out what happened on *Dead Girls*, to your dad and my mom."

Brett piggybacking himself onto my search struck me as a recipe for trouble. His version of events might be phony, like the scam he'd tried at the department store. Maybe he'd start another childish campaign, like his feud with Della.

I pulled out the *Dead Girls* reels, started through them, and challenged him: "Show me a shot of you in the movie."

He was silent until the middle of the second reel. "There," he said, and pointed to himself in a bar arguing with two thugs. "They were going to use my name in the advertising, but after Mom died, the release got delayed. I don't like thinking about her death, but I'm glad you found this."

Brett insisted we screen the reels once more to look for other shots of his mom.

The second time through, he stopped me every time she showed up and made notes about wardrobe and props from *Dead Girls* he'd seen on this shoot.

Because of the late hour and my concern about the phony PI, I appreciated Brett's company as we walked to the hotel and headed upstairs. When we left the elevator and approached Brett's door, the phone rang inside. He said good night and went in, closing the door.

Inside, he said, "Man, you'll never guess what happened tonight."

I knocked.

The door opened a few inches, and Brett peered

out. "I'm busy."

"Don't tell people what we're doing. If my dad's here, you might scare him off."

"The guy I'm talking to is my best bud in LA. He won't say anything. Don't be paranoid." Brett closed the door and told his friend, "Been viewing scenes from my mom's last movie. The dad of a girl here worked on it."

I knocked again. He didn't answer.

Chapter 30

The next morning, day five on our zombie epic, I called Lottie and asked her to remember who Dad and Mom might have known in Vancouver, someone with a Russian name.

"I'll do my best," she said, "but I'm worried about you."

After assuring her I was fine, I took Royal to the parking lot and threw a ball for him. He went after it like a shot, returned, and laid it at my feet. I was pleased he'd gained weight and muscle tone in the few days since I got him. While I was imagining him retrieving ducks or pheasants I'd shot, a big guy in a hoodie approached. Royal snarled, and the guy retreated. I scratched Royal's head, whispering, "I loved Scout. But I wish you'd been at the house to protect Mom."

****

At the set, the First AD, sporting a black beret with a Canadian army patch, gave an order on his walkie-talkie then had me distribute the revised shot list for the day.

As I made my rounds I passed near Brett at the craft service table, flirting with two young women. I made a zipper movement across my lips.

He came over. "Have faith. I've already asked about the outfits from *Dead Girls*. The wardrobe mistress and her assistants were on other projects."

I left Brett, went to Bob, the key grip, and said, "I know you worked on *Dead Girls Don't Lie,* so—"

"Not me."

"Why did you nudge Dale when we screened a clip last night?"

"It's always strange when somebody shows up in a shot by mistake."

It sounded like BS to me. I went to the camera truck where Dale handed me art books with reproductions of paintings by Hopper, Caravaggio, Corot, and El Greco. "These artists, except for Corot, feature dark images or somber settings, and I feel the same way. Hate to over-light, love unusual characters and faces." He handed me a Polaroid camera and packs of film. "It's my spare. Take a few shots."

I put the camera and extra film in my purse. "Tell me why at dailies your key grip nudged you when the footage from *Dead Girls* came on. You both worked on it, right?"

Dale nodded.

"Why did you lie?"

"You weren't following the movie business in 1982, when Vic Morrow directed a *Twilight Zone* episode which killed him and two children in a freak helicopter accident. People avoided any mention of that project like the plague. Freelancers have to job-hunt every time a film ends. You may not know that two people from the *Dead Girls* shoot passed away. Their deaths gave the film the same stink as TZ. We all worried the connection might hurt our careers."

"What two people died on *Dead Girls*?"

"Actors, both with small parts. According to the

rumor."

"But you knew the man in the fill stock. The one who stuck his head into frame and said, 'Sorry.' "

"He arrived one day, looking for work, and got a job. I didn't know him well, but he seemed okay."

The First AD approached and tapped my shoulder. "With me." I followed him to a black Mustang idling in the parking area.

He said, "Hop in. Give Jake a hand."

The grotesque special effects man sat in the driver's seat, staring ahead and drumming his fingers on the wheel. The folds and discolorations on his face were translucent in the midday light.

I stand in our bathroom, Mom on the floor below me, her face waxy, her eyes staring. Footsteps approach. A man looms in the doorway, wielding a knife with Cyrillic letters on the blade.

I whispered to the AD, "Someone more experienced should go."

"Jake asked for the new girl. That's you." His walkie-talkie crackled with a message, and he hustled away.

"Pleasure to meet you," Jake said in a gravelly voice. "Is it true your name's Tanya?"

"Why?"

"It means praiseworthy in Russian."

I tensed. "You have Russian friends?"

Jake's mouth curved into what might have been a smile or a sneer. "Met a few over the years." He studied me through scarified eye slits.

Recalling an old Lottie rule, I said, "Pleased to meet you, Mr. Kinsler."

"Jake will do fine." He extended a scarred hand,

and I gripped it. After a firm shake, he shifted the Mustang into drive.

Before I'd closed my door, he was accelerating out of the parking area. He sped down the ravine road and turned north onto the Barstow-Bakersfield Highway, the motor revving to an angry roar.

I said, "I'm curious why you asked for me."

"Your sneakers." He pointed at my tennies. "No good out here."

"Why did you—"

"Critters everywhere." He nodded toward two crows on the shoulder, pecking a squashed sidewinder.

"I didn't expect to be heading into the wilderness. I'm not clear why you asked for me."

"I wanted help. Brett said you were a no-bullshit girl." He pointed behind him. "Use my spare boots."

I pulled a pair of size twelves from the back seat. "They're huge."

"Slip yours inside 'em."

A dorky move, but I did what he asked. "What else did Brett say?" That you could do something weird or illegal or murderous, and I wouldn't tell?

"Coyote." He nodded toward the shoulder.

We whizzed past two vultures feasting on a gray, furry body half-hidden in the weeds.

"Why the fascination with dead things?" I asked.

"Everything dies sooner or later."

"You belong to some fatalistic cult?"

"Either of us might kick off today. From rattlers, scorpions, or some creature we've never heard of." He veered onto a side road, driving fast and sending brown dust billowing behind us.

Jake Kinsler. The name had a brutal ring. Like a

German U-boat commander who shouts, "Mach Schnell" and orders his crew to launch torpedoes at a freighter.

Jake turned on the radio and found a station playing a western song about a man in prison, missing his wife, his truck, and his dog, "but not always in that order."

We angled off the dirt road onto a rutted track and descended into a depression where we would be hidden from drivers on the highway. Jake stopped beside a patch of prickly plants. "Teddy bear cholla," he said. "Cling to your pants if you brush against 'em. Or sting you. Takes pliers to pull 'em out of your skin."

Our dusty wake drifted by us. When the air cleared and he killed the engine, the silence unsettled me.

"Should be a perfect place," he said.

Perfect for what? I hoped he'd leave the keys so when he came after me, I could sprint to the car and escape.

He stuffed them into his pocket, got out, and surveyed the terrain.

Was he trying to decide where to kill me? "Honest, officer, I warned her, but she ran right into the blast."

Lottie five, Charlie zero.

I opened the door and stepped into air as hot as a sauna and smelling of earthy creosote plants.

Jake closed his eyes and held still so long I thought he'd gone into a trance. I pulled out Dale's Polaroid and took shots of his misshapen face and hands. If I died, someone could figure out who I'd been with.

A print whirred out with each shot, but Jake's eyes remained shut.

I photographed a dead beetle, a vulture skeleton,

and a dried cactus shaped like a skull. I decided to make the best of my predicament. I stuffed the prints into my purse and gazed toward the horizon, inviting the beauty and the clean desert air to calm me.

My breathing slowed, and my pulse throttled back. If he planned to kill me, and I confronted him, he might be honest. And if he wasn't a killer, he wouldn't understand what I was saying.

When he opened his eyes, I said, "Are you working with the phony PI?"

He raised what remained of his brows.

"Did you kill Prescott and Shanahan?"

"Say again?"

"Are you planning to murder Jefferson Purdue?"

"What the hell are you babbling about?"

"I don't mean to be offensive, but—"

"Let's get started." He opened the trunk and grabbed a can of powdered explosive like Dad used to blow up stumps.

He pulled out a blasting cap and dragged the free end of a wire to a flat beyond a rocky wash, poured some of the material into a hole in a stump, and inserted the blasting cap.

Behind his grotesque features, Jake had a familiar brusqueness, confidence, and ease in the natural world. I longed to ask a question swirling in my mind but feared he would refuse to answer. While I searched for a subtle way to phrase it, he snapped his fingers. "Pay attention. Mess up with these charges, and we'll be food for one of those guys." He pointed at two turkey vultures, circling a half-mile away.

He attached the wire to the blasting cap, motioned me to back up, and payed the wire out as we retreated

214

twenty yards past a ridge of sand. He cut the wire coming from the car and connected the loose ends to a black box.

"Get down," he shouted. "Fire in the hole."

We ducked behind the sand ridge as he turned a crank. An explosion rocked the wash. The stump and several roots shot skyward and fell in a hail of sand and pebbles.

He set off a dozen more blasts and let me select roots to explode.

Jake didn't need me for his tests. Still, if he wanted to kill me, he could have done that right away. Looking like he did, I guessed he wanted a stand-in for the females who shunned him.

I hoped our explosions weren't hurting the environment, because I began to enjoy blowing things up.

A turn of the crank and *poof*, a log turned to wood chips. *Boom*, a rock became gravel. *Bang*, a root exploded. I wanted to do something similar to parts of my life. *Zing*, Dad hadn't abandoned me. *Zap*, Mom's murder didn't happen. *Crack, pop, snap*, my PTSD episodes were history.

To my surprise, though I'd been fearful and repelled by Jake at first, he began to inspire me. He had found peace and confidence after fate dealt him a terrible hand.

When we finished turning logs to wood chips, I faced him. "Did you ever hear of a movie called *Dead Girls Don't Lie*?"

"Funny you should ask. I worked that turkey."

"You knew my father!" I took a breath and told him the story: Mom's death; Dad's body pulled from the Skagit River missing his hands and jaw. "He played the actor who threw the waitress off the roof. Called himself Alec Hudson."

"The name I don't recall, the man, yes. Showed up one day, bruised, broke, and looking for work. Since one of our bit players had left for a better paying gig, they hired him."

"Did he mention a daughter?"

"Wouldn't discuss his past. Changed the subject when anyone asked, until one night when a few of us finished a bottle of scotch and he let slip he had a girl. That you?"

I nodded.

"Said you were strong and smart. Loved your spirit."

My heart raced. "I have to find him. Any idea where he is?"

Jake stowed his gear in the trunk and got into the car without answering. I joined him and we drove back along Three Flags Highway. A dozen telephone poles flashed by before he said, "I'm sad to have to tell you. If you're looking for your father, you wasted your trip. He passed away."

My hopes exploded like our stumps. "When? How did it happen?"

"Not long after the shoot. Car accident in Glendale is what they said."

A familiar cadence in Jake's voice turned my thoughts to Dad. A disfigured face and body offered perfect cover for a man trying to escape his past, Jake's recent scars and disfigurement making it hard to see the man beneath. He was the same height and build as Dad. No lopsided gait, but surgery might have fixed his limp.

Doubting Jake would answer if I told him my suspicion, I said, "All this fresh air makes me hungry for steak and eggs."

He nodded and drove to a restaurant off the highway, a converted gas station with 1930s Texaco pumps out front and two dust-coated Dodge pickups parked on the gravel.

Inside, a pair of stocky ranchers sat at the counter wearing overalls and John Deere baseball caps. They turned from platters of pork chops and gravy to stare at Jake.

He settled into a booth in front of windows facing a sea of cactus plants and rabbit brush.

I sat across the table. A waitress approached, her white shoes squeaking to a stop beside us. She set down two glasses of water and pulled out her order pad.

"How do you want your steak?" Jake asked me.

"Like yours."

"Two rib-eyes, well done," he told the waitress.

Strike one. Dad would have gone hungry before touching a steak that wasn't blood red.

I pointed to the words "root beer" on the menu.

"A root beer for my friend," he said, pronouncing it like *toot*, not *foot*. No Minnesota accent.

Strike two.

Our food arrived, and we ate in silence, while two red-tailed hawks rode thermals over the desert.

When we finished, I palmed my steak knife while Jake paid at the register. I followed him outside.

Halfway to the car, I yelled, "Heads up" and tossed him the knife. Dad would have flipped it and caught it in mid-air. Jake didn't move. The blade jabbed his bicep and fell to the ground.

Strike three.

"What the hell," he said, rubbing the spot on his sleeve where the tip poked him.

"Sorry. Game I used to play with a friend."

"Hate to be one of your enemies."

"Making enemies seems to run in my family. Some people claim my dad killed my mom."

"People say lots of things. Doesn't make them true. You should go home and get on with your life."

"A murderer is looking for my father."

"Best of luck to him. Like I said, your—"

"Father died. I know. But he played dead a few months ago when he was still alive." I picked up the knife. "Which of the other crew members worked on *Dead Girls*?"

"Dale, Bob, the key grip, and the editor. What's his name?"

"Allen. But he says he left the show early. How about our director, Ivan? Did he produce it?"

"Hard to say. Producers came and went."

"You can do better than that."

"Wish I could."

I wanted to punch him.

Chapter 31

"Star spat in progress. Better stay clear," the AD said as Jake and I pulled to a stop in the crew parking lot.

Aluminum foil reflectors on high stands hung like space antennas above crew members clustered in front of the general store on the mining town set. A furry boom mic hovered over the actors. Beyond the set, a road led uphill toward the taller of two peaks and a weathered trestle connecting it to the shorter one.

Imagining Brett accusing crew members of having worked on *Dead Girls* and hiding secrets about his mother's death, I hurried around the AD and arrived at the camera position as Ivan called, "Action."

The dolly followed Brett, walking with his arm around a young woman in her twenties, blouse unbuttoned halfway to her waist, as he led her past the mining office. Above it hung a sign decorated with a gold assay scale. In the story, the young woman played Della's romantic competition. The call sheet listed her real name as Carmen.

Brett kissed her passionately. She leaned back. He kissed her again. She pushed him away.

He threw up his arms. "Ivan, she's not giving me anything."

"Feels like he's attacking me," Carmen said.

Ivan talked with them.

The crew reset, and shooting began again.

Carmen pulled away during Brett's next kiss and wiped her mouth. "Feels like I'm at a high school make-out party."

Brett said, "You're wooden as a totem pole."

"Says the guy drooling like a Saint Bernard."

He grinned. "Remind you of your last doggy romance?"

She slapped him.

Ivan separated them. "We're behind. Let's get this."

Brett said, "Any woman here could do the scene." While several females on the crew smiled wistfully, Brett scanned the crowd. "Tanya, for example. She's a PA. Hasn't acted before." He headed my way.

Carmen propped her hands on her hips. "Go for it, champ. Can't wait to read the sexual assault article in *The Hollywood Reporter*."

He headed my way. "Would you charge me with sexual assault over a kiss?"

I looked at my feet, praying I wouldn't have a PTSD episode and kick him in the groin. "I'm here to do my job."

"So am I," Brett said.

Ivan pulled him away. "Leave her alone."

The camera moved to the start position.

Dale approached me and whispered, "I've seen you talking with Brett a few times. It's risky to get involved with actors. You're the flavor-of-the-week on location. Forgettable as yesterday's call sheet once the production wraps."

"I haven't been doing anything with Brett."

He pointed to the Polaroid sticking out of my

purse. "What did you shoot?"

While Ivan calmed his principals, I showed Dale my shots.

"Damn, girl," he said. "You have an eye."

The AD called people to their places, and Dale returned to the dolly.

Brett and Carmen gave Ivan two good takes.

The aroma of meat grilling in the catering van reminded me I hadn't considered the Latino cooks as sources.

****

When I approached the van's service window, the older cook was mopping his face with a kerchief. He flipped half-chickens roasting on the grill and stirred bubbling pots like a mad scientist in a laboratory. "Chicken or snapper?" he asked without looking up.

"Just the answer to a question. Have you been working for movie crews a long time?"

"Since I was thirteen. A helper at first, when my father cooked. What can I get you?"

From the set, the AD's bullhorn announced, "Lunch. Back in thirty."

Crew members mobbed the window.

"Chicken with asparagus," a grip shouted.

I said to the cook, "I'd love to hear about any strange things on your shoots during this year."

"I don't talk about the past." He dropped half a chicken on a plate and passed it to his teenage assistant, who added asparagus and mashed potatoes.

Orders swamped the pair.

The teenager cut his finger and hurried out, blood spurting onto his Los Lobos T.

I went to the end of the van and stepped inside. A

narrow passageway separated the window counter with its steam table from the grill, sink, and refrigerator. Pans sizzled with cooking meat while fans sucked smoke and steam out through the roof.

After a guy gave an order, I scooped rice and spinach onto a plate.

The cook said, "You can't be in here."

"You want to argue, or listen to Ivan explode when the crew gets back late from lunch?"

He eyed the line. "Knock yourself out."

The boy came back, his hand bandaged, and the three of us filled orders for half an hour.

When the crew returned to the set, I asked the cook, "What's wrong with the past?"

"Bad things." He grabbed a porous block and scrubbed the grill hard, as if the effort could erase some old hurt.

"I have painful memories," I said, "but burying them doesn't work for me." I washed a pot in the sink. "I'm Tanya."

"Adolfo." He kept scrubbing the grill.

After making him swear to keep my secret, I told him about my mom and dad.

"Someone murdered your mother?" He whistled. "*De veras?*"

"Last spring. Did you ever hear of a picture called *Dead Girls Don't Lie?*"

He nodded. "Papi catered it before he got sick."

"Were any of our crew on it?"

"A few."

"How about Brett? He says he had a small part."

"Don't know him." He carried a bowl of potato salad to a refrigerator, its door covered with dozens of photos—old, faded shots and recent ones in vivid color.

I studied them all—from brawny grips to waif-like wardrobe girls. The key grip, Dale, and Allen were there, along with bit players from movies Lottie and I had watched. A sensual woman in cowboy boots and a vest stood out—a younger Della, her complexion creamy, her lips lush and red as berries.

I pointed to a handsome young man with a moustache. "That's Brett. He's shaved his moustache now."

"¡*Híjole*! Looks like a different guy."

"But you knew him?"

"Not as 'Brett.' I called him Donny, for Don Juan, because he loved to chase the costume and makeup assistants."

"He's the male lead on this shoot. You haven't seen him come through here?"

"I don't pay attention to names or faces. Too busy staring at pork ribs and chicken breasts."

"Did you know his mother?"

"*Ay Chihuahua*. What a wild woman. One day Brett hustled a pretty assistant into the wardrobe trailer. His mother caught him and shouted he was giving her a bad name on the shoot. My father agreed. Told him to shape up." Adolfo chuckled. "But the next day Donny was back to his old routine. A few days later, after a problem on the production, I passed him sitting alone, head in his hands."

"Because his mom got injured." I studied the pictures again. "You have any of her?"

"This one." From the door, he pulled a print of a shapely brunette with dark eyes, posing, hand on her hip. She wore a red top and tight jeans, and had a small, star-shaped mole on her cheek.

****

I caught a ride to the editing room and while Allen left to eat lunch, I used the guillotine splicer to cut out clips of the two women, and a clip of my dad poking his head into frame. After I walked Royal, I sneaked him into my room and gave the chambermaid two dollars not to mention him to housekeeping.

I hitched a ride to the set with the clips, an extra loupe, and a new load of film stock for Dale.

I went to Adolfo, handed him the loupe, and showed him the clips. "Is either of these Donny's mother?"

He held the film close. "Their hair is blonde, not dark like his mom's."

"They wore platinum wigs. Did one have a mole shaped like a star?"

He handed me the clips. "I don't know."

I passed him the clip of my father. "Look familiar?"

"Yes. I recall his eyes. A nice guy, but always nervous."

"What happened to him?"

"Papi didn't say." He crossed himself. "I think he died."

"Do you know where? And when? Can we ask your dad?"

"He's at the house with my mother in Echo Park. Doesn't get out anymore."

"A short talk would be enough."

"I understand you want to find your father. But mine is weak with cancer. It's dangerous to over-stress him."

224

"Please. I would be gentle and respectful."
"No. He's sick. *Lo siento mucho.*"

Chapter 32

I returned Royal to the repair bay to avoid any problems with the hotel management. After the dailies screening, I followed Dale into the hotel lobby, hoping to quiz him again. But he joined his assistants and headed to the bar.

A hand touched my waist. I whirled. My purse, heavy with the Polaroid, swung in a wide arc, and brushed Ivan's face.

"Didn't mean to alarm you." he said. "We haven't talked since you arrived. Have people been treating you okay?"

I stiffened. "Everything's fine."

Through a window, I spotted Brett in the parking lot, stepping out of a van.

"I'm late for a meeting," I told Ivan, and exited through a side door. Out of his sight, I approached Brett. "What's new, *Donny*?"

"You ran into Adolfo."

I smiled. "Any more news about what happened with your mother?"

"The crew is still keeping mum. Scared they'll be sued or prosecuted. I've been checking *Variety* and the *Hollywood Reporter,* hoping someone might have let a detail slip. Nothing so far."

To raise his spirits, I told him about Adolfo's father and said he might know things about my dad and his mom. "Convince your pal to let us go meet him."

"Tomorrow's Sunday. I'll talk him into it and get a rental car so the production company won't know what we're up to. I'll meet you at nine thirty at Montara Park, across town." He headed into the hotel.

While a dozen of the crew strolled down the far sidewalk, Dale left them and entered a bar.

I went to a photo shop, pulled the *Dead Girls* clips from my purse, and asked the clerk to make eight-by-ten prints as fast as possible.

When I returned to the street most of the crew had gone. I went to the bar Dale entered and stepped inside. I walked past men watching basketball games on wall-mounted TVs, to a booth where Dale hunched over a glass and a bottle of scotch.

I said, "Okay if I join you?"

"If you're here to ask me about the person you're looking for, let it go. I don't know more than I've told you."

"You don't realize how important this is to me."

"And you don't realize you're not the only person on the planet. Let me drink in peace." He drained his glass, poured another, and watched Magic Johnson sink a jump shot.

I marched out, and, using his Polaroid, photographed the ugliest images I could find. Fat men's bellies hanging over their belts. Piles of dog crap. A muddle of overhead wires. And a dozen faces, green and bilious under the city's streetlights.

I headed toward the hotel, got lost, and found myself approaching the pinball bar. The phony PI, in an Angel's jacket, stood outside, leafing through a sports section.

He looked up. I smiled to hide my fear and stepped forward, reaching into my purse and easing the top off the hair spray can.

He said, "If it isn't my favorite client. Have an update about your father?"

"Wish I did. You're the pro. What should I do?"

"Keep looking. One of the operatives in our agency spotted him in LA. I found out the actress your dad made friends with is here or about to arrive. I have a photo of her in my motel room."

"Thanks anyway."

"Got it. Single girl. Man she doesn't trust."

"The sidewalk outside your motel sounds better."

He led me to the front door, went inside, and returned with a folder. He slid out the picture of Hannah Lynn with her phone number.

I squinted, as if trying to place her. "Beautiful woman, but the photo's old. She'd look different now. I'll keep my eyes open." I pointed to a shot behind Hannah's photo—a handsome teenager. "Who's that?"

"My brother. He died."

"What's his name?"

"Boris."

He looked like the bloody young man who had ended up in the news story about a Russian Mafia bust by the FBI in Canada. Was the phony PI part of their organization or a guy out for revenge against my dad for tips he gave the FBI?

I was sinking into a quagmire of Russian intrigue. Interesting—Tanya, the name I'd invented when I met Della, was Russian. Why had I done that? "Who are these guys?" I asked, pointing to a photo of two five-year-old boys on bikes, one with the PI's cocky grin.

"Not important." He closed the folder.

If I avoided this guy, he'd still do his worst to Dad. If I played dumb and pretended to cooperate, I might get a clue about what he had in mind. I agreed to tape a note to his motel's front door if I learned anything new, and went to my hotel, thankful he still wanted me alive.

****

"The good news," Nina said when I called her, "is that I've gone to your grandma's neighborhood lots of times without seeing any suspicious people. The bad news is I've searched the University library and haven't found anything about the crew of *Dead Girls*. The Russian Studies profs say they don't know of a Russian crime family working in Barstow."

I described my PI encounter and our meeting at his motel building.

"My God," Nina said. "You can't be so reckless."

"You're such a mother hen."

"Sometimes I think you need that."

"I have to take chances. I'm hitting dead ends. The cook on the movie last spring must have met Dad, but his son says the old man's too sick to talk to me. I'm sure the DP, who admits he met Dad, hasn't told me everything he knows. Feels like I'm in a river, swimming upstream."

****

The next morning, Sunday, day six on the film, I picked up the prints from the photo shop, hiked across town to the park, and found Brett and Adolfo waiting in the wide front seat of a rental Chevy. I climbed in, took the spot by the window, and we left.

Adolfo shifted position nervously and said, "Donny, I don't know about this trip."

Brett said, "What *I* know is, it's great to see you."

"Papi may not be well enough to talk."

"Is he still mad about the wardrobe assistant I hustled?"

Adolfo raised a hand for Brett to stop talking. "*Sabes que.* My parents live in a dangerous neighborhood."

"I'm sure we'll be safe as long as we're with you." Brett wrapped an arm around Adolfo's shoulder. "How about the time we went dancing at that scuzzy bar."

Adolfo grinned. "The lead guitar player's amp caught fire. Some drugged-out guy tried to warm a glass of tequila over it, and *poof*. No eyebrows."

The pair chatted and joked the rest of the way to Los Angeles.

****

When we switched to the 10 Freeway and exited at Echo Park Avenue, Adolfo directed us to Quintero Street and past stucco bungalows with waist-high chain-link fences. We stopped at a green house with a Honda Civic in the driveway and a pit bull in the front yard. Adolfo got out.

At the sound of distant gunshots, he glanced right and left, waited a moment, and beckoned us to follow him.

A short, brown-skinned woman with white hair swept into a bun stepped out on the front porch. Her dark currants of eyes crinkled and disappeared in her lined face as she hugged Adolfo.

After he introduced us, he led the way inside to a living room crowded with upholstered furniture and knickknacks on every table and shelf. A picture of Jesus and another of President Kennedy hung on one wall.

Over the fireplace was a memorial plaque with a photograph of a young man in his teens.

Adolfo said, "We should go see Papi before he's exhausted."

He led us down a hallway lined with photographs of men with full moustaches, and olive-skinned women with long hair, to a dark bedroom. The sweet scent from a candle decorated with a picture of the Virgin Mary mixed with a medicinal smell.

A barrel-chested guy with a thick neck lay propped on fluffy pillows. An IV ran from a plastic bag on a stand beside the bed to one of his muscular arms. His chest rose and fell every few seconds, his breaths soft as whispers. Adolfo touched his arm, and his eyes flickered open. The two exchanged a few words in Spanish.

The sight of their connection brought a lump to my throat.

Adolfo introduced us to his father, and we stepped closer. I pulled out the black-and-white photos I'd made from the *Dead Girls* clips and showed him shots of the two women.

Brett pointed to one of them. "Even though it's blurry, I hope you can tell if this is my mother."

Adolfo's father touched the shot of the actress with the star-shaped mole—the one who had run out of the building to the taxi. "Katrina," he said. "Laughed like an angel, or growled like a puma when things set her off."

Brett said, "I couldn't find out what happened in her taxi shot. Do you know?"

"They took her to the hospital." He crossed himself. "*Me dijeron que ella falleció.*"

"She passed away," Adolfo whispered.

"I know," Brett said. "I wondered how."

I handed Adolfo's father the third print. "This is my dad peeking into frame. People tell me he's dead. Do you know the film he and Brett's mom were in?"

"*Dead Girls Don't Lie*," he said. "It didn't open in the U.S., but I sent my relatives in Mexico a VHS copy, re-titled *Mentiras Amargas,* Bitter Lies. My cousin in Guadalajara told his friends I was a big cheese for working on it." His chuckle became a cough, and he covered his mouth with a handkerchief.

"Did my father die?" I asked.

"Two months ago, he came to a screening of a small film we'd both spent a few days on."

Hairs prickled on the back of my neck. "Did he mention me?"

"It was a dark theater, people wandering around." He sipped water through a straw. "We didn't come face to face."

"Do you know where I can find him?"

He shook his head.

Brett asked, "Where can we get a copy of the film?"

"*No sé.*" His eyes closed.

Adolfo whispered, "We should let Papi rest."

We thanked his dad and left. As we entered the living room, the old man called out something in Spanish.

Adolfo went to a TV cabinet and retrieved a VHS tape. "He says this is the version his cousin returned to him from Mexico." He handed it to me.

When Brett and I left, Adolfo stayed behind to spend time with his parents, saying he'd catch a ride with a friend.

As we drove away, Brett said, "We need to hire a private detective."

"And have some stranger snoop around, stirring things up? Scaring my dad off or doing something that helps whoever's looking for him?"

"We're getting nowhere. Your dad could be attacked any day."

I didn't tell Brett about the phony PI—he'd insist on a meeting and would want to tell the guy everything.

Chapter 33

When Brett and I arrived in Barstow we hurried up to watch the VHS copy of *Dead Girls.* Brett's room had a view of the mountains and a panoramic sunset painting above the bed. We played the tape in his VCR, Brett leaning forward in a chair, his attention fixed on the screen.

The story involved two waitresses who overhear the schemes of gangsters running a restaurant and planning to steal from the owners. The thugs catch the waitresses listening and decide to kill them. As I'd seen in the University screening, my dad's character throws one from the roof to her death. The other fights him off, flees the building, and runs into a taxi that catches fire. She escapes and runs away.

Earlier in the story, Brett's mom, the blonde who ran from the taxi, had a love scene with my father.

"Look at them," Brett said as the pair, half-naked on the back seat of an old convertible, kissed and hugged. "I bet they had an actual fling, and he screwed over my mom some way."

"We don't know he did anything wrong," I snapped, surprised at my anger in Dad's defense. "The important thing is finding out about him may help us learn what happened to your mom."

Someone knocked on the door. "Who is it?" Brett asked.

"You alone?" Ivan's voice.

I stepped onto the lanai and slid the door shut behind me. I sniffed wood smoke in the air and peered at the desert. The squirrel popped into my head and whispered, "Get with it, Charlie. Your dad's not camping out there." I peeked through the blinds.

Ivan entered and stared at the TV. "What's on the screen?"

"An old movie," Brett said.

"Where'd you get it?"

"From a friend in LA. I'm tired and—"

"Show me a few minutes." Ivan sat down.

Brett pressed the remote, and the picture played. "Ever see it before?"

"No," Ivan said. His face remained expressionless, but his fingers clenched and relaxed several times, what Grandma Lottie's poker pals would call a tell—Ivan knew about *Dead Girls*.

I gasped, then bent low as Ivan looked toward the lanai and asked, "What was that?"

Brett said, "Some drunk grip coming out of a bar."

"Is Tanya here? I know you two have something going."

"Forget that scrawny kid. She's about as alluring as a hat rack."

"I disagree," Ivan said. "The girl has a beguiling innocence. I put an actress like her in *Dog on the Run*. Audiences loved her." He tapped Brett's forehead. "Keep your mind on the job."

After Ivan left, we continued playing the movie. Brett kept going over the part where his mom, with the star-shaped mole, ran to the taxi, and got away after the crash. Several times, he asked, "Do you think she could have been a star if she'd started younger?"

"How am I supposed to know?" I walked away.

"You're angry."

"Tired." I went out and shut the door hard.

****

In my room, I stripped and checked out my image in the mirror. Brett had it right. I *was* scrawny, ribs prominent beneath my breasts. Since my parents' deaths, I'd been so nervous I'd skipped lots of meals. He liked girls with more flesh on their bones, not that it mattered to me.

The blonde without the star-shaped beauty mark, the woman Dad threw off the roof, reminded me of an actress I'd seen in better roles. I tried to recall which ones, cursed my foggy PTSD memory, and threw a brush at the mirror.

I was too embarrassed to mention my hurt feelings to Brett about his comment, but there was someone I could confront. I got dressed and marched to Dale's room. I gave myself a C minus on my mental PTSD chart and pounded on his door.

He opened it, his hair and beard unkempt, his eyes crusted, and his shirt stained and rumpled. He downed the inch of liquor in his glass and spread his arms, palms up, asking, "Why are you bothering me?"

I shoved my photos into his hands and walked away.

I'd gone halfway to the elevator when he yelled, "Not so fast."

I kept walking. "That's the way I see things."

He said, "These are fantastic. Even better than your earlier shots."

I went back. "Don't patronize me. They're bleak

and ugly."

"Sometimes the things we think of as ugly are the most beautiful and interesting."

"You're not going to give me the story about a pony hidden under a pile of horseshit, are you?"

"Ever see Diane Arbus's work?"

"Her mental hospital pictures? I've seen her biography with photos of men, women, and children, their blank eyes staring at the camera. Arbus committed suicide. I'm crazy, too. Deal with it."

He held up a photo. "I love this jumble of crisscrossing utility wires. When I first started shooting, I tried for perfect order and symmetry. Now I prefer images that distort places and people or show them from strange angles, like you did." He fanned the rest of my photos. "Impressive work."

His praise dissolved my anger. "I know you don't want to talk about *Dead Girls,* but you were the DP for the whole movie."

"No, I—"

"Your work on *Dead Girls* and *Zombies* is similar. It reminds me of the El Greco and Caravaggio paintings in your books. The long moments where Brett's and Della's faces are in semi-darkness, or distorted, intrigue me because they make me work. They're the best aspects of both movies."

He shrugged as if to dismiss the compliment, but his eyes brightened. "Apologies for not coming clean earlier. I don't like people raking up uncomfortable moments from my past. Need to keep my attention on the current film, but thanks for appreciating my work. I didn't realize what an artistic soul you are. Shouldn't have been so dismissive when you arrived. What's your obsession with *Dead Girls*?"

"My dad acted in the movie sometime after I found my mom's body on the bathroom floor with her throat slit."

"My God. How did you deal with that?"

"At first, I suspected my dad did it. But when the police dragged his body from the Skagit River, it made more sense for the killer to be an outsider. This fall I saw Dad in *Dead Girls* and figured he'd faked his death. I'm here to find him and I hope you know something to help. In Los Angeles, he called himself Alec Hudson."

"Do you still believe he killed your mom?"

"You've seen him more recently than I have. What do you think?"

"I was curious about him, showing up and asking for work with no film experience. So, I asked questions. He'd change the subject. One night after a bunch of us were dead on our feet, he conked out in the camera truck. He woke up at dawn, mumbling about a fox caught in a trap."

"And chews its foot off to get away. That's what he said the last time I saw him." I poured scotch from his bottle into a glass, took a gulp, and winced as it burned its way down. "People here keep telling me he's dead."

"Since he didn't want to talk about his life, I shouldn't say this, but…" He clamped his lower lip with his teeth. "My guess is he's alive."

I hugged him. "Not a come-on, I promise."

He flashed me an impish smile. "Let's hope our reputations survive."

"Have you worked with my dad since then? Is he on this movie?"

"When we shot *Dead Girls,* he stayed in the shadows. If he's around and can contact you, I'm sure he will."

"Are you saying he's here?"

He downed another shot. "I hope you find what you're looking for."

****

Back in my room, energized by Dale's suggestion, however vague, that Dad was on the crew or in the area, I reexamined a packet of family medical records I'd brought from home. Checked Dad's height, weight, birthmarks, and scars from a series of reports years ago by Dr. Lindahl, our physician in Concrete.

A VA form among the doctor's papers confirmed Dad's blood type as O POS, and a report of a well-baby visit for "baby girl Charlotte" agreed with what the officer had told me: I was AB positive.

I called the emergency room at the Barstow Hospital, and asked a nurse, "If my father's blood is O positive and he's injured, would you be able to get plenty for transfusions. Or if not, could you use some of mine? I'm AB positive."

The nurse said, "If you're AB, your father can't be type O."

I stand on the bank of the Skagit as the tow truck winches Dad's pickup from the water. I rush to the truck, yank a lever, and send the pickup plunging into the river.

"Dad, you might as well get in your truck and float out to sea. You never give me anything worth holding onto."

I charged into the motel lobby and kicked the cowboy mannequin, stomped on his plastic guns, and

239

punched his chest until he crashed to the floor.

****

I spent five minutes in my room calming myself and called Lottie. "I'm not my parents' real daughter, am I?"

"Charlotte, stop. You're on one of your PTSD tangents."

"Don't use my PTSD to avoid answering questions."

"What you need to do is stop dredging up things that don't make any difference."

"Knowing the truth about who I am makes a huge difference. I hate my life being a lie."

"Then put your energy into finding your dad, talk to him, and come back as soon as you can."

"Sure. Whatever."

When we hung up, I phoned Nina at the dorm. "This whole trip has been a joke. The man I've been looking for is not my father. Just some guy who married my mom, assuming she *was* my mom. That's why he didn't send for me."

"From what you've told me, he took you hunting and fishing and spent the kind of time with you most daughters would die for."

"I guess you're right, but—"

"If you want to talk about lousy families, I have a brother who's eight years older and spooky-strange. He'd tear the wings off butterflies and giggle as their bodies flopped around. He's a blood relative I wish I *didn't* have."

"You've got a father and a mother."

"I see my dad twice a year. And my mother has been complaining about our family forever."

"I know you're trying to help."

"I'm your friend, not your relative, but I'll be there for you anytime, anywhere."

"I'm dying to have you here in Barstow but afraid to stop you from checking Lottie's house."

That night, I had repeating dreams: Mom moaning she should have told me the truth and Dad apologizing. I swore at them both.

Chapter 34

My seventh morning on *Zombies* I awoke in a cold sweat. I called the California Department of Public Health to see if they had a death certificate for Dad, in case he'd died since he'd been in the movie. A clerk told me I'd have to submit a form to Sacramento, with the fee, and wait four weeks. In four weeks, our filming would have finished. I didn't want something with my real name showing up at the hotel or the production office.

I fed Royal and gave him a romp in the neighborhood. I skipped the van ride to the set, risked being late for work, and biked to the Barstow library. Doing a hurried search of blood type articles, I learned the nurse was correct—a type O person could not be the parent of an AB child.

As I left the library, questions spun in my brain. Did Mom have an affair and get pregnant? Had Dad found out, lost his temper, and hit her in the market, as Mary Sue claimed? Or had my parents decided an off-the-shelf or bastard daughter was better than no daughter at all?

"What are you doing?" a male voice called when I exited the library.

Jake's black Mustang sat by the curb, the driver's window open. He leaned out. "Karen's been trying to find you."

I shoved my bike into Jake's trunk and got in, huddling against the passenger door and staring ahead.

After we left my bike at the hotel and started for the set, he said, "When is the giant asteroid going to crash into earth and destroy life as we know it?"

"The man who pretended to be my dad isn't my real father." I told him about the AB and O blood types.

"That must feel like a slap in the face."

"Try a 12 gauge in the gut."

I planned to remain grumpy all the way to the set. But every time I glanced at Jake, his confident, cheery look said his life was as blessed as anyone's.

By the time we arrived at the location, I felt better.

Until I ran into a short zombie with green hair and goggle eyes. "Annie?" I said, "Is that you?"

"We don't know where she is," the zombie said. "The rest of us are panicked about the food. Some bring meals from town." She pointed toward the makeup trailer. "Annie's replacement is in there."

I went to the door. Inside, a stylist fitted a statuesque female with a spiky orange wig and added ghoulish makeup. Three special effects artists, wearing smocks and using makeup, plastic appliances, and foam, were turning other actors into zombies.

If the PI had sidelined Annie, since everything the guy did seemed aimed at finding Dad, any dirty tricks he pulled had to relate to him.

Karen approached, trailing her signature smoke cloud. "You're late. Go see Della. She's frazzled about something."

****

Face ashen, fingers trembling, Della sat on her motor home couch, lacing a pair of hiking boots.

"We're going to the mine so I can practice my big shot."

"The call sheet says the crew works down here until mid-afternoon. We should wait for them."

A horn blared.

Della slapped a flashlight in my hand and led me outside into a passenger van. We headed up the road from base camp, drove by the set sheriff's office, the saloon, and a corral where Della's bay and the gelding were drinking from a trough.

The van left us at the base of the taller mountain, by the mouth of a tunnel posted with a KEEP OUT sign. A handwritten note taped to it read, "Leo Dvorak's crew on *The Gold Mine Murders* ignored the warnings. Ten men died in a cave-in."

Narrow-gauge rails extended out of the opening, under the sign, and past us.

The dark, narrow tunnel opening tried to drag me to our spooky hallway in Concrete, but I focused on two fluffy clouds and stayed present.

Della led me to an outcrop from where the tracks extended across a trestle as long as a football field. A lattice of cracked and broken timbers supported the structure which spanned a deep ravine strewn with boulders. At the far end, the tracks entered a tunnel in the smaller peak.

The rusted, warped rails showed no sign of use. On them rested an aged and dented ore car. The brake lever, designed to press blocks of wood against the wheels, showed fresh welds.

A sign taped on the mine car read, "DANGER. STAND CLEAR, Jesse Dorr, stunt coordinator."

"Get in," Della said.

"It's not safe."

"I know. So does Ivan."

"Then why get in?"

"My character has to cross that trestle in this ore car to escape the zombies. I'm fine riding a bucking quarter horse, but not this piece of junk. At eight I got thrown out of a roller coaster and had to cling to a girder until they rescued me. Let's go. We'll run my lines in the car."

"I'm not sure we should touch this thing. I saw Jesse Dorr when I arrived. She didn't look like a do-whatever-you-want person."

"Brett's telling the crew I can't do this shot. If I panic in the tech rehearsal, he'll needle me so much I'll screw up my scenes all week. I have to practice in the ore car where I'll be working."

I waved at crew members below in the parking area, but no one responded. I said, "It will help you get the lines if you tell me the story."

"Brett and his girlfriend plan to kill me and take my gold claim. But I overhear them plotting and head for the mine because I know every inch of it. They follow and corner me and give me a choice: sign my claim over to them, or they'll push me down a shaft and forge my signature." Della banged on the car. "Now, hop in."

While she reviewed her script pages, I waved again to the crew but still got no response. "You're sounding more confident," I said. "Please go on."

"What Brett and his lover don't know is that I've made friends with the zombies who live in the mine. I bring them food, roadkill, and prospectors who die on the mountain. The zombies attack Brett's girlfriend.

When they kill her and turn on me, Brett and I run outside, jump into this mine car, and escape by riding to the far side of the ravine."

"What a cool story," I said, glancing toward the parking lot.

She thumped the car. "Hop to."

For extra protection, I laid pieces of wood in front of the car's wheels. As I climbed in, the clouds shifted and a shaft of light fell on Della's face, accentuating her cheekbones, making her eyes luminous, and giving her lips a sensuality I hadn't seen.

Actually, I had—in Ray India's office at Sunset Vista Productions. The former Hannah Lynn was Della, older, with different hair color and styling, and without the exaggerated makeup in the porn poster.

She climbed in and drank again.

I reached for her hand. "Please. What you need—"

"What I *don't* need is a minder." She shoved me.

I toppled backward. My arm fell against the brake lever which released with a snap. The car shook and moved a few inches.

Della grasped the edge, threw her leg over the side, and tried to climb out. The car tilted and moved again. As Della continued to struggle, the wood below crackled and snapped, and we rolled toward the cliff edge, ten feet away.

I tugged the brake lever, but we kept moving.

Della gripped the edge of the car like a shipwrecked passenger clinging to a lifeboat.

We rolled onto the trestle, the ground sliding away, revealing an animal skeleton on the jagged rocks. Timbers groaned, wheels screeched, and the structure swayed.

While the car accelerated across the chasm, I pulled with all my strength on the brake lever. Halfway across, the lever gave a loud pop and went slack. I hoped the car might stop on its own, but the downgrade kept us rolling.

We continued into the far tunnel. Cobwebs pulled at my face. Acrid air stung my nostrils and filled my lungs. While we moved at a slow pace, I could have climbed out, but Della's screams reminded me of my own terrified moments. I couldn't abandon her.

The tunnel, unused for decades, showed signs of cave-ins. I pictured the roadbed giving way and dropping us to our death.

When the car stopped, Della ceased screaming.

I sniffed the air. "Smells breathable. Are you okay to walk out?" She nodded.

We climbed down to the track and hiked back, following my flashlight beam past fallen debris. When I shined my light on Della, she was calm and breathing with ease.

I said, "If I ask a question, will you give me an honest answer?"

"This tunnel might collapse any second, and you want to play Truth or Consequences?"

"Your photo is taped on the catering van fridge beside crew members who worked on a movie called *Dead Girls Don't Lie*."

"My picture is taped to dozens of refrigerator doors. Lots of lonely actors and stuntmen in California."

"*Dead Girls* must have been a strange shoot. People talk about somebody dying on the set and someone else killed in a car crash."

"You might check with Ivan."

"He hates me. Thinks I'm after Brett, which isn't true."

"Good. Girls get location crushes on the sleaziest guys."

I stand over Mom in the bathroom, studying her bloody tile scribbles. "What did you write? Dad's name? The name of my real father?"

She doesn't answer.

I faced Della. "I have to find out about my dad."

"Sometimes when we turn over a rock, we don't like what's underneath it."

Had Della just advised me, or threatened me? Realizing how fast she recovered from her fright, I grew suspicious. Was she terrified of riding in the ore car? Or pretending, as a way to get me into the mine?

What if she heard my phone message to the 818 number, feared I'd identified her as Hannah, and decided to finish me off before I revealed her past?

Icy air drifted over us. I shuddered. Della touched my shoulder. "Easy, hon." She offered her flask. "If you're nervous, have a bit of courage."

I shook my head.

Della drank again. When she returned the flask to her purse, my light reflected off a knife blade next to her lipstick.

I stepped away from her.

Our rail tracks came to a V. We took the right fork until it dead-ended in a rubble pile. We turned around, chose a different tunnel, and followed my light beam to another dead end. We tried again, this time stopping inches short of a crevasse. My breathing quickened.

A shout echoed from somewhere in the blackness.

Footsteps approached on gravel. When a rock crashed to the rails, I lost my balance.

Della grabbed my arm. "Easy, dear." I swung my light to her. Expecting to see the knife, I grabbed a broken two-by-four.

"Put it down," Della said. "There's nothing to be afraid of."

"Don't lie."

Gravel crunched behind her.

I cocked the two-by-four.

A light blinded me. Behind the glare, I made out a white Van Dyke—Clint.

Della flung her arms around his neck. "See, Tanya. We're fine. I told Clint I'd be rehearsing in the mine car."

"Sorry." I dropped the two-by-four. "I...uh...panic in tight, dark spaces."

Clint put his arm around my shoulder. "I understand."

I felt better. But were my suspicions wrong?

Chapter 35

At base camp, the First AD announced the crew would work through lunch break, which meant Ivan would be busy for half an hour. I picked up a six-pack of water from craft service, walked to his trailer, went inside, and put the bottles on his desk. The space contained a couch, a blackboard-sized production schedule covering the far wall, and a file cabinet.

While the AD's bullhorn commands sounded from the set, I picked the lock on the file cabinet with two bent paper clips. In a manila envelope in the top drawer, I found a statement from an accounting firm, showing revenue from film rentals and sales on several movies, *Dead Girls Don't Lie* on the third line. The column to the right of the title listed the estate of Zolton Baron, the original producer, as the owner of record.

I returned the papers to the drawer, locked the cabinet, and left. Whether Ivan was the son, brother, or business partner of Zolton Baron, he had to know something about *Dead Girls* and about Dad.

****

At the hotel after wrap, I found Brett, took him with me to throw a ball for Royal, and described what I'd learned.

He said, "Your best way to get information from Ivan is by flirting."

"No thanks."

"I'm not suggesting you sleep with the guy. Just play up to him."

"Playing up to men is not on my résumé. And why would Ivan want a scrawny girl like me to do that?" I regretted the remark—it sounded weak and petty.

Brett took my hand. "If I offended you, I apologize. I wanted to keep Ivan from thinking we were involved."

I pulled free. "The man gives me the creeps."

"Forget it. Dumb idea."

"Besides, I am scrawny. I know—"

"You're not scrawny. You're very attractive. But even if Ivan didn't think so, he'd try to get you into bed. Ditch that notion. We'll face him together."

"Come to think of it, I should have a drink with Ivan. Nothing bad would happen. If I unbuttoned my blouse, he'd run."

"Too risky."

"Don't worry. I'm seduce-proof. Since Mom's death I've been emotionally numb, like a robot whose romance software has been deleted."

"Ivan might sense that and be more interested."

"I'll take my dad's .45."

"What are you doing with a .45?"

"I have to protect myself while I look for my dad. I'll try this 'playing up' stuff."

"Don't worry. We're making progress."

"We're not. If the wardrobe women know something, they're not saying. Allen claims he didn't go to the set. Jake may know the truth, but he suggested I go home. Adolfo's father says my dad is alive but doesn't know where. Dale hints Dad is here but won't tell me how to spot him. We have to get to Ivan. He wouldn't have a *Dead Girls* revenue report if he didn't have a connection to the original film."

"You want to do this because of my 'scrawny' comment."

"Everything's not about you," I said, borrowing Dale's line.

****

I phoned Nina from my room and told her I planned to flirt with a disgusting old man to get information. "What the hell am I doing?"

"Using your feminine advantages."

"I don't have any."

"Sure, you do. My advice about the old man is that males are programmed to pursue. When you're together, nature will do the rest."

"How many times should I let him kiss me before I push him away?"

"You'll know. And in case you're wondering, everything's quiet around your grandma's house."

When we hung up, I showered and put on clean slacks and a knit top, adding a touch of lipstick and eyeliner. I snapped a loaded magazine into the .45, slipped it into my purse, and went to dailies.

When they were finished, I made a point of walking ahead of Ivan through the lobby. He passed me without a word.

The lobby emptied, leaving me alone with the lopsided and mutilated cowboy mannequin (D minus on my PTSD chart). I went outside and stared at clouds drifting past the Man in the Moon. Were my claims I had no feelings about sex and romance like those clouds? Camouflage, hiding my fear men wouldn't find me attractive? Or worse, that I wouldn't care?

"Nice night," said a male voice behind me.

My arm whipped around and struck a glass. It fell, shattering.

Ivan picked up the pieces. "Didn't mean to alarm you. It must be difficult to be a young woman away from home with a male crew."

A ghostly figure in the moonlight, he had white skin and obsidian eyes glinting with reflections from the streetlights. I fought a PTSD pull, trying to bring me to the hallway in Concrete.

Ivan said, "I brought down one glass. There are more and a full bottle of champagne in my room. Perhaps you'd like to tell me your career plans. We need new blood in this business."

I clutched my purse, feeling the hard outline of the Colt.

Ivan led me to a three-room suite on the fourteenth floor with expensive ash furniture and a panoramic view to the north where peaks stood silhouetted against a pale tangerine sky.

"Called Black Mountain." he said. "Petroglyphs by the dozen. I'd be happy to show them to you when the picture wraps."

Beneath the window, a basket of fruit and a greeting card lay on his credenza. Above the king-sized bed, an oil painting of Black Mountain glowed under a frame light.

Ivan inserted a disk the diameter of a pancake into a device and pressed play. Sinatra's "All the Way" filled the room.

He beamed. "One of the new compact disc players." He poured champagne for us both, ushered me to his couch, and sat beside me. He took the phone off the hook and raised his glass. "To our challenging but exciting profession." He drank.

"People say you worked on a film called *Dead Girls Talk*."

"Not that I remember."

Hoping for a jolt of Della-courage, I drained my glass. He filled it. I drained it again. "Correction, it was *Dead Girls Don't Lie*."

"I don't think so."

He poured. I drank. "I'm sure that's what I heard."

He edged closer. "Tell me about yourself."

"I'm studying philosophy at Bellingham University in Washington State," I said, struggling to make my rubbery lips behave.

"What inspired you to work in film?"

"Lots of things. First—"

"I've found it a romantic and exciting career. Movie stars, exotic locations. I had a fabulous shoot in New Orleans." He wrapped his arm around my shoulder. "A balmy night, the strains of cool jazz in the air and scents of spicy gumbo and jambalaya drifting from bustling kitchens." He drew me toward him.

I stiffened and tried to edge away. "You remember the words Dead Girls in a title?"

He kissed me on the lips. Kissed me again. I eased the .45 partway from my purse. "Try to remember."

His hand slid off my shoulder.

My fingers found the trigger of the .45.

His hand inched toward my breast.

Even the slightest touch and I'll—

Pounding shook the door.

"We're busy here," Ivan said.

The pounding grew louder. "Phone call," a voice

shouted from the hall.

"This better be important." Ivan marched toward the door.

I shoved the .45 into my purse and followed. I caught up as he flung the door open.

Brett faced us, hair askew, face flushed. "I was walking past the front desk when a call came in for Tanya. They paged her but got no answer. Someone saw you together, so—"

Ivan said, "Have them transfer the call up here."

"They said it was Tanya's dad."

I pushed past Ivan. "I have to take it." I joined Brett, and we walked to the elevator. As the doors closed, Ivan stood in his doorway, staring after us.

On our way down, I asked, "Did you hear my dad's voice?"

"No one called. I couldn't let you go through with your plan. Sorry if you wanted to. Did you learn anything?"

"Ivan's a liar. I need to find out what he knows about Dad." I wanted to punch Brett for getting my hopes up, and hug him for trying to save me. "Ivan will be furious. He figured he had me."

We got out in the lobby, and Brett went to the front desk, handed the receptionist a ten-dollar bill, and whispered, "If anyone asks whether Tanya got a call, tell them yes."

****

As I readied for bed, the phone rang. I picked up. "Brett, I'm exhausted. Let's talk tomorrow."

After a long silence, I said, "If you're my dad and don't have the guts to speak, to hell with you. And if you're someone else, you don't scare me any more than

255

you did my grandma. Don't call again."
   A feathery breath. More silence.
   I hung up.

Chapter 36

The next morning at dawn, day eight on the film, I was hurrying toward the editing room when Ivan intercepted me. "What did your dad have to say?"

"He hung up before we got there." I studied his face for signs of anger, but his eyes were bright, his features relaxed.

"I'd feel like a charlatan," he said, "if I filled your mind with expectations about movie making, without following through."

"I'd be happy hearing about all the films you've worked on."

"I can do better than that." He led me to the Ford building lobby. "I'm pulling you off PA duties. Come to the trestle location this afternoon and see production value in the making."

He went outside and got into a waiting car. It pulled away, and I rode a van to base camp.

****

After lunch, I rode another van, which followed one carrying Ivan, Dale, and Bob, the gaffer, the quarter mile up the road to the trestle, where grips were pushing the ore car up the grade. Assistants mounted two cameras on tripods beside the nearest mine tunnel and on two others farther along the ridge. Gaffers adjusted reflectors while welders repaired the ore car's brake.

Jesse, the stunt coordinator, emerged from a van, wearing a dirtied Kelly-green shirt and blue jeans. She approached Ivan. "When I did my tech rehearsal, I was dubious about this scene and made trestle and mine car suggestions. Not enough have been done. Besides which, there's no ambulance and crew of medics ready. I can't give my okay."

Ivan said, "The scene is crucial to the story."

"My stunt man and I will do it, but it's going to cost you $8000 for the pair of us."

"That's way over our budget."

Della emerged from a van, wearing jeans and a Kelly-green western shirt, dirtied to suggest she'd been scrambling through the mine. Face ashen, she glanced around.

Jesse said to Ivan, "I bet you're pressuring your actress to do the stunt. I can't go along with that."

"Lots of actors do their own stunts. Della's a first-class horsewoman."

"She won't be riding a horse."

Brett, wearing a soiled denim shirt and faded jeans, sauntered after Della.

She glanced over her shoulder at Clint, who mouthed, "Break a leg."

Jake announced he'd set charges along the trestle to create harmless explosions and smoke during the car's run. He handed Della sticks of special effects dynamite. "Throw these at the zombies."

Jesse passed Ivan her walkie-talkie. "I can't have any involvement with the risk you're asking your actress to take." She walked to a van and left the set with a guy wearing a Stunts Unlimited patch.

Ivan said, "We don't need them. Della, are you

ready?"

She gave a faint nod.

Dominick's assistant fitted Della and Brett with wireless microphones.

Ivan guided them from start positions inside the tunnel to the mine car outside, having the zombies follow, moaning and grasping at them.

On rehearsal takes, Della stopped short of the car, each time citing a different excuse: "I tripped." "Way off my marks." "I looked at camera."

While the grips taped final start marks on the dolly track, and electricians adjusted reflectors, Della sneaked a drink from her flask.

I approached her and whispered, "You've got this."

"Position one," the AD announced on his bullhorn.

Della, Brett, and the zombies retreated into the tunnel. The AD called for sound and picture. Both rolled.

Ivan called, "Action."

Della and Brett ran out, the zombies after them. Brett climbed into the car. Della threw dynamite sticks and climbed in behind him, while he released the brake.

After a few feet, she yelled, "Stop."

The grips returned the car to first position.

"Off my marks again," she told Ivan.

"Not a problem."

They tried five more takes. Della shouted, "Stop" each time.

Ivan huddled with her.

As they spoke, Della's voice rose. "It's no use. I don't trust the trestle. It's going to collapse and kill us. You have to make the repairs the stunt coordinator asked for."

"We don't have the time or the budget."

Brett leaned against the production van, watching.

Mouth dry, heart thumping, I approached Ivan. "I'll stand in for Della."

Dale rubbed his chin, nodding. "It might work if we have Tanya face away from camera in the wide shot and shoot close-ups of Della for Allen to cut in later."

Ivan nodded. "All right, kid."

I said, "On the condition you answer my questions."

"Fine, but you have to sign a release."

I did.

A crew van started, ready to rush me to the wardrobe and makeup departments at base camp, when timbers snapped, and the trestle sagged two feet.

The key grip shouted, "We're done for now."

The crew broke and headed down to film a scene on the mining town set.

Brett hurried to me. "Don't do the shot. It's super risky."

"Della's been on my side from the beginning. If I can help her, I'm going to. Besides, Ivan agreed to answer my questions afterward."

"He won't do it. Don't be stupid."

"You can be such a jerk." I took a deep breath. "But trying to save me last night was sweet." If we hadn't been surrounded by crew members, I would have hugged him and kissed his cheek—a scary idea, but it didn't set off a PTSD reaction.

As Brett walked away, Jake approached me. "Don't do the scene."

"I can't bail."

"You don't have to prove your courage to anyone.

Tell Ivan you've changed your mind. Say you're afraid of heights."

"Talking to Dale, I got the impression my dad is here or close by. In case he killed my mom, I want him to understand I'm not afraid of him. If he didn't do it, I want him to be proud and contact me."

"I've already told you, your father—"

"I have to do the shot."

Jake threw up his hands and walked away.

Chapter 37

At night, on the way up in the elevator to our rooms, Brett put his hand on my shoulder. I flinched. "Please don't do that scene tomorrow," he said, his voice calm and gentle. "I'll refuse, if you do. The stunt coordinator said it's dangerous."

I liked this gentler, kinder Brett. "Thanks for your concern, but I'm doing the shot." I expected him to make fun of my bravado, but he stared at me in a way I didn't recall from any guy, including Tony—his mouth curving into an earnest smile, his eyes seeming to see the me inside, the one I didn't let show.

He said, "Before you get maimed or killed in that insane stunt, let me take you out to dinner."

I grinned. "You're asking me on a *date*?"

"It might be nice to discuss strategy in a fancier spot than the set or the hotel dining room."

"Fancy dinners aren't my thing."

"There's a roadhouse up the highway with a rep for the best steaks around. Go to your room and decide. I'll be in the lobby in half an hour, ready to go with you or by myself."

When I undressed in my room, Brett's kind offer took second place to a hot bath and a night's rest.

I opened my bureau drawer to get a T to sleep in and found, tucked in with Lottie's cash, a second photo. Lottie, in her twenties, eyes alight with mischief, hair glowing in the sun, posed in a formal garden, wearing a prom dress with a corsage pinned at her breast.

On the back of the photo Lottie had penned, "Charlotte, frightened girls deserve to have a good time, too."

I showered and put on a burgundy blouse and a black skirt crushed like a fossilized flower from when I jammed it into my pannier. I ran an iron over it and phoned Brett in the lobby. "I'm hungry, but I don't want Ivan to see us together on this non-date. I'll go down the back way."

When I descended the rear stairway and stepped outside, Brett's company BMW sat, idling. He stood beside it, holding the door open.

After I got in and we drove off, I turned around, looking for the phony PI, but I didn't see him.

****

The roadhouse turned out to be Francisco's Escondite. It wasn't fancy, but atmospheric, with old timbers, rough-plastered walls, and hand-hewn tables lit with flickering candles. The manager, a Latino in his seventies, with a white beard and droopy brown eyes, led us past several couples to a secluded alcove. He beamed as if he thought we were lovers having a tryst.

I didn't need a menu to select a porterhouse steak, baked potato, and salad.

Brett ordered the same items, plus a bottle of Cabernet Sauvignon. He offered me a glass.

I stuck to water.

The steak was juicy and delicious, the potato huge and overflowing with sour cream and chives. During our dinner, a guitar player in a pirate-sleeved white shirt sat in the corner singing a Mexican song in a sweet, sad voice.

I kept expecting Brett to push me to try the wine or to take my hand. But he didn't mention the wine again and kept his hands to himself. Reverse psychology, I decided.

The manager approached our table and said to Brett, "Rodrigo will play a waltz if you and the señorita would like to dance."

Brett said, "Very kind of him, but I suspect the lady would prefer to listen."

I nodded. "Have him play one of his favorite songs."

While we had chocolate flan and coffee, Rodrigo strummed his guitar and sang Spanish lyrics to a sweet waltz tune that made me picture Mom and Dad dancing as they had in our living room last New Year's Eve.

****

On the drive to the hotel I said, "What happened to discussing strategy over dinner?"

"I decided good company and good food beat talking set politics."

I didn't trust him and prepared a speech for when he suggested we go to my room. I'd explain how it wouldn't do to chance Ivan seeing us together and how it would hurt my reputation with the crew if they found out. How it had been a lovely evening, but I had eaten too much and needed to call it a night.

When we pulled up to the rear entrance and Brett headed around the car toward my door, I shoved it open to short-circuit whatever strategy he had in mind. He extended his hand.

I grasped it and stepped out, inhaling the smell of chocolate on his breath.

"The hills close by have hiking trails," he said.
"I...uh...and...petroglyphs."

Brett leaned close.

I closed my eyes.

He slapped my neck.

"What the hell."

He wiped a bloody mosquito from his fingers.
"Lucky our rooms are air-conditioned. Keeps these
buggers out. You have a decent view from yours?"

"The rail yard." Here it comes.

"Ivan wouldn't care if we looked out on a sea of
dumpsters. If he found a cheap enough hotel, we'd have
coffee-stained carpets and tiger paintings on black
velvet." Brett gestured toward the town center. "There's
supposed to be a museum. We could explore it when
the shoot wraps."

If you're going to kiss me, get it over with.

He peered across the parking lot. "Is that a
coyote?"

I looked. "A mutt."

"I guess you're right." He sighed. "It was an
awesome evening. By the way, you look terrific." He
stepped back to let me pass.

His gallant manner unnerved me. I rushed toward
the door, expecting a PTSD eruption to show I resented
his bait-and-switch tactic. Instead, what came out was,
"My real name is Charlotte." I clutched my skirt and
hurried inside.

****

In my room I glanced in the mirror, surprised to see
an amused expression. My non-date with Brett hadn't
been frightening, miserable, or uncomfortable.

I phoned the dorm in Bellingham. After a delay,

Nina came on, yawning. "Found your father yet?"

"Still looking. Your exams going well?"

"I'm acing them."

"What's the report from my grandma's house?"

"A van came by yesterday with a man wearing a clerical collar."

"Interesting." I pictured the clerical collar I'd found in the trash. "How do you know he was a real pastor?"

"The church's name was painted on the van. The man brought two women in their seventies. They carried bibles and lugged suitcases inside. Good company for your grandma."

"What a relief. I appreciate all you do."

"Sometimes I'm afraid I'm interfering in your life."

"No way. When do you finish exams?"

"Tomorrow."

"Then you have no excuse not to come see me."

"At your service, ma'am."

I laughed, pleased with myself. I'd gone on a date. And my best friend was coming to keep me sane in the midst of the craziness. Life was looking good.

Nina said, "A suggestion. You might not want to tell Lottie you're happy about her new housemates. From what you've said, I'm sure she'd hate to admit she listened to your advice about living arrangements."

"You're right. And if these church ladies are half as tough-minded as Lottie, they'll keep her safe."

Chapter 38

On my ninth morning on the production the call time had been delayed until noon. I lounged in bed, daydreaming about hiking through the Cascades.

A girl screamed. I snapped upright, then realized it was children playing in the hallway.

Their voices reminded me of a day after school at Concrete elementary.

****

Four older girls chased me on my bike, yelling for me to give them the giant Tootsie Rolls I bought at the Loggers' Landing grocery. I pedaled hard down Route 20 until I couldn't hear them. When I stopped to look back, a long black car pulled up beside me. The rear window rolled down.

Inside, a man wearing a dark suit with a red handkerchief in his pocket regarded me with slate-gray eyes. The expression on his bearded face softened. "Hello, Charlotte. How are you?" he asked with a foreign accent.

"How do you know my name?"

"I'm an old friend of your father's."

"Are you here to buy one of his cabins?"

He shook his head. "Did you study hard at school today?"

"Yes."

"What do you do for fun?"

"Hunting and fishing."

"With your father, I'm sure." He said something to the driver in a language I didn't understand, and the car pulled away.

I didn't tell Dad. He'd warned me not to talk to strangers.

****

The children were still playing in the hallway when I called Lottie. "Tell me about the Russian Dad dealt with."

"Russian?"

I believed that was what the limousine passenger had spoken. "Please don't pretend you've forgotten the man my parents consulted about adoption."

"Your parents loved you."

"But—"

"As I told you before, when they couldn't have children of their own, they tried to adopt. An expensive process at the regular agencies. Your dad had financial problems with his fancy cabins. An acquaintance mentioned someone who had money to invest, and who sometimes knew about children needing parents."

"So, now you're admitting what you waffled on last time I asked you. I *was* adopted, wasn't I?"

"Honey, none of that makes any difference."

"Did the killers attack Mom, your daughter, because someone stole me from my real mother?"

"People adopt for all kinds of reasons. It doesn't mean the children aren't loved, or that adoption leads to murder. Your parents wanted to tell you, but they delayed, worried about upsetting you."

"Did my birth mom know my parents in Concrete? If she went crazy when they took her baby and she sent someone to get revenge, that makes me responsible for Mom's death."

"Not at all, child."

"Where are my real mom and dad?"

"I don't know. When your folks brought you home, your dad said the arrangement was legal but he wouldn't talk about it."

"You must have some records about my birth parents."

"Sorry."

I was shaking but made my voice calm. "Lottie, you've saved every Christmas card and phone bill since Columbus discovered America. Please go through them. You told me Mom and Dad dealt with, and I quote, 'some man with a foreign name.' See if a Russian is listed anywhere."

****

I hustled to the repair bay with sausages from the restaurant, fed Royal, and gave him a long run. When he started after a squirrel I called him back, and he came.

I biked to Barstow Community College and searched for material about Pacific Northwest agencies offering Russian babies for adoption, but I didn't find any, though I did find newspaper articles about people selling babies under the guise of doing legitimate adoptions.

The man in Concrete who'd pulled over in the limousine to talk to me was dressed too well to be a hunting pal of my father's. I guessed Dad had built a fancy log cabin for some rich man and got me in the deal.

As I read about a sex slave's infant left in a car

trunk, about a baby tossed into a dumpster, and about prostitutes' newborns given away or sold or adopted out, I wished for a PTSD episode to take me to another time and place. It didn't happen. I stood in the library thinking, I'm better off than those poor girls. But for how long?

Chapter 39

The next morning, day ten on the shoot, loud knocking woke me. I grabbed the .45. "Who's there?"

"It's me," Nina called from the hallway. "I flew in this morning."

I put the .45 away and opened the door.

Nina stepped in, wearing fawn-colored pants and a white halter-top, her hazel eyes brighter than usual. With every hair in place, her eye shadow, liner, and lipstick perfect, she looked as glamorous as any of our actresses. "Stunning outfit," I said, thinking we were the same dress size. When we returned to school, I'd borrow a few of her clothes.

She put her suitcase down. "Love the new haircut but not the circles under your eyes. We need to de-stress you."

"I'll call Lottie and ask what she's found out about Dad's Russian connections so we can figure out how the phony PI is linked to them."

Nina sat me on the bed. "Forget about the Russians. What else have you been checking out?"

I described Brett's mother's death after the taxi shot on *Dead Girls,* and how he and I were working together. I told her about Annie and said I suspected the phony PI of poisoning her. I added I'd sneaked into his favorite bar and viewed folders from his briefcase while he played pinball.

"How do I find this bar?"

"You warned me to stay away from him."

She winked. "He won't have a clue who I am."

I gave her directions.

She grabbed her purse. "I should talk to Brett."

"He's very busy."

"Is that a fact?"

"It's...I'll see what I can do."

"You two have sex?"

"No. Is sex all the girls at school gossip about these days?"

"I won't talk to him if you're not okay with it."

"You can talk to him or anyone else. If you keep your eyes open and tell me when you see something suspicious, I know we'll be okay."

****

I gave Nina a tour of the set. I loved seeing her fascination as Dale's crew prepared the camera, electricians set lights, and art department people dressed the mining town buildings. When I told her about Ivan's mine car shot, she said, "If you get injured in that stunt, you'll have to leave the movie. Never find your father."

"I'm going to do it," I said with conviction, but Jake's and Brett's warnings were unsettling me. I skipped lunch, and while Nina wandered around observing, I went to the wardrobe trailer to be fitted with a Kelly-green western shirt, jeans, and cowboy boots.

I kept checking on Nina, pleased she seemed interested in the movie.

Next, I moved to makeup. Doreen, cheerful and relaxed, sat me in a chair and applied foundation, eyeliner, and lipstick. Plus, dark smudges to dirty my face and neck. She added a wig matching Della's hair.

Two chairs away, a makeup artist applied blotchy red eye shadow, facial scars, and black lips to the statuesque zombie with the orange wig who had replaced Annie.

****

I was at the opening to the mine tunnel, staring at the rusty ore car when Ivan joined me. He said, "My instincts tell me you'll have terrific screen presence. I see a career for you in front of the camera."

The boom man attached a radio microphone out of sight on my bra strap and asked me first to say, then to shout, a couple of lines so Dominick could set record levels. Ivan and Karen, both wearing earphones connected to wireless receivers, sat on high folding chairs beside the main camera. Other operators and assistants set camera positions along the ravine.

Nina caught my eye and mouthed, "You're going to be fabulous."

I returned a nod, but when Brett checked her out, I looked away. Silly—I had no interest in dating him, or anyone.

First, Ivan did a wide shot of Della and Brett. Even with her soiled wardrobe and dark smudges covering her face she drew my eyes like a fourth-of-July sparkler when she ran out followed by a dozen zombies.

Brett, tan, grim-faced, and weaving his way through them like a football running back, looked every bit the rugged movie hero.

Della raced beside him toward the ore car, fighting off the grasping zombies.

Ivan leaned forward, eyes on the video monitor,

and made comments. After three takes, he called, "Cut. Print."

My turn came to double for Della. Jittery and breathing fast, I had to pee and wished I'd gone to the honey wagon.

Della approached me. "If you're nervous, pick a brave person in your life and use her strength." She grasped my hands. "I don't know how to thank you for today."

"I know a perfect way. From the photographs of you, Dad, and Officer Shanahan hunting in Washington—"

"You're Jefferson's daughter?"

"I respect your old life, as well as your new one. I've been slow to figure out you played the blonde thrown off the roof in *Dead Girls*. I assume my dad called you when he came to Los Angeles last spring, and that he's here. I promise to honor your privacy, but please tell me where and who he is."

She whispered, "It might be dangerous for your dad if you two connected now. I can't do that to him. He changed my life."

"So, you had an affair."

She gave me an amused smile. "Not every close relationship involves sex."

"But you fell in love?"

"With life, with nature. I met your mother on one of his hunting trips. Seeing your parents together inspired me." She sighed. "I failed your father once. I'm not going to do it again."

"How did you fail him?"

"After he paid off his mortgages, he needed more cash for his cabin business and asked me for help. I'd had boring parts since my stint in the adult film world and wanted a more interesting role. *Dead Girls Don't Lie* came along with a decent role as a waitress, but the production insisted on an investment. I put my savings into the movie and got hired."

"Through your friend Zolton Baron. I know he's connected to Ivan somehow."

"I've had enough pain in my life to want to ease yours. But I can't put you or your father in jeopardy."

"You saying he's in the crew?"

"Wherever he is, let him find you if and when he's ready. You're braver today than any of my western heroines. Thanks more than I can say." She patted my shoulder and walked away.

The AD's voice blared over a megaphone. "We're up in five. Let's get this."

The crew on set was about fifty people. Inspired by a combination of wishful thinking and PTSD, I'd had moments when I imagined each man of the right age being Dad.

But when I calmed down, I couldn't see any as my father: Allen was a pothead, while Dad preferred alcohol; Jake had failed every test I'd given him; Clint was old; Dale was more fastidious and artistic than the father I knew. Ivan pushed himself on me in a way Dad wouldn't have.

Whom had I overlooked?

Jake approached me. "It's not too late to back out."

"I can't."

He let out a resigned sigh and handed me sticks of dynamite to throw at the zombies. "These are fake and safe. We'll do the explosions as opticals in the lab later."

One of the production assistants, about Brett's size and build, headed our way in an outfit matching Brett's.

"No doubles," Brett said. "If Tanya takes this crazy ride, I will, too."

Ivan said. "Out of the question."

"It's all right, Brett," I said. "I'll be fine." *You keep surprising me.*

Ivan and Brett turned to the video monitor. Jake bent over his special effects panel.

"Settle," the AD said. "Roll sound."

"Hold it," the key grip shouted. He pointed to a muscular guy, heading toward us, brow pressed against the eyepiece of a video camera.

A graying, crinkly-haired blonde in sturdy heels and a pantsuit strode beside him. Stocky, with a nose, eyes, and chin one size too large for her face, she announced in a hoarse Brooklyn accent, "Kiki Benson, *Hollywood Movie Beat*" and extended a hand to Ivan.

"Closed set," he said and signaled to the guard. "Get them out of here."

"We can create a buzz for your movie on television tonight in LA or say you're afraid to reveal your shot's dangerous as hell."

"Leave."

"Fine. We'll work from another spot."

"Stop taping now."

When the guy kept on, the First AD tried to wrest the camera from him. They tussled, and the camera popped free like a fumbled football and bounced down the rocky slope, landing in a clump of brush.

Kiki glared at Ivan. "You've bought yourself a lawsuit."

"You accepted the risk by entering private property

and taping without permission."

I caught Brett's eye and mouthed, "Did you call them?"

He shook his head.

A grip retrieved the scratched and dented video camera and handed it to the cameraman.

Kiki said, "That's fifty thousand dollars' worth of gear."

Jake cast a concerned look at the rusted tracks, dissolving what remained of my bravado.

I pressed my eyes shut, hoping for a jolt of courage from Lottie.

"Roll sound."

"Roll picture."

The slate closed with a crack. I opened my eyes as Ivan called, "Action."

I repeated my run to the mine car with Brett's double to escape the zombies. I jumped in and, as we rolled, I hurled dynamite sticks at the ghoulish creatures attacking us. Jake's explosions erupted around the car. The farther we went, the louder the trestle groaned, the car weaving on the uneven rails, tossing the two of us about.

I feared I was going to die, and my PTSD snatched me away.

I'm five, Grandma Lottie's hand hanging inches from my face. I grip her fingers and walk with her and Mom, whose belly is huge and round.

Waddling like a goose, Mom smiles at me. "I have a new sister for you in my tummy."

We enter a doctor's waiting room filled with big-bellied ladies. The nurse leads Mom through a doorway.

The mine car lurched. I toppled backward, reached for support, and yanked the release lever by mistake. The hopper flipped, dumping me and the PA. Our feet danced, grappling for footholds on the car's jostling frame.

When Mom, Lottie, and I come home from the doctor's office, Lottie tries to send me out to play.

I cling to Mom and ask, "What's wrong?"

She doesn't answer.

I point at her tummy, round as ever. "My sister's in there, right?"

The PA heaved upward on the bucket and righted it. A support timber split with a boom. The trestle dropped a foot. A gap opened in the track ahead, and we sped toward it.

"Help me stop this death trap," the PA shouted.

We threw our bodies against the brake lever. The shoe smoked and squealed, and the car slowed, stopping inches short of a two-foot gap in the track.

"Cut. Print," Ivan shouted on the bullhorn, his voice echoing down the canyon. "Cut, print. Cut, print. Cut, print."

Dad drives Mom home from the hospital. I run to her, looking but not seeing her giant belly, or a baby.

I ask, "What did you do with my sister?"

Mom rushes to the bedroom.

I try to follow, but Lottie holds me back. "They had to leave her at the hospital."

"Mom didn't want her?"

"The baby died, honey. Nothing anyone could do."

I punch Lottie. "Why did the baby die?"

"Nobody knows."

I break free and catch up with Mom. "When did my

baby sister die?" I think Mom must have dropped her,
like she always drops the baseball when we play catch.

"A month ago."

"Then why did you keep her in your tummy?"

"The doctor said I had to."

When the car stopped, I stared ahead, numb and
shocked that I'd forgotten about Mom's pregnancy.
Someone grabbed my arm and helped me out of the car.
Grips and mechanics scrambled onto the trestle,
welding, bolting, and replacing broken struts and track.

Nina stood above on the embankment, grinning.
She gave me two thumbs up. I made my way up the
trestle to the main camera position, spotted Brett hiding
behind a group of crew members, went to him, and
jabbed his chest. "You called those TV people."

"Reporters have been poking around since the
beginning."

"Not while everyone was paying attention to me."

"No one knows anything about you. And they
won't make a connection to your dad."

"Someone will put my name together with my
questions about him." I punched his shoulder. "Swear
you didn't invite that woman."

"She'll make you look heroic. You want your dad
to see how brave you are, right?"

"TV people focusing attention on Dad will send
him deeper under cover." I stomped away. "Once a
spoiled brat, always an asshole." Kisses I'd imagined
planting on Brett's lips blew away like dandelion
thistles in the wind. I pictured a TV story by
"Hollywood Movie Beat" with my real name, my
photo, and a narrator describing my search for Dad.

I approached Ivan. "I need to know what happened

279

to my father and Brett's mother on *Dead Girls*."

"No time now. We'll talk after the second take."

"We can't do that shot *again.*"

"You didn't make it all the way across."

I balled my hands into fists, ready to walk away. Then I recalled the dead baby in Mom's belly. I almost had a younger sister. Damn it, I should have a sister.

"I'll do a second take after you tell me about my dad and Brett's mother."

"You're not irreplaceable."

"No one will do the stunt now it's clear how insane it is."

Ivan mopped his face with a handkerchief. "Not much to tell. I worked away from the set most of the time, making deals about locations, trying to get film stock and extra lenses on the cheap. Your dad may have worked on the show. I don't know. As for Brett's mother, I don't have a clue. Do you, Jake?"

Jake made adjustments on his control panel.

I faced Ivan. "I'm not getting back in the ore car until you tell me who got killed."

"Someone went to the hospital after wrap, from a car crash. I don't recall anyone dying. Now get in the damn car, and let's do this."

The second take terrified me more than the first. Timbers burst loose, and the trestle swayed as if we were in an earthquake. The car twisted and squealed like a wounded beast, tossing me and the PA up, down, and sideways.

Once more, we threw our weight against the brake lever, slowing the car and stopping it inside the far mine tunnel.

Drenched with sweat, legs and arms bruised and

aching, I welcomed a grip's help on my way up the trestle to the cliff edge. I didn't trust Ivan's version of what happened on *Dead Girls*, but it didn't matter. I was proud of having done the stunt and awed by my mother's heroism in carrying the dead baby inside her. I scanned the crew, hoping to see my father beaming at me.

No one except Nina noticed my return, everyone intent on wrapping gear. On the set you were either the center of attention or the last shot's mess to clean up.

****

When vans brought everyone to the hotel, Nina went for a walk. I was sorry for having been hard on Brett. After I showered and changed into a skirt and top, I bought a humorous friendship card in the lobby and walked toward his room.

I was halfway to his door when he emerged with his arm around a busty redhead in a short black skirt and a turquoise top clinging to her curves like wet paint. She undulated along the corridor, gazing into his eyes and whispering to him. Neither noticed me when he kissed her.

Chapter 40

As I entered the hotel bar, crew members were huddled in groups, talking and drinking. I tossed the greeting card in a wastebasket.

Brett and his slinky friend arrived and went to a big booth where Kiki sat drinking with her cameraman. She had changed into a white blazer over navy slacks and had brushed her hair, which made her look feminine, but still more like a gym coach than a TV personality.

Her cameraman, in clothes dirtied from his scuffle on the set, introduced himself to Brett as Ralph, and downed two drinks in quick succession.

Dale, in a clean shirt, his hair and beard trimmed, sat with his assistants in a booth near me. "Be smart," he whispered. "Don't get yourself hurt."

"Nothing romantic is going on."

"Not sure I buy that. When this girl leaves town, you'll be the featured attraction."

"I don't care," I said. But I did, a little. And I didn't want to spend time around Brett and his girlfriend, or date, or whatever she was.

As I headed back toward the lobby, Brett called, "Tanya, come join us."

Unwilling to give him the satisfaction of seeing me flee like a frightened twelve-year-old, I walked to their booth.

Brett introduced me to his date, Bonnie. "She's a

star on a hospital series."

I wanted to say, "You mean a mindless soap?" But I didn't.

Kiki's wrinkles deepened as she studied me. Brett scooted over, hip-to-hip with Bonnie to make a space. I sat on the opposite side, next to Kiki, who extended a hand, her forearm clinking with turquoise-inlaid silver bracelets. We shook.

"Didn't I see you on the set today?" she asked.

"I'm a production assistant."

"I swear, the up-and-comers in film today get younger by the year. Names like Billy Wilder and Frank Capra wouldn't mean a thing to you."

"I could watch Wilder's *Sunset Boulevard* and *Some Like it Hot* over and over. My grandma loves Capra's *It's a Wonderful Life,* which cloys for me. I prefer *Lost Horizon* and *The Bitter Tea of General Yen.*"

Kiki's raucous laugh made me want to nudge her drink into her lap. She pressed her hands together, as if she was offering an apology. "Since you're such a smart cookie, how do I get the production to pony up money to replace our camera?"

I could see Ivan gnashing his teeth at the prospect, but remembered Sally, the dialogue coach, saying, "You'd be surprised how many people in Hollywood think they're making art."

I said, "Instead of confronting Ivan, you could do a retrospective of his films. He might be flattered enough to find some dollars hidden in the budget."

Bonnie put her arm through Brett's. "Enough boring movie talk. Let's go dancing."

Ralph got to his feet and slapped a five on the

table. "See you all in the morning."

He left, and Brett and Bonnie walked to the exit. I stayed behind with Kiki. Having no doubt she could tap into the dark and secret side of the movie business, I said, "If I wanted to track someone down—"

"I'd be your magic carpet to his door. I know everything and everyone of interest in Hollywood." Her broad grin reminded me of porn producer Ray India's and made me just as uncomfortable.

"Ever hear of an actor named Alec Hudson?" I asked.

"Damn. Stumped right off the bat."

"How about *Dead Girls Don't Lie* or the film's producer, Zolton Baron?"

"Drawing a blank on them too. I'm sure I can find out but I have to warn you—I drive a hard bargain."

****

In my hotel room I found Nina sitting on a daybed, leafing through the papers I'd brought from Lottie's house. She beamed. "You can forget about your favorite PI for a while."

"I'm afraid to ask."

"I play a mean game of pinball. Wandered into the bar you mentioned, found your mystery man, and racked up a couple of mega-scores. He challenged me to a duel. I let him win, and we had a few beers. Next thing I knew, he offered me a ride on his new Harley and an evening of wild sex."

"Tell me you didn't agree."

"Said I was in if he rode to LA and brought me a burger and a menu from the Hard Rock Café."

A motorcycle backfired in the parking lot below.

I hurried to the window.

"Don't worry," Nina said. "While he paid to gas his bike, I stuffed a couple of scrunchies into his tank. The elastic dissolves and clogs the fuel filter—a tip from one of my true crime books. He's stranded somewhere between here and LA."

****

In the morning, Nina and I found Kiki and Ralph having breakfast in the hotel coffee shop. After introducing Nina, I asked, "Have you had time to research Zolton Baron, Ivan, or *Dead Girls*?"

Kiki dunked a croissant in her coffee and finished it in two bites. "On Zolton Baron and *Dead Girls,* no luck, but on Ivan I found something strange. For the last year, he's made and distributed films you can rent or buy anywhere. Before then, the items on his resume are phony."

"Did he produce *Dead Girls Don't Lie*?"

"I'm not sure, but his career is going to make a good story. He'll love being interviewed—directors have such needy egos. We'll air the piece in a few days."

I made a face. "If you go public now, it will screw things up for Brett and me. You can broadcast everything after the movie wraps in a few weeks."

Kiki snagged another croissant. "Story's current. Besides, the camera damage has my LA bosses apoplectic. I need to jump on this to take their minds off the loss."

"I have to keep my research project secret a while longer. What can a broke college girl do to convince you?"

She dipped the croissant into the jam jar on the table and took a bite. "If I could get an interview with the intriguing man who controls the explosions, I'd be a happy girl."

"Jake? With the messed up face and hands?"

"Our audience would love to know about his life. Where he got those scars."

"How do you think that would make him feel?"

"Proud. I'll paint him as a brave man who's overcome incredible odds to do the work he loves."

"Jake's a good person. I can't put him on the spot. Besides, I'm sure he'd say no."

Nina smiled, pleased I hoped that I'd stood up for Jake. Kiki pulled a micro recorder from her purse and held it out.

"I can't," I said.

She placed the recorder on the table. "Hide this in your bra. He won't know where I got my information."

"You don't believe that."

She looked at Nina. "You wouldn't tell, would you?"

Nina covered her mouth with her palm. "Mum as the Sphinx."

Kiki dipped the rest of her croissant into the jam and finished it. "I have a tidbit for you about Ivan and *Dead Girls*, what you're looking for—if you do this for me."

"I couldn't."

As if I'd agreed, Kiki demonstrated how to use the recorder and slid a couple of micro-cassettes toward me. "I need personal stuff—when he started in film, how he got injured, his experiences since. Do we have a deal?"

Kiki was tough, and certain to find something to help me. I sucked a rueful breath and took the recorder.

Chapter 41

Karen intercepted me as I left the dining room. "You didn't get rid of that mutt." She pointed to Royal, thirty feet away, nudging a sausage patty off a recently vacated table with his nose. "You can't be a pushover and get on in this business. Take him to the pound."

I said I would and led him out. The shoot wouldn't start for several hours, so I biked into town and bought a collar for Royal. "Now you're mine," I told him. I set out a dish of dog food and a pan of water in a far corner of the repair bay and replaced his rope leash with a piece of chain.

He wagged his tail and licked my hand—I read it as doggie absolution for my sleazy deal with Kiki.

When Nina and I went upstairs, we found a shipping carton in my room.

A note inside from Lottie read, "I was listed as executor on your dad's estate when your mom died. I closed his accounts and emptied his safe deposit box. But I found another stash of his papers in an old filing cabinet."

She'd filled the box with financial documents, letters to banks asking for money to underwrite spec log homes, and replies refusing to lend him a cent. There were threats to foreclose on our house and land. And a promissory note signed by Dad and by a man named Aleksey Dorokhov, listing our property and home as collateral. The agreement was for "$100,000, due six months." A paper scrap mixed in with the legal documents listed a phone number—the one that called our house the day of Mom's murder.

I said, "I'll bet Dorokhov is from one of the Russian crime families we've read about."

"Crazy of your dad to borrow from those people." Nina said. It sounded like she was judging him, but I shrugged it off. I tried the B.C. number. Got an error message. Phoned newspapers in Vancouver, British Columbia, the *Seattle Times,* and the reference librarian at Bellingham University. None of them reported having anything on Dorokhov.

"I'll keep checking the papers in the box," Nina said. "Go for a walk and unwind. Try to be patient. We're close to finding your dad."

On an envelope from Mary Sue Brasher addressed to Charlotte Purdue, Lottie had written, "This arrived in my mailbox." A Bellingham hospital name was printed on the envelope. I stuffed it into my jeans pocket to read later and headed downstairs.

In the lobby, I found a house phone in an alcove and had the hotel operator call Lottie's number so I could thank her for the package.

A man answered. "Detective Lansky, Bellingham Police Department."

I went cold. "My name is Charlotte Purdue. I'm calling to speak to my grandmother."

"That's not possible. We've been trying to reach you to arrange an interview. If you come to the department, I can answer your questions."

"I'm out of state. Is my grandma hurt?"

"I regret I can't give out information without

identifying you in person. It will help if you come here as soon as possible."

My mind raced. A detective wouldn't be at Lottie's house...unless she was dead. Which meant I was as guilty as whoever murdered Mom and Prescott and Shanahan.

The phone fell, and I collapsed, squeezed my eyes shut, and curled into a fetal position.

"Is your name Charlotte Purdue?" a woman asked. When I opened my eyes the desk clerk was kneeling beside me, saying. "Are you all right?"

I lay still. She hung up the lobby phone, helped me to a chair, and felt my forehead. "You're feverish. I'll get a doctor."

"Please don't. I'm okay."

"Your party said to call again when you feel better." She headed toward the reception desk.

Hands trembling, I rose, stumbled to the phone, and gave the operator Lottie's number.

When the detective answered, I said, "You have to tell me what happened to my grandma."

"I'm sorry, miss, I can't."

"Did you find papers with Russian writing in her house?"

"I can't discuss that, Miss Purdue. I need your address. Where are you?"

"Hiding. Someone's killing everyone in my family." I hung up.

I placed a call to the *Skagit Valley Herald,* identified myself, and spoke to a reporter who had returned from Lottie's house. She said the place had been trashed. The *Herald* viewed it as a robbery/homicide. I rang my room and told Nina about

Lottie.

"My God," she said. "I'll come right down."

"I need time alone. When you're finished with the papers, put them in the hotel safe and be on the alert when you leave the room."

Outside, a hot wind was blowing through town. I wandered, letting gusts sting my face and arms with flying sand. I did my best not to think about the grandmother I'd never see again. Still, with each step, memories rushed into my mind—dinners Lottie had cooked for us to share; evenings together on the couch, eating popcorn and screening movies; and her efforts to support me no matter how misguided or bratty I acted.

Compared to Lottie's murder, my mission to find Dad seemed trivial, a personal quest to satisfy my curiosity or settle an old score. I was on the point of heading for Bellingham to help the detective when Jake waved to me from a window table in a restaurant across from the hotel.

Lottie's death offered a perfect excuse to return the micro-recorder and cancel my deal with Kiki. But if I quit, I'd reduce my chances to get justice for Lottie. And what if the secret Kiki had promised could help me save Dad's life?

Jake beckoned again.

I put the micro-device on record, slid it inside my bra, and entered the restaurant.

As I approached Jake's table, his scarred lips curved into a smile. He opened a tin of mints and held it out.

I shook my head.

He popped two in his mouth and chewed. "Crazy doing that mine car ride, but a gutsy performance." He drank from his coffee cup. "Why aren't they working your butt off to prep for the shoot tonight?"

"How come you're not eating at the hotel with the crew?"

"I get tired of people."

A waitress came to the table. "Our special is short ribs, candied yams, and green beans. The soup is chicken tortilla."

Jake ordered the ribs.

Stomach knotting, I stuck with water. "Della told me about your decision to avoid being a victim and to concentrate on the positive parts of your life."

"You beat the demons, or they beat you."

"How did you beat yours?"

"You're asking about this?" He touched his scarred jaw.

"To help me deal with my own dark days." The lie made my cheeks go hot.

Jake said, "I worked on the crew of a sixty-foot ketch, sailing the Caribbean in a storm. The electrical system shorted out, and I went below to fix it. Tripped, and knocked a half-open can of paint thinner onto a sparking wire. The boat went up in a flash. We put it out, but the fire messed me up. I had an amazing doc in Mexico. After his cosmetic surgery and skin grafts, I was able to work again."

He described being hired by a blasting company in Colorado because he took chances no one else would. Said he ran into a film crew that needed spectacular explosions and became their special effects man.

As he talked about connections with friends and satisfying days on the job, I bristled. "You're describing life like a pleasant amusement park ride. It's a minefield, ready to blow us up any second."

"I considered ending mine more than once—downing a bottle of barbiturates, jumping off a bridge, or eating the barrel of a 12 gauge. Until I went to a Fourth of July parade. The wheelchair vets with no arms or legs gave me a new perspective."

He studied me with such intensity I was sure he knew I was recording him. He smiled, which made me feel worse.

I excused myself and left, with enough recorded material to satisfy Kiki, and wandered toward the hotel, feeling weak and small.

****

I tried to shove my guilt to the background by going to the Ford repair bay and playing fetch with Royal. I found Dominick and asked him to help me edit a less damaging version of Jake's comments.

"I don't have time now," he said. "My boom man's back is out. If you want to pinch hit for him, we can do it between takes tonight."

In the Ford showroom, I ran into Nina. She hugged me. "I'm so sorry about your grandmother. Mine is in the hospital. I'm going to town to find a gift for her. After, I'll hitch a ride to the set."

I caught a van and arrived at the set at dusk. Dominick gave me a belt pouch with adhesive tape, a box cutter, black and red Sharpies, and a penlight. "Using the boom microphone might be tough for you," he said. "Put radio mics on Della, Brett, and Carmen."

As darkness settled in, the camera assistants mounted a dolly on tracks while art department people dressed store windows, and grips set black flags to mask unwanted flare.

Dale did light readings, ordered adjustments, and told the AD, "Camera's ready."

I struggled to keep my mind off Lottie as we shot takes with the three principals. During pauses, Dominick helped me transfer some of Jake's dialogue onto a micro cassette in a second recorder.

****

When Ivan broke the crew for dinner, I took the recorder and edited cassette to Kiki at a catering table where she sat bundled in a cardigan, reading the *New York Times*.

She listened to a few seconds of my edit and slid the cassette and recorder into her purse. "As promised, *Bubeleh*—you ought to know a bit of Yiddish—here's your reward." She leaned close. "I located an eighty-year-old producer who knew Zolton Baron. Had a fistfight with him over a cut of their movie—knocked out two of his front teeth. The word was Baron had died. This fall at a bar mitzvah in Long Beach he came across a guy who had Zolton's voice and new bridgework in front. His beard had been shaved and he had scars from recent cosmetic surgery on his nose and face. Zollie was calling himself Ivan Shervek."

"That's our Ivan?

"Down to his chintzy soul."

"Why the cosmetic surgery?"

"He'd been stiffing a few creditors."

While the crew ate dinner, I returned to Dominick's sound cart and picked up a spare radio mic, a wireless transmitter, and a couple of batteries. I knocked on Ivan's trailer door and went inside.

From the bathroom came the sound of a mechanical toilet and Ivan grumbling, "Nothing works on this goddamn production." He came out, carrying the shooting script, and pointed to the door. "No time. I'm busy."

"I have to replace your wireless battery." When I stepped behind him, I made out recent surgery scars by his ears. I pretended to fiddle with the receiver clipped to his belt, taped the transmitter to it, and ran the mic cord up under his shirt, explaining that Dominick needed to try a new antenna. I finished, got halfway out the door, and turned around. "Tell me if my father is alive and on this crew."

"Tell me which film's going to win the Oscar for best picture. Who do you think I am, Ivan the Omniscient?"

"You were Zolton Baron when you went hunting with my dad in Washington and when you produced *Dead Girls Don't Lie* last summer."

"No idea what you're talking about."

"I bet you owe back taxes, plus penalties and interest from your old productions. Maybe a few of your creditors are still looking to collect. So, if you want to play dumb, we can let them all decide."

A vein on his temple pulsed. "I have a scene to shoot."

"My dad's real name was Jefferson Purdue. Called himself Alec Hudson when you hired him to throw the blonde off the roof in *Dead Girls*."

"If working here is too stressful, you should go home."

"A killer murdered my grandma there yesterday. Someone's keeping track of me and trying to kill my dad. Going home's not an option."

Knocking rattled the trailer door. The AD

announced, "We're up in five."

Ivan ushered me out. "Terrible about your grandmother. As people have told you, your father passed. Nothing we can do about that now." The party line from everyone except Dale and Della.

As I approached Brett's motor home to tell him the news about Ivan, a woman moaned inside.

I knocked. "Five minutes."

The moaning stopped. The door opened, and Brett peered out.

I said, "Glad to hear you're having fun."

"As if that were your business."

I expected to see Bonnie with him. Instead, in shadow behind his naked shoulder, Carmen was wriggling into a red tank top. Brett went for women who gave him a hard time.

As he buttoned his shirt, I leaned close and whispered, "Ivan was the producer on *Dead Girls*. He faked his death sometime in the last six months. I told him I knew what he'd done. And, in case you're interested, some maniac murdered my grandmother."

"How awful. We'll talk during my first break."

I taped a wireless mic on his chest under his shirt, plus a transmitter on his back. I put similar gear on Carmen and followed her into a waiting van. Brett climbed in along with Doreen and a hair stylist.

Nina ran toward us, waving. I made a space for her. She got in, and the van pulled out. We passed Kiki standing by the steps of the mining town's general store, her cameraman videotaping Jake with a small camera.

Shoulders hunched, Jake sat on a chair, staring at the ground.

Nina nudged me. "I'd love to hear what he's telling her."

I closed my eyes, ashamed to recall my betrayal of Jake wasn't my first. In various ways, I'd let both Mom and Lottie down.

Chapter 42

The van let us out near a pile of tailings at the mine entrance. The electricians had laid heavy cables from a humming generator into the tunnel. Grips carried in a small camera dolly and sections of aluminum track.

When another van arrived and Della climbed out, I put a mic on her.

I headed into the tunnel with Nina, following hand-printed signs indicating the way to the set. The exterior light fell away, and we walked in darkness except for occasional ceiling bulbs. The warming temperature, narrowing tunnel, and foul-smelling air tried to drag me to our hallway in Concrete. To stay in the present, I reminded myself that Dominick depended on me to fill in for his boom man, and that Ivan's microphone might reveal something.

We passed a battered arc light—no bulb, two sticks of carbon meant to glow white hot under heavy current. It was discarded equipment from the *Gold Mine Murders* shoot.

After walking several hundred feet, we entered a chamber the size of my English lecture hall at the U. Pieces of equipment lay stacked around the perimeter, between openings to three side tunnels.

Electricians, their T-shirts and cargo shorts soaked with sweat, adjusted lights on stands while grips placed the miniature camera dolly on its narrow track amid a cloud of dust motes, swarming like insects.

Carmen, her breasts on display in the V of her top, sat on a high folding chair. Perched on a second chair, Della wore her Kelly-green shirt, jeans, and cowboy boots. Hair and makeup people did finishing touches on them.

Two women from wardrobe adjusted the zombies' bloody, torn costumes—a police uniform, farm overalls, a tuxedo, and a prom dress.

Jake arrived and looked my way, his face expressionless. I was sure he knew I was responsible for Kiki publicizing details of his life. Wishing he'd scowl at me instead, I retreated to the sound cart where Dominick was patching cables into his mixer.

More zombies in bloody, shredded clothing followed an AD into the chamber, their wide vacant eyes and bared teeth iridescent in the semi-darkness. We were about to shoot the scene preceding their attack on Brett, Della, and me at the surface—the setup for my ride across the trestle.

I stayed close to Nina, scanning the dark chamber for the phony PI but I was distracted by the zombies staggering and groaning as the First AD rehearsed them. Actors mocking the idea of death while my grandma lay cold and lifeless in the Bellingham morgue put a chill in my heart.

The curvaceous zombie with spiky orange hair, Annie's replacement, sidled up to Brett and pressed against him. He nuzzled her neck. He'd been intimate with Carmen minutes earlier. Now, five feet from her, he was flirting with someone else. The guy was hopeless.

I couldn't see the female zombie's face, but as I

passed close to her, I detected citrus-tinged perfume. Brett and the woman locked arms and wound their way through the crew.

I returned to Nina, shaking my head.

She said, "He'll come back to you."

"Who cares?"

The AD shouted, "First position." Della, Carmen, and the zombies took their places. He scanned the crew. "Where's Brett?"

I said, "He was talking to a zombie with orange hair a few moments ago. They headed that way." I pointed.

Karen and the ADs hurried around the dark chamber, looking behind piles of equipment.

A garbled transmission from Ivan's walkie-talkie crackled over my earphones. A male voice, echoey as if coming from an enclosed space, said, "Ivan, listen up. We—"

"Who's that?" Ivan broke in over the mic I'd placed on him. No one else reacted. His walkie-talkie must have been working on another channel.

"Give me the name of the man you hired last spring for a small part," the voice said with a foreign accent.

"I don't know—"

"Came here from the state of Washington. Tell me who and where he is, or your male star won't finish the movie."

Sex-obsessed and juvenile, Brett was impossible in lots of ways, but I ached, thinking I might not see him again. At least the killers had no better idea than I about Dad's name or appearance.

I glanced at Dominick who had removed his

earphones and wouldn't have heard the walkie-talkie conversation. Nina pulled off one side of mine. "What's going on?"

"Some thug's telling Ivan he has Brett."

The walkie-talkie voice crackled again. "What name does the guy use?"

"I knew him as Alec Hudson," Ivan said, "but he's been dead for months."

"Bullshit. His daughter followed him here."

"She's working on out-of-date information. I haven't seen Hudson since the *Dead Girls* shoot."

"You have twenty-four hours to come up with a better answer, or your movie is finished. We'll contact you tomorrow morning. If you call the authorities, Winner gets carved up and served to the coyotes." The walkie-talkie crackled and went silent.

I repeated the conversation to Nina. She said, "If we hurry to the mine entrance, we can catch them."

Flustered, I answered, "You go ahead. I want to look around."

Nina grabbed my arm. "They'll have to leave through the tunnel. Come on."

Ivan shouted, "We're shut down until we find Brett. Anyone who isn't wrapping equipment, leave."

Assistant directors ushered me and Nina and various crew members along the tunnel toward the outside. While we walked, I thought about the echoey voice quality of the man on the radio, slipped away from the group, and returned to the set. Radio transmissions couldn't have carried from outside the mine, so the logical places to explore were dark, claustrophobic tunnels. Perfect terrain for one of my PTSD disasters.

While Karen, Ivan, and the remaining crew members searched the chamber, an AD escorted Della and Doreen toward the entrance along with a few zombies. None with spiky, orange hair.

I skirted the cavern perimeter but found no sign of Brett. I hoped I would not detect the zombie's citrus perfume at the side tunnels and could join Nina outside. There was none at the first tunnel and none at the second. But when I approached the gate in front of the third, I sniffed citrus. Heart racing, I pushed through the gate and leaned over a vertical shaft beyond it. Faint air currents whistled below. I knew there was arsenic in old mines. Was toxic air waiting for me?

I stepped onto the top rung of a ladder leading down. The rotted wood crunched, but I descended to the second rung, then the next. My breathing grew shallower with each one, and the sound beneath me lower in pitch—less like moving air than flowing water.

If I fall into an underground river, I'll drown, but if I tell Ivan Brett might be down there, he'll say it's teen girl nonsense and send me to base camp.

A few more rungs, and darkness swallowed me. I pulled the small flashlight from Dominick's tool kit and aimed it down. Dust swirled in the beam. Even if I managed to catch up with the kidnappers, I'd have no gun. Dad's .45 was in my room, my only weapon a box cutter.

I held the flashlight in my teeth, gripped the ladder with both hands, and descended another rung. It gave way, and I slammed against the wall. The light fell and glowed beneath layers of dust.

A dozen more rungs, and I stepped onto a rocky surface and retrieved my flashlight. I shined the beam at an opening in the rock and passed through it into a tunnel with narrow car tracks leading to the right. Beside the tracks, a shallow stream flowed.

A few steps and I found a balled-up tissue smelling of citrus. I walked on, illuminating my way with short flashes from my penlight.

Hot, humid air washed over me, and beads of sweat ran down my face, joined by drips from the ceiling rocks.

When a faint voice echoed in the darkness ahead, I quickened my pace. The stream shrank to a trickle, then became dry gravel. Vibrations under my tennies grew stronger. I ignored them and rushed on.

A loud crunch, and the ground gave way. I tried to grab a mine rail but missed it and plunged into an icy current. As it swept me away, I clawed at the channel wall but found no place to grip.

I gulped metallic-tasting water and spit it out. A faint light glowed ahead, reflecting off the surface. I arrived beneath an opening and glimpsed a figure above.

"Help," I yelled, but water filled my mouth and covered my cry. The figure moved on.

Another light glowed ahead. I floated to a spot beneath it and clasped a rock. "Help," I yelled again.

Footsteps approached, but my fingers lost their grip, and the current snatched me away.

When my feet bumped into a split rock, I wedged one leg between its two halves. Footsteps thumped above and passed on. A light shimmered on ripples fifteen yards ahead. I tried to move, but the rocks wedged my leg like a vise.

"I'm here," I yelled, but got no answer. I strained

to pull my leg free. It stuck fast. "River," I shouted, "you can't drown me. I'm a girl from Concrete. Tougher than some stupid rock."

A light moved toward me under the water. Something broke the surface in the darkness and splashed my face. "Please," I yelled, "don't kill me."

"Shush," said a voice. The rock pinning my leg shifted. Strong hands supported me as the current carried us onward. When we approached the next hole, the hands raised me toward it. I climbed up and out onto the mine track.

The man, his features hidden in darkness, joined me.

I asked, "Who are—"

"Follow me," he murmured. I stepped forward. My leg buckled. Callused fingers gripped my hand, and an arm wrapped around my waist.

My wet tennies sloshing, I limped on my bruised leg, the man half-carrying me with such deftness we made only a faint shuffling noise. I whispered, "A radio message from one of the gangsters said if Ivan doesn't reveal Alec Hudson's identity, they'll kill Brett."

"Shhhh."

We rounded a bend. A hundred feet ahead, four figures walked away silhouetted by the light of a swaying electric lantern. The curvy female zombie, who'd replaced Annie, had removed her orange wig to reveal blonde hair pinned in a bun to her head. The second figure had a thick moustache, a broad chest, and bandy legs. The third, a beanpole of a man, held Brett's taped wrists behind his back.

"I have to rest," Brett moaned.

"Keep going," the big guy said.

Brett moaned louder, and the trio halted.

When the heavy guy turned to Brett, the lantern swung sideways and cast a faint glow on my arms and hands and on my rescuer's face—a mass of scars and gelatin-like skin. Jake.

I was dying to pull him aside and question him, but he pressed me against the wall and whispered, "Stay here when I attack."

"If you do, won't they shoot?"

"Let's hope they know wild shots will bring down the overhead rocks."

For a moment the three figures turned away as if they hadn't seen us.

All three drew weapons—two handguns and a machete—and they charged, the heavy guy in the lead. Jake chopped his throat with the side of his hand and dropped him. He put the thin guy down with two blows to his head and turned to the female racing at him. She was shouting in Russian and swinging a machete like an Amazon warrior. I feared she'd sever Jake's arm, but he dodged her blade, karate-kicked her temple, and she collapsed.

I raced to Brett and freed his hands with my box cutter.

Jake checked the men. "These two are out for a while." He ripped open the muscular man's shirt and stared with such fierceness I expected him to tear the skin from the guy's chest. The tattoo across it was a winged skull.

"It stands for Bop," Jake said. "Cyrillic for VOR. He's a made man in the Russian Mafia."

Mom's blood drawings flashed in my mind, three crude versions of the "bop" she'd seen on her attacker's chest.

"Why are the Russians after you?" I asked, surer by the second that Jake was my father. "Did you inform on them? Was that what caused this feud?"

"I did what I had to."

Gunshots boomed. A barrage from the prostrate female zombie's pistol zinged by us and slammed into the rocks above.

Jake/Dad, Brett, and I stumbled back as a cascade of boulders crushed the female and blocked our route to the tunnel and shaft leading to the movie set.

Chapter 43

As dust eddied around us, men's voices drifted from beyond the rock pile.

Brett said, "Jake, you were amazing. I never moved that fast in any of my action roles."

I grabbed a rock from the pile.

"Stop," Dad said. "No point in clearing the rubble to greet those guys. They're not on our side."

Brett pointed to the tunnel opening ahead of us. "My kidnappers said something about a back way out."

I grabbed a flashlight from one of the unconscious Russians and hobbled as fast as I could along the tunnel, Dad and Brett behind me. We arrived at a debris pile, pushed through a side opening, and hurried on a path slanting upward.

After a brief climb, we came to a level stretch. Eager to cut short my time in the claustrophobic space, I rushed ahead, turned a corner, and plunged forward into blackness.

A hand grabbed me. "Careful," Brett said, pulling me back.

Dad took the flashlight and aimed it ahead, illuminating a vertical rock face five feet beyond a deep crevasse. The top of the opposite wall stood a yard above our feet, too far and high to reach by jumping.

Shouts in Russian echoed from behind us. Dad shined the light at a six-inch ledge on the far wall at foot level. "I'll step onto that," he said, "and help you two over." He extended his leg, planted his boot on the narrow ledge, and straddled the gap. Bits of rock broke free and pinged against the walls as they fell.

"Hold my hand and jump," he said.

"We won't be able to pull you across."

"Do it."

I seized his hand and leaped toward the narrow ledge, landed off balance, and yelped in pain. Dad steadied me while I hauled my butt onto the flat surface above.

Brett came next and clambered up beside me.

From a distance, came faint thuds of rocks being tossed around and voices arguing in Russian. Dad attempted to transfer his weight to our side but couldn't bring his body across the gap.

Again and again, he tried, his legs shaking more each time.

I stretched flat on the upper ledge and extended my hand.

He said, "My weight would drag you down."

"I'll take that chance."

"No."

"Those guys will kill you."

"Leave."

"Not without you."

Dad made a final lunge. He tottered, arms windmilling. Brett and I each grabbed a wrist. Straining and grunting, we hoisted him up to a spot between us.

I said, "I have a few questions."

"Not now."

Shouts from the far side of the crevasse grew louder.

Bullets zinged past us and broke chips from nearby rocks.

Dad grabbed the flashlight and headed off through a tight passageway. I followed, Brett behind me. Fifty yards later, we squeezed through a slim opening into a sea of cool night air. Millions of stars glimmered in the black sky. Toward the horizon, headlights inched along like luminescent snails between ranch house windows, glowing in the hills.

We emerged on the side of the mountain opposite the mine entrance and struck off on a trail circling the peak. Before we'd gone a hundred yards, shouts issued from the tunnel opening behind us.

I tugged Dad's sleeve. "Where's the limp in your left leg?"

"A surgeon fixed it."

"I have to know why you never contacted me."

Brett pushed close to Dad. "You're Charlie's father? The actor who threw the blonde off the roof in *Dead Girls?*"

Dad veered into a gully leading down. Stumbling over rocks, we descended to the dark parking lot, where a dozen crew people were loading trucks.

I said, "We should stay out of sight so no one will see either of you."

Dad said, "My only chance to survive is to convince the Russians I'm dead."

Actors in zombie costumes and facial prosthetics milled around the makeup trailer. I grasped Brett's arm. "Those zombies give me an idea, but we're all going to have to be on board for it."

"I'm not sure. I bet your dad manhandled my mom on the roof before she ran down. Injured her so she had a hard time escaping the burning taxi."

Dad said, "Stunt people on the roof made sure everything was safe up there."

Two wardrobe assistants headed our way. We ducked behind the humming diesel generator and waited for them to pass.

Brett whispered, "On the VHS, my mom stumbled while she was running from the burning taxi. Did the fire cripple her?"

"Your mom never got into the taxi. A stunt woman did."

A shot ricocheted off a truck across the lot. The two crew women sprinted to a car and drove off. On the mountain, lights moved along the trail we'd traveled and headed toward the gully. Dad led us between two trucks.

Brett grabbed his arm. "I want the full story."

Dad said, "The stunt woman got out fine, and we were about to do the shot of your mom running away. Somehow her apron caught fire."

"I don't believe it."

"Word of honor. The flames spread from her apron to her dress."

"Didn't anyone put them out?"

"The stunt crew was right there with firefighting gear, but your mom panicked and raced around the set, screaming."

"Why didn't someone stop her?"

"Everyone did their best."

Flashlight beams moved along the ridge and down the gully we had descended. Dad hurried ahead.

Brett pulled him to a stop. "How can I be so dense? You caught my mom and carried her back so the crew could put out the flames. That's how…" He raised a hand toward Dad's face.

Dad said, "Doesn't matter."

But it did to me. I pictured him hugging the woman as her flames spread to his clothes and scorched his face and hands. Love welled in my chest. I reached out to embrace him.

He tugged my hand. "We have to keep moving."

Brett bent forward. I feared he might bail on us, but after a deep inhale, he stood up. "What's your idea, Charlie?"

"If our special effects people can make zombies out of actors, they could turn my dad into a replica of himself before the fire. That's how the Russians remember him. We can make it look like he dies again."

Brett said, "Russians might be hiding in our makeup crew. My friend Esteban in LA is the perfect guy to help us. He created a terrific vampire appliance for me last year."

The First AD stepped from behind Della's motor home and shined a flashlight around the parking lot. We ducked into the shadows. As the AD got into a car and drove away, a half dozen dark figures emerged from the gully behind us.

Brett led us to his BMW at the edge of the lot and pointed to a young man asleep in the front seat. "He's my driver. Keep quiet about our plan." He roused the guy, and we pushed the car, lights off, onto the road leading downhill and jumped in.

****

When we arrived at the hotel about one a.m., Brett called reception from a phone booth in the lobby and left a message for Ivan, saying he would be gone overnight.

I pulled out the letter Lottie had forwarded. Soggy from my time in the water, it was in pencil and printed in a child-like hand.

"Dear Charlie," it read, "you'll laugh after the way I criticized your dad. The joke's on me. I've ended up in a hospital. Maybe you'll say I'm nuts, but I'm sure a guy put something in my coffee. He approached me in the dining hall and was charming while we chatted. Half an hour later, I went nuts. I didn't find out his name, but I remember seeing him talking to your friend the day before you left. Are you sure you can trust her? All the best, Mary Sue."

As I returned from the repair bay after checking on Royal, a figure loomed out of the darkness. I stumbled.

Nina stopped my fall. "Looks like you've been swimming."

"I went as far into the tunnels as I dared. An explosion rocked the walls. I fell into an underground stream and got out of the mine fast."

"Did you find Brett and your dad?"

I hated not telling Nina about Dad and the Russians, but since he had kept his identity secret, I wanted his permission before I told her anything. She might slip and let one of the Russians know we'd found him.

Nina said, "Lots of crew people were out searching. I scoured the town but struck out." She folded her arms across her chest. "I feel so useless."

"You're an inspiration, always smart and loyal. But keep your eyes open. The PI and his pals are desperate. They might grab you."

"This production is such a cauldron of intrigues. I don't know who to be suspicious of."

"Speaking of suspicions, here are a couple." I handed Nina the letter.

She read it. "Sounds like she panicked and tried marijuana, LSD, or something stronger. I'm not sure what she means about me talking to a strange guy. You know how friendly I am with everyone."

"Does it bother you I didn't throw this away as soon as I read it?"

"I'm glad you have a friend as concerned for your safety as Mary Sue."

I wouldn't have been so gracious, and I decided Nina and I were not as alike as I'd imagined. While she headed to the bar for a drink, I went to my room, showered, and changed. I slid the loaded magazine into Dad's .45 and put it in my purse along with his old driver's license. I added the blowups of the two blondes, the one of my father peeking into frame, plus the Vietnam War shot with his buddies. I left a note in the room, telling Nina I had received an emergency call to help a crew member hurt in the mine. I hated lying to my best friend and couldn't wait for Dad's plan to be over.

Chapter 44

Five minutes after Adolfo, Brett, Jake, and I started toward LA in the company BMW I said, "Dad, did you call Lottie's house after you left, but never speak when we picked up?"

"I wanted to talk to you but feared having the Russians listen in to my call or figure out I had phoned. They'd have abducted you to draw me into the open. How often did those calls come?"

"Once at our Concrete house, once at Lottie's, at college, and again at the hotel in Barstow."

"Any idea who called?"

I shook my head. "Why didn't you apply for witness protection for us?"

"Law enforcement had me on the books as your mom's killer. I found out the Mafia stole a knife with my prints, smeared it with her blood, and left it in the neighborhood for the police to find. The FBI would have insisted I stand trial for your mom's murder first, and I had no way to guarantee the feds would look out for you. Besides, in witness protection you wouldn't have been able to see your grandma again. She'd have resisted leaving her church and friends behind. My best bet, and yours I was sure, lay in staying dead until I could connect with you in a safe way. Not your fault, your mom's death, or my leaving."

I stiffened. "I know."

"Sometimes kids blame themselves for family problems."

"I don't need your amateur psychobabble. I had more than my share of it after Mom died and you walked away."

"That's on me."

Brett asked, "Why didn't you take Charlie with you?"

"That would have clued in the Russians I was alive. They'd have searched until they found us both."

I said, "I'm guessing you satisfied your original mortgages with money from the Russians. Why didn't they beat you to a pulp when you were late with your payments? Why start a homicidal vendetta?"

"Dorokhov, the family boss, sent some goons when I got behind. I told them I'd pay, but they started to knock me around. After a couple of their punches, my mind was back in 'Nam. I lost control, killed one, and beat the other unconscious. In their car trunk I found papers and a small black book with their family's secret information. I revived the guy I'd knocked out, told him to inform his boss I needed more time, and sent him on his way. "

I said, "That sounds as dumb as the plot of our movie."

****

Sometime after three a.m., we drove down a tree-lined street in Silverlake, a neighborhood north of Sunset Boulevard not far from Dodger Stadium. We parked in front of a Craftsman house with dormers, and shingles cut in curves and triangles. Weeping willow branches hung over the front porch, and a sprinkler click-clacked spray across a brown lawn.

The door opened. A broad-shouldered man, with muscular arms and a tuft of hair peeking from the front of his Hawaiian shirt stepped into the glow of the porch light. He had long hair streaked with gray and a grin creasing a brown face with warm eyes.

Brett said, "Great to see you, Esteban."

Dad held out his hand. "I met you on a quick shoot this fall."

They shook, and Esteban led us to his home studio at the rear of the lot. Inside, two beauty parlor chairs faced a bank of mirrors and shelves filled with jars of makeup, hairpieces, containers of powdered plastic, dyes, and tubes of colored liquid. Plus, an assortment of tools and brushes.

Esteban sat my father in a chair. He used a magnifying glass to study Dad's license photo and the blowup print of him in *Dead Girls*. He poured a cup of coffee and sipped as he made sketches of Dad from front, side, and three-quarter angles.

I showed him the Vietnam photo of Dad in his twenties and asked, "Can you make him look like this?"

"I'll use clay and latex to build replicas of his original chin, nose, cheekbones, and ears. We'll glue those to the mask of his head. Don't worry. I've fooled lots of movie audiences."

I said, "Dad, I've got more questions. Would you rather wait until we're alone to answer?"

"I suspect Esteban has heard people's scariest secrets from his makeup chair."

"In one ear and out the other," Esteban said. "I worked on an ex-hit man. You'd be shocked at the stories he told."

I said, "Okay, my first question is, how did your

315

truck and mutilated body end up in the river when you were still alive?"

Esteban smeared plastic material over Dad's head, leaving openings for his nose, eyes, and mouth.

Dad said, "Not long after you left for school, I went to work. Got a call in my trailer-office from your mom as the killer burst into the bathroom. I raced home. Found her dead. A motorcycle roared away through the woods. I followed the sound to my building site. As I arrived, a guy rushed out of my trailer and headed into the woods on the bike."

While Esteban applied plastic material, Dad said, "I started toward our house, met you on the way, and went home. Found a thug ransacking the living room, looking for his crime family's black book. He made a run for it. I caught up and snuffed him. Hauled his body and bike away in my truck, altered his features, and put my dog tags on him. I dumped his bike and body into the river and pushed my truck in after."

Brett cringed. "Altered his features?"

"Got rid of dental and fingerprint-matching possibilities. I had to fool the Russians."

****

When the material on Dad's face set up, Esteban applied a plaster cast on top of the gel and made a latex mask to go over Dad's skull.

I said, "Tell the truth. Did you have an affair with Della, or should I call her Hannah?"

"I wasn't the best husband, but I didn't cheat on your mom. Hannah and I were friends. When I called her, broke and desperate, she convinced Ivan to give me a job. I wanted to work behind the camera, but they had lost an actor and insisted I take his part. A low-budget film and my small role seemed a decent place to hide as long as I kept my face in shadow and turned away from the camera as much as possible."

"Did Ivan know about your Russian connections?"

Dad nodded.

Esteban put a hand on his head. "Hold still."

Dad said, "I owed him the truth about the risk I posed. Hannah said he'd dealt with tough guys and understood what it was like to get behind paying them."

While Esteban molded facial features matching Dad's youthful ones, I asked, "How did the Russians know I'd come looking for you?" I described the geek/priest/phony PI. "Have other Mafia people had their eyes on me since I was in grade school?"

"No doubt." Dad stared into my eyes. "Did you believe I'd slit your mom's throat?"

"I was a high school girl, and you left me with blood on your shirt and a half-assed explanation. What did you expect me to think?"

"I understand."

"Our AB and O blood types mean it's impossible for me to be your biological daughter. Why didn't you tell me?"

"I wanted to but I knew it was a strange thing we'd done and I feared if I leveled, I'd lose the connection with you I loved."

"So, was I some prostitute's baby your Russian financier was getting rid of?"

Brett and Esteban exchanged a look.

Dad said, "Before we adopted you, we tried over and over to have a child. The miscarriages devastated your mom. A contractor friend said a Canadian named Dorokhov lent money and sometimes knew of babies needing parents. I mentioned our desire to have a child when I went to meet him about financing my cabins. You were a couple of months old, his daughter by a woman he loved, but not his legal wife. You seemed to stare right into my heart, gurgled, grabbed my finger, and wouldn't let go."

"And you said, 'Wrap her up. She'll look perfect next to our TV.' "

"I signed the loan papers, took Dorokhov's envelope of cash, and went home. He called a month later, said all hell had broken out between his 'wives,' as he called them. He worried harm would come to you and asked if I would adopt you. He'd arrange the papers. You'd captivated me with those big brown eyes. I couldn't say no."

"You're saying my gurgles and entrancing eyes were to blame for you adopting me and for some goon killing Mom?"

Dad touched my face with his scarred fingers. "If I'd turned down his offer, who knew what would have happened to you?"

Another excuse; you have a million of them. "Lottie's dead," I said, my words clipped and cold. "The detective wouldn't give me details when I called her house. A *Skagit Valley Herald* reporter claims she was murdered."

Dad slumped. His eyes went flat behind the cosmetic mask. Head wrapped up, he reminded me of the Invisible Man in the movie of the same name. I suspected if I unwrapped Dad, he would be as invisible as the movie character.

He said, "If I hadn't been obsessed with building those fancy log houses, I wouldn't have had to borrow from the Russians, and your mom would be alive. I screwed up big time. In your place, I wouldn't forgive a father like me. So, I can't ask you to."

"I'd like to blame you for Lottie's death. But my asking her to search for a Russian connection to our family caused it. I'm sure the phony PI killed her."

Dad grasped my hand, his rough fingers as comforting as they had been when he'd saved me from the underground river. I settled beside Brett on a sofa in the corner.

****

I awoke to a rooster crowing in the darkness outside, sat up, and rubbed my eyes. "Did we move to the country?"

"My neighbor's chickens," Esteban said. "He doesn't even share the eggs." He stepped away from Dad and waved his hand like a magician presenting his big finale.

Before me stood the father I joked with the morning the killer murdered Mom. From across the room, Dad's face appeared smooth, his eyebrows, nose, and ears reincarnated in their original shapes. When I stepped close, I could see the new look was fabricated.

"Dad—"

"You like me better this way?"

"The selfish teen-Charlie might. The more grownup me is content knowing you're alive and well. Esteban's illusion works, but how do we use it to trick the Russians into believing they're seeing you die? Special effects bullets?"

"They'd want to examine the body. I'll need to keep my distance. Incinerate myself and leave them nothing to ID."

I cringed. "Incinerate?"

"Think movie magic."

"The Russians won't be easy to fool," Brett said, sitting up, his face lined by the pillow seams he'd slept on. Hair mussed, beard bristly, he looked roguishly handsome.

Dad said, "During your snooze I worked out an idea with Esteban. You two can leave for Barstow. I'll get back on my own. When I show up at the set later today, insult me with all your anger from the past months. Follow me on foot when I drive away but stay fifty yards back."

I wanted to ask questions, but Dad's jaw muscles were tight, his mind made up.

Brett pulled a check from his wallet. "The production pays me more than I'm worth. If you'll permit me, I'd like to cover Esteban's bill." Dad nodded. Brett got Esteban to fill in an amount and signed it.

Dad stayed behind while Brett and I drove toward the desert under a sky changing from grape-juice purple to orange. I kept wondering if our cheap trick had a prayer of fooling the Russians.

Chapter 45

When Brett and I entered the hotel lobby in Barstow, I calculated it was my thirteenth day on the movie. A lucky one? Or a calamity waiting to happen?

Ivan, shirt rumpled and eyes bloodshot, hurried past two sunburned couples in Hawaiian T-shirts and madras shorts. He grabbed Brett's arm. "How did you get free from those goons?"

"Tanya caught them off guard. Together we put them out of commission. She must have taken karate in high school."

"Cut the bullshit. Who helped you?"

"No one," I said. "You didn't give away Alec Hudson's identity, did you?"

"Considered it, but those bastards don't keep their word even if you do what they ask. They'll want an answer this morning."

"Coming right up," I said.

"The investors have threatened to pull the plug unless we start filming."

Brett grinned. "Then, let's shoot this sucker."

Ivan stared at me. "I don't want you confusing Brett today."

When the others left, I said, "You helped my dad when he needed it last spring. Can you do that again?"

"What are you talking about?"

"Production value. If you don't get thrown by

surprises, you'll see something interesting."

I conferred with Della and Dale, with Bob, the gaffer, and with Karen. Thanked them for their loyalty to Dad, told them to expect a surprise, and begged them to play along.

****

Nina had left my room by the time I went up. I showered and changed into clean jeans and a cotton top and slid the loaded .45 inside my jeans in back. I went downstairs and hurried to the phony PI's motel, stood on the sidewalk, and threw pebbles up at his window. I'd point the .45 at his chest and make him tell me if he'd killed Lottie.

A maid stuck her head out of his window. "If you're looking for the man who stayed here last night, he checked out."

I went to the hotel and found Nina asleep on a couch in the lobby. She opened red, puffy eyes and said, "You didn't come back. I was worried."

"My bad." I hugged her. "I spent most of the night at the ER with a friend. I need you on the set today, ears and eyes alert for any suspicious-looking guys."

"Half the guys on this crew look suspicious to me."

"Now you know how I've felt since a killer murdered my mom."

We drove to the set in her rental car. When we arrived, Dominick told me his boom man was laid up and asked me to help him. I put a radio mic on Brett, another on Della.

Loud chugging noises stopped us in the middle of our first scene.

Crew heads whipped around as a '50s vintage Chevy pickup backfired its way onto the set and kept coming, despite the AD's frantic shouts for it to stop.

Ivan played his role, shouting, "Cut. Get that wreck out of here."

Fenders hanging at odd angles, front bumper dragging, the truck halted twenty yards short of the camera. The driver's door opened, and Dad stepped out, looking like he had before he'd been burned.

Della gasped and pressed her hand to her mouth.

Nina tapped my shoulder. "Who is he?"

I walked toward the pickup, shading my eyes. "That bastard is my father."

Ivan started toward Dad.

"Take it easy, Mr. Director," Dad said. "I came to talk with Tanya."

I said, "You're too late."

Ivan signaled to Dale, twirling his forefinger.

Dale grabbed a hand-held camera and swung it toward Dad and me.

Dominick did the same with his shotgun mic.

I said, "I guess you're here to finish me off now you've killed Mom and Grandma Lottie."

"I didn't kill your grandma or your mother."

"Why did you run away?"

He pulled a small black book from his shirt pocket. "Got a couple hundred reasons in here. The mob's secret deals. You want me to give it to them?"

Crew members glanced between me and Dad.

Nina whispered, "What's he talking about?"

Dad waved the little book. "If you don't trust me, come take a look."

Nina tugged my arm. "Is he really your father?"

I said to Dad, "The book's a prop. No more real than our zombies."

"Seems you don't care about the truth. Just want to be mad at me."

"Unless you've got something better than a five-and-dime notebook, leave before we call the sheriff. You never even said, 'Sorry for running out on you.' "

"Time to decide." He tapped the Timex he'd worn since my grade school days.

Nina said, "Go look at the book. See if it's real. Give him a chance."

I aimed the .45 at his chest. "Read us a page."

"Don't shoot," a wardrobe woman shouted.

Dad said, "The Russians would have killed me, and you, to keep the items in here secret: their schemes, offshore accounts, and the names of the judges and politicians they bribed." He turned a page. "The first heading is extortion, thirty-five thousand. Second is prostitution, a take of twenty thousand dollars in November 1980 in British Columbia."

I shrugged.

"Seems my information isn't worth much. Me either." He stuffed the notebook in his pocket and got into the Chevy. He gunned the engine, spraying dirt and gravel as he backed off the set.

Nina said, "We have to talk to him." She pulled me with her as she ran after the pickup, now roaring away.

The crew remained motionless, except for Dale, who headed after the Chevy, the hand-held camera on his shoulder, Lori with him, carrying an extra magazine. Dominick followed with his recorder and mic.

Enveloped in a dust cloud, the truck disappeared around a curve.

"Keep filming," Ivan shouted.

A thunderous explosion shook the ground, toppling light stands, breaking vehicle windows, and setting off car alarms.

I shrieked as a smoke cloud mushroomed, carrying brush, rocks, and truck parts a hundred feet in the air. The debris hung motionless a second and started down. Chunks of the truck body, panes of window glass, and wheels crashed twenty yards ahead. Bits of bone and flesh landed around me.

"He used too big a charge," I screamed.

"Too big for what?" Nina said, whirling. Her elbow hit my jaw. I collapsed, and my head slammed on a rock. I groaned.

Nina bent down. "God, I'm so sorry." She pulled me to a sitting position.

The smell of burnt oil, spent gunpowder, and seared flesh made me nauseous. A bone fragment landed on my shoulder.

"Dad, you can't leave again," I moaned, and sank to the ground. Nina tried to raise me, but I pressed my face to the earth, wanting to dissolve into it.

Brett rushed to me, Della and Clint beside him.

"Dad's gone," I cried.

Brett said, "I'm here for whatever you need." He lifted and half-carried me, my feet tripping over each other, toward the set. Nina came with us, clutching my hand.

Chapter 46

A San Bernardino County sheriff's cruiser roared up the canyon road, lights flashing, siren wailing. It maneuvered between chunks of smoking truck debris and skidded to a stop.

Two deputies stepped out, donned trooper hats, and settled their leather belts and holsters into place. The six-foot sheriff scanned the crowd, eyes narrowed as if he'd decided we were all guilty of something. After a brief conversation with Ivan, he sent his deputy our way.

The deputy, in his fifties, adjusted his aviator glasses. "I worked security for a Burt Reynolds shoot years ago. Looks like the film world's as crazy as ever." He unwrapped a yellow plastic roll, and payed out crime scene tape.

I held Brett's arm for support while crew members came by and hugged me.

When the sheriff asked for the person responsible for explosives on the production, Ivan said, "Jake Kinsler."

The sheriff called, "Mr. Kinsler?"

There was no answer.

"Jake Kinsler, are you here?"

Ivan turned to me. I was about to say Jake had gone to town, when a voice said, "Right here." The pre-Esteban Jake, scarred features more gruesome than ever in the midday sun, approached the sheriff. "After the explosion, I went to the far side of base camp to get a piece of gear from my locker. Someone had broken into it."

Nina whispered, "I'm so distressed about your father."

I bit my lip to hide my excitement.

"You need to get your mind off everything here," she said. "Come home to Bellingham with me. We can move into a dorm room together and brighten our place with a colorful rug and a painting or two."

Ivan said, "Tanya, I can't imagine how awful you must feel. The authorities will ask questions and close us down a few days, but I'm determined to finish the movie. It's small comfort, I know, but your mine car shots add exciting footage. If you want to work, call Karen." He patted my arm and headed toward Dale.

"Did I hear my name?" Karen said as she approached, Royal tugging her toward me on a new leash. "Looks like this guy wants to say hello."

I bent to let him lick my face, and said, "Karen, you can't take him to animal control."

"I won't. He keeps me sane."

When Royal turned to Nina, I got ready to pull him away before he started his crotch-smelling routine. She startled and backed away. "I'm sure he's nice, but dogs make me uncomfortable."

Karen laid a hand on my arm. "I'm upset about your dad, and I'm sure you're undone. As soon as the sheriff interviews you, feel free to go to the hotel and start packing to leave for Washington."

Nina asked, "Will he want to talk to me?"

"I imagine," Karen said, "since you were with

Tanya."

Nina glanced toward the sheriff, who stood a few feet away, quizzing Dale. She said, "I'd love to help, but if I'm on record as being connected to whatever crime is going on here, my chance to join the FBI will be gone. I'd better take off."

I said, "You aren't responsible for any of this."

"The FBI doesn't want recruits who've been in the same galaxy with scandal."

"I understand," I said, but I didn't. I couldn't see how she could bail while she thought my dad had been blown up. I sighed. "If you head to the honey wagon, you can sneak away."

While she hurried off, I whispered to Brett, "Ivan's playing along like a pro."

"He'll still talk with Allen tonight about editing the explosion footage with news coverage of your dad's death into a promo to hype the movie."

The AD approached Brett with an envelope. "This arrived earlier by messenger."

Brett ripped open the envelope, glanced at the letter, and walked away with it.

When the sheriff finished interviewing Dad, I went to him.

"I'm lucky," he said. "John Law here seems convinced I had nothing to do with the explosion."

"Why didn't you warn me bits of skin and bone would rain down on us? I thought they were parts of your body."

"If you knew the truth ahead of time, you might have given our scheme away by accident."

"I hate to think what you blew up."

"Beef and pork trimmings. I bought the old Chevy

from Esteban and stopped at his cousin's butcher shop."

"Won't the cops check the bits of flesh on the ground and find out they're not human? Won't the Russians?"

"The cops might, but they may not publicize it. A medic friend of Esteban's drew a pint of my blood. I poured it over the animal meat. Traces will test as mine and confuse a few techs."

"What if the Russians come after you again?"

"We'll blow up that bridge when we get to it." Dad walked away.

The sheriff approached me and offered his condolences. He asked for my name and address. I gave him Tanya Becker and a fictitious street number in Bellingham, hoping to blur my connection to Dad and reduce the chances for the Russians to find him.

The sheriff scribbled in his notebook and said I was free to leave.

I said good-bye to Dale and returned his Polaroid with a bunch more shots I'd taken: Diane Arbus-style portraits of the crew, caught in strange expressions and poses. "Thanks to your artistic advice, I realize having a weird perspective on life isn't so bad."

"How about bringing your weird perspective to my next job, as an apprentice?"

"I'd love to take you up on that down the road, but I have things to deal with first." I kissed his cheek. "Rumor has it some idiotic female rejected you. You'll find a better girlfriend before this movie hits the theaters."

I found Della in her mobile home. "Thanks for helping my father when he came down here." I told her I'd be clearing out and got her address and phone number. "You'll be amazing in this movie," I said. "Your beauty and kindness left Officer Shanahan with a perfect romantic fantasy. And your invitation to him to visit Sunset Vista Productions helped me find Dad." I hugged her.

I searched for Brett and found him sitting on a wooden step by the tavern set, staring at his letter. I tugged the paper. "Good news, I hope."

He didn't look up.

I said, "I'm heading to Bellingham."

He rose. "I need to check with wardrobe about my outfits for the next shooting day, whenever that will be. It's been fun. I hope you enjoy the rest of your time at college."

He patted my shoulder and walked toward the wardrobe trailer.

I stared after him, recalling Dale's warning not to get involved with an actor.

Despite the hot sun, I shivered and put on a sweater I'd slung over my purse. But it didn't ease the chill in my heart from Lottie's death and my part in causing it. If I'd still been keeping score about the risks of going to LA, it would have been Lottie a zillion, Charlie close to zero.

****

Dad and I met in the production office and parted with a handshake. We'd catch up later out of the sight of watchful eyes.

When he headed to the Ford repair bay to check his gear, I went to Karen's office, ready to hear a list of complaints about my screwups during the production. I said, "Thanks for the chance to work on your movie. You must be worried about it."

"We'll get past our troubles."

"And thanks for helping Dad."

"I don't know what you mean," she said, but a hint of a smile told me she did.

Royal rose from a pad behind her desk, stretched, and nuzzled my hand. I hugged him. "I'm going to miss you, boy." I stood up. "I hope things get better on the show. I know I've been trouble for you."

"Didn't believe you could hack it when you first showed up. But you turned out to be tough and smart. If you decide to apply for another film job, have them call me as a reference." She gave me two hundred-dollar bills for the mine car shots. "And here's a bit of production swag." She handed me a black baseball cap with "I survived Zombies from Gold Mountain" embroidered beneath a zombie face with gold eyes and teeth.

She offered me Royal's leash.

I shook my head. "You two are a perfect pair."

"I insist. After all you've been through, you'll need his unconditional love. I'll find another pooch to keep my mind off the yahoos Ivan hires for peanuts. Give this guy a good home in Washington."

"I doubt he'd be allowed on a Greyhound."   ·

"One of our grips plans to drive up in six weeks to hike the Cascades. I'll keep Royal until he can bring him to you."

"Thanks," I said. I tried to feel optimistic, but as I left her office, I imagined the phony PI and the other Russians figuring out our trick and hunting Dad and me down.

Chapter 47

When I arrived in Bellingham two days later, I phoned Detective Lansky from the bus depot. He had me come to the police station.

Minutes after I mentioned his name in reception, a rangy man with a pencil moustache and arms a bit long for his suit jacket entered from a side door. Lansky introduced himself, directed me to an interview room, and turned on a tape recorder.

When he'd announced my name and the date and time into the microphone, I said, "I want to know who killed my grandma. And how."

Lansky gave a pained smile. "We don't know the killer's identity. Hate to say it, but he slit her throat. You can view the body if you want, but you don't have to. Her minister and two members of the congregation ID'd her."

I pictured the PI grinning and balled my fists. "I can tolerate an edited photograph."

Lansky showed me one with the wound blacked out. He questioned me for hours about Lottie, her friends, and her possible enemies, and asked about my activities since I'd left Bellingham.

I expected he would find out why I went to California, so I said I'd gone to search for my dad, adding he'd been killed in an explosion. I hoped if Lansky or any of his investigators went to LA, crew members would confirm that Dad died.

Though I had committed several crimes by not telling Lansky everything, I didn't know another way to handle the situation. If word got out Dad survived, the Russians would keep after him. He and innocent crew members would be tortured or killed.

Lansky said the autopsy and toxicology reports had taken longer than expected, but I could claim Lottie's body. For the moment, her house would remain a closed crime scene.

I called Dr. Kraig and filled him in on what I'd been doing. He'd read Lottie had died but didn't know anything more. "Come in for an appointment," he said.

I summarized what had happened and told him I'd been making progress on my mental PTSD chart. "Not ready for an appointment yet."

****

I moved my belongings into a double room Nina had arranged in Ridgeview Delta. Based on reports of my father's death—*Variety*, *The Hollywood Reporter,* and the *Skagit Valley Herald* described it in detail—I received permission from the university to take my exams late.

I made Bs and Cs in my courses, and, thanks to what I'd learned from Lottie, Dad, and Dale, I wrote a philosophy term paper based on the idea that ugliness can hide beauty, and pain can open the door to rewards and growth. Having made peace with my father, I had been able to forgive the universe, and it offered me several bonuses, including a B plus on the paper.

Nina invited me to join her family for Thanksgiving. I thanked her but stayed at school, holed up in our dorm room, reading novels, and trying not to be distracted by thoughts of Mom, of Lottie, or of the possibility I might never find the phony PI.

In the University Library's periodical room, I checked out the current issue of *Daily Variety* to see if *Zombies from Gold Mountain* had started shooting again. It had, according to an article quoting Kiki. I was relieved she didn't mention Jake, but shocked to read Brett had been rushed to Beverly Hills Hospital in Los Angeles, on hiatus from the movie.

****

While Nina signed up for the next quarter's classes, I packed an insurance card Lottie had gotten me before my PTSD problems, and used Christmas money and the cash from Karen to buy a ticket from SeaTac airport to LAX.

In LA, I searched the yellow pages until I found a super low-price car agency that claimed to accept female drivers under twenty-five. After I showed my license and the insurance card, and they rented me an old Pontiac, I fought my way through traffic to the hospital.

Brett had a sixth-floor corner room with a view of the Hollywood Hills and vases of flowers from the cast and crew. None of the cards had Bonnie or Carmen's signatures.

Face pale, hair matted, he lay on his bed in a hospital gown, half-buried in a mound of pillows, looking skinny and limp, like a marionette with nobody working the strings.

"What are *you* doing here?" he growled.

"Let me guess. You were so jealous of my acting in the mine car shot you collapsed in embarrassment."

"Haven't seen the dailies. Why aren't you in

Cement or whatever backwater you came from?"

"Concrete. Named for a mixture of Portland cement, water, rock, and sand or gravel. My backwater town produces beautiful, strong girls."

He frowned. I moved closer. "What's with the grouchy attitude?"

He clamped his jaw.

"Stop the nonsense and give me a hug."

He pulled the sheet to his chin and stared out the window. Stayed that way until a petite nurse named Divina bustled in, all business. She handed him a pill in a tiny plastic cup.

Brett pushed it away. "Later."

"Now." She held out a cup of water.

Brett plopped the pill in his mouth, downed it, and covered his arms.

But not before I spotted the bandages. A kid at a high school downriver had acted normal for months, until he slit his wrists before Christmas.

"Be nice to your guest," Divina said, and left.

I poked his knee. "You want to tell me what's going on? Something to do with the letter you received on the set?"

"My agent didn't have the guts to tell me in person. I had two terrific parts lined up. Lost both."

"Don't all actors go through that? You didn't get fired."

"I did. I had signed to do a movie with a major star. His agent told him I was a troublemaker on *Zombies,* and he said he wouldn't do it if I got the part. I can't go to Barstow. Everyone reads the trades. They'll know what a loser I am."

"You're not a loser. And no matter what anyone

thinks, Ivan will keep you on. It would cost him a fortune to replace you since you're in so many scenes. Besides, you have an obligation to finish. I bet the crew will support you."

"How come you're Ms. Life-Is-Beautiful all of a sudden?"

"I've got lots to be thankful for. And so do you," I said, suppressing a smile—I sounded like Lottie. "Let's go to Barstow and check things out."

"Have they started shooting again?"

"A couple of days ago. When can you get out of here?"

In an hour, it turned out—after the attending doctor gave his okay and Brett answered enough questions to satisfy an LAPD officer he didn't present an imminent suicide risk or a danger to anyone else.

We put his clothes and effects in my rental car and headed out on Interstate 10. Brett dozed while I drove. To pass the time, I listened to the radio. When a western singer kept on about his lovely darlin', I couldn't resist a glance in the vanity mirror. Though I had no blood connection to Janine Purdue, the woman who raised me, I had her expressive eyes, wavy hair, and lips fuller and more sexy than I'd thought.

"I love you, Mom," I whispered, tasting salty tears that came easily. More progress in my PTSD journey.

****

As I expected, when we arrived at the hotel in Barstow and met the crew returning from a day of shooting, no one made fun of Brett.

Dale and his assistants, and the grips, electricians, and wardrobe women chatted with him and said they'd missed his energy on the set. Ivan gave Brett a photo book of vintage race cars. When Brett asked about Jake, Ivan said he had been replaced by another special effects man.

"I don't know if I can handle starting up again," Brett told me on the way to his room.

"What if I come to work, too? We can spend the days telling each other what shits we are. You can seduce all the women. They love tragic heroes."

He bopped me on the shoulder. "Being here is dangerous. The Russians planted the zombie actress. I'm sure others are hiding in the crew, as grips or makeup artists. We might mention your dad's trick by mistake and give it away. They'd off us in a flash."

"Coming back will suggest to the Russians, if any, that we're here to help with the production."

"Is this a mercy mission? Help poor Brett through his crisis?"

When I said no, he sent me from the room.

I booked one of my own for a night and ordered a steak from room service. Afterward, for exercise, I wandered the floors, checking behind me and peering around every corner. If the phony PI followed me, so much the better. I'd defend myself somehow without the .45, which I'd left in Bellingham.

On the top floor, I found a stairway I hadn't known existed.

At nine o'clock when I climbed it, I discovered a rooftop pool open to the sky and reclined on an aluminum chaise lounge. I scanned the heavens and located the constellation *Aquarius,* Latin for water carrier, and one of my favorites.

A wind blowing off the desert, carrying the aromatic scent of wild grasses, put me in an adventuresome mood. I hadn't brought a swimsuit, but since I was alone, I stripped to my bra and panties and slid into the water.

Voices and laughter drifted from the street below— the crew leaving a bar.

I pulled myself onto a blow-up pool chair and floated on the glassy surface, staring at *Aquarius*, hoping Dad, who had schooled me about the constellations since our earliest camping trips, might be seeing it at the same time.

I must have dropped off, because the next thing I knew, a hand grabbed my foot. I screamed and tumbled into the water.

Brett's head burst through the surface. "Hi, kiddo."

I kicked him. "Don't ever scare me like that."

"I wanted to say thanks for staying on, which I'm sure you didn't want to do."

"Not true."

He sculled toward the pool ladder. "Forgive me for disturbing your bliss-out."

"You're not." His strong jaw and cheekbones, shimmering with the light reflecting off the water, sent a current zinging down my tummy. I whispered, "Come here a second."

He moved a few strokes closer and lowered an eyebrow.

Did I see an interested look? Had the phony PI captured something attractive about me in his photos? It didn't matter. I felt pretty—until my PTSD brain whipsawed me through feeling numb, curious, agitated, and terrified.

I gripped my float, about to tell Brett to move away, when I recalled Lottie saying, "Frightened girls deserve to have a good time, too."

I managed a nervous smile and beckoned Brett to come nearer.

He cocked his head and sculled toward me. Water glistening on his face and strong shoulders made me think of the sea god, Poseidon.

I didn't know if my grin looked wicked. That's how I meant it.

He moved closer and whispered, "I'm not sure we should...I don't want you to—"

I stopped him with a kiss and said, "I didn't thank you for that wonderful dinner."

He kissed me back. Kissed me again. And slid his tongue between my lips.

Seductive fantasies spun in my brain and set my body tingling with tiny eruptions like the candies that fizzed and crackled in my mouth when I was six.

He pulled back. "Are you positive you want—"

I kissed him over and over, getting so excited I would have had sex right there.

Brett lifted me from the pool, grabbed my clothes, and carried me down two floors. Part of me hoped someone would see us, but no one did. He entered his darkened room, eased me onto his bed, and removed my wet underwear.

Despite the compliment I'd extracted from him about being attractive, and despite the PI's entrancing black-and-white photos, I doubted Brett found me pretty. I expected him to make an excuse and say it was time to call it a night.

He undressed.

Any second, he'll send me away.

But he didn't.

We explored each other like five-year-olds opening Christmas presents. To my surprise and joy, I grew more and more excited. I wanted him. Didn't care if we met again. He found sensitive places on my body I didn't know existed.

As my pleasure grew, so did my panic at the loss of control. Life still seemed arbitrary. Mean. Ready to kick you when you were vulnerable.

I pushed Brett away, thinking, now he'll be furious. Jam me down. Force himself inside.

He kissed me softly and whispered, "It's okay to stop. This is perfect already."

His patience calmed me like a summer breeze, dissolving old demons and allowing me to lose myself in the slow, easy touch of his hands.

"I mean it. I could stop," he said.

"Don't you dare."

He kissed and guided me through moments of rising pleasure.

Long before he eased inside me, I soared like a bird, riding updrafts over a cliff.

He brought me to the edge again and again, easing back each time. Then he sent me higher, moaning so loud I expected hotel security to break down the door.

At last, I cascaded over the crest, surfing the most beautiful wave imaginable. Then again. And one last time.

Not until the end did Brett enjoy his own pleasure.

That night surpassed the romantic fantasies I'd begun to imagine before Mom's death. Life was random and full of disappointments, but far from a wasteland. I lay in Brett's arms and drifted off to sleep, imagining his lips and hands everywhere on my body.

****

When I awoke the next morning, Brett had gone. A note on his pillow read, "Went to the set. I loved being with you last night but I know that might have been an impulsive move on your part. If you want to take off, I'll understand. I'm staying to finish the shoot. Thanks more than I can tell you for being an amazing friend and lover."

The production was wrapping. Some of the departments had already packed up. Others were stowing gear. With few vehicles around the parking area, the place was like a town being abandoned in the face of rising flood waters.

Karen paid my hotel bill, and I spent the next couple of days working in the editing room, which would close soon and move to Los Angeles. Allen had me pull sound effects from his cassette library and showed me how he laid them in, improving scenes with sound and subtle picture changes.

He'd snap a short rough-cut sequence into the Moviola gate, press the pedal, and send the film clacking through. Stop the Moviola with the hand brake. Trim or add frames, splice the pieces together, and repeat the process until the sequence pleased him. He worked so fast—whir, screech, cut, splice, whir, screech, cut, splice—that I pictured him as an editing Rumpelstiltskin, spinning film straw into gold.

Reel by reel, Allen transformed our corny story into a scary, fast-moving adventure. He amazed me when, by moving one shot, or by shortening or lengthening it a few frames, he could alter the sense of a moment or a scene—or the whole story. I loved that notion. I wished I could do something similar—alter, remove, or replace an event, or a thing I had said or done, or failed to do—and give my life a different meaning.

Chapter 48

In December, soon after I'd said good-bye to Brett—we agreed to connect again when we got our lives on track—and I'd chatted with my other friends on the crew, I returned to Bellingham.

Detective Lansky called me at the dorm. "Your grandmother's body is ready to be released. I don't mean to intrude, but have you made arrangements for a memorial service?"

"I'll speak to the funeral home."

A few days later, Nina and I described the circumstances of Dad's death to the University housing people. I argued I needed solace away from the hustle and bustle of dorm life, and they let us out of our contract.

We moved into a two-bedroom apartment near campus in a brick building with a garden outside our front window, a wood-paneled entry, and a view of Mount Baker. We bought beds, a couch, a TV, a dining table, chairs, and kitchenware. I signed up for a phone, my first.

****

One Sunday, Karen's grip delivered Royal to our front door and left to go hiking. After wolfing down a leftover piece of meat, he went for a walk with me around the neighborhood. He sniffed every inch of the apartment, settled at the foot of my bed, and went to sleep.

During the next days, he trailed Nina around the house at a distance, sniffing her hands.

She acted nervous again, but I knew he'd win her over.

I didn't tell Nina my dad was Jake but I hinted he hadn't died.

"He's *alive*?" Her eyes brightened. "Wonderful. Where?"

"I don't know." Dad and I had agreed if we needed to get in touch, we would communicate through a lost-pet personal for a dog named Scout in the *Los Angeles Times* and *Bellingham Herald*. I'd neither written nor read any notices about Scout. And I hadn't told Nina about our plan.

"If he comes, should we meet him after the memorial service?" she asked. "Invite him to dinner?"

"I'm sure he'd want to keep to himself." Nina made me nervous with her questions, but I chalked it up to her delight I had Dad back and to her pleasure in quizzing me like the FBI agent she planned to become.

The next day, she found the notice I received from Lottie's church, announcing her desire to be buried in the Concrete cemetery next to Mom. I had scheduled the service for the coming Saturday.

Nina clasped my hands. "I bet your dad will be there."

Her jubilance while I struggled with guilt about causing Lottie's death unsettled me. "I'm sure he won't show," I said.

"That would be a shame, but I'll be with you for moral support."

****

Detective Lansky phoned to say they were ready to hand over possession of Lottie's house. Nina and I left Royal at home and drove there in her VW.

While a uniformed officer removed the crime tape, a Crown Vic pulled up and Detective Lansky stepped out, wearing dark glasses and his dark suit with a weapon evident under his arm. He stepped from the car and scanned the house and nearby properties before heading toward us.

I was prepared to hear him announce his investigations revealed Russians had been involved in the film shoot, that he knew my dad had not died and was charging me with a felony for withholding information. But Lansky shook my hand and introduced himself to Nina.

"Miss Purdue," he said, "you had asked about Russian names in papers among your grandmother's things. We searched. The killers ransacked the place. I don't know if they found anything, but we didn't." He gestured toward the house. "It's all yours, unless you want me to stay."

"I'm okay, thanks."

"If you attend your grandmother's service in Concrete, be on guard. Sometimes killers show up to gloat about their work. I'll be there to keep an eye out. Let me know with a wave if you see anything strange." He returned to his car and left. The other officer followed.

I said to Nina, "I'm not sure we should go to the service."

"We have to honor your grandma's memory."

Nina meant well, but she sounded bossy to me. I said, "Why don't you head to the apartment? I'll walk home in a while." I wanted to search the house by myself on the chance Lottie had squirreled away personal items I might not want to share. Nina hugged me and got in her car, casting a long look back as she drove away.

I went inside past what remained of the grandfather clock—the door and face had been broken, the weights dropped on the carpet. I climbed the stairs to the second floor, biting my tongue to keep tears back.

I kept expecting to find myself in our bathroom in Concrete, staring at Mom's body. But I stayed present while I entered Lottie's bedroom and stepped onto the wood floor. The rug, her nighties, dresses, underwear, and bedding were gone, removed as evidence. The faint scent of her signature French perfume remained in the air.

On my way out of the bedroom I noticed between the mattress and frame the postcard I'd sent from the hotel in Barstow. Lottie had glued dried Baby's Breath sprigs to it in the shape of a heart. I put it in my purse.

Outside my bedroom window, the three-legged squirrel scolded me until I found a bag of almonds in my purse. I opened the window, scattered the nuts on the sill, and said, "Be well, my little friend."

Downstairs in the living room, furniture had been ripped apart, and swaths of wallpaper torn away. Pots and pans lay scattered about the kitchen. I checked everywhere, including the chimney above the fireplace, the toilet tank, and the freezer.

After looking for an hour without finding any notes or documents, I went outside, stood on the creaky front steps, and let out a long sigh. My imagination of Lottie's last horrible moments and my part in causing them had so poisoned my feelings I knew I'd never return to her house.

Taking a last look at the yard, I noticed Lottie's sundial was out of alignment. I went closer and checked. The dial and vane were intact, but the vane's shadow was three hours off the correct time. Lottie would not have set her prized device so far off. I tipped the pedestal over, pried the metal cover off the bottom, and drew out a plastic bag filled with news clippings. I flipped through item after item, chronicling the activities of a Russian Mafia family.

A note in Dad's handwriting said the crime boss had ordered a falcon the size of a wood tick tattooed in the crook between the two smallest toes of the right foot of each of his children. "Strange," Dad had written, "but I guess it made sense in a family where any of his kids could end up in a morgue, burned or mutilated beyond recognition." I shivered as I pictured the brown mark between my toes I'd always taken for a mole.

A manila envelope, also encased in a plastic bag, contained lists of enterprises: money laundering, extortion, drugs, prostitution, gambling, and smuggling. A color photo of Aleksey Dorokhov made him look as imposing as he had in his limo in Concrete years ago.

A newspaper article said law enforcement agencies in the U.S., Canada, and Europe were after Dorokhov. Another article discussed the family's operations shut down by the FBI—based on tips from Dad?

I put all the pages in the plastic bag, slid it under my top, and hiked the twenty minutes to our apartment.

At home, Nina stood waiting when I opened the door. "Find anything interesting?"

"No."

****

I had considered wearing a somber outfit to the memorial. But on Saturday morning a warm spell arrived, and I imagined Lottie saying, "No Gloomy Gus attitude when you send me off, Charlie. I want to see a joyful expression, and an outfit that says, 'I'm lucky to be alive.' "

I borrowed a sleeveless dress of Nina's, pistachio green with a quince blossom print.

I called Lottie's minister, apologized for having upset his church service last spring and for not having helped prepare for the memorial. He told me not to worry. The congregation had been eager to pitch in.

I said, "Thanks so much for having a few of Lottie's friends stay with her over the last month."

He said, "I didn't arrange for anyone to live with your grandmother."

"Oh," I murmured, and we said good-bye. I hung up, unnerved Nina had told me something untrue.

Other things about her seemed off as well. I hated doubting my friend, but Nina's earlier queries about Dad and her increasing excitement at the prospect of meeting him rattled me.

When she went into the bathroom to shower and wash her hair, I turned the manila envelope upside-down and shook it. An old photo-Christmas card slid out. On it, Dorokhov stood erect and proud beside a raven-haired woman in a glittery dress. A girl about eight with big eyes and golden tresses and a boy in his teens knelt before them on a Persian rug. Flanking the parents were two young teen boys.

While Nina finished her shower and dried her hair, I checked my Russian dictionary and translated the printed greeting in Cyrillic script as "Merry Christmas, from Aleksey, Marta, Andrei, a capital H, a backwards N, a smaller capital H, and a lowercase a—*Nina*.

My best friend, my half-sister, my blood, belonged to the Mafia family plotting to kill the father I loved. Every kind thing she did had been a ploy.

I'd been slow to recognize the clues: Nina's convenient appearance as a victim in the arboretum, while her attacker (who had to be the phony PI) ran away; her choice of a Polish major—a Slavic language and a cinch for a Russian speaker; her questions about my family history; the fact she had convinced me to attend the noir movie screening where I "discovered" my missing father in *Dead Girls,* and had to go find him.

Aside from Mary Sue, who I now considered damaged rather than dangerous, Nina had been the one person at the U. aware of my departure for LA. Not long after I called her from the Greyhound terminal, a familiar guy had shown up on the bus. She had played along with my illusion that he was Stephen and interested in me. Several times Nina had pushed to join me in California.

She had looked in on Lottie at my request, fool that I'd been, and must have described the house's layout to the phony PI. She created a preposterous story about sending him to the Hard Rock Cafe. His departure from Barstow came too close to Lottie's murder to be coincidental.

"Damn you," I said, louder than I meant to.

"What?" Nina called from the bathroom.

"Take your time." I retrieved the .45 from my bureau drawer, checked it—one round in the chamber, seven in the magazine—and put it in my purse.

Over the sound of running water, Nina hummed a familiar tune in a minor key. Was it a Russian song I'd heard as an infant?

If I brought Nina to the funeral, she might kill Dad when he arrived. If I asked her not to come, she'd be wary, show up anyway, and attack Dad before I could stop her. I had to bring her with me, keep her close, and hope if she invited the phony PI to the funeral to finish Dad off, I could neutralize him.

I added an eight-inch boning knife from the utensil drawer to my purse. I was about to phone Detective Lansky to tell him about Nina, when she came out of the bathroom.

I hung up, whisked Royal outside for a quick pee, left him a dish of water and another of canned food, and rode away with Nina in her VW.

Chapter 49

As we headed east on Route 20, I studied Nina, wondering how old she'd been when she learned her family ran prostitutes and drugs and murdered people.

We drove into Concrete past a few pickups parked outside the Logger's Landing grocery, then to Dad's favorite spot, Cascade Supply, where several men poked and prodded snow blowers on "Spring Special."

By way of putting off the moment when I would have to see Lottie's face in the casket, I turned back and directed Nina along Main Street, where small patches of grayish-white powder lingered on rooftops and in protected crevices.

We passed a few boarded up storefronts, casualties of the cement plant closure seventeen years before. I pointed out the Concrete Theater, where I'd sneaked in as a girl to see *The Breakfast Club*. Now, it advertised *Stand by Me,* the title a sad comment on my present situation. I repressed an impulse to stop at the Hub Coffee Shop and directed Nina to Compton Lane. She parked her VW at a row of maples near the Forest Park Cemetery sign, and we got out.

Twenty yards away, a crowd clustered near a fresh grave where women smoothed their skirts, and men moved like mannequins in stiff suits, mothball scents mingling with hints of perfume. Nina and I walked toward a group surrounding Lottie's Bellingham minister. His demeanor was as sedate as his dark suit, except when he greeted two of Lottie's close church friends.

As we neared the gathering and I sensed Nina studying me, I made a point of avoiding eye contact with any of the men, in case Dad was among them.

While Nina glanced at the crowd near the casket, I checked out a group of retired men with beards and flannel shirts, standing in the shadow of the maples bordering the cemetery. When Nina gazed at them for several seconds, I thought I might see Dad in the group. But I didn't.

Nina asked, "If your father shows up, should we say hello, or ignore him to protect his anonymity?"

"What do you think?"

"I'm not sure, but please let me know if you see him. We can signal we'd like to meet somewhere in private."

An unmarked Crown Vic pulled up. Detective Lansky got out and approached the gathering. If I went to him, Nina would follow me. And if we whispered together, she would realize something was up.

I gave Lansky a faint nod when he looked our way.

"Dad isn't here," I told Nina. "I didn't let him know about the service."

"I'll bet he's been checking the local papers, seen a notice, and decided to come."

I stayed a few feet back from the open casket to command a wider view of any newcomers and also to avoid seeing Lottie's face and dissolving in tears before I offered my farewell thoughts.

Eyes radiant, the pastor began, "In addition to appreciating Lottie's kindness, I marveled at her spunk.

A few years ago, when a teenager hurled a rock through the sanctuary window, she chased him halfway down the street in her Sunday suit and heels. She impressed us as a devout Christian and a loyal supporter of the church. For a few months earlier this year we feared she'd given up on us, but she returned, more vibrant and loving than ever. A beacon of strength for everyone."

After he finished, I stepped forward. "My grandma didn't give up on the church, on God, or on me. When my mother was murdered last spring, Lottie was a life preserver keeping me afloat. Sometimes I didn't appreciate her old-fashioned ways, but she was more often right than wrong. She will always live in my heart, an inspiration to be brave and worthy."

Lottie, dressed in her favorite lavender Pendleton suit, lay on a bed of white satin, a crown of lilies of the valley pinned to her coiled braid of silver hair. Her eyes were closed, her lips curved in a subtle smile, the fine lines on her face like delicate lace. She looked…hopeful.

I kissed her cool brow, dappled with light streaming through the maple leaves, as it had months before when she drove me to my dorm, hugged me, and said, "You're stronger than you know." Lottie realized before I did that I would become a real Concrete girl.

"Rest well, Gram," I whispered. I lingered a moment and rose.

There was no point getting Lansky alone to reveal what I'd learned about Nina. I had no proof she'd committed any crime and if I aroused her suspicions, I'd lose the element of surprise and the chance to find Lottie's killer.

After the ceremony, I knelt before Mom's headstone in the plot beside Lottie's and kissed the inscription, "Janine Purdue, beloved wife and mother."

Nina pressed my hand. "I'm sure you're disappointed we haven't spotted your dad. Why don't we stay around in case he's here and hanging back, waiting for a chance to talk with you away from everyone else?"

"There's a place we could go. Dad knows about it. If he arrives and joins us, we'll be alone." I gripped the .45 in my purse.

Chapter 50

People were mingling at the reception table as Nina and I drove away from the cemetery. Lansky's Crown Vic pulled out and headed downriver toward Mount Vernon.

I had Nina drive in the opposite direction, across the Henry Thompson Bridge, up the winding Baker River Road through stands of maples and alders, with views to the left of Lower Baker Dam.

We left Nina's VW at the side of the road near a locked gate. We went around it, hiked fifty yards up a gravel road to an open parking area rimmed with birches, and stopped in front of the two-story Worldstar Cement Plant. Spray-painted swear words, love declarations, and cartoon figures in fluorescent colors covered the outside walls.

"What a fabulous place," Nina said. "I bet you and your friends loved hanging out here."

"Be careful when we get to the upper floors. If you fall through a hole, you could break your leg."

The company had boarded up the front entrance, so I led Nina to the left and down a steep bank, my heels skidding and twisting on the moist soil. We entered through a break in the basement wall and crossed an area resembling the bombed-out World War II buildings I'd seen in movies with Lottie. The area hadn't changed since the previous spring, except for recent piles of beer cans. Nina and I threaded our way between the charred remains of bonfires.

"What are those?" she asked, looking at two round, twelve-foot openings above us.

"Holes for the crushers that pulverized limestone from the quarry across the road."

She pointed through one of the holes to a catwalk three stories above. "Can we go up there?"

I nodded and started up the concrete stairs, recalling my desperate climb last spring when I planned to throw myself from the catwalk. Nina followed. As we ascended, part of me hoped I'd find a reason to look past her betrayal and reconnect. Another part of me wanted to put a bullet in her heart, though I doubted I could.

She touched my arm. "Is something wrong?"

"Everything's fine."

When we reached the second level I led her to an opening with a panoramic view of the aqua waters of Lake Shannon, a hundred yards down a rocky slope.

I said, "I need your help with something."

"What kind of help?"

I gripped my purse, feeling the gun inside.

From outside the building came a raspy "*chuck*," a louder "*chukar*," then "*chuck-a-ra*." A call by a type of partridge living among the basalt cliffs of eastern Washington. It had to be Dad. I stuck my head out the opening and scanned the hillside.

Twenty yards to the left, my father in camouflage gear moved from tree to tree, silent as a shadow and looking like his old, disfigured self without Esteban's special makeup and appliances.

"My God," Nina gasped. "That's Jake from the

movie. What's he doing here?" She stared at me. "Is Jake your father?"

"Something like that."

A figure in a checkered shirt and jeans, from the line of retired men at the edge of the cemetery, was following my father and gaining on him.

"Watch out, Dad," I yelled.

He darted from view into the basement below us. The figure behind him ran through a sunny patch, and light flooded his face.

I said, "The second guy's the phony PI who's been following me since I left Bellingham. A member of your Mafia family, I'm sure." I opened my purse, ready to pull out the .45 and blast him.

Nina grinned. *"Dobro pozhalovat' v real'nyy mir.* Welcome to reality." At the sound of Dad's shoes scuffing across the basement floor, she moved to the circular opening.

"Dad," I shouted, "there's a Russian behind you." I pushed Nina away from the edge as Dad's head poked up through a hole a level beneath us. Shots ricocheted in the basement.

Dad climbed through the hole and stepped behind a concrete column.

Nina reached into her purse and pulled out a handgun, like one of Dad's—a Czech CZ-75. I tried to knock it from her hand, but she pushed past me and raced up the stairway. I scrambled after her. She whirled, slammed her elbow against my cheek, and sent me tumbling.

My head hit a step, and lights flashed in my brain. I struggled to my feet and watched Nina's CZ-75 jump as she shot at Dad.

He stepped behind another column and fired back, until a metal "click" and his "Damn!" told me his Glock had jammed.

The phony PI climbed from the hole in the floor while Nina fired four shots that hit near Dad.

I aimed the .45 at her and pulled the trigger. My gun made a dull click. I ejected the magazine. It was empty, the chamber, too.

"Surprise, girl." Nina tossed a handful of my .45 cartridges through the big crusher hole. "You should have paid attention to your purse during your grandma's funeral." She fired more shots at Dad, missing as he ducked behind the column again.

"Slick move, emptying my gun," I said. "But if you people are so smart, why did it take you years to come after my dad?"

"Papochka, my father, hated you losing your mom. Made us leave your family alone for a while." She climbed higher.

I followed. "What changed?"

She fired two shots that landed inches from Dad. "A few months ago, Papochka got sick, and Andrei took charge."

"The phony PI?"

"Yes." She fired again. "He sent me to the University to find you and your father. Now, he's here to finish the job."

The guy shot several rounds at Dad. Concrete chips erupted from the column in front of him.

Nina shouted, "Hey, Jefferson Purdue, you can still save your girl, if you give up."

"Don't do it, Dad," I yelled.

She fired another burst, and her gun clicked,

empty. While she bent forward to snap in a fresh magazine, I leapt at her and thrust the boning knife into her gun arm.

She swore and dropped the CZ-75. I smashed her face with the handgrip of my .45. Sent her toppling down the stairs, blood streaming from her nose and mouth. I dove after her, and we rolled across the floor, grappling for her gun.

Dad got his Glock working and traded shots with Andrei.

Nina pulled hers free, inserted the fresh mag, and aimed at Dad.

"What a joke!" I laughed to distract her.

She spun toward me. "You think what we're doing is funny?"

"Not *us*. Andrei with his ridiculous disguises." I reached for her gun.

She pulled it away. "He watched too many horror movies when we were kids."

"So, he's your brother." I grabbed her CZ-75 but couldn't pull it free.

Dad fired and creased Nina's left shoulder. She staggered, shouting "*Blyad! Blyad Blyad!*"

Andrei's bullet hit Dad's Glock. Sent it skidding across the floor. He fired again, and a red stain bloomed on Dad's sleeve.

With my free hand, I hurled a chunk of concrete.

Andrei dodged it. "Be nice. I reserved a beautiful room for you in our best whore house in Moscow. They love your photos."

"Nina, you were my best friend," I said as we grappled for the CZ-75.

"After you were born, I was nothing. Papochka

would hold you and coo, *'Moya milaya malen'kaya Katya.'* My sweet little Katya." She yanked the CZ-75 free but lost her grip. It spun into the air and fell through the crusher hole. She grabbed the knife from the stairs.

Andrei sent a shot whizzing past my ear. Took aim to fire another.

Nina shouted "Wait!" I jumped back as Andrei's muzzle flashed and a round thudded into Nina's chest. She dropped the knife. I tossed it to Dad.

He jammed the blade into Andrei's arm. The gun fell. Dad caught it and put the muzzle to Andrei's temple.

Nina sank to the floor.

As I pressed my hand on her wound, blood oozed through my fingers. Her eyelids fluttered. "You're like us. Dog-eat-dog to the end."

"You took a bullet to save me."

She shook her head.

Dad pinned Andrei's arms behind him and bound his hands with a scrap of wire. Andrei's shirt flopped open, baring a winged skull on his chest—what Mom must have seen as he slit her throat. What she copied on the bathroom tiles with her blood.

Nina groaned and grasped my hand. "Find my dad. Tell him I love him."

"*Me?* Find your gangster father?"

"He's your father, too."

"I couldn't."

"In my bureau," she wheezed. "*Please...*" Blood burbled from her lips. "Won't take long."

"I'll see."

Her eyes closed. After a rattling breath, her face

went slack. I felt her carotid. The artery pumped a few thready beats and went still. Distant thunder shook the air, and black clouds roiled in the sky above the lake. Hail rat-tatted on sheet metal.

Dad said, "If we wire concrete chunks to their bodies and dump them in the water, no one will find them for years."

I pictured Nina splayed out on the lake bottom, decomposing, and recalled my thoughts as I watched Allen editing. *By my actions, I can alter, remove, or replace an event, or a thing I had said or done, or failed to do—and give my life a different meaning.*

I said, "We leave Nina so her family can bury her, take Andrei to the hospital, and notify the police." I checked a B plus on my mental PTSD chart.

"You have your mother's forgiving nature," Dad said. "I hope it doesn't do us in."

I rushed down the stairway to him, and while he supported Andrei on one side, I held Andrei's other shoulder, and we dragged him outside.

Our feet sloshed through puddles. Raindrops splattered on our heads and shoulders as we shuffled down the road to Dad's rented Buick, hidden behind a clump of brush. We put Andrei in the trunk, left his Harley in a thicket beside the road, and drove downriver.

****

In Mount Vernon, we parked in the Lower Valley Hospital garage near an ER where a line of patients waited outside the door.

Dad said, "We have to find an entrance where I won't be seen."

We pushed past a barrier of orange netting and

slipped through a construction area. We dragged Andrei up a stairway to the second level and made our way between piles of plywood and metal studs to a landing above another door where doctors and nurses were entering and leaving.

I asked Andrei, "Why did you murder my grandmother? She didn't have any money. Wasn't out to hurt your family."

"Loose ends are bad for business."

I searched his eyes for the sensitive, talented artist whose photos made me look more beautiful than I had imagined possible. It was like staring into a void.

We pulled Andrei across a plank bridge toward a stairway leading down to the door we'd spotted. A wall bordered the plank on one side, construction netting on the other. Below, a cement truck roared, belching black exhaust as it pumped slurry into a wide form.

Halfway across the bridge, Andrei pushed off the wall, flung himself at Dad, and knocked him halfway over the netting.

As Dad started to fall, I saw what must have been Mom's last view—Andrei's cocky grin. I yanked Dad from the edge, put a foot against Andrei's back, and drove him over the net.

The crew below, dealing with a river of concrete flowing from the truck, didn't look over as Andrei landed and sank into the cement.

I expected to see his hand, forehead, or shoulder rise from the gray swirl. When no part of him surfaced, I walked from the bridge with Dad. Placed an E on my PTSD chart, content with a low grade to be rid of Mom and Lottie's murderer.

Chapter 51

I gave Dad my home number when I dropped him off at SeaTac Airport. After a goodbye that left me feeling more alone than I had in months, I drove to Bellingham and spent a sleepless night in the apartment, my arm around Royal, my mind replaying images of Andrei sinking into the concrete and blood burbling from Nina's mouth.

The next morning, numb and unsteady, I walked Royal in a park near the apartment. He seemed to sense my distress and stuck by my side even when squirrels crossed our path.

That evening, Dad risked a phone call to tell me he'd learned from his friend Esteban about a first-rate cosmetic surgeon in Tijuana who promised to bring his appearance to a version close to his old self.

"Fabulous," I said. "Can't wait to see the new you." I hoped I'd be able to forget he had left Concrete without ever sending word of his survival. If he believed I would chew my foot off to escape a trap, why hadn't he trusted I could keep his secret?

On the other hand, Dad had rushed to our house, risking his life to try to save Mom. Risked it again and become disfigured when he bear-hugged Brett's mother as she raced around the set, her clothes ablaze. He had also been ready at the chasm in the mine to die so I could live.

My excuses for betraying him to Kiki were no better than Dad's. The dozens of times I had disrespected or disappointed Mom removed any chance for me to feel superior.

Grown-up love, I decided, meant caring about people when you knew their worst failings.

At my request, Dad had left the black book with me. If I turned it and Dad's papers over to the FBI and they raided crime family houses and bank accounts, the Russians would believe Dad was alive. But if I destroyed everything, they would still suspect one or both of us every time the FBI cracked down. Any day, a former crew member might give away our scheme.

"As well hanged for a sheep as a lamb," Lottie once told me. I made two copies of the black book and the papers I'd collected. I mailed one copy to the FBI. I also made an anonymous call to the Concrete PD, reporting gunfire at the old cement plant.

I dropped out of the U and found a respected female attorney in Seattle, had her sell Lottie's house and deposit the proceeds, and any money I'd inherited, into an account the Russians couldn't find. The attorney rented me a one-bedroom Seattle apartment in her firm's name.

I gave her a copy of the black book and the files to put in a secure place.

I had her locate Mary Sue—living at home with her mom in Concrete, recovering from her psychological troubles. I sent her an anonymous envelope of cash to help with her studies and therapy. I wanted to thank her in person or with a signed letter for warning me about Nina, but I couldn't risk revealing my name, in case the Russians were checking on Mary Sue.

****

When I cleaned out the Bellingham apartment, I found three ginger-colored wigs in Nina's dresser—her disguises for pretending to be a redhead and creating clues to lure me to LA. I also found a letter from an extended-care facility with an address in British Columbia.

I took my passport, used a car my attorney rented, went to Canada, and drove north through miles of countryside to a mansion on park-like grounds overlooking a river.

At a reception desk in the walnut-paneled foyer I approached a gray-haired woman and said, "I'm here to see Aleksey Dorokhov."

She offered me a chocolate from a crystal bowl on the counter. "I'm not familiar with that person."

"He's my father."

She said something in Russian.

"I don't speak it," I replied. "I'm adopted. Have a different last name." I showed her my passport and the letter with Nina's name on it. "She's my stepsister."

The woman made a phone call, conversed in Russian, and led me along a plush hallway lined with gold-framed oil paintings, including a Corot of a dark forest with a lake in the background I'd seen in one of Dale's art books. Had Nina's family stolen or counterfeited it?

My palms went clammy as we approached an open doorway where gloomy orchestral music and a baritone voice singing in Russian flowed into the corridor. I wished this Mafia boss who'd caused so much pain would be a shrunken husk of a man.

The receptionist left, and I entered a room filled

with antique Italian furniture. In a chair before a large window sat the man I'd glimpsed in the black limousine.

He wore a dark suit with a red pocket handkerchief, as he had years before. His hair and beard were grayer, but he had a ruddy complexion. He studied me with slate-gray eyes.

Should I hate or love you? I have both options with the fathers in my life. "My name is—"

He silenced me with a raised hand. "Russian's not good enough for you anymore, eh? That's a shame. We'll speak English." He sipped from a steaming cappuccino cup. "Are you angry because you don't believe I love you?"

I shook my head. *I'm disgusted you raised a monster who killed my mom and grandma and tried to kill my dad.*

He touched my hand. "I know you resented my gifts of clothes and dolls to Katya. She was so tiny and helpless, her mother always frantic and crying. I had to show the child some kindness."

Katya's mother...frantic and crying? My PTSD brain was up to that one—I was Katya, and Katya's mother was my birth mother.

He stroked my hair. "Ninotchka, I hope you're not disappointed I phoned the girl so often after Andrei killed her mother. I wanted to promise I'd keep her safe, but each time she answered..." He sighed and turned to the window.

You think I'm Nina. Those calls were from you, Da...Papochka.

On a side table, among dozens of framed portraits, sat a black-and-white photo of two "Andreis" about eight years old—both with wild eyes and roguish grins—arm in arm, standing thigh-deep in frothy ocean waves.

Dorokhov shook his head. "Inseparable, those two. Always scrapping. That was before you were born, but I'm sure you know the stories. Such a wicked undertow that day. We told Andrei not to feel responsible, but since he had dared Kolya to swim out past the breakers, he couldn't forgive himself. Our priest took him under his wing, started him taking photographs, and helped him survive. But the boy never stopped feeling guilty. It's hard to lose the dearest person in your life, when you believe their death was your fault."

I pictured Lottie's face and jammed my fingernails into my palms.

Dorokhov relaxed his brows. As if forgetting the poignant sentiment he'd expressed, he gestured toward the stereo speakers, pouring out operatic voices in Russian. "Remember *Boris Godunov?* We played it often when you were a baby. Do you believe Boris would have gone mad from guilt after killing the son of a man like Ivan the Terrible?"

I said, "I don't know, but I've gone mad myself a few times. Hate that happening to anyone."

His eyes turned moist, and he took my hand. "Don't worry. I'll always love you, Ninotchka."

"And Ninotchka will always love *you.*" I squeezed his hand. "I want to be clear. You called Katya's house the day her mother was killed. Phoned her grandma's number. Called her at college and at the hotel in California. Is that right?"

He closed his eyes halfway and gave a hint of a nod.

I asked, "Why didn't you ever speak to her? And please tell me what happened to Katya's birth mother."

He kissed my fingers, aimed his remote at the stereo, and turned up the volume. "If they're serving sturgeon tonight, please remind them not to overcook mine."

Maybe his evasion allowed him to forget all the brutal things he had done. Maybe it came from embarrassment at not identifying himself to Katya on the phone—I suspected he had been unable to bear speaking with her after his son had killed the mother who raised her. Maybe he didn't remember the calls at all or had forgotten who he thought I was. It didn't seem to matter.

I left him conducting *Boris Godunov* with his cappuccino spoon.

A cool river breeze played through my hair as I walked to my car. "You see, Nina," I said, "in the midst of losing everything, including his memory, your father loves you more than ever. His attentions to Katya show his humanity endured during his cruelest days."

Chapter 52

On my first day in Seattle I ran across a cluster of girls dressed in styles I'd never seen. Layers of flannel shirts over ratty dresses over baggy pants and Doc Martens boots (soles thick as cheesecake slices, laces top to bottom). And hair so wild or tangled or dyed such weird colors the group would have fit into my PTSD nightmares. I asked one girl, "What do you call your clothing style?"

She laughed. "Where have you been, on Mars?"

"No, an even scarier planet."

She smiled. "Grunge, slacker, or slouch. Take your pick." She walked on with her friends.

I had no desire to go all in on any of those styles, but in case the Russians were poking around, I dyed my hair orange and blue and always wore a hat, tilted to cover part of my face. Royal took the change in stride.

Together, we explored the Seattle parks. He watched TV with me, slept at the foot of my bed, and followed me everywhere. His affection and loyalty reminded me of the carefree years I spent with Scout and brought me a sense of normalcy I hadn't known since before Mom died.

A few weeks after my trip to Canada, I checked the Vancouver papers for news members of the Dorokhov family had surfaced in response to Nina and Andrei's deaths. I came across an obituary notice—Aleksey had

passed away.

From Alzheimer's, I imagined, unless he'd been dispatched by one of his remaining offspring, worried he might leak an incriminating tidbit to the wrong person.

****

During our walks near my apartment in a Capitol Hill neighborhood, Royal sniffed every tree and fire hydrant. I decided the smells, each with its own rich story, were canine equivalents of the starry constellation myths Dad and I loved.

One mid-May afternoon around dusk, while Royal and I idled past taverns and restaurants in the Broadway shopping district, he marked a telephone pole with a pee. Above it, a fresh poster caught my eye. Four teen boys with tousled hair and pimples glared from a photo beneath gothic lettering announcing, "ACID REFLUX IN CONCERT." The performance was to take place that evening in Volunteer Park, a few blocks away. Now that the boys had made it, at least to a Seattle Parks Department stage, I wondered if they were still kind enough to offer a girl in distress their company and a walk to share burgers and fries, like they had to me.

****

As darkness settled over the city and birds swooped between the park's maples and horse chestnuts, Royal and I shared a blanket on a grassy slope while the young rockers performed on a concrete stage for a crowd of several hundred: adults over forty, clusters of twenty-somethings, couples with children, and teens with dyed hair, tattoos, and piercings—echoes of the zombies on our shoot.

Marijuana smoke drifted over the crowd. I inhaled,

pulled Lottie's Baby's Breath-decorated postcard from my purse, and pressed it to my heart.

Acid Reflux sang several of their old favorites with vocals as vulgar and grating as ever. They switched to new tunes in a mellower, more polished style, with sweet melodies and uplifting lyrics.

One song spoke of surviving life's knocks with courage and ingenuity, another of finding satisfaction in small pleasures. My favorite, "Dynamo," described how one player's Irish setter saved his life by sniffing his oncoming insulin shock and barking for help.

People applauded, and the boys took a bow.

It might have been a PTSD relapse or the effect of the thick marijuana smoke in the air, but as we clapped, Principal Dalton walked onstage and raised his hands. "When you go out into the world, if anyone makes fun of your hometown, you can tell them concrete from the limestone processed here built the Grand Coulee Dam and skyscrapers in Seattle. Two thousand years ago, the Romans used concrete like ours to make the Pantheon dome. You can see it today, still beautiful as ever. You students are like our concrete, strong enough to weather troubles that would undo most people."

The class cheered, or maybe it was the crowd.

Royal rested his chin on my leg as I savored an encore by Acid Reflux and gazed at the night sky. Beyond the city's glow, one constellation stood out— Orion, named for the hunter from Greek mythology. I hoped Dad was looking at it.

I hope you are, too, Mom, I thought as a tear made its way down my cheek and left a salty trace on my tongue. I wished on the myriad of stars overhead to have hunts and adventures with friends and lovers. I smelled the flowery scents of spring, felt the cool earth beneath the blanket, and made up my own lyrics: "If you're caught in a river that runs dark and deep, hang in there, keep swimming. The end might be sweet."

A word about the author...

Arthur Coburn got a BA from Dartmouth College, and an LLB from Harvard Law School. He was a first Lieutenant in the infantry and jumped out of airplanes at Fort Benning.

He moved to Hollywood in the 1970s and is a member of the editor's guild, ACE, and the Motion Picture Academy.

He edited more than two dozen films, including Spiderman, A Simple Plan, The Cooler, and Beverly Hills Cop. His short story "Some Creature I Care about" was published in a Sisters in Crime anthology entitled LAndmarked for Crime, in 2006. "Backswing" appeared in a recent Sisters In Crime Anthology.

Three other novels: Boys Will Be Boys, Mostly; Rough Cut; and Murder in Madrona, await revision.

Thank you for purchasing
this publication of The Wild Rose Press, Inc.

For questions or more information
contact us at
info@thewildrosepress.com.

The Wild Rose Press, Inc.
www.thewildrosepress.com